SECESSION
2041
Beyond the Melting Point

MIKE BUSHMAN

www.mbushman.com
Twitter: @m_bushman
mike@mbushman.com

ISBN: 0988336936
ISBN 13: 9780988336933

Library of Congress Control Number: 2013906862
AltFuture Publishing Naperville, IL

Printed in U.S.A.

Cover by Peri Poloni-Gabriel, Knockout Design, www.knockoutbooks.com

DEDICATION

I might never have had the opportunity to pursue this passion if I hadn't been fortunate enough to meet my wife, Cathy, at the University of Illinois when she was running for student government president and I was editor-in-chief of *The Daily Illini*. Weeks later, I wrote a column accusing her of nefarious political deeds, a column she somehow said was endearing on our first date right before graduation. Twenty-five years of marriage later, we both now work in our dream jobs and are proud parents of Matt and Shannon.

When the column I wrote later passed from my memory, I learned that written words, even those seemingly forgiven and forgotten, always have a time and place at which further discussion is deemed appropriate.

ACKNOWLEDGMENTS

Life is highlighted by and sometimes endured in order to reach meaningful moments and experiences. For me, the best of these are shared with people who open my eyes or maybe even bring a momentary smile. Over the years, I have been blessed by many who have done this, including my: parents, wife, son, daughter, three sisters, two brothers, cousins, classmates, co-workers, teachers, aunts, uncles, in-laws, nieces, nephews and friends, along with people I just enjoyed being around or met for a brief shared experience.

Some of these people have been part of my life for decades. Others have come and gone, always leaving an impact and memories that I cherish.

Bryn Collman Henning was a colleague at a previous employer known for her exceptional proofreading, among many other skills. As I hiked around the Southwest in 2012 while writing *Melting Point 2040* and pre-paring this book, I dropped by Bryn's house for an enjoyable morning of sharing stories, inspiration and memories before heading south to Nogales, Arizona for the rest of the day. Bryn provided valuable insights and edits that made this book better.

When our daughters were very young, Dick Riederer and I began a multi-year soccer coaching collaboration to help develop a number of very talented and hard-working young ladies. After both daughters moved past park district soccer, years sometimes went by without us meeting up, but we reconnected recently. After *Melting Point 2040* was published, I learned that among Dick's many talents is a keen eye for language. He volunteered to help proofread *Secession 2041* and I am grateful for his many contributions.

Another good friend and former colleague, Luisa Fernanda Cicero, again took time from her busy family and professional life to offer guidance and a sharp eye. I have had countless discussions with Luisa over the years on the travails of being a Colombian working through the U.S. immigration process to become a U.S. citizen. I admire Luisa for many reasons, not the least of which is her willingness and ability to make it through that process.

Two siblings and a sister-in-law also provided thoughtful assessments that helped me improve the flow and context of the story.

As a child, my brother Bill endured the trauma of a third-grade teacher who didn't appreciate the difference in his learning style from that of his older brother and sister. As I took notes on his advice for this book, I couldn't help but think how wrong that teacher was to not recognize Bill's intellect. I know Bill would never try digging a posthole with a weed whacker, as my wife enjoys telling everyone I tried – twice. Bill's wife Cathleen came into Bill's life at a time he needed and deserved joy. She brought that happiness back to his life, and has enriched our extended family ever since. Her insights into what makes a book interesting are exceptional. I have incorporated some of it here, but am even more excited about what her thoughts will add to my third novel.

My youngest sister, Christine Hudzik, grew up in many ways in a different family than I did. It wasn't long after she was born that I started working almost full time while going through high school to save enough money to afford college. When she started elementary school, I was in college and then moved to Washington, D.C. for six years, so didn't spend enough time with her in her childhood. One of our favorite family memories is of Christine singing a collection of Christmas songs to the family, with me backing her with my nearly tone-deaf guitar skills. After missing so much of her childhood, it is truly a gift to be part of her family life. Christine shared her thoughts on an earlier draft with me during an hour-long soccer practice that kept her two young boys occupied. This book is better because of that discussion.

While many helped make the book better, any errors that remain are clearly my responsibility and likely resulted from my inability to stop tinkering with the text until the very last minute.

PROLOGUE

A.D. 2041

During the past century, nations have shaped, reshaped and divided at an accelerated pace. In the past 70 years, the trend toward separating nations by race, ethnicity and religion has sped to the point that even printed global maps contain coding to allow for wirelessly dispersed updates. More than a dozen nations gained independence in just the past 30 years and a dozen other city-sized nations gained effective independence from federal control. These nations formed from remnants of previously diverse societies.

Most new nations are small and resource poor enough to be left alone. Those with anything to protect – food, water, energy sources, minerals and, most of all, money – quickly build alliances to prevent external exploitation. Ironically, many new nations struggle more with internally generated exploitation. It turns out that political classes are rarely as magnanimous as they portend when leading independence movements. As has long been the case in the United States and elsewhere, the debate is rarely about whether or not there will be political spoils. Disputes are almost always over who collects these spoils. Still, hundreds of millions have hoped that a new ruler for their territory would act as the exception.

Finding sustainable alliances is difficult. During its second great depression, which finally came to an end in 2035, the United States dramatically reduced its international military involvement. This left many smaller U.S. allies scrambling to deter nations with odious ambitions from entering their borders.

The year 2040 was an eventful, nerve-wracking span – with stark implications for the future of the United States. Challenges triggering traumas that year had built, though, for generations. While secession calls occurred frequently throughout U.S. history, those calls had largely been marginalized since the Civil War. In 2040, following two generations of deep political division, secession again found a receptive audience inside U.S. borders. Powerful politicians seized the opportunity. In November, by approving secession initiatives in four Southwest states, voters gave this effort at division the legitimacy many had craved.

The United States long stood as among the most multi-cultural nations in world history even as racial, ethnic and religious separatism prevailed globally. In 2040, U.S. whites lost majority status for the first time since the nation's founding. Meanwhile, immigrants from Latin America, Asia and the Middle East bolstered the political and economic power of Latino, Asian and Arab communities to the extent that large segments of the U.S. population no longer felt compelled to integrate with people who did not share their appearance or language.

The United States is superficially multi-cultural. A closer look, however, shows that races and ethnicities are segregated inside the nation's borders and even within its political subdivisions. Racial and ethnic divisions took a troubling, deadly turn last year. Sparked by language, employment and federal control disputes, majorities of voters in Texas, New Mexico, Arizona and the recently split state of South California voted in the November 2040 elections for secession and alignment into an independent republic. The U.S. Supreme Court first determined in 1869, in *Texas v. White*, that states could not unilaterally secede. Secession could only be won, the Court determined, through either approval of the union or successful revolution.

Though the Honor to Mexico (H2M) group promoted secession referenda votes as advisory, strong majority approval of pro-secession initiatives in all four Southwest states provided legitimacy to the secession movement.

Even before the votes took place, U.S. Senator Manuel "Manny" Jones argued, and the United Nations agreed, that U.S. military or police forces might be used against pro-secession advocates if voters approved separation. The United Nations agreed to send troops to the U.S. border to provide rapid peacekeeping response in the four states, particularly to prevent genocide against Hispanics who voted to secede. Publicly, these troops were intended to prevent the U.S. military from attacking U.S. citizens.

As the Nov. 6 secession referenda results were announced, U.N. troops began amassing in large camps 10 to 100 miles south of the U.S. border. Nearly two million U.N peacekeeping troops from Russia, China, Mexico, Iran, Egypt, France, Germany, Indonesia and dozens of other countries set up camps in the Mexican provinces of Baja California, Sonora, Nuevo León, Chihuahua, Coahuila, and Tamaulipas, as well as in several provinces farther south. Large segments of the Russian, Chinese and Iranian navy fleets joined the Mexican Navy for exercises along the Yucatan Peninsula on Mexico's East Coast and around Los Cabos on Mexico's West Coast.

While angered by the United Nations' actions, reelected U.S. President Marc Phillipi did little to respond to the U.N. military build-up, in part because he had enabled it with a lie to cover a foreign policy failure just before the November elections. In addition, extensive U.S. debt held by China, Germany, Japan and other countries gave these countries substantial leverage over U.S. policy. Many countries in the U.N. coalition made clear their involvement in the "peacekeeping" mission was predicated on a need to protect their investments. Though the United States has shrunk in economic power, a civil war here will still harm lenders and drag down the global economy. Lender countries have a disproportionate stake in a U.S. recovery only recently fully emerging from the stark depression that began in 2029.

As foreign troops amassed on the U.S. southern border, President Phillipi continued to send substantial numbers of U.S. troops to urban and suburban America to protect U.S. cities from the ravages of ethnic and racial violence. These redeployments were done to uphold a 2040 campaign promise. The redeployment move was sold as proof of the President's concern for the safety of all Americans, even those he knew would not vote for him.

Terrorism has been an ongoing scourge for two generations and worsened during 2040, one of the most violent years in American history. The Harvard Massacre killed more than 100 students in late spring. Ethnic conflicts at a Washington D.C. March for Freedom event erupted into street violence that left nearly 1,000 dead and many more wounded. The leader of the Honor to Mexico movement was assassinated, a death quickly followed by coordinated highway bombings that killed several hundred more. H2M protégé Juan Gonzalez was also the target of at least one shooting.

Tensions in the United States reached another extraordinary level on New Year's Day 2041. President Phillipi elevated the U.S. military threat response level to DEFCON 2, the highest military alert level since the Cuban Missile Crisis and just a step below maximum readiness for imminent nuclear war. On that day, U.N. alliance fighter jets raced toward the U.S. border from several Mexican air bases. These jets flew at full speed to the edge of Arizona's border with Sonora, Mexico before moving into what appeared to be airborne patrol along the U.S./Mexico border.

President Phillipi dropped the military alert status back to DEFCON 4, just above normal readiness, several days later after learning that the U.N. fighters had been chasing an unidentified flying object believed to have been involved in the assassination of Mexican drug lord and economic powerhouse Cesar Castillo. Castillo, beyond running the primary cartel shipping more than 50 percent of the drugs entering the United States, was the de facto ruler of large parts of Mexico and undisclosed owner of nearly a dozen large multi-national companies. Mexico's President had called President Phillipi five minutes into the New Year's post-midnight jet scramble to seek fly-over permission. President Phillipi denied the request, but guaranteed that the U.S. military would continue the search on Mexico's behalf and bring to justice anyone involved in a crime.

Tensions are elevated between the United States and Mexico. In an angered state, U.S. President Marc Phillipi made comments to Mexican President Daniel Suárez last fall that he believed Mexico was involved in deadly U.S. highway bombings. President Suárez worried that the highway bombing accusation was a pretense for the U.S. to invade Mexico. He responded by inviting in and hosting the U.N. peacekeeping troops to protect his citizens. He also told the media that he believed that the U.S. government orchestrated the highway bombings to provide justification for territorial theft.

In addition to focusing on tensions with the United Nations, President Phillipi is restocking his Administration for his second term after a wave of post-term resignations. Recently, he began negotiating with congressional leaders to develop changes in federal-state relations that he hopes will reduce anxieties in many states. These negotiations have bogged down over tax-sharing, federal authority and language mandate issues. The President has announced plans to present a substantial package of policy changes at his State of the Union address scheduled for early February.

Since the New Year's Day scare elevated these tensions, nerves on both sides of the border have calmed only modestly.

"When we focus on which politicians win and lose in public policy disputes, we lose sight of what really matters: the people whose lives are affected by what is done for or to them."

–Professor Paul Stark

The Elements of National Destruction
August 2040

CHAPTER 1

Early January 2041
Punta Mita, Mexico

Ramon Mantle is smiling more comfortably than he has in a long time, watching his little sister Celia doing a water ballet version of her ice skating long program. She's alone in the massive infinity-edge pool at his vacation estate, enjoying extra vacation days without worrying about school.

Celia is the family prima donna, the youngest child and still a precocious pre-teen. She also can't skate right now, having injured herself just after Christmas. While sending messages to friends on her Lifelink device, the all-encompassing communication devices that dominate daily life, she walked off a ledge four feet above a parking lot and landed on both knees. The scabs are healing, at least the parts she doesn't pick at, but she's still sore enough to need a break from her ice-skating regimen.

Ramon's parents are sitting in the shade near the other end of the pool, holding hands intermittently while watching Celia continuously. Since Ramon was first brought into the Castillo cartel, family time has been rare. Ramon's father is required to work in the cartel's production operations in Mexico's Sinaloa Province whenever Ramon is working some place where his capture and death at the hands of the cartel's Protection Corps might not be immediate if he, in any way, endangered cartel profits.

Ramon first heard that cartel boss Cesar Castillo was assassinated early on New Year's morning. With his brain still highly fogged from a long night of New Year's Eve drinking, Ramon had enough sense to gather his family and get to his Punta Mita, Mexico estate before anyone in the U.S. government connected Ramon to Castillo.

Even without knowing why they were being urgently rushed to leave their home, Ramon's parents and little sister Celia were driven off in one of Ramon's off-grid vehicles. Ramon later joined his family at a private jet hangar after cleaning up and dressing in a well-tailored suit. The car Ramon drives, like all cartel vehicles, carries a system Ramon developed to evade police detection. Before following, Ramon wiped out digital traces of his connections to Castillo from his home's sub-sub-basement.

In the intervening weeks, the Castillo cartel's U.S. informants determined that suspicion of U.S. government involvement in Castillo's death was misdirected. Potential killers are under house arrest, but the informants can't access data on who they are or where they are being held. Ramon isn't sure who would be brave enough, skilled enough and stupid enough to take out Cesar Castillo, but he is sure revenge by the cartel's Protection Corps military wing will be swift and severe.

Ramon gazes at the Islas Marietas from beneath his poolside canopy. He wears only a loose silk shirt, knee-length swimming trunks, dark sunglasses and a physically embedded earring that has been his constant companion ever since he met Castillo. A 30-year scotch rests in a crystal-glass-lined platinum tumbler. The tumbler's exterior is embossed with the shape of an Aztec temple known as the Templo Mayor. He sips slowly as he ponders what new risks or opportunities he faces with his long-time protector and enslaver gone.

Ramon doesn't mind a little sun. His skin darkens quickly, but he likes how deepening his tawny color highlights his smile and his eyes.

Ramon assumes that the Protection Corps security team is still watching and listening, even as he sits within their easy grasp. For years, Ramon has been forced to wear a soldered ear-stud recording and tracking device. If any of the solders detach, he and family members could face execution. Those who attempt to escape the cartel don't last long. The consequences of capture aren't limited to cartel employees either.

Nothing coming back from cartel sources embedded inside U.S. law enforcement suggests Ramon's cartel involvement is exposed. Only his dedicated bodyguards and three senior cartel leaders had known about Ramon. One of the three, Castillo, is now dead.

Finally, after 10 days at Punta Mita, Ramon's tensions ease. It's good to be a real family again. Ramon doesn't have to play the role of father to Celia now that their father is allowed to stay with the family. Ramon enjoys treating his family to time at the beach, swimming in his pool, shopping trips down in Puerto Vallarta and up in Mazatlán, and sailing trips around the Islas Marías.

Ramon has to do some work, of course. He never fully escapes either his public profession or his cartel work. Turmoil in the cartel following Castillo's death has many watching their backs anxiously. A general inside Mexico's official military made clear the day after Castillo was killed that he planned to leave his public post to run the cartel directly. The other self-nominated contender to replace Cesar Castillo was Castillo's eldest son. He announced in Haigist fashion that he was in charge only minutes after hearing his father had been killed. After having spent the past decade in a series of drunken stupors and one-night stands, few took his declaration seriously. The risk of becoming a stated contender to run the cartel became clear when both Castillo's son and the Mexican general went missing. Hearing this, Ramon told the two high-ranking cartel leaders who knew of his work and were still alive that he would not seek greater cartel involvement.

Mexico's unofficial military wing, the cartel's Protection Corps, is led by General Raúl Hernández. Hernández retired as a general in the Mexican military after being passed over as the Army's top general and Minister of Defense. In the Army, he had been responsible for expanding the nation's elite operations capability to fight drug trafficking. Post-retirement, General Hernández turned most of his former Special Forces teams into the Protection Corps. Fifteen years later, he operates the most powerful non-government military in the world and is turning his attention to greater goals.

General Hernández is one of the two cartel leaders still alive who know Ramon's role in the cartel. Ramon's dedicated bodyguards know Ramon is as important to scrutinize as he is to protect. They know that grave consequences would follow either his death or escape.

Ramon's 12,000-square-foot Punta Mita estate includes a tennis court, movie theater and cascading infinity-edge pools leading down to a clear-encased Olympic-size pool. One-third of the Olympic pool juts out over the shoreline, hovering above the ocean supported by long, wide, clear plastic beams.

Ramon's Shady Shores, Texas home is nice, but not so overwhelming as to invite criticism that Ramon's wealth has gone to his head. At home, Ramon wants to be known as a man of the people. For years, he has thought he might someday become a U.S. senator. At his Punta Mita estate, Ramon's desire to live in opulence is indulged. A collection of Aztec and Mayan artifacts spreads through many of the compound's rooms. Ramon sees these artifacts as important reminders of centuries during which his ancestors created the world's most advanced civilizations.

Ramon's desire to live in opulence at Punta Mita is protected by men assigned by General Hernández's Protection Corps. Though Ramon trusts the Protection Corps soldiers to be concerned for his wellbeing, he understands their ultimate loyalty lies with General Hernández.

As Celia twirls around in the pool, Ramon hears commotion coming from the front of the home.

"Celia, Mom, Pops, get to the safe room," he yells. *"Now."*

In advance of an unscheduled meeting with Ramon, General Hernández sends 20 additional men to surround the Punta Mita estate.

Ramon always worried that his cartel involvement would lead to early death, but he never identified an escape path from the business. As he hears the Protection Corps soldiers surrounding his estate, he watches his parents and Celia lock themselves inside the safe room. Ramon calmly refills his scotch, grabs and fills a second tumbler and walks to a shaded poolside table. If this is going to be his last day, Ramon wants to spend it looking at the beauty of the Pacific Ocean. As Ramon takes his seat, General Hernández emerges from the home to join him. He happily takes the offered tumbler, sniffs it, takes a small sip and then guzzles the rest.

"General Hernández, I'm certainly surprised to see you today," Ramon says, in what the General clearly knows is an understatement. *"If I'm in your way in any of this, I'm happy to step aside and leave with my family."*

"Step aside, where are your cajones, hombre? You can't just let people walk all over you and take what belongs to your family," General Hernández tells Ramon.

"True, certainly, but my security team is your men. Even more importantly, this is not the business I love. You may recall that I have had no choice but to be successful to ensure my family's survival. You know this better than anyone, General."

"I do know this, Ramon, which is why you are alive today."

"So what can I do for you?"

"You, Ramon Mantle, can become the new head of the Castillo cartel."

"Me? Why?" Ramon responds, trying to keep his shock from fully displaying on his face.

"Very simple. Your technology is what has made us successful and funded my ability to build the Protection Corps. It has given me the ability to create the world's greatest and best-trained private military," General Hernández says as he stands in front of Ramon and blows cigar smoke at him. *"There are many people who think they should lead the family. But I have watched them long enough to know they would destroy what I have worked so hard to build. These people, if they took charge, would cost me my money and make it impossible for me to achieve my plans. So these people, well, they are gone. You are a successful business leader. And, I know you have noticed, you are alive."*

"So . . . you want me to lead the cartel?" Ramon asks.

"I want you to run business operations and make more money for us. If you do your job well, and I'm confident you will, you will help the Protection Corps expand our operations and eventually control other militaries to create a combined force that is the best military in the world. With your business sense and technology expertise, and my strategy and military expertise, in a few years, we will run many countries and be the most powerful and richest men in the world. There are many powerful people who want me – want us – to succeed. And they will help."

"So will I run the cartel with the support of the Protection Corps, or will you run it, and I run the business side?" Ramon asks, careful to be as non-threatening as possible.

"We'll tell everyone that you are running the cartel. The people inside will respect you once we tell them what you have done for them. They will want to follow you the way a baby attaches to his mother. Only you and I will know who gives the orders and who controls the ultimate power," General Hernández responds.

"Is this an offer or an order?"

"If you are not smart enough to answer that without my help, I may need to reconsider my offer, . . . or order as you suggest," the General responds.

"I guess this is a better deal than I've had, but I need to cash out my U.S. businesses first if people are going to tie me to the cartel," Ramon tells the General. *"The U.S. government will confiscate what they think I own once they understand the connection."*

"Then do this quickly. Once we announce to the leaders that you are running the cartel, word will spread fast. More importantly, these people do not fear you, so I will make it clear that the drunk and the General were killed on your order. From that day on, you must stay within my security for your protection."

Sensing that he has little option, Ramon accepts the offer from General Hernández. Though worried about the General's ambitions, he knows that refusing to accept the partnership will mean the end today for his family and him. The safe room can't protect his family from a man who knows its combination.

In the following days, Ramon is anxious to sell his part of his businesses, and needs a cover to enable his rapid exit.

"One more thing," General Hernández adds, now speaking in English so his guards won't understand. "I need you to work on a small technology adaptation that will put us on the path to our true goal."

CHAPTER 2

Inauguration Day, 2041
West Nogales, Arizona

At 4 a.m., Juan Gonzalez wakes to a familiar tap on the shoulder. Looking around his sparsely furnished room, part of a rental unit he shares with his mother when he's back in town, he's quickly reminded of what he has accomplished in his 19 years. His hospital volunteer-of-the-year plaque hangs from a nail. Certificates and trophies collected from his high school soccer years sit above the pressed-wood shelving unit that serves as closet and dresser. Trophies and ribbons from statewide Mandarin speaking contests are stacked up on the right side of the table he uses as a desk.

His most impressive achievements have just one visible symbol – a rather substantial award from the national Honor to Mexico (H2M) social service agency recognizing him as the H2M Medal of Honor winner for 2040. The trophy is tall enough that it rests on the floor and still rises above his table.

None of Juan's accomplishments makes it easier to wake at this early hour.

His mother, he calls her Mama, shakes his shoulder again, trying to get him moving.

"We need to leave in 30 minutes, Juan, so I'm back in time for my shift."

It is to be another interesting day in a year filled with firsts for Juan.

He's headed by private jet to represent H2M at President Marc Phillipi's inauguration into his second term. Between the inauguration ceremony and inaugural balls, he'll conduct dozens of media interviews to help sell fulfillment of H2M's secession agenda.

A year ago, Juan led a successful protest against the massive FirstWal supercenter store in West Nogales after he was denied employment because his English wasn't fluent enough. Most public school courses in West Nogales are taught in Spanish. Juan had emphasized learning Mandarin over English as a second language to increase his global job prospects, so he wasn't good enough to pass FirstWal's English fluency requirement.

Following the success of that protest, Juan became the public voice for an Arizona state law naming Spanish as the state's official language. Success there gained H2M's attention, and Juan was recruited to take a year off before starting college to become national spokesman for the H2M-driven secession referenda in Texas, New Mexico, Arizona and the recently split state of South California.

During 2040, he was threatened, chased, shot and grilled in both Congress and the media. To this day, he's uncertain which of these experiences he enjoyed least. Juan also became a cover boy for numerous national publications, attracted enormous crowds to rallies and caused a sizable number of female admirers to toss assorted garments onto stages during public H2M rallies.

Some of the attraction is certainly appearance driven. At six-feet tall, Juan has a slender but well-defined, muscular frame. He has a strong chin with dimpled cheeks, open brown eyes and a broad smile with teeth that look almost straight out of a denture catalogue, particularly contrasted against his modestly tanned skin tone. His strong, youthful appearance helps gain attention for his causes, but his life story is what makes Juan a national sensation.

Raised in West Nogales by a single mother who moved from Mexico just as the second great depression began, Juan has long known what it's like to not know where tomorrow's meal is coming from. He often was left to feed himself while his mother put in overtime to keep the electricity on and food in the cabinet. Juan's development has been his mother's single-minded obsession.

Though others have much easier lives, Juan never lets it bother him. He always has a kind word for others, works hard and plays sports with a dramatic flair. Juan frequently says he believes God intends for him to be somebody, but acts with a natural humility in his everyday interactions.

Ten minutes after hearing they must leave immediately, Juan makes his way down the concrete stairs outside their unit, holding the tuxedo, suit, winter coat and shoes purchased for him by H2M in one hand, and his normal clothes and hotel toiletry assortment in a bag with the other.

Mama, dressed already in her company uniform, has borrowed a friend's car to drive Juan to a private hanger at an airstrip in Tucson, Arizona. The irony of leaving the apartment he has been raised in – a place sometimes lacking even in necessities – to ride an opulent, amenity-stocked private airplane is not lost on Juan. He always grabs a few snacks, drinks and soaps for Mama whenever he is flying home.

While the automated car Mama borrowed drives them to Tucson, she keeps Juan busy talking, at times holding the outside of his hand when she raises a point she wants to be sure he understands. He'll have time enough to sleep on the plane, she tells him. She misses their time together now that Juan is so busy flying around the country to speak for H2M about the benefits to the rest of the United States of allowing the secession states to leave.

Because they're running late, Mama drops Juan off outside the hangar, hugs him and pulls his forehead down to kiss him as she pushes to resize the car for her single-person return trip. She resets her destination with the hope of making it to work on time. The automated software that controls these cars determines the pace and route each car will take, never surpassing speed limits. She can't make it go any faster, even to avoid being late for work.

Mama dozes off during the drive back to West Nogales.

After saying goodbye, Juan stops in the hangar restroom and rechecks his bags before walking out to an H2M jet he has taken many times to get to Washington, D.C. and other cities where he speaks for H2M.

Fifty steps out of the hangar, Juan stops suddenly.

His face turns pale. His eyes open fully. Eyebrows elevate.

Gabriel Herrera is looking at him from the jet window. Gabriel runs H2M, having replaced his father after an unsolved assassination of Ángel Herrera last year. Juan remains convinced that Gabriel has tried to have him killed to consolidate his power in H2M. Gabriel even publicly threatened to take him out at a massive Washington, D.C. rally before saying his comments were taken out of context. Despite this fear, Juan continues working with H2M on the condition that Gabriel must stay away from him anywhere hundreds of people are not present. Juan's commitment to the cause is stronger than his fear for his own life, but he refuses to be alone with Gabriel.

Sensing trouble on seeing Gabriel, Juan turns and starts running back to the hangar.

As he does, two bodyguards emerge from the hangar and one from the jet, all with weapons drawn. Juan quickly realizes these are Gabriel's personal bodyguards. He might be able to outrun them, but he can't beat a bullet.

Gabriel emerges from the door of the plane as the bodyguards walk Juan up the stairs.

"Get him in here," Gabriel orders the bodyguards, two of whom now are firmly squeezing Juan's triceps and biceps, forcing him toward the plane.

Juan swivels his head as he is being pushed, looking for an escape route or for someone who might call the police. No one else is around at this early hour.

Shoved down into a thickly padded leather seat inside the H2M jet, Juan stares at Gabriel as he sits reclined two thirds of the way back. Seeing Juan looking for a way out, Gabriel sits up and leans forward, stopping his face just inches away from Juan. A guard continues to hold a gun pressed up to Juan's ear.

"Today is going to be a far more momentous day than you can imagine Juan," Gabriel assures him.

"What do you mean?" Juan asks, trying to hide his fear as a bodyguard grabs a hood to pull over his head.

"I can't give you any more details until it happens," Gabriel tells him. "We need to be somewhere secure when it happens and that's where we're headed."

"What's 'it'?" Juan asks.

"If I tell you now," Gabriel says, looking toward the nearest bodyguard, "my friend here would need to clean both of our brains off the cabin wall after he puts them there. It would be such a shame to mess up such beauty."

Gabriel caresses the soul patch below his bottom lip between his thumb and index finger. Then he rubs the thin beard line that connects elongated sideburns along his chin as if outlining his face for a portrait. "Don't you agree?" he finally asks after creating an outline of his face with his middle fingers.

With a hood being pulled over his face, and one hand cuffed to his chair, Juan can no longer see Gabriel's face, let alone a way out. He tries folding his fingers and thumb in to slide his hand out of a cuff, but it has been closed too tight.

"You really think you can escape all of us," Gabriel says, watching Juan's machinations. "You're such a naïve little boy sometimes. But don't worry. You'll be happy with what happens today. You'll see I am actually doing you a great favor to prove my belief in you, but I have to follow the security precautions I've been given."

With the jet taking off, Juan tries calming himself. He tries to visualize what direction the jet is heading by feeling which way his body is pressing as it turns. Then he tries keeping track of how long he's in the air by counting to 60 repeatedly. He's well past counting 70 times before he loses track of his count and decides that knowing he's been in the air for more than an hour has to be enough. His only relief from isolation comes when the hood and cuffs are removed for a short restroom break, during which the guard's primary concern is that he not see outside.

After landing, Juan tries listening to the sound of the vehicle he's being driven in. It sounds like an old-fashioned engine – not the quiet, fluid cars driven on city streets and run by automated Easy Ride control. Juan's trip to his holding cell includes an elevator and numerous flights of stairs. Once in the room, his hood and cuffs are removed. The only window in the room is on the door. A guard peers through that window to check on him.

Looking around the room, the only other potential exits are through the ceiling or through a manhole in the floor. The manhole, however, is easily within view of the guard and the ceiling won't be quick or easy to reach.

He decides that escape won't work. Even if he makes it out of the room, he has no idea where to go from there.

Despite being frisked and having much of what he had with him taken, Juan still has an emergency device tucked away in an underwear compartment his mother had sewn for him. Professor Paul Stark gave him the device after helping to save Juan from Gabriel's last threat on his life. He already made one quick, quiet contact from the jet restroom using the device.

While being searched on the jet, Gabriel's guards found Juan's normal Lifelink multi-function device and his bag of fried peanut butter, refried bean, rice and poblano balls that Juan eats frequently when he needs comfort food. But they missed the underwear-sewn emergency contact chip phone in patting Juan down. Gabriel's guards had known Juan for more than six months and didn't consider him a real threat. Thinking about how the chip phone could help him, Juan searches the room for cameras and audio bugs. After finding none, he stands in a corner, pulls out the chip phone and tries to make a call.

He can't get a connection.

***

U.S. Southwest

As the sun sets, truck traffic streams out of the massive West Nogales Border Flooring distribution center, a scene that repeats at more than 200 other large distribution centers linked to a dozen companies within 20 miles of the U.S-Mexico border. The first movement starts in southeast Texas. Trucks in Texas have as much as five hours to get cargo in place. By the time trucks roll in South California, cargo only has three hours to reach delivery destinations.

Nearly 20 highway-like tunnels deep beneath the U.S. border are lined up with advanced weaponry and troops being lifted to the surface on the U.S. side and sped to target destinations. The tunnels were built and used for decades by the Castillo cartel, or the Caskillo cartel as the group was often called during its heaviest days of mass executions. The tunnels were built to supply U.S. citizens with the world's largest supply of illicit drugs. Now, they transport a speedier tool of control.

At sites throughout the Southwest, U.N. troops meet their trucks and delivery vehicles. More than one million U.N. troops are entering U.S. territory under a peacekeeping plan in which not every participating country shares a common understanding of the objective. Several nations are sending troops as peacekeepers after being told that intelligence agents have determined that the U.S. military plans to attack secession supporters at midnight tonight. Others send their troops with a more insidious purpose. Many of these invasion-minded troops entered U.S. territory through the cartel's deep underground tunnels in recent days. Others came as tourists or through border inspection sites run by agents who don't dare question their secondary employer and controller.

It helps greatly that the four border state governors are all in on the plan, and have built massive National Guard centers near the Mexico border to confine and confuse view of so much movement.

Road traffic in the four Southwest states is unusually high to those living in the area. However, law enforcement agency systems don't show unusual activity. Law enforcement agencies use traffic data produced by Perfect Logistics Company. Perfect Logistics pulls data from its Easy Ride operating software that is required to operate every public road vehicle. Perfect Logistics is essentially owned and controlled by the Castillo cartel, though both the ownership and control are well hidden from public view. Ramon controls a sizable portion of what is known of the company's ownership.

Inside the FBI's counter-terrorism center, an agent on duty takes a call from a college friend working highway patrol near San Antonio, Texas.

"I must'a had 1,000 trucks just roll past me out here, man," he tells the agent, "but our dispatch folks tell me they ain't on the system. Y'all got some kind of exercise goin' on down here y'all forgot to let us know 'bout?"

"Hell if I know. I'll check into it and get back to you," the agent responds. "You see anything that worries you?"

"It's just odd. I've never seen nothin' like it, and now it looks like a wave of doublewides comin' through," the patrolman says. "I mean, like hundreds and hundreds. Hell, I can't even see the end of the line. It's not tornado or hurricane season, so where could they be goin'?"

"No idea, but I'll make some calls," the agent says. "But if you really want to know, you'll find out a lot faster by pulling one over."

"Maybe so. They ain't doin' nothin' illegal, but I'm sure I can find a busted tail light somewhere."

"Let me know what you find out. Meanwhile, I'll check around."

The agent starts searching through federal agencies for anyone who knows what's happening.

Meanwhile the patrolman decides to take his friend's advice, and pulls up next to one of the doublewide trailers. Normally, he can force any vehicle to stop by scanning its identification code from its plates. Then, traffic dispatch connects to and disables that vehicle's Easy Ride system and pulls it over at the next safe location. This vehicle doesn't pull over until the patrolman flashes his lights and the driver spots him. As he pulls over, a bit of the doublewide sticks out into the driving lane.

With a long trail of doublewides moving around him, the patrolman pulls behind the truck. He walks toward the passenger side of the truck, away from traffic, with his flashlight on in his left hand and his right hand on his pistol. As he reaches the truck cab, he turns to look back when he hears the front door of the doublewide, halfway back on the trailer, open up. A woman pops her head out to ask if she can help the officer.

"You can't be ridin' around in a trailer while it's being hauled," the patrolman tells her. "Y'all need to get down from there."

As he finishes the sentence, she steps a few inches to the side. The last sight for the patrolman is a flash. Before he can move, he has a hole punched straight through his forehead and out the back.

"*Roll him to a ditch,*" the shooter shouts in Urdu. "*Who can drive an old car? Okay, drive his car to a remote area and ditch it. Stay hidden until we have base control and then catch up.*"

With troops and weapons in place, U.S. Senator Manny Jones calls for Conversion Hour attacks to begin. Simultaneous assaults take place at 23 military targets in Texas, New Mexico, Arizona and South California. Only 20 of the U.N. countries are aware of and take part in these military base assaults. The rest of the nations are sending their troops to cities and borders to prevent what they are told is a planned midnight U.S. assault on secession support targets.

At Cannon Air Force Base in New Mexico, 300 semi-trailer trucks and 200 trucks carrying double-wide trailers come to stops along 60/84, County Road R and Wheatridge Drive. Tank-like vehicles mounted with anti-aircraft missiles emerge from the mobile homes and race toward the air base. Other assault vehicles emerge from the truck trailers and break through the guard stations, shooting down anyone trying to stop them from entering. More than 10,000 U.N. troops emerge from the trucks as well as from school and tourist buses arriving at the base. Those trucks and buses had converged on the nearby city of Clovis just ahead of the assault.

On-site defenses are light. Most special operation units housed here have been reassigned to support National Guard and police in maintaining peace in Boston, Kansas City and other mixed race communities. Several other companies are out on training exercises when the Egyptian-led U.N. contingent takes control of the base, killing dozens in the initial assault. The remainder of U.S. troops withdraw to avoid a massive threatened explosion of family housing; an explosion they are told will occur with the families still inside if U.S. troops do not back down. From there, a handful of defectors align with the secession movement and help finalize the United Nations takeover of major portions of the air base. Several pilots stationed at Cannon don't wait for orders. They reach their jets and get airborne before their planes are destroyed.

Within minutes, the base commander communicates the assault to the Pentagon. His instructions to troops to repel the attack at all costs go nowhere with his communication system quickly compromised and destroyed. Airborne pilots are unable to connect to either base command or directly to the Pentagon, so they start circling the base awaiting orders until they are chased off by in-bound jets from Egypt and other U.N. invasion nations.

A separate Russian-led U.N. contingent shuts down Dyess Air Force Base in Texas after an initial struggle. With site communications again compromised, a coordinated U.S. response is stifled. Dozens of U.S. officers organize companies to attack U.N. troops. Within 20 minutes of surrendering operating control of the base, Iranian, Saudi, Russian and Egyptian fighters are landing on the strip, adding to the U.N. troop contingent at the base.

Deaths on both sides from the U.N. "peacekeeping mission" are repeated at nearly two-dozen bases throughout the Southwest. The success of the United Nations takeover is sped by the dearth of combat-capable troops serving on base at the time of the attack. These troops were moved as part of the show-of-force peacekeeping efforts President Marc Phillipi instituted to reduce racial and ethnic confrontations in urban and suburban areas the prior year. Several generals working with Senator Manny Jones on his secession plan gained undue influence on troop redeployments. Reassigned troops were those these generals deemed most likely to be effective in combating the invasion.

Most importantly, U.S. intelligence agencies missed hundreds, if not thousands of warning signs. A recent miss was the FBI counterterrorism agent who wasn't able to piece together the San Antonio truck warning from earlier that night with other information that would have suggested an invasion was under way.

As is usually the case in a disaster, no individual error accounts for all of a travesty. Tens of thousands of foreign troops had entered the United States illegally over the past several months. Many were sent with intelligence-gathering missions, but entered as tourists. As often as possible, Russian, Chinese and other spy agencies constructed families of older male and female spies and soldiers. These "parents" brought teenage children with them, most of whom were unrelated young soldiers. When several of the countries ran out of enough trained female soldiers and spies, they replaced the husbands in families that had already secured tourist visas with trained intelligence agents. To maintain security, they held the real husbands and fathers under arrest to ensure that families remained silent during their time in the United States. All were sent with what they believed was a human rights protection mission – until they were activated as the full launch began.

Large groups of other foreign troops had entered the United States through deep tunnels under the U.S. borders with Canada and Mexico. In Canada, the soldiers arrived at ports where foreign governments had well-established relationships with local customs officials, primarily in Vancouver and several locations throughout Quebec province where arms to support Quebec's independence movement were exchanged for easy access to U.S. territory.

In all, more than one million foreign soldiers reached Alta Texas territory ahead of the invasion launch. Another million are streaming into the Southwest by land, air and sea as Conversion Hour begins.

***

Washington, D.C.

Word of the United Nations attack reaches President Phillipi during an inaugural ball.

Ten minutes into Conversion Hour, the governors of the now provinces of Texas, Arizona, Nuevo Mexico and California del Sur announce their secession from the United States of America and the formation of the Republic of Alta Texas.

"We, the People of the Republic of Alta Texas, declare our independence from the United States of America and all others who lay claim to our lands, to live as free people in a nation that honors and respects our heritage and our aspirations," reads part of the first English translation of the Alta Texas Declaration of Independence.

Supported by the four state governors, Manny Jones is declared interim president of the Republic. He doesn't bother to resign as a U.S. senator from the State of Texas. President Jones issues a statement saying he and the governors invited U.N. troops to enter Alta Texas to protect the people of his new nation from "genocidal attack expected as a response from the U.S. military" to the formal secession announcement.

Just after formation of the Republic is announced, U.N. Secretary General Sudarto Suryasumantri issues a statement that the United Nations considers Alta Texas to be an independent country operating under full U.N. protection. In all, 67 countries are part of the U.N. peacekeeping mission. A total of 45 of these nations send troops into Alta Texas territory. Of these, 20 nations join President Jones in operating out of the true Alta Texas command center. The Secretary-General's announcement lists all 67 countries taking part in the peacekeeping operation, but doesn't separate the list by those countries in attack mode versus those with peacekeeping troops in Alta Texas and those nations whose troops remain in Mexico.

Leaders of several nations publicly pledge that their troops will fight and die to protect the lives of "those brave individuals who are securing independence from one of the world's most invasive nations." China, Japan, Germany and several other holders of large amounts of U.S. debt quickly announce that their nations will call all debt immediately and stop lending should the U.S. take retaliatory action against U.N. troops.

Air Force bases and air wings of other military units are secured inside
Alta Texas as these statements are issued. The United Nations soon announces that it has surrounded all major military facilities inside Alta Texas
to take control of the Republic's "fair share" of weapons at those bases. This
U.N. announcement calls for troops at these bases to surrender control of
all major weapons and relocate to protective custody inside family housing.

In the middle of a private discussion at his inaugural ball, President
Phillipi is surrounded by Secret Service agents and rushed back to the
White House to decide how to respond to this attack. At midnight, still
wearing a tuxedo he had worn to the inaugural ball, President Phillipi
takes to the national airwaves to issue his response:

"I had planned at the State of the Union to announce a new agenda
to turn many responsibilities usurped by the federal government over the
last 250 years back to the states – moving government closer to the people
where it belongs. Rather than patiently wait to resolve the critical issues
we debate, several power-hungry politicians are exploiting their chance to
seize power. What's worse, they are enslaving our people to foreign governments who do not share any interest in the survival and prosperity of our
nation, let alone its people," President Phillipi says in his national address.

"I am offering these treasonous politicians and the military officials
backing them a one-time deal. If, in the next 72 hours, they demand that
foreign troops withdraw from their invasion of the United States and fully
abandon efforts to force four states into seceding from the United States, I
will offer full presidential pardons and allow them to live out the remainder
of their lives comfortably at an enclave of the choosing of the President of
Mexico. If, in 72 hours from this moment, this deal is not accepted, we will
bring the wrath of the United States military down on all involved in a terror I am frightened to even imagine.

"Please pray with me and please pray to your God for intervention. God
help us all in the next 72 hours and, God willing, beyond."

CHAPTER 3

72 Hours

January 21, 2041
Chicago

Rachel Cruz calls home as soon as President Phillipi's press conference ends. Her Lifelink signal and alerts set by everyone around her are buzzing so continuously that within 60 seconds of the first sound, Rachel decides to stop her reading prep for graduate classes at the University of Chicago to see what is happening.

Alerted to the secession and simultaneous U.N. invasion, Rachel quickly contacts her parents at the family's Fresno, North California home. Fresno is only a short distance north of the border with the new Alta Texas province of California del Sur.

In 2029, California was broken in half, due in part to Democratic Party efforts to expand control of the U.S. Senate through adding two reliably Democratic Senate seats. After contentious court battles, the U.S. Supreme Court settled state boundary line disputes by redrawing legislatively planned borders to ensure that South California had a strong majority Latino population.

"Mom, is everyone okay?" asks Rachel, twisting her long, black hair into a ponytail shape and spinning it around her fingers.

"Oh God, please talk to Papa," her mother responds.

"Why? What's going on?"

"He pulled his guns out of storage and he's in the basement loading them now. He says he's going to the new border to fight."

"For who?" Rachel asks as her deep brown eyes begin to shimmer. Tremors take control of Rachel's cheek muscles. She slouches over in her chair to hide her face from those around her while tightly twisting her hair until she feels several roots pulling from the back of her head.

"I didn't ask. I'm trying to stop him. Just talk to him," Rachel's mother pleads, handing him her Lifelink multi-functional device and demanding that he talk to his daughter.

Rachel's father, Victor Cruz, was born in Mexico. Rachel calls him Papa. While proud to be an American, Victor is also proud of his Mexican heritage. Through Rachel's childhood, he spoke to her in Spanish while Rachel's white mother raised her in English. Victor Cruz is a hard-working man, having put in extraordinary hours throughout Rachel's life to give her a chance to succeed in the United States. Rachel, now a graduate student at the University of Chicago, sees the potential for a better life within her grasp.

"Papa, what are you doing?"

"I'm going to fight for my family," he says in a matter-of-fact tone.

"On which side?" Rachel asks with far less sense of calm.

"We're Americans now. I can't let invaders come and destroy my home," he tells Rachel while he continues searching for and packing the supplies and materials he expects to need.

"But you're Mexican Papa. What if the Americans think you're the enemy?"

"I'm wearing a flag so they know. Don't worry so much. I'm thinking about what I'm doing," he tells her.

"How do you know one of our Mexican neighbors won't shoot you if they decide to take sides with this Alta Texas country?"

"Rachel, I can't worry about something like that because I have to do what I know is right so I can live with myself," Victor Cruz says. He pauses for a moment, then smiles as he speaks. "I love you. I love my family. I can't live with thinking I let something terrible happen to you. Stay where you are. I'm putting Mom and your brother in the car and sending them to stay with you until this is over."

"Papa."

"Yes Rachel."

"I love you. Please come with them."

"I can't sweetie. You know I can't. I love you too," Victor Cruz says, ending the connection.

Rachel's heart skips a beat. She shrivels off her chair, down to the floor. Kneeling first, then hunching over. Finally, Rachel straightens on her knees to pray, one elbow resting on the seat of her chair for support and the other hand still actively twisting her hair.

After several minutes of prayer, she concludes: "Please God. I beg you to help all of the stupid men now threatening to pull us apart to come to their senses and bring peace back to our lives."

Looking around and realizing now where she is, Rachel sees dozens seated around the library looking at her. A few students she doesn't know come over to ask if she's okay. Rachel pulls on her coat, gloves, hat and boots. A few students keep watching, following her with their eyes as she walks to the door, trying not to be too obvious as they do so.

Minutes later, Rachel finds the doors to Rockefeller Chapel unlocked. She goes to the back row, pulls down the kneeler and drops to her knees with elbows resting on the back of the pew in front of her. Taking off her gloves, she cups her face in her hands.

Rachel is jolted from deep thought into realizing where she is when she hears the door open behind her.

***

Flagstaff, Arizona

John Coleman has lived for the past 45 years in Flagstaff, having moved here with his parents after his father retired from the Army. Even 10 miles away, shots taking place at Camp Navajo outside of Flagstaff are unusually loud. John, a sizable, gruff and sometimes awkward man, decides he needs to know what's going on. He turns on the radio and hears that United Nations troops have started to take control of U.S. military bases in the Southwest. He also hears the secession announcement and decides he can't waste any time getting north.

John startles his wife and daughters, screaming at them to grab whatever they need to survive at the New Rite compound in Utah. The compound is the first escape spot that comes to his mind. John and his daughters have gone there for survival training and weekend excursions several times over the years.

John attaches his pre-packed escape trailer behind their Right Size adaptable car and checks with his dad on whether he's joining them.

"Hell no," Grandpa Coleman tells him. "Someone's got to protect our property."

John has learned that arguing with Grandpa gets him nowhere. He isn't surprised when he sees his dad pulling a chair outside while armed with a Marimaster 1500 rifle and 100 rounds of ammunition.

Grandpa Coleman, as everyone calls John's dad, puts his Lifelink device into the Right Size car and does his eye scan so the car will expand to fit an additional seat that holds as much money, clothing, weapons and food as adds up to Grandpa's weight. He's not going with, but this provides more storage space for the rest of the family.

After setting their destination for the New Rite Utah camp, the Colemans travel up Fort Valley Ranch Road, avoiding the already closed Route 89. United Nations guards already have set up blockades on many major northern travel routes. Fully legal, unaltered cars that pass no exits before reaching the barricades simply shut down and wait in lines at these barricades. The Coleman family is fortunate. Easy Ride software recognizes the barricades ahead while the Colemans still have an alternative route north. When the software later shuts down and disables their car, John switches the vehicle to off-grid travel using a manual override he installed in all of the family's vehicles. John learned how to self-install the black-market overrides after taking up survival training.

Technically, it's a federal crime to drive on public roads with a vehicle not controlled by approved traffic and fuel management operating software. John knows now that it was smart to ignore that piece of excessive government limitation.

***

Republic of Alta Texas Headquarters

After the secession announcement goes public, Juan Gonzalez is surprised and relieved when Manny Jones enters his holding room. Juan met then-Senator Jones last summer through H2M at congressional hearings, at the funeral for H2M founder Ángel Herrera and at other public events in Texas and Washington, D.C. Throughout 2040, Senator Jones was the most prominent elected official speaking aggressively in favor of Spanish-only language requirements and particularly for secession of Texas, New Mexico, Arizona and South California. Now, Alta Texas President Jones fills Juan in on the secession announcement and U.N. troop protection arrangement.

President Jones takes Juan up several floors and briefly returns the Lifelink device confiscated from him by the guards so he can call his mother. Lifelinks are multi-functional devices needed to connect to any digital network, validate identity and pay for almost anything.

Juan tells his mother that he is safe, but can't tell her where he is. He will be unreachable for several days.

"¿Por qué no?" she asks. Why not?

"No sé estoy," Juan responds. I don't know where I am.

Mama Gonzalez assures Juan that she is safe. She doesn't understand why she needs to have four bodyguards to protect her door, she tells him, but it does make her feel better since there is so much military traffic streaming through the area.

"¿Le llamo a la policía para usted?" she asks. Should I call the police?

"Mamá, aquí todos hablan español," he tells her, letting her know that the people he is with are listening and they understand Spanish.

With U.N. troops having already surrounded most military bases in the four states, Alta Texas President Jones is no longer worried that Juan will give away critical Conversion Hour information. He stops listening as Juan finishes his call home.

Once Juan finishes the call with his mother, his Lifelink alerts him to another call. It's Congresswoman Jill Carlson. Alta Texas President Manny Jones tells Juan that this discussion can be his first official duty as ambassador to the United States, if he wants the job. Juan is overwhelmed at the idea that he might be Alta Texas ambassador to the United States. Going from ambassador for H2M on several issues to being ambassador to one of the 10 most important countries in the world is a big step for someone who hasn't even been to college yet, Juan realizes. Juan expresses immediate gratitude to President Jones and tells him that the offer of the role sounds wonderful, even as he responds to the call from Jill.

"Juan, have you heard what's happening? Did you know about the U.N. troops attacking our bases?" Jill asks.

Juan doesn't truly comprehend her question, having not been told much about the peacekeeping mission, let alone the invasion.

"Good evening Congresswoman. It's good to hear you're safe and sound. Have you heard from the professor? Is he okay as well?" Juan asks in rather stoic tones.

"Yes, yes, he's fine. He's right here. I'll put you on speaker," she says. "So are you part of this Juan?"

"I haven't decided, but I've been asked, in a way, to join President Jones' administration as ambassador to the United States," Juan tells the pair, with President Jones standing next to him, listening to the conversation. "I want this secession to be non-violent and President Jones doesn't believe there's any way to guarantee our safety without U.N. protection."

"I can't believe what I'm hearing," Jill responds, putting the call on speaker so Professor Stark can listen in. "This is treason. You're bringing foreign armies onto our land."

"No, no it's not. This is helping my people find the freedom and self-control we deserve. We have the right as an independent republic to invite foreigners to join and help us as we . . . as our President deems appropriate," Juan says, looking toward President Jones and speaking in a loud, tense tone.

"I can't even begin to tell you how disappointed and angry I am with you," Jill says. Professor Stark adds, "I'm afraid Juan, that you're being used. It's only a matter of time before those who understand the true elements of power will sacrifice you and your life to their aims."

"I thought about that. President Jones assured me that his first act of goodwill will be to turn over Gabriel Herrera to the U.S. FBI if I ask him to do this, particularly after today," Juan says, while scanning the military command center room surrounding him. "I hope I will be able to talk more soon, but I have to ensure our people are protected and decide what I need to do. Goodbye Congresswoman. Goodbye Professor."

Professor Stark tries to jump in on the call. "Juan, Juan, Juan."

"Yes, Professor."

"You say you want to create freedom and safety for your people as your primary objective," Professor Stark says.

"That's what I've been saying all year. I'm glad you understand," Juan replies.

"As you decide what to do, just think about what the nations who have come to supposedly protect you will expect of you and your people to repay that debt," Professor Stark says. "If you think through this carefully, I think you'll see you're making the greatest mistake of your life. Please think about it. They'll demand to set up military bases on your land and it will get worse from there."

"How's that any different from the U.S. paying down debt by selling away land? Oh, no, I need to go," Juan states. President Jones has left Juan's side. The guard assigned to Juan is moving quickly toward him, and has instructions to take Juan's Lifelink back.

After this tense discussion, Juan considers whether the peaceful separation he seeks for his people can be achieved. He hadn't been told anything about attacking U.S. military bases, and wonders whether it's smart to ask about this accusation.

Congresswoman Carlson, Jill as she demands to be called, is Juan's favorite legislator among the many he has met in the past year. Jill is nearly the same age as Juan's mother and shows a genuine, almost motherly, concern for Juan. Besides, Juan still believes that Jill and University of Chicago Professor Paul Stark helped save his life last year.

Though Jill and Professor Stark had opposed the Spanish-only language mandates and secession movements Juan championed last year, they had risked their lives to save him when Juan thought Gabriel Herrera was trying to have him killed during the bloody aftermath of the March for Freedom Rally. The passionate following Juan generated last summer remains unfettered even by speculation that Gabriel or others in the H2M leadership were behind at least one attempt to assassinate Juan.

After another 30 minutes, Juan secures permission to again speak with President Jones. Juan's guard, wearing a U.S. Army uniform with the U.S. flag replaced, escorts him back up to the command center. Juan studies the new flag on the guard's uniform as they walk. Juan decides it must be a State of Texas flag with the blue behind the star replaced by the green that appears in the Mexican flag. Walking in on President Jones, he asks for a couple of minutes to raise questions before confirming his decision to accept the ambassadorship.

"Juan, I can't do this now. Some U.S. bases aren't surrendering their weapons. The peacekeepers are demanding permission to attack everyone barricaded around the weapons. I'm trying to get them to show some patience. We'll find you once it quiets down," President Jones says, before nodding at security to have Juan moved back to a secure location.

Oh, maybe we did really attack some bases, Juan realizes.

Though he wants Juan to join his team, President Jones keeps him away from military decision-making. Until he's certain of Juan's allegiance, he can't risk compromising the Republic's military tactics. Who knows what he might learn that he could give away, even unknowingly, as ambassador.

***

Washington, D.C.

During the high-speed drive to the White House from the inaugural ball, Defense Secretary Xavier Mendoza calls President Phillipi with a brief on the invasion. Secretary Mendoza has already ordered troops at the attacked bases to barricade in place while maintaining weapons control rather than directly engage the United Nations troops.

Reluctant to enter full-scale war without considering alternatives, President Phillipi agrees. The President calls the U.N. Secretary-General and tells him that the U.S. troops inside the bases will stand down and not shoot if the U.N. troops stop advancing and attacking. The Secretary-General passes the message on to Alta Texas President Jones, who responds back that he will agree to hold back further attacks. Jones does not send this message out to his troops for an hour though. Even once he issues the orders, it takes another hour for his orders to reach troops through the U.N.'s convoluted communication protocol.

After arriving at the White House, the President and other leaders immediately drop to the Deep Underground Command Center (DUCC) to manage the war response.

"Can we slice the head of this treason?" President Phillipi asks on the extended elevator drop to the DUCC. "I mean, do we have enough of a bead on Manny and the governors that we can conduct drone strikes and take them all out as enemy combatants without killing too many civilians?"

"We're trying first to locate the city each is in, but there's no human intel on specific locations," Defense Secretary Mendoza acknowledges as he looks to a display screen for confirmation from the Central Intelligence Agency director. "I assume they're all smart enough to have lost their electronic tracking long ago. In fact, we've been told the signatures suggest all of them are in D.C., and I find that highly unlikely."

"No one has any visual on the ground?"

"Nothing yet. We're working on it."

"What about flight tracking?"

"We checked that. More than 100 private jets left from the metropolitan area right after the swearing-in, landing in almost 80 different locations," the CIA director responds.

White House Chief of Staff Vijay Chinh interjects. "So if we kill them all, then who's in charge? Does the United Nations take firm control? At that point, the Chinese or Russians or Mexicans are as likely to take control of the four states as any other political leader. Are we sure we don't want to be sure an American, or at least an ex-American, still has control of military decisions until we can end this?"

"Good point. Move everyone to DEFCON 2. Beef up our presence around borders with these states. What's going on at our Southwest bases?" the President orders and asks. The subsequent global U.S. military alert warns American troops that they must be ready for combat in less than six hours.

Display screens are lit up around the DUCC Situation Room. Secretary Mendoza points to a wall-sized map showing U.S. operations and personnel locations compared against estimated U.N. force locations.

"U.N. troops, and a few U.S. defectors, have surrounded most of our primary bases in the four states and called for everyone to turn over their weapons and leave the base," Secretary Mendoza says. "From satellite, it looks like several bases are emptying out where the on-site leadership has apparently defected. Following your orders, many of our other bases are hunkered down inside. Keep in mind, most of these bases are understaffed since we sent tens of thousands to serve as peacekeepers in troubled cities and 'burbs."

"Those troops came from everywhere. Right?"

"No, Mr. President. Turns out almost all came from our Southwest bases. Don't ask me why I didn't question these assignments earlier, because I have no acceptable answer. Generals responsible for making these assignments in three of the four branches defected to Alta Texas officially at the time the secession was announced, but clearly were working with Jones for some time."

President Phillipi pounds his desk, knocking some papers off to float to the floor. "Where the hell was our intelligence while this was happening?" he asks, balling both hands into fists. A second later, snapping his head toward Mendoza, he adds: "Any nuclear risk?"

"We're changing all of the codes as we speak," Secretary Mendoza assures him, "but we think most of the nuclear side is contained. We're more concerned that defectors have given U.N. troops access to all our secure communication. We're scrambling to work around this."

"So even if we want to respond immediately," President Phillipi says while cupping his hands behind his head and bending his leg to put his left foot on a chair, "they'll know exactly what we're doing?"

"Seems that way for now sir. We're working through alternatives, but some defectors took part in those exercises, so we're pushing to come up with a new communications protocol," Secretary Mendoza responds. "One more thing, Mr. President. It appears a battle has broken out around Camp Pendleton. The Chinese and Russian naval fleets are racing toward Tijuana as we speak and could provide air support to the U.N. invaders. We need to get air support in as soon as possible if it looks like the Marines there will be attacked or bombed."

"For God's sake, get President Suárez on the phone and if anyone knows how to reach Traitor Manny directly, get him on as well," President Phillipi orders.

A successful Tennessee business executive who founded and grew two successful companies, Marc Phillipi is used to working in a high-stress environment making dozens of simultaneous decisions. He began his first presidential race near the tail end of America's second great depression, wanting to bring common sense and business judgment to fix a long-faltering economy that left many families financially ruined. The poor economy accentuated racial and ethnic divisions that had been allowed to fester and sometimes were even nurtured by politicians and media seeking to dominate ever-narrowing niche markets and racially segregated constituencies. Those tensions exploded last year. In his first term, President Phillipi may have wandered cautiously into involving himself aggressively in military decisions, given his lack of military experience. But confidence built during four years as the nation's chief executive, combined with active engagement with the intelligence and military communities during that time, makes him comfortable calling the shots today.

Frustrated on hearing that U.N. troops continue to attack U.S. bases in the four states, the President asks to patch through to Mexico's President Suárez. President Suárez is a Yale-educated lawyer, credited with controlling violent crime in the southern and central provinces his government most directly controls and spurring good economic growth throughout Mexico. He's the most popular leader there in generations. Suárez's connection to the Castillo cartel is unclear to U.S. policymakers. Many take the reduction in mass executions in Mexico as a sign the cartel now has firm control, with the Suárez administration doing little to interfere with their operations. Others argue that Suárez has the cartel operating on its best behavior in fear of government encroachment into currently cartel-controlled northern Mexico.

After failing to reach President Suárez, Mexico's ambassador to the United States is escorted to the White House DUCC for an in-person session.

"Tell President Suárez that he has 15 minutes to get his troops, the U.N. and everyone else fighting this war on your behalf away from our

men and their families or we'll engage without waiting for my deadline,"
President Phillipi tells the ambassador. The ambassador is regaining ori-
entation, having entered a controlled room inside the DUCC under heavy
guard and wearing a blindfold and earplugs. His descent to the DUCC took
nearly 10 minutes.

"I can assure you, Mr. President, that . . . ," the ambassador starts to
respond.

"I don't give a damn about your assurances. Pass on the message or all-
out war is on your head," President Phillipi belts. For effect, he has U.S.
Defense Secretary Mendoza join him for the conversation, and issues orders
to Mendoza with the Mexican ambassador still in the room. "Mr. Secretary,
make plans to attack and support. Upload all video of our bases being attacked for the American public to see. I don't want anyone doubting that
we need to go hard at them if they don't back off now."

After the ambassador is escorted out, President Phillipi reconnects with
Secretary Mendoza. "I don't actually want orders issued to engage yet without my involvement. That was for show, to buy us time," the President
says, "and maybe to convince Jones that we may escalate this rapidly if he
doesn't get the U.N. invaders to back off."

***

Professor Paul Stark joins Congresswoman Jill Carlson in her congressional
office. Jill, an attractive, economically conservative independent from
Indiana, and Professor Stark, a middle-aged bachelor best known nationally
as a political reformist, had befriended Juan Gonzalez over the past eight
months as they met repeatedly for media debates and congressional
hearings on official language and secession issues. After Juan felt his life
was threatened by Gabriel Herrera when a DC-based March for Freedom
disintegrated into a violent street war, it was Jill and Professor Stark who
rescued him and brought him to safety. Gabriel, the son of H2M founder
Ángel Herrera, replaced his father as H2M's leader following Ángel's late
summer 2040 assassination, but was known to resent Juan's prominent role
in the organization.

Despite intense investigations in the months since, no proof has emerged that Gabriel Herrera physically attacked Juan or was involved in the earlier assassination attempt on him. Gabriel claims his public dispute with Juan at the September March for Freedom rally was all a serious misunderstanding. Without any public evidence that Gabriel had been part of his earlier poisoning and miraculous revival, Juan and Gabriel had rebuilt a workable but tense partnership in the final two months prior to the secession votes. That tense relationship worked well enough to help secure referenda passage in all four states.

Juan's defection decision dominates the attention of Jill and Professor Stark. Jill is not certain she can get Juan to change his mind. With her adrenaline fully charged, however, she is certain she can't stand to try nothing.

CHAPTER 4

71 Hours

New Rite Compound, Colorado

Ten hours into a grinding war game competition in his continuous adaptation New Rite pod, Pete Roote receives an alert call from JT Alton. JT is the wealthy founder of New Rite, a survivalist training company that has grown to become the world's largest combat gaming organization and a fast-growing advanced weapons developer. JT is about the only person important enough to Pete to get him to stop in mid-game, particularly a contest he is winning handily.

Pete has been confined to the New Rite Colorado compound since returning from his last mission for JT. In that New Year's Eve mission, Pete killed Mexican drug lord Cesar Castillo in a daring single-man attack where patience and technology outgunned Castillo's vast Protection Corps military advantage. The New Rite Colorado compound, based in a rugged, mountainous area of the former Arapaho National Forest, is closed to survival training and competition for the winter. The annual closure means only Pete, Ally and JT are aware of the nearly 200 hand-picked U.S. Army troops surrounding Pete and Ally inside the camp. Soldiers at the compound are tasked by sealed court order with both imprisoning and protecting Pete and Ally.

Ally Steele was Pete's air escort in and out of Mexico during the Castillo assassination. A former Air Force special operations pilot and now New

Rite special operations team leader, Ally brought Pete safely out of Mexico even while being chased to the border by nearly 100 Mexican and U.N. jets.

Shaken by the alert call, Pete signals his need to depart his game, taking out a competitor with a throat slash from behind before shutting down. The adaptable pod game center flattens the flooring, stops the multi-direction treadmill-like floor movement, and reshapes the walls back to flat surfaces.

"What's up, JT?" Pete asks through the secure communication device he and other members of the New Rite special operations team use only for confidential calls with each other. After taking a deep breath and quick swigs from the pod's water and feed tubes, Pete adds, "I thought you were at the President's party tonight."

"That's exactly where I was before the Southwest states declared their independence and the U.N. and Mexico invaded the United States. I was getting ready to ask the President to remove your guards, especially since it's now clear that he understands our work."

"Invaded?" Pete asks, raising his voice and disconnecting from the last of the New Rite pod hoists and monitors. Sweat still drips from every pore in his body. The rigor of the nearly all-day competitions keeps Pete in remarkable physical shape. He grabs a towel and rubs down briskly, starting with his closely cropped light brown hair.

"Yeah, Pete, you need to turn on the news. We're three days away or less from World War III. Might be time to turn off the games and prepare for the real thing," JT responds. He is still fully dressed from the inaugural ball. JT's tightly curled medium brown hair carries a slight red tint reflecting back from his seat in front of a hotel room sink. His lightly tanned skin carries an extra sheen from nervous perspiration that stands out against his neatly trimmed full beard and mustache.

"What do you want me to do?" Pete asks.

"Go find Ally. She hasn't responded yet. I need the two of you prepared for another mission. I'm offering you up for the target of the President's choosing for full pardons for any and all of our past sins," JT tells Pete.

"Last time Ally let me in the house, I left with a black eye. She wasn't feeling my magic the way I was," Pete says, checking in the mirror to see if he needs to shower before heading to the main house to find Ally. A better sense of smell would have given him his answer.

"So be a man, beg forgiveness for being a jerk and for the sake of all that is decent, promise to keep your hands off unless you have a written, notarized invitation that says you can do otherwise. Now."

***

Washington, D.C.

"Who has troops surrounding our bases?" President Phillipi asks his National Security team, now fully ensconced in the Situation Room deep under the White House.

"Looks like at least the Russians, Chinese, Iranians, Iraqis, Pakistanis, Indonesians and Mexicans all have ground troops surrounding various bases, joined by remnants of several U.S. battalions that have already defected," comes the response from an analyst. "Altogether, almost a third of the world's nations have troops inside or around our borders. Looks like most of our ally countries, though, held their troops inside Mexico or were sent to do border and city patrols instead of attacking our military."

"How could the U.N. get that many troops across our border without anyone seeing movement?" the President asks, sweat stains breaking through from his armpits to the front of his shirt despite the cool room temperature.

"We don't know, Mr. President. We saw caravans of trucks all round trip from ports or other Mexican bases into the northern Mexico U.N. sites. When the trucks headed south, U.N. camps emptied out. It looked like a drawdown in response to your demands to get non-ally troops away from our border. They all drove south hundreds of miles and emptied troops onto ships. We watched every step of the way by satellite."

"Did you count how many troops got out of each truck, and backtrack to see how many were in the trucks when they headed north to make the pick-up?" the President asks, looking around the room and to the screen where the CIA Director is connected for an answer.

"I don't know any counts, Mr. President," a National Security Council staffer assigned to CIA liaison duties finally responds. "All of the pickups and deliveries were made inside factories being used as base camps and inside ships."

"Seriously, people. We're three weeks out from learning about a massive underground tunnel, deeper and longer than any of us could have imagined, and no one thought to study whether these factories are entry points to massive tunnels. Are we trying to be dumb losers?" the President asks while his face turns bright red and his cheeks tremor from anger.

Everyone in the room looks toward the President, but most drop their eyes to the floor and some drop their heads.

"Don't we have underground sensors by the thousands along our borders?" the President asks.

"We do, but I assume we would have been told if there was anything unusual there," Secretary Mendoza responds, before realizing that assumptions aren't helpful. "Never mind. I'll check to see what went wrong."

"Get JT Alton for me. Bring him here if necessary. He seems to be the only person who has any idea what we might be up against with the ability to not have his communications intercepted," the President orders. "Maybe his boy and his toys can help us with a surgical hit on Jones."

***

Fresno, North California

Victor Cruz gets in his One Shot vehicle and sets the guidance system for Visalia. At Route 198, Visalia is one of the towns split between California del Sur and North California. The road could be the border between the United States and the Republic of Alta Texas if the secession succeeds.

Victor plans to park his car at the corner of Route 99 and Route 198 and then fight back any foreign troops trying to enter North California. Armed with two rifles, several knives, two baseball bats, rope and all the canned food and water he can fit in the tight confines of the car, Victor makes one last trip to the crawl space to pull out a handgun and bullets he inherited from his father.

His wife hugs him and begs him again to not go. She tries wrapping herself around him to keep him from leaving. Victor pushes her off, gets in and locks his One Shot. The car starts to back out of the driveway.

Mrs. Cruz runs around behind the car, forcing it to stop. Sensors in the One Shot controller stop it from moving when an object is in the way. Victor gets out of the car, picks her up, carries her inside the house while enduring her fists slamming into his back, shuts the door, holds it and then races back to the car. As he jumps in the car to pull away, she comes running around the back of the house and again dives behind the car to force it to stop. This time, Mrs. Cruz is lying behind a tire and wrapping her arms around it so he can't pick her up.

"Stop it, damn it. You can't do this to us. I won't be abandoned again. I won't. I won't," she pleads loudly as he steps back out of the One Shot. "Damn you. Don't do this," she continues to plead. Now lying on the ground under the back tires, her chest heaves and she soaks the area under her eyes as she thinks about how her father walked out and destroyed her upper-middle-class life at a young age, forcing her and her mother to fight through the rest of her childhood.

Hearing the anguish in her voice, Victor gets out of the car and cradles down next to her under the car.

"I will never leave you. I will never abandon you. I will always love you," he whispers softly into her ear, caressing her hair, stroking her shoulder and moving his hands slowly up and down the side and front of her body.

Victor lies behind his wife under the car, holding her. After a while, she begins to shake. Victor flips the back open, pulls out a blanket, lies back down and covers them both.

***

Washington, D.C.

With Martin Luther King, Jr. Day coming the day after inauguration this year, Professor Stark hadn't planned to return to Chicago until late Monday night. He hoped for quality time with Jill, a day of neither working nor being pulled multiple directions. Since they started dating, alone time was infrequent.

Paul Stark spent at least 20 years searching for the right woman. It hasn't been easy for him. He's pleasant enough in appearance, but never turns a head in a bar or restaurant unless someone recognizes him for leading passage of the Political Freedom Amendment to restore sanity to the nation's political process. He wears glasses that magnify too-small eyes and carries some of the wear of middle age on his face, with dark circles under his eyes only partially obscured by the rims of his glasses.

As a young professor, he dressed to gain professional attention. Years later, with his reputation well established, Professor Stark is more likely to dress to avoid attracting attention. Frequently, he looks more collegiate than many of his students, wearing flannel shirts when it's cold and t-shirts when it's warm. He does, however, have a particular fondness for tweed sportcoats when under any type of scrutiny. Part of his subdued dress pattern is understandable. Following a series of muggings a decade ago, he went through a long period of trying to go unnoticed. To women, at least, he largely succeeded.

Having found Jill, Professor Stark's patience is tested daily, particularly since they spend too little time together in his view.

Intellectually, Jill is at least the Professor's equal. Even with her intelligence, Jill's political strength is her grounding in reality. Despite years in Congress, she refuses to succumb to the gratuitous ego stroking that is part of daily Capitol life for Members of Congress, going so far as to insist that everyone call her Jill. She talks to Professor Stark openly about how satisfying it would be to believe that others were right when they told her she was smart, clever, savvy, witty or whatever other adjectives they used in obsequious attempts to gain favor.

To keep her sense of perspective, Jill keeps two plaques behind her desk. One contains a quote from the Congressman she replaced: "You'll never be as great as people say you are while in office or as irrelevant as these same people will make you feel the day you leave." The other plaque contains a quote her dairy farmer father whispered to her after she was elected: "Honor your Mother's memory. She sees everything you do." This plaque, the one with the quote from her father, is the one she touches before leaving her office to vote.

For Professor Stark, the sharp, challenging intellect, dignity and grace Jill displays is more than enough. But that is far from all he sees when she's in a room. Long, silky dark hair. Clear, creamy skin highlighted by a sprinkle of small freckles. Eyes that light any room she enters. A nearly visible personal warmth. Even more, he can't help checking out her backside curve every time she walks away, and battles internally to focus on her eyes and smile as she walks toward him. He's not sure he could have drawn Jill if asked to come up with the perfect woman. Actually, he's certain he couldn't have drawn her because he can barely color inside the lines. But his imagination wasn't even good enough to believe she existed, was single, and somehow seems interested in him. She has imperfections, of course. Scars where stitches were needed to heal farming accidents. One nostril that is slightly larger than the other. Unusually small ears she keeps hidden under her hair. But those imperfections only highlight how perfect the rest of her is to him.

In the months they've been together, Professor Stark quickly lost any pretense of cool, casual interest in Jill. After three days of not speaking at the end of December's lame duck session, he wrote a long message that bared his feelings for her, then immediately worried that he had opened up too much as soon as he tapped send.

"I hope it's not desperation, or your biological clock; something that will tick off the moment you know you have me," he wrote then. "I'm afraid what I feel for you can no longer be turned off or tucked away. This feeling can't be laid dormant or put on sabbatical. I wake with it each morning, wondering if this is another of the many great days we have had that will nourish my heart or instead be the one to singe it with unimaginable pain. I long for the former and cannot bear thoughts of the latter. So for now, I await the hours we talk. Your mind feeds me. Your smile warms me. Your eyes spark me. I yearn for our next moment together." He signed the note "Paul." Jill is one of few who refer to him as anything other than Professor Stark.

His hopes to turn those words into action this weekend have been shattered by Manny Jones and the United Nations. Reason enough, Professor Stark decides, to despise the person and the organization. The immediate threat of war further distracts him as the two sit in Jill's office at 419 Cannon House Office Building.

"I'll turn on the monitors so we can watch the news channels," Jill says as she walks around her office turning everything on, including her well-worn coffeemaker. "If I flip between all of them, maybe I'll get a complete picture of what's happening." Unlocking a drawer in the cabinet behind the desk, Jill offers Professor Stark his choice of her food stash. Almonds. Apple chips. Reduced fat, high-fiber crackers. An assortment of cheeses, several made using milk from her family's dairy farm.

"No chocolate?" he asks.

"No chocolate."

"I think I'll make some coffee," Professor Stark states, grabbing her mug, as well as a spare she had officially dedicated as his several months ago in a goofy, yet thoroughly endearing ceremony. "Any word on a declaration of war or votes tonight?"

"No, nothing yet. I can't imagine we'll vote on a declaration of war until the President's 72 hours are up, don't you think?" Jill asks, intending the question to be rhetorical.

"Makes sense to wait," Professor Stark responds, missing that no answer was expected. "Besides, it would help to know who to declare war against. You can't declare against Alta Texas, because that would acknowledge it exists. So, do you declare against the whole U.N., just the countries that crossed our borders, Mexico, or what?"

As he turns back with two coffee cups in hand, Jill has her head down in her hands.

"Are you okay?" Professor Stark asks before realizing the folly of the question. "I don't mean okay, but I mean, you know, physically okay."

Jill's eyes are almost blank as she responds, appearing to stare past Professor Stark as she talks.

"I can't believe Juan is going along with this. Senator Jones, easy to believe. He's always been megalomaniacal. He's not the first senator to lose a grip on reality. The governors, I don't really know them but the chance to run their states without D.C., especially with another four years of their party being out of power. Who knows about them? But Juan . . . , Juan . . . , he seems smart enough to know better," Jill says. "Don't you think we need him, someone wildly popular in the Latino community and who was in favor of non-violent secession, to come out against this particular move, to have a chance to end this peacefully?"

"Maybe," Professor Stark responds. "Maybe he can help pull this back, but with U.N. troops in, and China, Japan and Germany threatening to call our debt and collapse us economically if we respond militarily, I don't know that any individual can pull this one back."

"Maybe you're right. I'm calling a couple of staffers in. I wonder if some of your students we met might give me a young person's perspective. Think you can arrange that for early morning?" Jill asks him while rocking back and forth in her desk chair.

"I doubt many people are sleeping well tonight. I can probably arrange it now, if you want. These are graduate students. They don't understand normal sleep."

***

Republic of Alta Texas

The government of Mexico issues a statement on behalf of Alta Texas President Jones. It's clear President Jones knows that having his location traced will invite attack, so he communicates through the office of President Suárez, who maintains a single, controlled connection to Alta Texas headquarters.

The statement reads: "All U.S. military personnel inside Republic of Alta Texas borders who wish to go to the United States will be allowed to do so as soon as we sign a peace treaty. We also believe residents of both nations should declare their citizenship preference by January 31st, with one year to complete movement. We hope the U.S. government and people in both countries will see our deep concern for the fair treatment of all involved and will discuss in good faith the peaceful resolution of any modest differences."

***

Washington, D.C.

Minutes later, President Phillipi is reviewing intelligence data related to several military response options when an aide displays the Alta Texas statement on a screen in the room. President Phillipi holds his coffee mug in the air to call for a refill as he stands up to read from the screen. He shakes his head from side to side as he reads before turning to the aide, "Here's the statement I want to send out. The United States is prepared to negotiate in good faith to resolve modest differences over how Manny Jones will be killed and where he will be buried. Think that's clear enough."

"That would be clear, Mr. President. Perhaps, the press staff can propose some modest wording adjustments," responds U.S. Chief of Staff Vijay Chinh, with enough of a hint of a smile that the President knows the wording changes will be more than modest.

Twenty minutes later, a statement is released as coming from President Phillipi: "The United States maintains the sovereignty of its borders and will not engage in negotiations with any individuals who suggest any outcome that does not respect the exterior boundaries of our nation as they have existed since the addition of Puerto Rico as a state. As the U.S. Supreme Court decided in 1869, states do not have the unilateral right to withdraw from this union."

***

North of Dallas, Texas

Charlotte Lee stamps down the last embers from the fire her family had fueled throughout a robust game night. Kurt, the oldest son, won the first-ever Lee family contest of the children's version of a three-dimensional strategic global control game. With all three children asleep, and the familiar sound of husband Bob snoring, Charlotte passes from room to room cleaning up before heading to bed for the night. As part of her nightly routine, she checks her One World site for any news and family and friend updates. One World is the largest integrated social interaction site in the world, having surpassed and acquired dozens of other competitors in the past decade.

"What the hell?" Charlotte mutters out loud.

Charlotte initially assumes the invasion story is a joke. She remembers hearing about the "War of the Worlds" radio broadcast by Orson Welles that had the United States in panic about a Martian invasion. Surely, this must be someone's idea of humor.

During the Lee family's Sunday game night tradition, everyone disconnects from the outside world to spend uninterrupted time together. With husband Bob traveling frequently for his sales job, Sunday is often the Lee's most meaningful family time. Once she reconnects, Charlotte finds more than 200 messages from family and friends asking if they are safe. She sprints up the stairs and wakes Bob to tell him the news.

"Wait a minute, say that again," Bob responds, not believing what he is hearing. He shakes his head rapidly then looks at Charlotte, noticing she is still fully dressed in the blue jeans and loosely fitted Aggie sweatshirt she often wears for game night.

"Senator Jones started the secession. The United Nations, with the Russians, Chinese, Mexicans and a whole lot more, have all invaded Texas to take control for him," Charlotte says, sweeping the hair out of her face as she leans over to look Bob in the eyes.

"That's ridiculous. There's no way they can get troops into the United States without a war being started," Bob says, laying his head back down on the pillow, presuming his wife is overreacting.

"That's what I'm telling you. A war has started, and it's being fought in Texas."

"Well if that's true, I guess I don't need to catch my flight in the morning," Bob says, with more than a hint of sarcasm.

"I think we need to get out of here, Bob," Charlotte says, with an edginess and worry to her tone that Bob only hears when one of the children is temporarily missing.

"Okay. To where?"

"Back behind U.S. lines. We have plenty of people who will take us in."

"You might be overreacting," Bob responds. "I know you were vocal against the secession, but it's not like anyone's going to look at you and be worried you'll become a rebel commander."

"Have I ever told you that you can be a real son-of-a-bitch sometimes?" Charlotte says, pulling his face toward her by holding both sides of his cheeks firmly and staring straight at him.

"Yeah, I think I've heard that one before," Bob says as he rubs away the beginnings of eye crust and sits on the edge of the bed. "I'm not trying to offend you. Are the invaders already in Texas?"

"Sounds like they've taken control of most military bases in four states and have started to shut down entry and exit points into this supposed new country."

"Well then, let's check to see if we can get out and get somewhere safe without putting our lives at risk. I just want to make sure you understand that everything in our house will be gone if we don't stay here to defend it," Bob tells Charlotte as he grabs to hold her hand, stands up and wraps his arms around her shoulders.

"We can replace stuff. We can't replace our family. I want to go," Charlotte pleads, reaching up to hug Bob above his shoulders and around his neck. She reaches with one hand to rub her fingers through Bob's thick black hair and around the puffs forming in what was once a deeply ridged face before moving forward to kiss him. Firmly. Just as quickly as she moved toward him, Charlotte stops the kiss and tells Bob they need to decide what to do. Her kiss had a point. She wants Bob to focus.

Over the next 30 minutes, Bob and Charlotte consider whether they can get out safely. Quickly discovering that One World is the only electronic source still operating, they exchange information with friends and family. While mapping out an exit route that is not already blocked, the One World site shuts down. They lose the last of their outside contact mechanisms.

"What's the chance that they were able to shut down every form of electronic communication and didn't think to block the highways out of here," Bob asks, pulling on blue jeans yanked from the laundry basket and a hole-pocked t-shirt taken off his closet shelf.

"I don't know. Why don't we at least try?"

"Yeah, you're probably right. You get the kids and I'll try to pack in what we need in case we can't find a place to sleep the first night."

Over the next 15 minutes, Charlotte wakes the three children and tells them they're going on a surprise vacation. Bob gathers food, drinks, blankets and other items they'll need for the ride up Interstate 35 into Oklahoma. Assuming that hotels will be full for hundreds of miles, he expects they'll need to drive through the night until their electronics work again and they can connect with friends.

Charlotte holds daughter Kerry while walking toward the garage. Kerry's head rests on Charlotte's shoulder and her arms wrap around her neck. Bob walks back in from the garage, holding all five identification cards required to reshape the family's adaptable car. Right Size adaptable cars are designed to re-shape for optimal fuel efficiency, making them only able to hold as many passengers as can be identified through cards inserted into the electronic system. If the seated weight of riders in the car doesn't match the inserted identification, the car can only move 500 feet, enough to be started or parked.

Bob tries inserting the five cards and backing the car out of the garage to make it easier to load allowable levels of luggage.

"The car doesn't work," Bob says as he sees Charlotte glaring at him when he walks back inside the house.

"What do you mean, doesn't work?" Charlotte asks.

"I mean, it won't start, it won't adjust to fit us all, it won't move. That's what I mean."

"Didn't you plug it in?"

"I'm not stupid, dear. It's charged. And the tank is filled with natgas. The electronics don't work at all, except for a message that Easy Ride operating software is temporarily unavailable."

Charlotte walks back up and returns Kerry to bed. She tells sons Kurt and Kevin to go back to sleep. The car doesn't work, so they'll try again in the morning, she tells them, hearing groans of disappointment in return.

"Why didn't you check the car before you woke us up?" Kurt, the oldest, asks.

"Do you really think anyone would have expected the car not to work?" Charlotte responds angrily, the combination of stress over the invasion and the feeling of disappointing her children being too much to handle. While getting the boys into bed, she hears the door open and looks out the window to see Bob walking to a next-door neighbor's house. Running downstairs, she yells out to Bob: "What are you doing?"

"Going to find out if it's just our cars, or everybody's. If it's just us, then we need to run and run quickly," he yells back.

A few minutes later Bob walks back into the house. "It's everyone," Bob says to Charlotte. "Looks like we're stuck here."

CHAPTER 5

70 Hours

West Nogales, Arizona

Jia Lin, the Shanghai-based executive vice president of international operations for First Empire, calls Chet Leach. First Empire is the world's largest retail chain and recent acquirer of the massive U.S. retailer that is now called FirstWal. By title, Chet is head of U.S. operations for FirstWal. However, Jia withdrew his daily operating authority last year. Chet is now primarily focused on special projects involving government and supplier relations.

Chet's diminished role at FirstWal is Jia's punishment for Chet's involvement in setting an English fluency requirement for FirstWal employees. Until Jia stepped in to fix the problems created by Chet's policy, FirstWal and the Shanghai-based First Empire retail conglomerate suffered substantial brand damage.

Chet thought he was unfairly made the fall guy for a policy that had been developed to optimize WalCo's and then post-acquisition FirstWal's service efficiency. Though mid-day in Shanghai, it is late night to Chet Leach when Jia calls. Much of China is watching progress of the "peace-keepers" on official government programming, with particular focus on what is happening to Chinese troops who entered the secession states as part of the U.N. contingent.

Chet is one of few who see the start of a war involving China against the United States as a positive. The conflict is his opportunity to retake control of FirstWal U.S. operations from Jia's recently installed operations executive, the well-connected nephew of a high-level Beijing party official.

"Chet, what steps are you taking to make sure FirstWal is protected from harm in this dispute?" Jia asks, emphasizing the word "this" to make clear that she hasn't forgotten his role in the prior year's protests against FirstWal.

"I hadn't given it much thought," he responds, "since you made clear to me and everyone else on the team here that operating decisions are made by your new boy. I assume he has a plan and he'll let me know what I'm supposed to do to implement that plan. Then I'll comply fully as my contract requires."

"You know he has only been there for a few months," Jia responds, standing up as if that will make her point more forceful across 7,000 miles of digital connection. "I want you to help him take the right actions. What would you do?"

"I'd take directions from the person in charge. If you want to make me the person in charge again, I'll be happy to contemplate what the right steps are to take when I have the ability to deliver results unimpeded by an inexperienced bureaucrat."

"This is pure insubordination," Jia yells loudly. Always impeccably dressed, Jia usually places every eyelash exactly where she wants it. Any undone button has a carefully contemplated objective. Her hair generally moves with predetermined purpose. Not today. Jia's anger is quite apparent from the pursed lips, scrunched nose and rapid hand gestures Chet sees displayed on the video screen. She nearly rips the seams of the expensive, tightly tailored suit coat she has put on for this call as she flails her arms to demand his attention. Chet is surprised, and more than a bit satisfied, to see Jia come unglued.

"I fail to see, and I think the U.S. courts will fail to see, how it is insubordination for me to expect to follow the directions of the leader you have told the whole company is the person who will make all the decisions and give me my operating instructions," Chet states. He still has not turned on the video feed on his end. Even so, he makes the finger gestures that display his true anger out of range of the camera lens on his device just in case she has a way to turn it on from her end. Chet speaks in a calm cadence that belies his true emotion.

"You know damn well that you have ideas on what we should do that can be helpful to the company. You have to share those ideas," Jia tells Chet as she presses a button to record the remainder of their conversation to play for the chairman of First Empire.

"My ideas are useless without the ability to implement them," Chet responds while turning his camera on, forcing the ends of his lips to elevate to create a weak smile with still-clenched teeth. "Send out a note that lets everyone know I'm in charge. If I don't increase profits by 10 percent in the next week, you can take it all back."

"You're a real horse's mule," Jia states, confusing the phrase and pausing for several moments to think about her response. "Done, but you better deliver. What are you going to do?"

"Fix our prices and rearrange our distribution network. I'll give you more details once I see the note on the change," Chet says, clearly concerned that Jia will take his ideas and pass them on as her own if he doesn't force her to reestablish his control first.

"You're not worried about price gouging controls?" Jia asks, checking whether he can conceivably deliver the earnings improvement before deciding to commit. With her face more relaxed, more of her natural beauty comes through the video feed but Chet will always view her as his Bitch of Belsen for the way she torments him.

"We'll change system codes for everything that could fall under control. That way nothing will see a price increase. Everything covered will be introduced as a new product," Chet says. "Every regulation has a work-around if you know a system well enough."

Within minutes of shutting down the call with Jia and seeing her grammatically challenged note restoring his authority as head of U.S. operations, Chet orders price increases on all survival-related items. Non-perishable food and beverage prices are doubled, weapons prices are tripled and outdoor survival equipment prices are increased between 50 and 300 percent. Sign creation is automated to announce that all of these items are new in-store products. Several of the products will be displayed as selling at a discount to the even higher "new" product prices Chet has ordered artificially created. Chet also remaps warehouse delivery routes with the FirstWal logistics team. To the extent possible, FirstWal will start in the morning to supply secession-state stores from secession-state warehouses. Chet wakes up the head of FirstWal's Mexico operations to provide additional deliveries to the Alta Texas states from Mexico if necessary.

"Everything we sell is non-returnable until the crisis is resolved," he writes as part of his order to store managers.

Awakened by his wrist buzzer alert, FirstWal West Nogales Store Manager Mike Sanchez is shocked to find that Chet Leach is again issuing orders, and even more shocked at the price hike requirements he needs to have in place before his store opens. Typically an early riser, Mike slept as the inaugural balls were underway on the other side of the country. He was also one of the few West Nogales residents who slept through the loudly rumbling military convoys making their way across the border in Nogales.

Walking out to the family room, Mike sees the whole family gathered around the video display screens and can't believe what he sees. "Why didn't you wake me up?" he groans at his wife.

"I figured this would be the last peaceful sleep you'd get for a while," she responds.

"I have to go to work. We're jacking up prices on everything," Mike states.

"You can't go out there. From what I can see, we have a lot of militaries making their way across the border. You could find yourself in the middle of a war zone."

"I have to go or I'll be fired."

"You might want to worry a little more about being killed, and about us," Mike's wife says.

"I'll be fine. I'll stay off all the main roads."

***

Washington, D.C.

Secretary Mendoza tries to call all of the generals who are suspected of or are known to have defected to Alta Texas. None of the generals are carrying either their military communication devices or their personal Lifelink mobile devices. Knowing the military's ability to target bombs from 50,000 feet to land within a one-foot radius of any specific electronic device, Mendoza is not surprised the traitors have abandoned traceable communication devices.

President Phillipi orders that an immediate review be undertaken of all high-ranking military officials, with anyone suspected of harboring sympathy for the secession states to be placed on immediate paid leave.

"You know I have to ask this," President Phillipi says in a video call to Secretary Mendoza, whose heritage is one-eighth Mexican. "Do you remain loyal to the United States of America and your Commander in Chief?"

"Yes sir, Mr. President," the Department of Defense leader responds.

"I thought so and hoped so, but I had to ask," the President responds. "Now I need you to get anyone who might not share your loyalty out of any military positions of authority."

***

West Nogales, Arizona

Alta Texas President Manny Jones orders martial law in the four states, with citizens allowed to be outdoors only between the hours of 8 a.m. and 5 p.m. Mike Sanchez is nearly at the FirstWal West Nogales store when he hears the order and decides to continue that direction as quickly as his computer-programmed car will take him there. While traveling the last few miles, he sends a message to Chet Leach that the store will be open only between 8:30 a.m. and 4:30 p.m. to allow employees to get to work and home without breaking martial law requirements. He copies Jia Lin and the new executive from Beijing on his message to be sure there is no miscommunication about his required store hours. Mike predicts in his message that the store will be swamped immediately on opening with people seeking food, water, weapons and other survival supplies. He also informs the executives that he is calling in all employees to work the full shift until the initial demand surge passes.

Five minutes later, Mike gets a message back from Chet Leach. "I expect you to stop copying the Shanghai team on any and all communication, with immediate effect," the message from Chet says. Finding that Chet has coded the message to prevent forwarding or response, Mike takes a photograph of the message on his personal Lifelink and uploads it for off-site storage.

***

Washington, D.C.

The White House Deep Underground Command Center, or DUCC, is more than 1,500 feet below the streets of Washington D.C. From the White House, the President takes an express, generator-powered elevator straight down the first 40 stories, before exiting to another hallway. Once at the normal national security command center level, the President and two Secret Service Agents take an express elevator at a 30-degree southwest angle down the remaining 1,100 feet to the DUCC situated well below the Potomac River.

Encased in 12-foot concrete walls reinforced by alternating patterns of steel and titanium beams, the DUCC is protected by intense security. Six airflow pipes ensure that enough oxygen reaches the center to keep everyone alive, even if five of the pipes are closed for security or air contaminant protection. Inside the DUCC, an oxygen regeneration machine supplements air quality. One pipe extends underground to the Chesapeake Bay, where it rises to draw air from above the bay surface, protected by its disguise as an old fisherman's boat tie. A second extended air pipe takes in air above ground from Site R, the Raven Rock command center.

Those same long tubes provide back-up water connections for the DUCC, with four alternative water inlets connecting to the DUCC. One drops from the Metropolitan water system. Another connects from a controlled location in the Potomac River. A third enters from a pipe beneath Andrews Air Force Base. The fourth backup comes from the Chesapeake Bay, pulling water in just four feet above the bay floor. A DUCC-level water filtration system enables the freshwater intake to be cleaned continuously.

In addition to the highly controlled entrance to the DUCC that originates beneath the White House, the President has other methods of escape if the DUCC itself is attacked. Only the President can enter a tube angled up to the Potomac River. A bone structure and eye scan ensures no one else can enter this last-resort escape. From beneath the Potomac River, the President enters a one-man small submarine, closes himself in, floods his opening and then travels at the speed of water flow in the Potomac to one of four spots down the Potomac. Once on the Potomac, the President can guide himself remotely to whichever spot is the first one he is told has been fully secured. If remote control doesn't work, or no escape site is secure, the President can take manual control to travel up to 1,000 miles.

Two other tubes are intended for use if Washington, D.C. is hit with nuclear weapons. Under nuclear bomb attack, the President would be the first of 20 able to use encapsulated, rocket-propelled bobsled-shaped vehicles to travel at nearly 250 miles per hour. The first set of tubes in which these vehicles travel connects to where the Chesapeake meets the Atlantic Ocean. From there, the tubes elevate inside what appears to be a farm building. A second tube system would carry the President all the way north to Raven Rock as the underground military communications installation is known. At those sites, specially screened crews stand on 24/7/365 alert to get the President and, if time allows, the other 19, to safety. From the Chesapeake Bay site, safety is presumed to be through connection with a nuclear submarine that would then travel to a deep ocean oxygen and saltwater filtration station for the duration of the attack and fallout. From Raven Rock, the President has air, ground and deep underground security options depending on the outside environment.

If none of these escape alternatives work, a separate protected environment for the President is situated east of the DUCC that will provide the President and a few of his advisors protection for up to 90 days. All of these shelter and escape scenarios assume the first family has already been moved to a separate secure location when the President enters the DUCC.

Attacking the DUCC without security clearance means running through a maze of death traps. Located well below the levels reachable through conventional and even flight-released nuclear bombs, the DUCC entrances and escapes are set to enclose and kill unauthorized entrants at each step of the downward journey. Even if an invading force succeeds in bypassing the U.S. military to gain entry to the tunnels, access to the DUCC would remain unlikely.

The initial 1,100-foot drop from the normal underground Situation Room is broken into eleven sections that can each be penetrated only with appropriate security controls. From the White House, only the President's trip to the DUCC can be taken as an uninterrupted drop to the core. Every other entrant faces 10 security stops at 100-foot intervals. To gain entrance, a combination of physical screens and watch-officer approvals must be obtained — one section at a time. Failure to gain proper approval in set periods of time triggers nearly immediate death. The simplest kill form starts at the top.

If sealed in the first 100-foot section, attackers face complete oxygen deprivation. At this level, all oxygen is sucked out of the 100-foot tube length. Anyone not hooked to an oxygen source will die within minutes at most. Using oxygen deprivation first allows the DUCC authorization team time to fix entry errors before elevator occupants are killed. The second section is also survivable for a short time as the section is water-flooded for a 10-minute period, or longer if it appears anyone in the section remains somehow alive. Again, water is used here to allow for error correction.

Should an attacker get through the first two sections and manage to force open the titanium vault doors to the third level, the invader will face motion-triggered, armor-piercing gunfire attack from 52 gun sites spread through the section. Somehow manage to survive that section and the next tube section uses compressing walls to crush anyone inside. Each level requires a different skill set and equipment to survive, with the expectation that no attacker will be prepared to pass each level. Toxic gas fills one section, spiked titanium bars barricade another, a five-minute fireball another, and acid-mist-bath still another. The ninth level uses electrocution and the 10th level simulates explosive decompression. The eleventh and final challenge injects a cement-like substance through the section to permanently encase everyone trying to gain entry, and further seal off the DUCC to allow those inside additional time to escape through alternative routes.

Tunnels connecting the DUCC to Raven Rock are set up with a similar series of death traps.

"Mr. Alton from New Rite is descending," the President is informed as JT is escorted down to the DUCC wearing a blindfold and headphones from which he can only hear his Secret Service escort's voice commands.

Individuals entering the DUCC without system preclearance require an express authorization code from the President, thorough physical scan and individual clearance at every level. Under the new, recently installed clearance system, the entry process takes 10 minutes for those without full body scan details pre-installed in the security system.

JT Alton is a publicity-shy businessman. JT skipped college and started a survival training company nearly 30 years earlier that quickly gained extraordinary popularity. JT was content at the time, driving rapid New Rite growth that began with his wilderness survival obsession. In addition to expanding his on-line survivalist gaming membership, JT turned large parcels of formerly state and federal lands bought from debt-ravaged governments into survival training centers. His focus changed the day he learned of his young brother's drug overdose death. From that day forward, JT dedicated a high proportion of New Rite profits to developing a military special operations capability. Just a few weeks earlier, on New Year's Eve, JT's team finally succeeded in killing Cesar Castillo, the Sinaloa-Province-based leader of the drug cartel that he blamed for his brother's overdose death.

"I'm sure you understand now why our conversation was interrupted," President Phillipi notes to JT in a separate meeting room in the DUCC set up to host guests without proper security clearance. The meeting room is non-descript, with blank white walls, a door and two faux windows that provide artificial light. JT looks to the windows to see if he can see anyone watching the conversation from behind the windows. A Secret Service officer remains in the room with the President and him.

"Of course, Mr. President. I'm not one of these executives who think the world revolves around my schedule or how I feel. There is no need to take time away from the massive crisis you are addressing to worry about my feelings," JT says, still dressed in his tuxedo with uncomfortably tight reflective black shoes and simple black bow tie, but without the metal cufflinks, studs and cummerbund that had been removed before he entered the DUCC elevator.

"Actually, it never crossed my mind to be concerned about your feelings. I wanted to see if you can help us win this war," the President says, putting his arm on JT's shoulder. As he speaks, Attorney General Betty

Cooke enters the room and Defense Secretary Mendoza patches in by video connection displayed on one of the artificial windows.

"Help? Well, I'll certainly do whatever I can," JT responds as he sits down around the meeting table.

The President stands up and leans over the table to make clear to JT that he needs a quick answer to his questions. "When your people killed Cesar Castillo, tell me how they managed to get back to the border, evade us at the crossing, and move 400 miles north before one of our pilots physically spotted your team and forced them down," President Phillipi demands. "I hope you understand this is now a national security issue, not some simple criminal investigation. Attorney General Cooke is here to validate any deals we might make. I need you to be forthright. We don't have time for a prosecutorial path."

"There is no need for threats, Mr. President. This is my country as well, and I have as much desire to see it stay together as you have," JT responds.

"Glad to hear it."

"I presume that the pardons for me and my team will be forthcoming as discussed as long as we assist you in whatever way possible," JT says.

"They're already written and approved," Attorney General Cooke responds, "with just a final signature needed."

"Thank you."

"So how did you do it?"

"A combination of great technology, Castillo's tunnels and two decades of human intelligence gathering with the patience to wait until the right moments to make use of that intelligence."

"Explain," Secretary Mendoza orders from the video screen.

"You've known for generations about the small tunnels used to bring drugs into the country. The Border Patrol has found some of these over the years, but there are dozens of deep highway-like tunnels spread around the Mexican and Canadian borders capable of taking massive loads of deliveries back and forth deep under the border," JT states.

"Do we know about these?" the President asks Secretary Mendoza.

"I'm not sure what he's talking about," Mendoza responds. Secretary Mendoza is approaching 60, but remains in great shape, exercising regularly in his office on an adjustable machine that converts from treadmill to elliptical to bicycle to rowing to core workout – all of which he uses as he reads and talks. Gray spikes are starting to overwhelm blonde, closely cropped hair. His skin shows the wear of too many missions in intense sun without proper protection and pockmarks from intense bouts of acne that lasted into his twenties. His last name belies his Nordic appearance.

"Our drop-off into Mexico was done with a simple flyover because we know they can't track our APB – our aircraft – digitally. The pick-up was done using a Castillo tunnel; one I knew the U.N. troops were not stationed around. After the kill, we knew Mexico would scramble its jets and particularly guard the border. We needed to get back underneath them and decided to use one of the Castillo cartel tunnels we thought they had abandoned," JT tells the group.

"Why use a tunnel if no one can see you anyway?" the President asks.

"Good question. We haven't quite perfected our gecko visual appearance camouflage skin on our APB. We flew both ways for the drop-off, but knew there would be too much air patrol at the border after the killing to risk being physically spotted. We surprised and overwhelmed the cartel's light security on our southbound tunnel trip, leaving an easy path to head back north unseen. We landed fast and hard 20 miles south of the border, pulled our APB by truck through the main tunnel and then came up one of the openings on the other side, in West Nogales," JT tells the President, Attorney General and Defense Secretary.

"There's no way you could have made it 400 miles flying from there before we spotted you," Secretary Mendoza says.

"We didn't. We trucked out the first 100 miles. Still I think you were lucky because our APB camouflage takes just five seconds to adjust to new terrain below or new sky pattern above. Your jet caught us and then lucked into flying at the same altitude. Our camo only works top and bottom."

Mendoza starts to question the believability of the story.

"We had Border Patrol checkpoints and police stops all along the highways to inspect everything coming in that night. Remember, when we saw all the jets chasing after you, we thought an attack was starting and had every military force mobilized. There's no way you could have snuck something that big past us," Secretary Mendoza says.

"Yet we did," JT says, "again thanks to the cartel's decades of extraordinary profits that allowed them to build tunnels you never thought could run that deep. In addition to border tunnels, Castillo built skip tunnels, with warehouses at each end, located all along the highways. He knows where the police and patrols are set up and uses these tunnels to skip his cargo around them," JT says.

"How do you know about these, and we don't?" President Phillipi asks, looking to Secretary Mendoza and Attorney General Cooke to see if they knew any of what JT was telling them.

"Castillo's drugs killed my little brother years ago. Since that day, every ounce of my energy has been focused on building the capability to kill him and to kill his people. My intelligence shop identified several key leaders in his organization over the past decades. Most of what we learned came through good, old-fashioned human intelligence gathering," JT says. "When the U.S. decided to focus on digital intelligence gathering, you abandoned an abundance of resources, some of whom I managed to locate and employ, and a few of whom I'll need to add to the pardon list. You have one of my most important informants in custody now."

"You said you also killed people who did his bidding. Were any Americans in that group?" Attorney General Cooke asks.

"Are you sure you want to ask that question?" JT responds, staring directly into the Attorney General's eyes. "And why would it matter?"

"The pardon is for all U.S. crimes in connection with the death of Cesar Castillo, which we have thought primarily included border crossing violations, the use of unauthorized and undisclosed military technology and similar violations. It's a different matter if you killed Americans in the process," Attorney General Cooke says.

JT makes clear that the pardon may need to be broadened in how it is worded before he can disclose some aspects of New Rite's operations. He takes the President at his word that this will be done.

"Look, I'm not putting myself in danger here, so I'll tell you what I think you need to know to keep the country together. There are a series of border crossing tunnels and skip tunnels that can bring large volumes of trucks and people and equipment into U.S. territory and evade detection once it gets here. Castillo has technology built into his drug delivery vehicles that identifies and evades all police vehicles nationally, including unmarked cars. I assume they would have similar ability to identify the locations of and evade military vehicles, a capability that should be of great concern if this secession turns into war."

"How do you know this?" Secretary Mendoza asks, again using his voice inflection to suggest he doesn't believe JT.

"Single-minded obsession. Everything my team does has been focused on learning to take down an individual target," JT says. "And you might want to be particularly worried about the ex-General who runs Castillo's Protection Corps and is probably running the whole cartel now. As ruthless and power-hungry as Castillo was, this man is even more maniacal."

"You should have been sharing your information with us," Attorney General Cooke states. "You could have kept drugs from entering the country."

"Either that, or my team could have been identified by Castillo's sources inside the government and taken out long ago," JT says, adding examples of several individuals he suspects were killed over the years using information that could only have come from high-level U.S. government sources.

"But think of all the drug deaths that happened because we couldn't shut Castillo down."

"As angry as I am with the people who got my brother hooked on drugs, you have to realize at a macro level that the amount of drugs that come into the country will always at least equal the demand minus what we produce here. So you might have stopped a shipment or closed a few tunnels with the information we've gathered, but politicians will never be patient enough to wait for the viper's head to be exposed to get a clean slice."

"We don't have time for what-ifs right now," the President says. "How did you get Castillo at his compound?"

"The APB helicopter we used in the Castillo case is my best, state-of-the-art technology, and we had not yet disclosed it or sold it to U.S. military – or to anyone else since I'm sure that's your next question. We don't believe anyone, including the U.S., China, Russia and the Saudis, has the capability to detect the APB any way other than visual luck. But I only have two prototypes built of my most advanced model right now, and I'm sure your people are tearing apart the one you took from us. I have a few other pieces of technology that might help as well," JT says.

"I think it best that you just turn this all over to us," Secretary Mendoza states emphatically, before being waved down by the President.

"Provide pardons to me and my team, and you'll have our full cooperation," JT says. "But you won't know how to use it, so you'll need my team to do anything or train anyone with our technology."

"Hypothetically, if there were Americans killed in efforts to take out a drug lord, how many might we be talking?" Attorney General Cooke asks.

"Hypothetically, no Americans not employed by a drug lord would have been in harm's way at any time from me or any of my people," JT says.

"Can we stop playing this game? We have a country to save," the President states.

CHAPTER 6

69 Hours

Washington, D.C.

Congresswoman Jill Carlson and Professor Paul Stark are feeling the effects of exhaustion now. Jill wears very little makeup, but her eyeliner is smudged and a hint of darkness shows under her eyes. Professor Stark is doing his best to fight back yawns, but with little success.

A video call is set for 6 a.m. with Jill and several of Professor Stark's top students whom Jill met last fall. The two decide to get some sleep. Professor Stark lies down with his back against the back of the couch opposite Jill's desk. Jill turns off all but a small lamp above her desk, then walks over and spoons her body against Professor Stark, resting her head on his left bicep.

Ten minutes later, he feels something wet drip onto his bicep. Not sure whether it's a tear or drop of drool, he pulls himself in just a little tighter to comfort her, rubs her right shoulder with his right hand, and slowly moves his hand down until his hand rests on her hip. He distracts his mind to keep his blood flow from redirecting, a feat made easier by thinking of the hideous effects of war.

Thirty minutes later, exhaustion catches up and Professor Stark is out as well.

***

Shady Shores, Texas

Ramon Mantle and his family returned days ago to their primary homes in the Dallas area, well ahead of the invasion launch. Having finished his technology update, Ramon intended to start working on selling his shares in his companies. A team of eight Protection Corps soldiers returned with the family.

The soldiers wear Perfect Logistics company security uniforms, but carry the best personal weapons the Protection Corps makes available. They have orders to kill the entire Mantle family if any of the adults try to evade their security detail. Ramon and his father know better than to try escaping.

With the invasion launch now public, General Hernández changes Ramon's plans. He orders Ramon to be taken to the Austin, Texas base set up to appear to be Alta Texas headquarters. From there, he and four Protection Corps soldiers will be transported to the real headquarters location.

The other four Protection Corps guards take Ramon's parents and little sister Celia back to Punta Mita, Mexico for "their own protection" and to ensure that Ramon delivers on additional technology development commitments Hernández has made to President Jones.

As Ramon is driven south toward Austin, he realizes that the secession effort might provide good cover for him to sell his businesses. But that won't do him any good personally if he can't store a sizable amount of the profits outside the grasp of General Hernández. He can pitch that the businesses need to be U.S.-owned to protect their largest client bases. If that's not enough, he can ask for a position inside the Alta Texas government to help ensure the new country starts off strong.

Initially thinking that seeking a government role may help him sell his companies quickly, Ramon explores in his mind whether he could use a government role as a valuable excuse to turn down the offer from General Hernández. Then he remembers that General Hernández just killed the three-star general who ran a large part of the Mexican Army with no concern about any consequences.

Hearing that his family had safely made it back to Lakeview Airport, Ramon continues the ride south to meet with Alta Texas President

Manny Jones. He is still struggling to identify an escape path from cartel involvement.

***

Fresno, North California

Only a few stars are visible through the haze over the Cruz family home. Hours after stopping her husband from leaving to go fight at the border, Mrs. Cruz falls asleep behind a back wheel of the family's One Shot car. Failing to convince her to get out of the way, Victor Cruz cuddles next to her on the hard driveway surface. Victor still wants to leave, but with his wife behind the car and the garage in front, the car's automatic security measures won't let the car move.

Victor wakes his wife just enough to roll her away from the car and carry her inside. He walks gently and quietly with his wife in his arms. He feels several sharp twinges in his back as he tries to hold her up and open the house door simultaneously. Laying her down in bed, he takes a moment to catch his breath and then pulls a single sheet over to cover her. He lies with his arms around her to hold her back to a deeper sleep. As soon as light snoring makes clear she is deeply asleep again, he slowly lifts her head and pillow to slide his arm out. Gently, he rolls to his side of the bed, moving as lightly as possible to minimize squeaks from the mattress and floor. Waiting several minutes to be sure her sleep remains undisturbed, he rolls off the side of the bed and slowly walks toward the door. A few squeaks from the floorboard threaten to awaken Mrs. Cruz, but the emotional outpouring of the night exhausted her physically as well as mentally.

Back outside, Victor Cruz resets his destination for the intersection of Routes 99 and 198, the new border. The One Shot backs quietly out of the driveway and he lets the car get 10 minutes away from the house before sending a message to his wife on why he had to go and why she shouldn't see this as abandonment.

"Before I met you, I was a boy searching for meaning. Now, I know in my heart that my purpose is to be your husband, the father to our children, and the protector you were left without as a child. I hope you believe I have lived up to this. It would destroy me to find out any different. It would also destroy me to fail you now. I could not live with myself if I showed so much weakness to run when I know I must fight. I know that you want to protect me and want me to stay by your side. But I know in my heart that if an invasion reaches our home, I will have failed you even more than your father did. So, I hope you see I must go to the border. I have to protect you from a distance that means you are safe. Go to Rachel and live with her now, knowing that I am not abandoning you and I am willing to give my life to protect yours. Whatever happens, I will always be with you."

Victor Cruz clicks to send the message, looks up to see how far the car has gone, turns off the receiver on his Lifelink and reclines his seat, closing his eyes as he is transported south to the new border.

***

Washington, D.C.

Congresswoman Jill Carlson is awakened from a short sleep by a loud ring from her Lifelink.

Lifelink devices are essential daily life tools for most Americans. Generally carried in sealed and code-protected inside pockets that are now part of almost every shirt, dress and even swim trunk, Lifelinks are barely larger than a playing card in normal quarterly fold shape, with the same depth as a toothpick. The devices act as government identity, payment device, personal computer, phone contact, key entry and memory support device with still, continuous and audio record and display capabilities. Embedded software allows any class, meeting or expressed thought to be recorded, with digital transcripts produced almost instantaneously. Optional software uses artificial intelligence to produce auto-generated notes from any session to highlight the most salient points of a presentation or discussion.

Because each person's Lifelink is so crucial to daily life, theft of the device can leave a person helpless. To combat this, Lifelink Inc. established intense security measures for device use. For basic operating purposes – note taking, recording and other basic functions, fingerprint identification opens the device and enables the programs. Government identification requirements mandate insertion of the device into government scanners that conduct facial feature shape and separation scans and a retina scan in addition to fingerprint checks. When the device is used to make large payments, similar scans are conducted and payment alerts are sent to each person's encrypted contact method for final approval. Lifelinks can only be set up for payment and government identification within specially created government identification offices that begin capturing blood samples at birth, dental analysis at age 10 and bone structure analysis at age 15 to ensure accurate identification. The largest payments are only confirmed following instant DNA analysis typically conducted through blood pricks for everyone except hemophiliacs. None of the security measures yet requires proof of life.

Jill presses her thumb on her Lifelink to click it open and is surprised to see and hear Juan Gonzalez. She says hello and fixes her now-compressed, gnarled hair. After moving to an adjoining office, Jill clicks to share a video feed as well.

"I'm surprised to hear from you. Have you decided what to do?" Jill says, seeing that Juan is listening to her in an earpiece and speaking quietly into a microphone cupped on his lips with what appears to be a flush handle for a toilet behind him.

"I thought so, but now I'm not so sure," Juan replies.

"Why's that?"

"Well, can we keep this between us?"

"Sure. Paul is in the other room."

"Professor Stark is with you. Are you two, well, uh?"

"Yes, Juan. Dating."

"Well, it's not him I'm concerned about. It's the media and any military people. No one can know that I spoke to you. No one. They took my communication devices, except for the tiny one the Professor gave me if I got stuck in another emergency."

"The media I can protect you from. If you tell me your side is about to attack somewhere else, I have to share that."

"No, nothing like that," Juan says. "It's just that when I went to see President Jones, most of his leadership isn't our people."

"What do you mean?"

"There are a lot of generals from different countries in with him."

"I'm sure that's the U.N. military command, Juan," Jill notes. "You shouldn't be surprised if they are in constant contact because a lot of U.N. troops helped swarm our borders, attack our bases and kill thousands of people."

"Really. They didn't tell me that. But I did hear he's declared martial law. People can only be outside nine hours a day. People I guess can be arrested, tried and executed on the same day. Food and fuel are going to be rationed," Juan says. "I don't even know where I am, and I'm not allowed to go anywhere on my own."

"Juan, you sound like you're surprised by all of this. What did you think was going to happen? Did you really expect secession was a good thing for the people in those states?"

"It will be. It can be. Senator Jones, I mean President Jones, has given me just three more hours to decide if I am with them or against them. He says he needs a public commitment on me being ambassador so he knows he can trust me. But I'm starting to wonder if I'm safe here," Juan whispers, now looking under the bathroom stall door to make sure no one has entered.

"What makes you worry about that?" Jill asks.

"They have security people around me at all times and won't let me go anywhere."

"Then you have to assume they're listening to this conversation."

"They think they have my device," Juan whispers. As he finishes the sentence, Juan stands on top of the toilet, looking over the tops of the stalls and around the ceilings. "Professor Stark told me this one doesn't carry identification."

"That doesn't mean they won't trace that a communication is occurring and be able to track where from. They just won't automatically know it's you. Maybe Jones doesn't have the capability, but China, Russia, all the others are bound to track calls coming out of the area you're in, wherever that is," Jill says. "For your own safety, I suggest you get out of there Juan and get somewhere I can help make sure you are protected."

"I haven't done anything wrong, so even if they're listening, I'm not worried. I'm just asking questions."

"For such a smart kid, you can be naïve. I'm telling you that you need to watch your back. The only way you can be protected is to get back to D.C. or somewhere else under firm U.S. control and let me know where you are so I can ask the President to protect you," Jill contends.

A loud argument starts outside the door of the room Juan is locked in; loud enough that Jill can hear the noise.

"I need to go," Juan says suddenly. Without closing the device, he drops it in the toilet and flushes it, something Jill sees for a few seconds before the feed cuts out.

Jill calls a contact at the Department of Homeland Security, someone she has known for years. "I have a recording of a video conference that may offer clues to the locations and actions of the Alta Texas leadership, but this needs to be treated as top secret," Jill tells her. "There are lives at stake if this leaks out."

"I'll go right to the director with this and get his top person," the Homeland Security liaison responds.

Ten minutes later, a senior FBI agent arrives at Jill's Cannon building office in civilian clothes to confiscate her Lifelink.

"You're not taking this. If my contact calls back and I don't respond, we'll lose an opportunity to see what else we can learn. Plus, there are lives at stake with what's on here," she yells at the agent. The agent starts to physically grab the Lifelink away as Professor Stark walks in and helps pull it back into Jill's hand. His intervention gains the Professor a violent shove up against the wall from the agent and a gun pointed directly at his face.

As the agent pulls his gun, a Capitol Police officer who followed the agent, wondering what would draw him here in the middle of the night, draws his weapon. He tells Jill and Professor Stark to walk around through an adjoining office and out to the hallway behind him. Then he calls for backup and restrains the agent.

Jill opens her Lifelink and calls her Homeland Security contact to explain the situation. Five minutes later, Jill gets a call from the director. "I apologize for the rough handling. The only good news is you may have helped us identify one of our moles. The agent who showed up doesn't even work in the section that would handle this type of case. We'll send our analytical team to you. Here are the names of the individuals you should let in," the director says before listing off the agent names and suggesting Jill get added security from the Capitol Police around her office.

"What's going on," Professor Stark asks, groggy from recently waking, having his head and chest shoved into the thick wall and staring at the barrel of a gun.

"I talked to Juan, but no one can know this because Jones is holding him against his will right now. He's seeing that some of what we said would happen is starting to happen," Jill tells Professor Stark.

"Sounds like this may be the only part of what's going on that could be called progress. Not the part about our predictions coming true, but the part about him starting to understand how serious this is."

"He talked to me without thinking through how much more sophisticated government surveillance techniques are than what he saw at H2M," Jill says. "I'm not sure he's safe wherever he is."

"I know that feeling," Professor Stark responds. "What was the FBI grunt supposed to be here to get?"

"Probably better that you not know anything more," Jill tells him.

***

Defense Secretary Mendoza, a Seattle native with a Mexican great grandfather as part of his mixed heritage, wants an individual follow-up meeting with JT Alton.

As JT walks from the White House north gate back to his hotel room, an Army jeep pulls up. The fully armed troops on board tell JT to get in. Crossing Memorial Bridge, JT notices the streets are barren except for military vehicles. If he didn't know better, he would have thought he was playing a game inside one of New Rite's combat game modules.

Arriving at Secretary Mendoza's office, he views the sprawling office, sparsely furnished with a darkly stained desk and matching table and chairs to the side. In the corner, Secretary Mendoza towers over a small, elevated table, hanging at an incline over his multi-functional exercise machine.

"Come in, Mr. Alton."

"Please call me JT, Mr. Secretary."

"Okay JT, we do need to cut through the formalities. We think we have a window to shut down this secession, but we have several possible operations where your team might have advantages we need. You've operated outside the bounds of the law for several years, and with some obvious success since we had no idea what you were doing until a few weeks ago. If your team can pull your magic one more time, you may help save the country."

"You know my conditions."

"The President has agreed."

"And if my team gets caught on this mission?" JT asks, looking around the expansive room for recording devices. Spotting his roaming eyes, Secretary Mendoza lets JT know he doesn't want any evidence of this conversation either.

"So, to your question. We'll disavow any knowledge and deride them as a right wing, white supremacist cell. I doubt they'd survive the day in any case so what we say won't really matter," Secretary Mendoza acknowledges.

"I give you credit for honesty and clarity. However, my having been seen with the President at the Inaugural Ball last night will complicate your ability to disclaim any responsibility," JT reminds him.

"Perhaps you'll have to disavow your team as well if anyone connects them to you and New Rite," Secretary Mendoza says. "This isn't a slam dunk, but we're hoping to have a bead on a location soon."

"I'll talk to the team and let you know if they're up for it. We'll need to get the team to a secure location for planning," JT responds, standing up and backing toward the door.

"Agreed. I'll get our commander guarding your camp to bring your two to Cheyenne Mountain."

"Give me five minutes to talk to them first, and then I'll work on getting the rest of the team there as well."

After quick hallway discussions with Pete and Ally, JT gives Secretary Mendoza the go-ahead. "We'll see if we can make it happen."

***

Republic of Alta Texas

Military base skirmishes continue breaking out for several hours. To Secretary Mendoza, the skirmishes seem to pop up and disappear like prairie dogs leaving holes to find food while avoiding being eaten. Different units sneak out and make runs at Alta Texas and U.N. forces until they escape or are forced back inside. Some don't make it either direction. Units of varying shapes and sizes, cut off in many places from official communication channels, search for attack or escape routes. Many of these escape attempts and attacks turn deadly. With the toll from deaths and injuries shared in equal part by U.S. and Alta Texas/U.N. alliance troops, Alta Texas President Manny Jones finally orders U.N. troops to pull back one mile from bases where the alliance doesn't have firm control.

At numerous bases, including Camp Pendleton in South California and Camp Navajo in Arizona, recruits and others out on extended training exercises are stuck outside the perimeter of U.N. troops now surrounding each base. Seeing Russian troops surrounding Camp Pendleton and Iranian, Saudi, Pakistani and other troops surrounding Camp Navajo, some of the recruits remain on perimeters with highly restricted views of the U.N. troops. After failing to figure out what is happening, a Camp Navajo drill sergeant breaks training radio silence requirements and contacts the exercise commander. Camp Navajo's base commander is barricaded inside the communications control room with many others who refused the Alta Texas defection offer.

After identifying himself and apologizing for breaking radio silence, the drill sergeant on exercise asks the base commander for orders. Quickly, the commander tells him that the United Nations has invaded four U.S. states as part of a secession effort and that all U.S. bases in the four states are now surrounded. "There are several people here who defected. If there's anyone in your command who you think would defect, lose 'em and get north before you're captured," the commander tells his long-time colleague. "Now get silent again and get moving before you're spotted."

Minutes later, the drill sergeant instructs two Hispanic members of the group to take the role "for exercise purposes" of being wounded. He explains to both squads that their orders are to secure reentry into Camp Navajo, and then fight back out to recover the wounded. All but the two designated wounded soldiers will travel with the drill sergeant to circle the exercise troops looking for an opening to get to base, he tells them. The two wounded trainees are not allowed to communicate for 24 hours, the drill sergeant adds.

The two "wounded" soldiers watch as the rest of their unit circles away from the base, then work on camouflaging their location to keep from being spotted prior to the training unit's return. The rest of the unit feigns that they will circle the U.N. troops before the drill sergeant leads the team into a heavily wooded area and turns north at intense pace. Three hours into their run, the sergeant takes a five-minute break to gather his remaining troops and fill them in on what is really happening and where they are going.

***

Military forces loyal to Alta Texas President Jones meet Ramon Mantle and his Protection Corps escorts north of Austin. Ramon is dressed like he is ready to head out to the finest restaurant in Dallas. His escorts still wear their Perfect Logistics security uniforms but are heavily armed with guns, grenades and small explosive packs.

As Ramon arrives at the temporary base, he sees a structure purposely set to look like it could house Alta Texas leadership. All but one of those inside are unaware they are being used as bomb bait.

After being informed by Protection Corps escorts of Ramon's relationship to President Jones, Mexican troops at the base relay a message through the still-forming alliance leadership chain. Thirty minutes later, they receive word back. They drive Ramon and his Protection Corps escorts to a waiting helicopter. It will take some time, he is told once airborne, before they reach President Jones.

CHAPTER 7

68 Hours

North California

Thirty minutes into the drive south on Route 99, Victor Cruz is caught in a 10-vehicle line at a police roadblock near the town of Traver, North California. Each vehicle in front of him is stopped by police and directed to exit onto Avenue 368 and turn back north.

As he bangs on Victor's window, the patrolman reaches for his holster, flips open the holster latch, releases the safety and holds his finger on the trigger. "What are you doing out at this hour, sir?" the highway patrolman asks while still knocking on Victor's window with his flashlight.

Victor responds: "I'm heading to the border to help protect my family." Victor offers to step out of his car and show the provisions he brought for the fight. The officer tells him to stay inside and keep his hands out of the window.

"What do you think you're going to do?" the officer asks as he steps forward to where a side-view mirror would be in an old-fashioned car without automated drive software.

"Keep anyone from coming north," Victor responds. "My family is in Fresno and I'm going to keep them safe."

"You're Mexican, right," the officer says, pointing his flashlight now directly in Victor Cruz's eyes and telling him to step out of the car. As he spreads his legs and bends over the car, Victor asks why he's being stopped when all the cars in front of him went on their way.

"We're just being cautious. We're not letting any Mexicans head south so they can fight against us."

"I'm going to protect my family, not to fight against my country. I was born in Mexico, but have lived here most of my life. This is my home," Victor tells the officer.

"Look, there's a lot of you facing this choice, so we've been told to take you all in until you decide. If you want to fight for the U.S. of A., you'll get the chance to join the Reserves or National Guard. If none of them want you, the best thing you can do from there is go home and go to work," the patrolman says.

"If I was white, would you let me go?"

"Not to the border. We're trying to keep all civilians away from the new border. That's why we're making the others exit. We don't want anyone heading south to start shooting people and create a civil war the government might want to avoid."

"I don't want to hurt anyone. I just want to make sure no one comes here to hurt my family," Victor says as he is placed in a patrol car, hands tied with plastic, disposable handcuffs. "Why am I being arrested when I haven't done anything wrong?"

"You're not being arrested sir. Just detained until someone who knows what's going on better than I do can figure out what to do with you," the officer says as he closes the door behind Victor. The officer keeps Victor's Lifelink inserted in his car for identification and sets its course for the makeshift prison the county is setting up. After putting weights on the seat to match Victor's identification weight, the car departs.

Victor is placed in the back seat of the patrol car, where he joins two other Mexican Americans already in handcuffs.

***

Alta Texas Headquarters

Breaking through the lock on the deep basement bathroom door, the muscular, gruff Army guard responsible for controlling Juan Gonzalez confronts him.

"*Who the hell were you talking to in there?*" the guard asks in Spanish, with the conversation continuing in Juan's native language.

"*No one. There's no one here. Go ahead and look.*"

"*I know there's no one inside, you smart-ass punk. Who were you talking to and with what?*"

"*I wasn't talking to anyone except myself. I talk to myself when I have tough decisions,*" Juan replies while thinking he better start talking to himself regularly to make this lie believable.

"*That's a load of crap, kid. How stupid do you think I am? I wasn't born yesterday.*" The guard grabs Juan by the collars on his shirt. He shoves him up against the bathroom door. Juan's head bounces forward after slamming into the door fast enough that it appears Juan is trying to headbutt the guard. The guard extends his arms to keep Juan at further distance. "*You don't want to test me kid.*"

"*Officer, guard, sir, I talk to myself when I'm thinking. I'm an only child. What do you think I did all day when my mother was at work? I had to talk to someone or I would have gone nuts,*" Juan argues, shaking his head to try getting his equilibrium back.

"*Talking to yourself is crazy, kid. Regardless, we need to strip search you and run you through all our security traps. We can't have any traceable connections out of here,*" the guard states, still looking at Juan with lips pressed tensely together, eyebrows crunched and eyes fully focused.

"*Strip search. You must be joking. Isn't that ridiculous? They're asking me to be ambassador to the United States, not a prisoner,*" Juan argues, straightening out his stance and clenching his fists.

"*I'll care about that when we're alive for it to happen. Until then, my job is to make sure the U.S. military doesn't know where we are so they can't wipe us all out.*"

"*Hey, I'm interested in being alive too. Do you think I want to die?*"

"*Doesn't matter what I think. Get your clothes off,*" the guard orders Juan, with enough menace that Juan realizes he's going to have to comply.

"*Right here?*"

"No, stupid. Outside."

As Juan starts to walk toward the door, the guard pushes him back into the bathroom. *"You're not even bright enough to be ambassador to the maintenance staff. Have you ever heard of sarcasm?"*

"What are you putting gloves on for?" Juan says. A wave of nausea hits Juan. His skin turns pale. His fists are fully clenched. A burst of vomits hits his tonsil before he can control the spasm.

"Do you think we let people strip search themselves?" the guard responds.

"If you have to do this, can you at least get a girl to do it?" Juan pleads as it becomes clear the guard is going to deepen his physical search.

"Bend over the sink. Now."

Juan tries to step away from the guard, begging again to have a female soldier do the inspection, if it needs to be done at all. Juan starts to tear up as he feels a shove below.

After thoroughly checking Juan, his clothes and doing a visual inspection of the bathroom, the guard calls for metal detectors and an electronic bug sweep of the room. The guard clears Juan, allowing him to dress and taking him back to his holding room. The room is adjacent to a larger holding room for other expected top Alta Texas officials who have publicly declared their allegiance to Alta Texas. Though the walls are thick, air vents make it easy to hear between the rooms.

"I told you I talk to myself," Juan barks at the guard, still upset at the rough treatment he received. His skin is a paler tone than when he arrived. Nausea and tear-inducing sadness has been replaced by anger. *"What a disgusting way to treat an ambassador."*

"It's not like it's a good time for me," the guard responds before walking back out and locking the door behind. *"Maybe after this, you'll stop talking to yourself. It's a bad habit."*

Gabriel Herrera is apoplectic when he confirms from his guard that Juan Gonzalez has been offered the ambassador's position. Gabriel and Juan have a testy, strictly formal relationship. Gabriel sees Juan as infringing on his rightful place as inheritor of all the goodwill and power Ángel Herrera, Gabriel's father, built up in his decades of running Honor to Mexico.

Gabriel asks to see President Jones, but is told he will need to wait for a calm moment with U.S. and U.N. militaries still mobilizing against each other.

"I made our independence possible, thimble prick," Gabriel yells at the security guard, a statement Juan hears through the air vent. "None of this would have happened without me so when I say I want to see President Jones, it's not a request. It's an order."

"With due respect, sir, you're not in my chain of command so you can't order anything from me," the guard responds in English to Gabriel since Gabriel is speaking to him in English.

"I don't care what you say. If you want to stop me, you'll have to shoot me," Gabriel says as he starts running for the door of the room.

"As you wish," the guard says as he pulls out and triggers his stun gun, sending Gabriel splattering to the floor. Quickly, the guard is on top of him, rolls him over, pulls his arms behind his back and handcuffs him.

The guard gets up and leaves Gabriel lying on the floor.

After a few minutes, Gabriel yells, "Aren't you going to help me up, at least."

"I didn't hear you say please," the guard responds, pausing for several seconds. "Sir."

"When I'm running this government, one of the first things I'm going to do is make your life a living hell," Gabriel barks.

"That doesn't give me a lot of reason to assure your safety now does it? . . . Sir."

***

Chicago

Rachel Cruz responds late to Professor Stark that she would certainly be happy to talk with Jill in the early morning. "My dad left to go to the border. Can Jill do anything to be sure nothing bad happens to him?" she writes back in her confirmation message. She can't sleep, but sets her alarm in case she dozes off to have time to fix her hair and at least put on a little makeup before being on a video call.

Rachel is happy to hear that others on the call will include Jeremy and Tamika. Rachel became friends with Jeremy and Tamika while enduring Professor Stark's two-quarter undergraduate course at the end of their senior year. That friendship strengthened during the even tougher two-quarter master's course they started in the fall. In between talking to her mother, who was awakened when she received the message from Papa Cruz, Rachel takes notes on what she wants to say to Jill about what it means to be proud of both her American and Mexican heritages.

She tries outlining what messages from the U.S. government would appeal to the Latino community, particularly Mexican Americans like her father, and, well, like her.

***

Washington, D.C.

President Phillipi is back inside the DUCC control room, with 30 dedicated systems controllers and national security personnel housed with him. A thick, bulletproof glass wall has been raised to surround the President and senior-level national security aides, giving them visibility to others in the center without others being able to hear their discussion. From his seat, the President maintains view of everyone inside the larger DUCC Situation Room.

President Phillipi asks to have Secretary Mendoza patched in again with video. Several wires running into the DUCC Situation Room have direct feeds that operate from a rotating series of single source lines. Even if a nation broke through all of the U.S. system computer security, these direct feeds would need to be physically tapped for the full content of any discussions to be stolen, a near impossible task given the deep, isolated routing of the wiring.

"What happens if we send all of our troops to bases where our troops are surrounded and start firing away?" the President asks Mendoza. "They have enough troops on our land to control the four states, but not to fight against the full force of our military."

"I understand you don't want to sit and wait, but if we attack, we'll end up fighting most of the world. We don't want to trigger World War

III until we've exhausted all other options," Secretary Mendoza responds, with the few national security staff inside the glass-encased meeting room nodding their heads in agreement.

"What if we go after a single base surrounded by one of our core enemies and leave our normal allies and others alone, just to send a message? Don't we know it's mostly Iranians around Camp Navajo? We have no reason to believe that this regime will be any friendlier than the extremists they replaced. Flagstaff is pretty far from the Mexico border. We can take Navajo back before they can get reinforcements up there," President Phillipi states.

"At what risk? It's a big training facility. Would we use it to push troops further south? At some point, we'll encounter the big boys and a lot of people will die. Don't you want to give your surrender efforts a chance?" Secretary Mendoza says. "Besides, it sounds like they'll see us coming since they have our communications protocols."

"They'll see us coming, but we don't see them. How's that possible?" the President says loudly and sharply, the joy of being elected and inaugurated to a second term as President of the United States having long since subsided.

"I think the deep tunnel explanation is the only one I can even fathom as possible," Secretary Mendoza states.

"If they really have tunneling capabilities we can't see or hear when tunnels are being built or operating, especially when we have, what is it, 15,000 underground sensors that turned up nothing, we need to carefully assess what other assets and capabilities we have at risk," President Phillipi states, ordering a connection to the director of the Central Intelligence Agency to get an assessment started.

***

Cheyenne Mountain, Colorado

A handpicked officer loyal to Defense Secretary Xavier Mendoza, who introduces himself only as Branch, escorts his guests to the Cheyenne Mountain secure military base. Five miles short of the base entrance, the officer stops his vehicle to place hoods over the heads of Pete and Ally from

New Rite. Ally had never been to Cheyenne Mountain during her military years, but is sure she knows where they are headed. This is Pete's first visit inside any operating U.S. military base.

Ally and Pete are assured by the officer that the hoods are for their own security, not to keep them from seeing the base but to keep anyone on the base and anyone watching the base from seeing them. Pete is angered by the intrusion, seeing it is as a sign of lack of trust. Ally speculates that the objective of the hoods is to minimize the number of military personnel on site who see them, so that the White House has plausible deniability of any involvement if their mission fails.

With hoods in place and now plastic handcuffs around their wrists and ankles to make it look like they're being brought in for interrogation, Branch guides Pete and Ally through a series of corridors. Nearly 15 minutes later, they arrive inside a secure planning room, equipped with all of the latest military surveillance technology. The officer removes their hoods and handcuffs. Ally is surprised and delighted to see other officers from the New Rite special operations team, all of whom she has worked with on various missions over the years. Ally introduces Pete to each member of the team. Only two participants in the room are not members of New Rite's special operations team. The two, hand-picked by Secretary Mendoza, introduce themselves only by single names: Koz and Branch.

Minutes after the group is fully gathered, the large screen display in the front of the room turns on. Defense Secretary Mendoza and New Rite founder JT join them virtually.

New Rite team members quietly express surprise at seeing the Secretary of Defense, but quickly focus as JT speaks: "I've asked a lot out of the people in this room over the years. I'm afraid I may ask you to take on perhaps the most difficult challenge we've ever encountered. Each of you knows the political situation, but to make sure I'm going to go over it in detail and ask the Secretary to interject if I miss anything. As you know, former U.S. Senator Manny Jones has instigated a secession move with full U.N. backing and military involvement. Already, thousands of U.S. troops, Border Patrol agents, police and civilians have been killed as U.N. troops snuck in unnoticed and attacked, wholly unprovoked. Voters approved the concept of secession. They didn't vote for a hostile military takeover and states don't have the right to secede unilaterally anyway. The legitimacy of this secession effort, including the ability of the United Nations to claim they are on a peacekeeping mission, is driven by a very small group of extraordinarily politically ambitious people."

Everyone in the Cheyenne Mountain room, except Pete, is leaning toward the screen where JT and Mendoza are displayed. Pete rocks back and forth in his swivel chair. Suddenly, he grabs the table to keep from falling backward, earning glares from the team. "We know that Senator Jones and the governors of each of the four states are part of this cabal," JT continues. "We know that many other elected officials who used to represent these states in Congress are taking up roles in the Alta Texas government. We also know that several generals and a small, but increasing number of officers and troops are defecting to create an Alta Texas military. Finally, we've been told by important, but unnamed, public officials that the one person in the secession movement who could and might help us destroy public support inside the secession states is a young kid named Juan Gonzalez."

"That's right JT," Secretary Mendoza interrupts, stepping slightly ahead of JT toward the camera. "Before we go any further, I'll make something clear. Anything you decide to do has to be actions you take independently, with no fingers pointed to the U.S. government. That includes me. I will deny ever having spoken to you, as will the two officers in the room with you. I trust these men with my life, so I'm comfortable they will do their part to take care of your lives. But given a choice between protecting you and me or millions of Americans, they will choose the rest of America."

"Understood sir," Ally responds, along with the other New Rite officers. A second later, Pete adds his response: "Got it."

"Thank you, Mr. Secretary, for that clarification. My team certainly would understand that, but it's best to get the rules of engagement set up front. For the time being, we're in a holding pattern. We know that if we can take out a small group of people, we can destroy the chain of command and maybe unwind this peacefully. At this point, however, we haven't zeroed in on a target location or locations. What I'm asking you to do right now is to eat, sleep, exercise and prepare yourselves as a team for the roles you could take in an assault designed to take out a small number of targets."

"I hate to say this JT, but what's in it for us?" Pete asks.

"In reality, probably nothing of great enough value to make it worth taking the risks I'm asking you to take. But, since you asked, you will each receive full presidential pardons for any and all illegal activities you may or may not have engaged in during your lifetime up to and including any actions you take here, along with an addition of 10 years to the pension value for all of you who have military service and an equivalent financial value for you, Pete."

"How much is that?"

"Enough to help survive on, but not enough to live on," Ally tells Pete. "But given your lifestyle, you'll be happy."

"Is it more than welfare?" Pete asks.

The military officers and New Rite special operations team members look at Pete. Secretary Mendoza pulls JT away from the speaker and asks a question. JT nods his head up and down, assuring Mendoza that Pete has special skills the group may need.

***

Washington, D.C.

President Phillipi meets with Attorney General Betty Cooke, Homeland Security Secretary Ray Peyton, Chief of Staff Vijay Chinh and a top press aide to determine whether it's possible to undermine the legitimacy of Manny Jones by publicizing an ongoing Justice Department investigation into his actions last fall.

Just days before the November 2040 election, Senator Jones convened a private D.C. meeting with U.S. Ambassador to the United Nations Hugh Brent. At that meeting, Senator Jones convinced the ambassador to agree to resign in return for not publicly disclosing his affair with his Brazilian counterpart. That meeting took place, not coincidentally, at exactly the same time as the United Nations Security Council voted to approve using U.N. peacekeeping troops to protect U.S. territory. As of today, knowledge of the purpose of Jones' meeting with the U.S. ambassador to the United Nations is limited to Jones, his committee staff director, the ambassador, the President, his chief of staff, three members of the President's cabinet, and a select group of FBI investigators and Justice Department prosecutors.

However, speculation about the ambassador's presence in Washington and firing the day of the U.N. vote was rampant in the days leading to the election and continues to this day.

The U.N. vote could have been an immense foreign policy failure for President Phillipi just days before voters were set to decide on his potential reelection. After short, intense debate, the President agreed with Chief of Staff Chinh's plan to characterize the U.N. action as a U.S. foreign policy victory that would ensure the safety of all Americans. In reality, the vote was an immense failure, but the President decided he could not admit to a foreign policy fiasco so close to the general election. The firing of the ambassador was justified publicly as the President's disappointment that the ambassador did not cast the U.S. vote in favor of the resolution. Ambassador Brent validated the President's public story to avoid even greater public embarrassment with the real cause of his firing; that the ambassador had failed to prevent U.N. passage by using the U.S. Security Council veto to keep U.N. troops away from the U.S. border.

President Phillipi's statement that day, publicly corroborated by Ambassador Brent, suggested that the United States had authorized the United Nations to proceed in order to assure voters in the Southwest that they could vote without any fear of harm. Senator Jones considered the White House public position to be one of great fortune, even if he knew that the contrived statement virtually assured President Phillipi's reelection. Democratic Presidential Candidate Sue Appling had been ardent in her pro-secession support. President Phillipi's action undermined enthusiasm for her by showing he would take extraordinary measures to protect the rights of even those Americans who disagreed with him.

If his actions in conspiring with the United Nations to bring U.N. troops to the nation's borders became known, Jones knew he could be arrested for treason. He had carefully covered his tracks, concealing a trip to New York to meet with the United Nations Secretary-General that led to the U.N. vote.

No one on Senator Jones' staff or in his family knew of his New York trip. That trip, coming only a few weeks before the U.N. peacekeeping vote, had been carefully arranged. The senator's close political ally, Ramon Mantle of Perfect Logistics, arranged for the senator to be transported back and forth to New York in an off-grid, gasoline-powered car driven by a trusted member of Ramon's security team.

Ramon, the founder of Perfect Logistics, created the world's most sophisticated public traffic management software and devices. He also created an even more sophisticated private law enforcement evasion system known to and used only by the Castillo cartel. Meeting at several political events in Texas, Ramon had bragged to Senator Jones about his street drag racing skills and how he had created software that enabled him to escape capture. Through a series of careful conversations, Senator Jones eventually became convinced that Ramon's team could get him back and forth to New York without being seen or traced. In return, Jones told Ramon that he would assist him in securing national defense contracts for a revised version of his technology to assist in military battles – contracts potentially worth tens of billions over the next several years. Jones always planned to make good on his commitment, but hadn't clarified to Ramon that he had Alta Texas in mind as the source of the contracts.

After meeting with the U.N. Secretary General in late October of last year, Senator Jones covered his tracks well. For their part, the United Nations had refused efforts by the F.B.I. to interview U.N. leadership and staff about the days leading up to the Security Council vote. Secretary-General Sudarto Suryasumantri told President Phillipi that the United Nations would not suffer any intrusion on its sovereignty, and suggested that if the United States had any problems with the actions taken by the Security Council, it should take those up through its ambassador.

These stalling tactics angered President Phillipi, but his administration was unable to figure out how to legally arrest and interrogate U.N. employees with full understanding of diplomatic immunity benefits.

Senator Jones found out about the FBI efforts to interview U.N. personnel the same way he found out when to hold his two-on-one meeting with his staff director and Ambassador Brent. A trolley-like shuttle runs between the basement of the U.S. Capitol and the lower levels of the U.S. Senate office buildings. While walking on the path alongside the shuttle, Senator Jones was asked for an autograph. At first, he didn't recognize the young woman handing him paper and pen. When he went to hand them back, now signed, the young woman slid him a small note. Realizing now what was happening, Senator Jones folded his hand quickly and shoved the paper into his shirt pocket with the pen he had just used.

Later that night, he took a candle from his house and walked outside under his garage overhang. He pulled the note out, held it above his head and read it, "WH sniffing at our door. We're locked up tight. Just so you know. Be careful." The note did not contain a signature, but Senator Jones recognized the type. He burned the note.

President Phillipi was so caught up in electoral politics in the days before the election that he lied outright to the American people at a press conference right after the United Nations "peacekeeping" vote. It wasn't his initial instinct, but he knew it would assure reelection.

Though the President is now certain Senator Jones committed treason in making the Security Council vote possible, admitting he knew this before will mean admitting to the American public that he lied right before an election to avoid responsibility for a massive foreign policy failure. Still, if President Phillipi could prove now that Senator Jones invited the U.N. troops to invade rather than keep peace in the four states, it might cost Senator Jones support of his people. With thousands already dead, it will require artful explanation to discredit Jones without destroying his own reputation. The U.S. government also needs to circumvent Alta Texas controls on news flows into the four states. Martial-law-enforced censorship allows people inside the four states to be executed for spreading information not approved through official channels.

"We're in a tough spot here, but we need to undermine this supposed government. What are investigators finding on Jones?" the President asks the assembled group. The President holds up his hand to tell everyone in the room to stop talking. "Wait, have we turned off all recorders?"

Once Vijay Chinh confirms the devices in the room are disabled, Attorney General Betty Cooke responds.

"We've had taps on Senator Jones and his top staff and family for the past 80 days. We haven't been able to get much out of this, though we did catch Jones' staff director telling someone he suspects that Hugh Brent resigned over an affair," she says. "In subsequent FBI interviews, he denied knowing anything about Hugh's decision or anything about his personal life. It's not much to go on, but we can charge him with lying to federal investigators and pressure him to talk."

"Won't the charges open up the bait jar with Hugh?" the President asks, drawing a confused reaction from those in the room.

"Sure, if I understand the question. More importantly, it doesn't get us much and will irritate senators who admire the staff director unless they understand how the lie connects to secession," Attorney General Cooke responds.

"What else do we have?" the President asks.

"We've ruled out any public connections between Jones and the U.N. leadership for at least three months prior to the security council vote. We can track his actions day-by-day through that time. He's very active, but very easy to trace because his Lifelink and other devices are always with him. We've checked hundreds of the locations he was supposedly at through that time and confirmed him at every one of them. The times we're struggling to confirm visuals are on two days he called in as too sick to work," Homeland Secretary Peyton says. "And we've found nothing on any form of electronic communication those days. His Lifelink sat in his house and wasn't used."

"So those sick days . . . ," the President begins to ask.

"That's the focus of our investigation," Peyton continues. "We've ruled out air travel, train travel, taxis, anything like that on those days. And the only place he took his car was to go to a mall on one of those days. Checking his Easy Ride records, he stayed for just 10 minutes before returning home."

"Okay, could he have met any U.N. people at the mall?"

"Best we can tell, anyone who was anyone in the U.N. was involved in meetings in New York at that time, so highly unlikely."

"Anything else?" President Phillipi asks.

"Yes, he took his car back to the mall for another 10-minute visit in the middle of the night that night," Secretary Peyton continues, describing information gathered by the Federal Bureau of Investigation.

"Strange."

"We thought so, too."

"So you checked satellite to make sure it was Manny in the car?" President Phillipi asks.

"We tried, but couldn't verify," Peyton responds. "He entered his car inside his garage so overhead visual couldn't see him and he parked underground at the mall so we couldn't see him there. By the time we figured this out, most street camera records were destroyed. The few we have show the driver in a hoodie, with a thick sweater over it and sunglasses. Hard to tell for sure if it is him."

"Sounds like you may have found our best hope of tracking a contact between Jones and the U.N. leadership," the President suggests.

"One last thing. We have the FBI conducting a very detailed traffic review comparing satellite data in the months prior to the Security Council vote with Easy Ride operating records of vehicles on the road. We're taking a chance that Jones used one of the off-grid vehicles still sneaking onto our roads to get back and forth to New York. But I need your authorization to put another 100 people on this to see if we can find something. This is very detailed and time-consuming work. We think we might find something, but it'll be months if we're limited to the three-man team doing the investigation now."

"We have nothing more to lose," the President says. "Doesn't sound like we have anything that can be used against Jones yet. Add as many investigators as you need. This is now a matter of national security, Ray. I'm also rescinding acceptance of your resignation. I can't have a transition at Homeland Security while this is going on, so you're just going to have to put off your retirement. Please tell your wife that I'm so sorry to do this to you, but your country needs you now."

Ray Peyton had been looking forward to some rest, but smiles at the thought he is still needed.

***

President Phillipi's face looks increasingly pale and wrinkled with each passing hour. A spot of acne pops up off to the side of his right eye, an area he has taken to rubbing while thinking. Inauguration Day is a long one even without a war starting. Now, the President is wondering what he was thinking in running again, knowing the intense difficulty of the job even without a secession crisis.

White House Chief of Staff Vijay Chinh pulls the President back into the glass-enclosed conference room inside the DUCC for a private conversation. "You realize, Mr. President, that if we find anything on Manny and publicly disclose that we knew he brought the U.N. to our borders against our wishes, it will expose our story. Your enemies might look at this as impeachable," Chinh tells him.

"You may be right, Vijay, except that I'm sure you recall that everything I did was in the best interests of the nation," the President responds. "I truly never expected the U.N. to take a peacekeeping mission this far. I was expecting maybe a thousand troops, but realize now that we gave them an opening they jumped through like an acrobat through a fiery hoop. I still think we did the right thing. We can say we tried to protect the country while we investigated the real cause of what was happening, with every intent of acting once we secured proof."

Chinh puts his hand on the President's elbow. "I know your intentions are good," Chinh says, "but it might be tough to prove national interest to everyone when it turns out what we said a few days before the election also served our political objectives. You must keep that in mind."

President Phillipi sits down at the well-padded, leather chair at the head of the table inside the private, glass-encased meeting room. Looking at the team of national security and systems analysts continuously tracking movements of U.N. and U.S. troops, he cups his chin inside his left hand and yawns.

"At the end of the day, we have to do what we must to save and protect the United States," the President tells his long-time aide. "If that means resigning because the public can't forgive some of the things I've done in their interest, then so be it."

"This might be one of those decisions that we shouldn't make without a good night's sleep," Chinh responds, before exiting the room and leaving the President a few moments to think. Several minutes later, the President puts his head down on the table and dozes off.

CHAPTER 8

66 Hours

Washington, D.C.

At just before 6 a.m. eastern, Professor Paul Stark and Congresswoman Jill Carlson are back awake. In the adjoining staff office, the properly assigned FBI agents are downloading digital copies of Jill's discussions with Juan. The agents also start tracing Juan's call, using tracking information on the device that Professor Stark kept in case he needed to track Juan down again. Professor Stark had bought the tiny communications contact device for Juan several months earlier for emergency use.

Jill grabs her overnight kit and spare clothes from her coat closet to head to the House gym. As she does, Professor Stark tells her he's going to take a "whore's bath" across the hall.

"Don't tell me you know how a whore bathes," Jill chides him. "I would hate to find out that this has something to do with the reason you're still single."

"Sorry, poor choice of words. That's the phrase I grew up with."

"How about trying, 'I'm going to wash up and shave," Jill tells him.

"Okay, let's go with that."

Forty minutes later, the two are back in the office. Jill wears a fresh black pantsuit, lightly ruffled white shirt, and dark, paisley-patterned scarf. Professor Stark is still in his tuxedo from the inaugural ball, sans the too tight clip-on bow tie and an undershirt he deemed offensive enough to require disposal.

A display screen shows Professor Stark's graduate students Rachel, Tamika and Jeremy each connecting from their individual rooms. Jill's chief of staff walks into the office carrying six 12-ounce coffees; two each for her, Jill and Professor Stark thanks to an ordinance limiting the allowable amount of caffeine or sugar in any individual drink in Washington, D.C.

"Thank you all for taking time early this morning to talk about this," Jill says. "With the secession announcement last night and the clear threat of war, I want to be sure I do everything I can to push for peaceful resolution. I'm seeking input from multiple perspectives."

"Happy to help, if we can, in any way," Tamika responds. Tamika Jackson was born and raised in a rough, low-income neighborhood on the south side of Chicago, not far from the University of Chicago. She earned tuition scholarships to pay her way through undergraduate studies, and saved money by living at home with her mom. Now, she earns enough as a graduate teaching assistant to move out, but won't leave her mother alone.

"It's an honor," says Jeremy McBride, a Milwaukee native who continues to surprise Professor Stark with sharper insights than his physical appearance or demeanor around women would suggest was possible.

"Thank you for the invitation, Congresswoman, I mean Jill. Before we start, can I just tell you that my father has been arrested? He was heading south from our home in Fresno when he was pulled over by police, cuffed and hauled away just because he's Mexican. I thought we were past this kind of racism," Rachel says. "Is this going to be like the Japanese Americans during World War II again, except for Mexican Americans?"

"Oh my God, Rachel, I'm so sorry. Paul mentioned that to me. What is he charged with?" Jill says.

"Nothing. They're just holding him because they want to keep Mexicans from defecting and fighting against us. He was going to the border to fight to protect us, not against us," Rachel says.

"That makes me sick," Jill states, looking over at her chief of staff and telling her to get direct contact information for the Attorney General and Secretary of Homeland Security.

"I'm glad we did this call if just so I know to work on fixing this," Jill tells Rachel. "You'd have thought we would have learned from the horrors of our history. If your dad's situation is any indication, I need to pass on some quick history lessons inside our government."

"Jill," Professor Stark interjects. "Thank you for anything you can do for Rachel and her family, and for everyone else in that situation. But, I know you have a lot of calls planned this morning, so this group might be particularly helpful with the one topic we talked about last night."

"Okay," Jill says. "So you all met Juan Gonzalez last fall, and I know that some of you keep up correspondence with him."

"Yes," Rachel responds. "Sure," Tamika says. "He's a smart kid," Jeremy adds.

"Without going into too many details, we believe Juan may be heavily involved in this secession move, though it's not clear to me that he had any advance idea of the U.N. military action."

"Oh my God, that means he has to leave the U.S.," Jeremy states.

"Well, that is unless the secession is stopped and he is pardoned," Jill says. "Or if we find out he never took part in actual acts of treason. And, of course, he has to live through this conflict as well, to be blunt about it."

Rachel covers her face, but quivering of her lips and cheeks is still visible. After a few seconds, she stands up and walks away from the camera. Though Jill sees how upset Rachel became after her comment, she decides to continue with her questioning.

"So my question," Jill continues. "If you are Juan, what are you thinking right now? You're closer to 19 than I am, so I need to know how a young man's mind thinks."

"Well Rachel knows Juan better than we do," Jeremy says, "but he struck me as very smart, very confident, very brave. People tried to kill him twice over his work with H2M and he still didn't stop. He even went back to speaking for H2M thinking the head of that group wants him dead. You have to be extremely committed or extremely stupid to take on that risk. I don't think he's stupid."

"Jeremy's probably right," Tamika adds, "but do you think he really expected his work to lead to a U.N. invasion and the potential for a civil war or even World War III? I know that Juan believes in letting Latinos rule themselves in places they're a clear majority, but I don't think he's the kind of person who would say millions of people should die to make that happen."

Jill looks up to the ceiling and then looks at Professor Stark. Professor Stark realizes he's being asked to help the discussion along.

"Let me put this another way," Professor Stark states. "Juan is such an important leader in the whole movement that if he disavows this action, it will hurt the secession's legitimacy and may help make clear that this is simply a U.N. territorial intrusion. If you are Juan, what information or argument would convince you that this secession movement is bad for the people you care about most?"

"When I was 19, all you would have to say to me is that no hot girl would ever touch me if I stayed with the secession movement," Jeremy responds while Tamika shakes her head in disgust. "So I'm not sure I'm the best person to answer that question. But if I try to think like Juan, he seems pretty logical. So maybe just give him evidence of what typically happens when countries break apart through civil war."

"I don't know," Tamika interjects. "He's 19 years old and he would be a huge deal in this new country. He's so popular there that he could probably be President some day in this Alta Texas. Most 19-year-olds don't think they'll ever die and Juan has more reason than most to believe he's invincible. So if he has the chance to be President of a country some day, he might be willing to take a big risk to make that happen."

Though distracted looking at the bars on Tamika's bedroom window behind her as she talks, Professor Stark tells her she may be on to something. "He's already survived what he sees as two legitimate efforts to kill him. That could either shake him up or make him feel he's even more immortal than most teenagers believe they are. From talking to him, do you have any sense how he feels about his mortality?" he asks.

"I get the sense he thinks he's on a mission from God and that bringing control back to his people is the reason for his existence," Tamika responds, between sips of a steaming drink. "He really, really believes in this separation. I don't think this is just a power grab for him."

"Where did Rachel go? Rachel, are you there?" Professor Stark calls out.

After a few seconds of no response, Tamika speaks up. "I think Rachel may be closer to Juan than any of the rest of us."

"What does that mean?" Jill asks.

"I'm not sure exactly what it means, but adding Juan being gone on top of her dad being imprisoned makes this a pretty rough day for Rachel to take," Tamika tells them.

Another five minutes of discussion later, Rachel returns to her screen.

"I've tried everything I can to contact Juan," Rachel tells the group. "He's not responding to any of my attempts."

"I wouldn't take it personally," Jill tells her. "I'm betting his ability to talk to any of us has been flushed away for the time being."

Rachel asks what she means by that.

"I can't answer that," Jill responds. "For his safety."

***

New Rite Compound, Utah

The first cars arrive at New Rite's Utah camp. Located largely in former federal lands between Kanab, Utah and the Glen Canyon Recreation Area, large parts of the camp are set in dry, tough terrain. Over the years, tens of thousands of survivalists, war game competitors and adventure vacationers have come here for weekend, weekly and extended stay survival training. With the Arizona/Utah border now the separation line between Alta Texas and the United States – at least in the eyes of Alta Texas leadership – many are concerned this border will become a new combat zone.

The earliest cars arriving have Arizona plates, driven by Americans of all backgrounds, but dominated by whites, blacks and Asians. Every car is crammed full, both of people and whatever possessions could fit.

Arriving at the New Rite camp, the Coleman family is greeted by compound leader Sarah Osborne. Sarah is a highly decorated former Navy Seal who sought the chance to lead this camp to gain non-military leadership experience and practice several survival skills. In addition, Sarah continues to be a key part of New Rite's special operations team. As John Coleman pulls up to the New Rite gate, he stops to show his New Rite membership and training identification. He drives past the main parking area, already overrun with vehicles, to park alongside a gravel road. From there, the family walks toward the main camp area, carrying their tent, blankets, John's weapons and a cooler of perishable food.

Finding flat, dusty land open near the main camp, the Coleman family pitches their tent as instructed and starts walking around to introduce themselves to other families sharing their trauma during the harrowing night.

"I can't believe our government let us be taken so easily," John says to one of the family's new neighbors.

"Never in my worst nightmares did I imagine America could be invaded without a fight. I'm sick to my stomach about voting for Phillipi so he could just give us away," the neighbor responds. "That's what happens when you trust the U.N. to be peacekeepers."

"It just doesn't even make sense," John Coleman adds.

The compound quickly organizes into 10-family cooperative groups to ensure the camp remains orderly and functional. The groups divide up duties, including watching the youngest kids, gathering firewood and supplying food and water in order to maximize the number available for combat if needed. Clarissa Coleman, John's 14-year-old and youngest daughter, takes responsibility for mapping water sources and learning what wild food sources can be hunted or gathered on site.

Seeing the wave of cars entering the site, compound director Sarah sets up new entrant briefing sessions every hour. She holds a separate security review for those with military background or advanced survival skills.

"If the U.N. is gonna send scouting parties into Utah, they'll likely come through our land since it's not heavily guarded," Sarah tells those at her initial security gathering. "We have a lot of challenging terrain requiring knowledge to cross. We're gonna have to fill in protection gaps around us. We can't stop an invasion, but we can send advance warning if one comes. We'll focus on finding scouts or advance parties and taking them down."

"What invasion are you worried about?" John Coleman asks, straightening his hulking frame and furrowing thick black and gray eyebrows as he speaks. Though John spends occasional survival training weekends with his family, his profession is designing massive recycling centers that separate garbage into its reusable parts.

The company John works for was founded to alleviate global supply shortages in electronics and household parts materials. Initially, the company focused on extracting mercury, cadmium, indium, tellurium and other resources in limited supply from the garbage, particularly rare earth minerals and those with human health consequences when spread in the environment. Now, nearly all household wastes in most modern countries are separated through massive conveyor-like systems that use robotic arm, air blast, water flotation and other physical means to move wastes to their proper recycling conveyor. John develops analytical eyes that trigger the waste separation, focusing on real-time, limited intrusion chemical composition analysis that allows waste such as lights to be separated robotically into various physical components, including glass, metals and mercury. More than 90 percent of household wastes are recycled, composted into fertilizer or converted into fuels. Basic material separation reduces the need for massive resource extraction growth as the world's population expands and average consumption levels increase in many other countries. Fuels produced inside the centers, including waste-based ethanol and methane, work in the multi-fuel cars that dominate the nation's roads.

"I'm not sure which way things are gonna go, but if I were the U.N., I'd be preparing for us to counterattack," Sarah tells the group. "They're gonna want to get scouts up here to call in early warnings. I can't imagine we're just gonna give up our land, so it's only a matter of time before we take our country back. They gotta know this."

"I wish I could believe that," John Coleman says. "From what I see, the President just had us all bend over and take it up our waste release pipe. "

"Sir, if that's the plan, it won't end with the secession states so we need to think through what that means. I take the President at his word that he's giving them 72 hours to put things back together or all hell will break loose," Sarah tells the group.

"If all hell is going to break loose, we really need to think about getting our families further north," another meeting participant says. "I came here because it's the first place I thought of, but wasn't really thinking how close we are to this new border."

"A reasonable consideration," Sarah acknowledges. "Let's schedule a discussion for all group leads after dinner tonight. That gives everyone a chance to get a few hours sleep, get some food in, and find out what's going on everywhere else before we start separating families."

When John gets back from the security briefing, he checks in with his wife. She and two of the kids are inside the tent, trying to sleep on the hard ground with their clothes and a few blankets spread out underneath them to provide a small amount of cushion between them and the ground.

"Where's Clarissa?" John asks his wife.

"She went out to try getting a better Lifelink connection so she can research native foods and water locations," Mrs. Coleman responds.

"It's too cold for her to be out too long," John says.

"I'm sure she's sticking near one of the fires. She's got to be somewhere to see and daybreak's still a couple of hours away. Don't worry. You know Clarissa. She'll be fine."

"That girl's going to be the death of me," John says to his wife, before lying down for a quick nap.

***

Alta Texas Headquarters

Calmer now, Juan Gonzalez is escorted to the temporary command center for Alta Texas. The command center is several levels up and several long hallways over from where he is confined. Told he will meet with President Jones, he's sure he'll be asked for an answer. The Army guard escorting Juan can't restrain his curiosity, having heard Gabriel's rant against Juan when he went to help his fellow guard.

"What is it with that jackass we had to stun," he asks Juan as they wind through poorly lit underground passageways, with pale paint covering the large concrete bricks walls. Now that he realizes Juan's English fluency is nearly as good as his Spanish, the guard speaks to him in the guard's childhood language.

"That's a really good question. He hates me more than anyone I've ever known. I never did anything to him," Juan responds.

"Aren't you supposed to be on the same team? I mean you're all part of the Alta Texas leadership, right?" the guard asks.

"I think that's what President Jones is still settling."

Arriving at the control room, Juan is rechecked for weapons before being escorted in by the command center security team.

"Juan, I hope you have a good answer for me," President Jones prods.

"I have the right answer for our people," Juan says, causing President Jones to start smiling. "I'll do it and with your permission, I'd like to tell the people of Alta Texas why I want to do this. I do have one condition – no more invasive strip searches," Juan adds, turning to look at his guard.

President Jones looks at the guard, who quickly tells him he heard Juan talking to someone and needed to make sure no calls or connections were going out that weren't routed through the command center scrambler.

"Juan, the guard has to protect us all, but now that it's clear you're on our team I think we can be a bit more open. Are you going to write a draft, or do you want our press team to write what you want to tell the people for you?"

"I'll write it."

"Great, then have the press team review and I'll sign off before you record it. We need to move quickly so we can get the video feed distributed from somewhere well away from here. This will help our momentum," President Jones says, reaching out to formally shake Juan's hand. "I look forward to working with you to build a great country."

"You too. Mr. President. One more thing. About Gabriel. He was threatening me again inside the holding room," Juan says.

"Understood," President Jones says, turning to one of his security guards. "Please send Mr. Herrera to our Austin base. Tell him he'll be needed for a special assignment and I'll be in touch after he arrives at his new location."

As Juan is escorted to an adjacent room, he passes someone he knows he has seen before, but can't quite place. Despite his clear youth and shoulder-length straight black hair, the man is conservatively dressed. A crimson red silk shirt and silver cufflinks draw Juan's attention. The man is carrying his black jacket over his shoulder. A folded crimson red and emerald green handkerchief sticks out of the top pocket. The floor triggers clicks as what appears to be cowboy boots underneath his slacks slam heavily with each step. The man has a thoroughly confident stride and is being treated with the type of kindness that Juan had hoped he would receive.

As he passes, Juan waves hello to the man and smiles. Ramon Mantle recognizes Juan Gonzalez, but is 10 feet past when he makes the connection to someone he didn't expect to find in this environment. "Good to see you, Juan," Ramon yells back, turning as he opens the door to the control room.

Now even more certain he knows this man, Juan struggles for a minute to figure out where they met. Unsuccessful, he realizes he needs to focus on his public statement supporting the secession and U.N. presence.

"Mr. President," Ramon says to Alta Texas President Manny Jones after shoving open the doors to the command room and drawing startled turns and drawn guns from the in-room security team.

"I asked him to knock and wait," Ramon's escorting guard says sheepishly, as President Jones tells everyone to relax. He greets Ramon with a handshake, half hug and strong slap on the back.

"So good to see you Ramon," President Jones says. "I had been worried at first when the police reported you missing in the middle of the night several weeks ago."

"Ah, yes. I was afraid I needed to permanently disappear for my own safety," Ramon says. "But now that my house is in your territory, I feel much safer in Texas."

"*Ramon, meet General Ramírez. General, this man is a master at using satellite technology to provide safe passage in and around the United States,*" President Jones says.

"*So, aren't you also the man replacing Castillo?*" General Ramírez asks, well aware that one of his colleagues linked to Castillo's cartel recently went missing. President Jones looks at Ramon in shock, having never made the connection between Ramon and Castillo before, let alone between Ramon and General Hernández. That connection explains the technology Hernández delivered to help the U.N. invasion succeed.

General Ramírez has long known of Mexico's military links to Castillo, but had always kept a distance from the cartel. Yesterday, Ramírez was sent to Monterrey by President Suárez in an attempt to regain control of the military action being orchestrated there. President Suárez was one of many global leaders who had thought the U.N. action was going to be a peace-keeping mission run from Mexico City.

"Nobody replaces Cesar Castillo. I simply have provided some technology he found helpful. I'm glad you find it useful as well," Ramon responds. *"But I'd rather not discuss anything else related to Castillo."*

"Well, your technology has proven its value to my men, so I'll forgive what has happened to my friend," General Ramírez tells Ramon. *"I'm afraid we need some additional support."*

"What can I do?"

"What happened to your ear?" General Ramírez asks, looking at burn marks on Ramon's ear where Ramon had the soldered joints melted to remove his tracking earring.

"I had an appendage removed that I no longer need, though I'm not sure how that matters," Ramon responds, dropping his jacket over one of hundreds of display monitors. Ramon was delighted he had been able to convince General Hernández that no one would believe he was leading the cartel if he was still wearing a tracking device.

"It doesn't. Here's what I need. I understand from your Protection Corps that you know where all the police, Border Patrol, FBI and DEA agents are in and around the United States. What would it take to acquire that same tracking capability for the whole U.S. military?" General Ramírez asks.

"It certainly would take some time, but it can be done. After all, the U.S. makes sure all of their troops and major equipment can be tracked. So we can do much of this by adapting my system. But we'll need to crack some pretty secure systems to have 100 percent tracking, and that could take me years," Ramon responds.

"What percent of their military could we track in 48 hours if I tell you we've already taken control of their encryption and communication technology from every branch of government?" President Jones asks.

"Maybe 95 percent in 48 hours, if you're right about what you have. But the last five percent never comes easy."

"I'll take 95 percent. Then help us figure out what the five percent is that you can't follow and we'll focus human intelligence on tracking them," General Ramírez states. *"Please get started."*

"I could do this work just as a thank you for giving me the chance to return home, but I hope you'll consider some additional service payments, Mr. President," Ramon says quietly and directly to President Jones.

"What do you have in mind?"

"I want to do something that makes people respect me for my humanitarianism," Ramon says without any visible expression.

"Then you better get away from politics," President Jones jokes, laughing heartily at his own comments, with others joining after he starts laughing. He turns to check on military movements. Finding nothing urgent, he turns back to Ramon.

"No, seriously, what did you have in mind?"

"I'm going to need a lot of new tunnels with the new borders, and I won't have 30 years to build them all."

"Done, as long as you keep our own kids clean," President Jones commits.

***

President Phillipi orders another 250,000 U.S. troops to relocate to the new borders, adding to the 100,000 sent within minutes of the secession launch. Two squads from different companies are assigned to each road, rail or human crossing point to stop traffic both directions. One goal of the blockades is to minimize the risk that squads or whole companies will defect to Alta Texas, taking weapons with them. Heavy armor, including tanks, are stopped three miles short of the border. Only cleared civilians are allowed to head north from the four states or east from Texas' eastern border. The U.S. military is stopping all efforts to enter Alta Texas from the United States.

Each Alta Texas border squad has discretion to allow U.S. citizens to walk north from Alta Texas once the individuals are cleared as being U.S. citizens, but not a potential security threat. While the few white, black, Arab and Asian families within walking or biking distance of the border are generally allowed to leave Alta Texas, Hispanic families are routinely turned back by Alta Texas border patrols before they can reach the new border. Many are forcibly enlisted on the spot to serve in the Alta Texas military.

The United Nations, which now includes the Republic of Alta Texas but no longer includes the United States, meets in Geneva, Switzerland and approves the dispatch of 500,000 more peacekeeping troops to Alta Texas. Several countries sending troops, including Germany and Japan, express dismay at the skirmishes that have already left many soldiers and civilians dead. Many nations believed they were entering U.S. territory strictly to defend the general public against attack. Still, the U.N. decides that increasing its show of strength is the best way to minimize the risk of a U.S. attack against the peacekeepers or participating countries.

Alta Texas President Jones calls the generals together from countries that helped take control of U.S. military bases. "For the most part, your troops have accomplished what we needed. We have major weapons control at most target bases and we have U.S. troops controlled and confined at almost all. We don't need to rush this," President Jones tells the group of generals. "Some of you followed my orders to create separation from U.S. troops but many of your men continue to attack. So get your men to stop attacking and into defensive mode at the bases. Now, we need to focus on controlling the cities and borders. We need to get reinforcements to bolster some of the 'peacekeeping countries' that didn't understand the full extent of what we're doing."

"You mean, pull our men away from the bases we've taken?" the Russian general asks.

"Not all your men, of course," President Jones responds. He turns his head, connecting with the eyes of each general in the room. "Just as many as you can spare while maintaining base control."

"You're not backing out of your commitment, are you sir?" the Russian asks, sternly and while staring directly at President Jones.

"No. No. Of course not. But there won't be any bases to give to you until it's clear we won and the U.S. pulls its troops out," President Jones states.

"As long as that's clear, we can redirect 15,000 troops," the Russian general states. Other generals follow, offering up some of their troops to redeploy.

***

New Rite Compound, Utah

Clarissa Coleman stands out at her high school. At an even six feet tall, she is among the tallest girls at Coconino High School and is already taller than most boys there. An influx of Mexican Americans to the district in the past 15 years has left this previously racially mixed high school largely concentrated with Hispanic and Native American students. The Coleman family is one of a small group of white families that continues to resist moving out of their long-time family home to relocate to a "whiter" school or state.

Clarissa goes to school most days in gym shoes, loose clothing and a ponytail. Her clear plastic braces push her lips outward. Those braces, combined with the sunken cheekbones of a thin, athletic girl and a long neck earned her the nickname Rattler during her middle school years. As that nickname devolved into something more mean-spirited, she increasingly wore baggier clothes and confined her interaction at school to a small group of friends. Her objective is permanent escape from Flagstaff. She studies without prodding to ensure she has multiple departure options.

As much as Clarissa wants to leave Flagstaff, leaving in a car in the middle of the night without saying goodbye to friends Angela, Catalina and Dezbah was never what she had in mind. The four have been close for several years, spending a disproportionate amount of their free time with each other.

An hour after Clarissa went out into the cold night to try and find a better satellite connection for her Lifelink, John Coleman wakes from his short sleep in panic. He looks around the tent. Seeing she's not there, he brushes his wife awake. "Has Clarissa been back yet?" John asks.

"Can you please let me sleep? I'm sure she's fine," Mrs. Coleman responds. Long suffering from severe sleep apnea, Mrs. Coleman only recently got herself on an apnea machine and feels more physically connected to the world than she had in more than a decade. Still, she never contemplated joining John and the girls on survival weekends, so hadn't bothered to get the battery pack connection for her apnea machine. Exhaustion comes quickly.

Far from reassured, John Coleman is fully awake. After grabbing the battery-powered flashlight from his car emergency kit, he starts searching for Clarissa by stopping at every fire. It's barely 20 degrees Fahrenheit to-night and even in hat, gloves and three layers of clothes, he's already cold. She has to be near fire. After climbing a series of large rocks, he overlooks the camp area and counts more than 20 fires, some raging, but most in the dying ember stage. In his mind, he maps out a pattern to make sure he gets to each. He starts walking between tents, looking for his overly independent youngest child.

After inspecting areas around 10 of the fires, he checks the time and sees it's still nearly an hour until sunrise. Trying to get his bearings, he heads back to his family tent to see if she has returned. Looking in, he sees his wife sitting up.

"You haven't found her yet?" she asks.

"No."

"Damn. Then I'm looking too."

***

Republic of Alta Texas

It's a bit after 7:30 a.m. Eastern time when the primary news networks carry Juan's announcement, promoted as live by satellite from Alta Texas headquarters. A backdrop of the Austin, Texas early morning skyline displays behind Juan. As Juan speaks, Professor Paul Stark hits his fist on the arm of his chair, enough for dramatic effect, but not enough to damage his hand. Jill puts her head down and shakes it from side to side.

"I am deeply honored and humbled to announce that I have accepted the position of ambassador to the United States for the Republic of Alta Texas. It is a great honor to be able to help build our new nation – one in which our people regain control of their lives from an over-bearing, unre-sponsive and, far too often, uncaring government in Washington, D.C. As a new nation, we can redefine this relationship from a position of strength, one that recognizes that we, the people, are the source of government's power and not its servants. We can demand respect for who we are as a peo-ple. Respect for the many of us who are descendants of Mexico, certainly. But also respect for those who join us from other backgrounds," Juan states, as the skyline of Austin, Texas shot from the Alta Texas base rolls live to display behind his green-screen recording.

"Under the leadership of President Jones and the governors of our four provinces, we will be a nation of economic opportunity, of safety and security for our people, of education to create a better tomorrow and of cooperation with the nations around us," Juan continues. "As ambassador, it will be my privilege and my responsibility to build a strong working relationship with the United States, starting with resolving minor differences over the establishment of this new nation. I'm confident that, now that we have made clear our intent to retain only our fair share of military property, President Phillipi and the American people will agree that creating the Republic of Alta Texas is in the best interests of our people, of prosperity and of peace."

Jill turns to Professor Stark: "Did he say 'resolve our minor differences'?" I didn't think Juan was a pothead, but he has to be smoking something to think these are minor differences."

"I have to hand it to him," Professor Stark responds. "That's not a bad speech for someone who probably didn't have much time to put it together. Do you think he really means it?"

"Means what?"

"Means he's committed. Or is he caught in a place where the only way to be safe is to be part of the team?"

"I don't know," Jill says, shrugging her shoulders. "I just don't know. You don't think he was actually shooting this with Austin's skyline in the background?" Jill asks, with Professor Stark missing that she was again asking a rhetorical question.

"Doubtful, but your new buddies at the FBI should be able to do a satellite audio voice search to find out. If he was outside shooting this, they should be able to find his voice on satellite searches," Professor Stark responds. "But if I were a traitor, I would know better than to tell the U.S. military where I am."

***

New Rite Compound, Utah

Clarissa Coleman's Lifelink is either turned off or can't connect to the satellite. Lifelink devices work best with strong satellite connection, but even faint connections are enough to be tracked.

Mrs. Coleman tries a GPS (global positioning system) check for Clarissa's Lifelink and turns up no response. From her device, she calls the emergency search team at Lifelink to find out that, with Clarissa's unit turned off, the Lifelink team can only identify and disclose Clarissa's location with a police warrant. Helpfully, they connect her to the Kanab police, who quickly agree to get a warrant given the unusual circumstances.

Minutes later, with the warrant in hand, they respond to the Kanab police. "We're showing no evidence of her Lifelink anywhere. Even with a dead battery, there is enough juice left in the system for tracking. I'm not sure what else we can do to help, but we will put her Lifelink on automated search to look every 15 minutes and let you know when we find it," the Lifelink team reports.

With this bad news relayed to them, the Colemans are now deeply panicked. They wake the other two daughters, and John Coleman goes around knocking on the poles holding up other tents to ask parents if they've seen Clarissa.

Quickly, they have 25 teenagers and adults gathered near what remains of the fire, sharing photos of Clarissa from Mrs. Coleman's Lifelink that are tapped to everyone else's devices. With the group now spread out searching for her, John Coleman wakes compound leader Sarah Osborne to inform her that Clarissa is missing and ask for help.

He shares basic physical and clothing descriptions, while also clicking photos onto Sarah's Lifelink.

"You sure she didn't meet some boy and just fall asleep talking to him?" Sarah asks.

"Doubtful, but I'm not ruling anything out. For all I know, she could be out doing some type of environmental project. She tends to keep to herself and takes time to be comfortable around new people. Even if she had liked some kid, she'd never stay out all night. She knows better," John Coleman says about his daughter.

"Does she have a Lifelink or any electronics on her?"

"Already tried that. The Kanab police helped, but her Lifelink can't be tracked by satellite."

Sarah straightens up and leans forward in her chair.

"Okay, Mr. Coleman. I'll get my team on it."

After John Coleman walks out the door, Sarah locks the door behind him, walks back into a small closet, pushes in a security code to open up the floor and descends into a tunnel.

CHAPTER 9

63 Hours

Utah New Rite Compound

The small tunnel system under the New Rite Utah camp compound is similar to tunnel systems at every New Rite facility. At every compound, JT Alton installed tunnels between the site's headquarters and aircraft landing spot.

Each tunnel contains disguised connections to two areas in other than the landing spot. One connection is always to a remote shed. Each shed houses normal operating equipment for the site, and is designed to attract attention from anyone planning an attack as a potential escape route or hiding spot. JT assumes the Castillo cartel will some day identify him and seek retribution. In order to survive a surprise attack at one of his properties, JT had survival tunnels built to blend so well with the natural environment that even JT might not see the outside opening when standing in front of it. At the Utah compound, that exit is hidden inside a north-facing rock wall recession and is protected by an overhang from ever being illuminated by the sun. Even the other end of the tunnel, which is connected below the tunnel between the headquarters and the shed, is difficult to find without knowing it exists as well as specifically where to look.

The survival tunnel exit is the quickest way to get to an outdoor area that JT sets up at each camp to hold confidential discussions free from any surveillance concerns. Sarah is the only person stationed at the Utah compound aware of the survival tunnel exit. JT and the tunnel's builder are the only others who know how to get in and out of this tunnel stretch.

After pushing her head through the opening of the survival tunnel exit, Sarah reaches down two feet to the ground with both hands. She drags the rest of her body out of the tunnel entrance by walking her arms forward. As she does this, the rest of her body slides out of the opening. After standing, Sarah bends back down to seal the tunnel opening.

Sarah checks the first of five hiding spots within a two-hour walk of the compound, though she doesn't expect to find Clarissa at this one. After taking the Utah camp role as her between-special-assignment work at New Rite, Sarah scoured the area for alternative escapes in case the camp is attacked by Castillo's Protection Corps. JT warned Sarah when she joined New Rite's special operations team that it was only a matter of time before Castillo figured out who was behind the cartel's losses.

Not finding Clarissa at the first location near the tunnel exit, Sarah continues to the spot where she really expects to find Clarissa. Nearing the mesh overhang carefully designed to look like part of the landscape, Sarah sees a young girl sleeping in the enclosed area.

Pushing against her shoulder, she asks, "Clarissa?"

The young girl looks up and tries to get her bearings.

"Clarissa Coleman?"

"Yeah, that's me," the shivering girl says as she realizes daylight is breaking and she has been gone all night.

The area is protected from the wind and has a shelf-like rock area elevated from the ground. Clarissa intended to just take a short nap here, but exhaustion caught up with her and she fell sound asleep. She had become lost while searching for a better satellite connection to search for local water sources and wild food collection and capture techniques.

"Oh my God, my dad is going to kill me," Clarissa tells Sarah.

"Maybe, but only after he's thrilled to see you. There are a lot of people out searching for you right now," Sarah tells her, pulling Clarissa in by her shoulder and putting her coat over Clarissa to help her warm up.

"I'm so sorry. I didn't mean to fall asleep."

"I'm sure you didn't. It's okay. We'll head back now."

"Why didn't they just call me?" Clarissa asks Sarah.

"I think something must be wrong with your Lifelink. Let me see if I can fix it as we walk and we can call on the way back," Sarah says, though she knows perfectly well that the area Clarissa was sleeping is overlaid with a buried mesh that blocks out any satellite signals. Clarissa hands her Lifelink device to Sarah, who pretends to move around some wires and play with the battery connection as they walk away from the covered area where Clarissa slept. Clarissa jumps as she steps on what appears to be recently shed snakeskin.

A few minutes later, Sarah hands the Lifelink back to Clarissa. Heading back over land requires some semi-serious rock climbing, a much more physically demanding trip than the tunnel path Sarah took more than half way to the site.

"It should work now. I've had this happen to my Lifelink before," Sarah says, lying to keep Clarissa from seeking the real answer. "Do you want to call your father or do you want me to call him?"

Seconds later, Sarah is connected to John Coleman.

"Mr. Coleman. I found Clarissa. She's cold and tired, but otherwise okay."

"Oh, thank God."

"We'll meet you back at camp headquarters in about 45 minutes."

"Thank you so much. Thank you. Thank you."

At camp headquarters, the whole Coleman family is waiting when Sarah and Clarissa reach the front door. Sarah realizes she had locked the front from the inside, so she hands Clarissa over to the Coleman family in front of the building and walks around to the coded entry on the side.

"How did you find her so quickly?" John Coleman asks once they are all inside for Clarissa to warm up.

"The benefits of knowing the whole camp site," Sarah responds. "I just thought about where I would have wandered if I were a 14-year-old girl searching for a good satellite connection."

Sarah didn't mention that as soon as she heard that no satellite could trace Clarissa, she knew the most likely spot for Sarah was an overhang area where she and New Rite founder JT Alton held their most confidential discussions.

Before walking away, Clarissa walks back and looks eye-to-eye at Sarah. "Thank you for finding me," she says.

"You're certainly welcome Clarissa. Just make sure you follow the buddy system from here on out. It's always better to be part of a team and save our individual efforts for those challenges we can only tackle alone."

"I will. I will," Clarissa promises. "Do you know where I can get the best satellite connection?"

***

Flagstaff, Arizona

Back at their Arizona home, Grandpa sits at the front door of the Coleman family home with his rifle in hand and loads of ammunition by his side.

One of the Coleman's neighbor mothers sees Grandpa sitting there, holding his rifle, as her children run around in the front yard. Fearful for them, she yells at them to get inside right away. Then she calls local police to tell them about her gun-wielding neighbor. Fifteen minutes later, three squad cars arrive around the home, stopping 100 feet short of the driveway. An officer pulls out a bullhorn.

"Put your weapon down, sir, or we will have to open fire," the officer orders.

"I haven't done a damn thing wrong. I'm just protecting my house from looters," Grandpa Coleman yells back.

Over the bullhorn, the officer responds: "Sir, martial law has been declared. You're required to be indoors except between the hours of 8 a.m. and 5 p.m. You're also required to turn in all weapons to local police by the end of the day. So why don't we take care of both issues. You go inside, but leave your weapons and ammunition outside," the officer suggests.

"If I don't have any weapons, how am I going to protect my home from all the invaders who come to take our property and rape our women," Grandpa responds.

"No one has come to do that sir. The United Nations is only here to provide security to assure our safety," the officer responds.

"It's not just the United Nations I'm worried about. It's all you damn foreigners trying to steal our country."

"I'm not going to sit here and listen to you insult me and my family," the officer yells over the bullhorn.

"If you leave, you won't have to hear anything," Grandpa responds, amusing himself and displaying a wry smile.

"The only reason I haven't shot you already is it's clear you're a senile, old bastard," the officer yells. He's loud enough now he is audible even without the bullhorn.

"I'm crazy all right; crazy enough to believe that I can defend my home any way I want. Unless you want to shoot an old man, or want an old man to shoot you, I suggest you just get on your way," Grandpa Coleman says as he stands up, holding his rifle pointed to the ground.

The officer's face turns crimson red. His partner grabs him by the collar as he starts to stand up and walk toward the Coleman's home.

"Let's call this in and see what the captain wants us to do," his partner implores.

Several minutes later, the three squad cars and five officers back up another 300 feet. Neighbors around the Coleman home exit their homes under police escort from rear doors, led away out of sight of Grandpa Coleman.

***

West Nogales, Arizona

Two hours before he is allowed to open the West Nogales FirstWal store, Mike Sanchez already recognizes this will be a rough day. From the hilltop location of the store, Mike sees the border crossing is wide open. Cars coming north don't slow down at the border. Neither do jeeps, tanks and trucks carrying all-terrain vehicles headed straight to the northern border of Arizona.

Though the sun hasn't yet peeked above the horizon, darkness is passing. As the sky further lightens, Mike forgets about the store long enough to look at the flags on the vehicles he spots in the distance. Pulling his Lifelink out, he zooms in to see they all carry a U.N. flag. Most carry flags of other countries as well. Eyeing the Nogales crossing, he quickly counts 20 countries before arriving at work. It is little shock then when he sees a Chinese- and U.N.-flagged military vehicle pull up in front of the store.

A West Nogales police officer meets the vehicle before the occupants start pounding on the main door.

As he hears banging on the door, Mike faces a dilemma. He's alone in the store so he can't let non-employees enter or be fired for breaking company policy. Still, he knows martial law has been declared and the men outside are likely here on official business. Realizing the military and police can enter the store whether or not he lets them in, Mike invites them to join him for coffee or tea.

"You the manager?" the police officer asks.

"Yes, sir."

"These men from the United Nations are here to protect your store. You will show them all the courtesies of a gracious host," the officer orders.

"Under martial law, customers buy only two supply days of food and drink. No weapons. We take your weapons away," the U.N. lieutenant from China directs in halting English. "You sell everything else you want. Prices must stay same, or you arrest. We check prices and compare."

"We aren't carrying any products we've had before," Mike responds. "Starting today, everything we're selling is a new product under orders from our national leadership."

The West Nogales police officer intervenes: "You realize that's absurd on its face, so don't even go there. You're not part of the U.S. any more, and the laws of Alta Texas dictate that you cannot raise prices on anything for at least 90 days. You'll only sell items at yesterday's prices, using either pesos or dollars, or my friends here will arrest you and charge you with treason."

"That's clear, sir. I'll let management know," Mike responds.

"No need for that. What's so difficult to understand that you aren't part of the United States?"

"I understand, officer," Mike says. "But if I can't communicate with the company, I can't get resupplies. We'll very quickly have nothing to sell."

"Do what we have told you and we'll check with our chain of command on whether you can communicate outside your new country."

"Yes sir. Got it."

The police officer leaves to his next location, but the Chinese peace-keeping troops are left behind to enforce martial law requirements.

As Mike walks back to his office, he pushes the emergency notification button on his wrist alert. In the years he has been required to wear this so Chet Leach could reach him 24/7/365, Mike never contemplated using it to contact Chet.

The Chinese troops track behind Mike to make sure martial law orders are being followed, asking questions Mike struggles to comprehend.

"Where go you?" the U.N. lieutenant asks Mike, drawing a puzzled look from Mike as he tries to understand what he's being asked.

"To my office," Mike responds after figuring out the lieutenant's gestures. "I need to connect to the computers to reprogram all of the pricing I just finished raising, and make sure that central controls don't override my work."

"You do law," the other states in return, reading from his translation program.

Chet Leach slept briefly last night, but has been back to work for several hours already when FirstWal's security director informs him of Mike's emergency alert. The security director connects the West Nogales store views to Chet's control screens. Chet calls Mike on his secure store Lifelink connection. No answer. He looks through the security screens and sees Mike talking to a military officer who is wearing a uniform Chet recognizes from traveling to China. He calls again. Mike doesn't answer.

Thinking Mike may have hit the emergency alert code accidentally, he sends an alert to Mike. The loud sound and vibration catch the troops by surprise.

"What noise?"

"That's the senior leader of our company telling me I have two minutes to call him or be fired," Mike responds.

"Okay. Call, but I talk," the man who appears to be the more senior of the two directs.

Following orders, Mike looks to make sure his actions are visible to a security camera, then slowly clicks to connect to Chet and enter his security code for the call. After dialing, he hands the earpiece and mouth clip over, again in clear view of the security camera.

"Yes," the official says.

"Who the hell is this?" Chet asks as he stares at the control screen to figure out what is going on.

"I am lieutenant with U.N. peacekeeping. Who this?"

"This is Chet Leach. I am in charge of FirstWal in the United States. I called to talk to the store manager. Put him on the phone."

"First, I make thing clear. West Nogales is not in United States so Mr. Mike here follows our orders. Not yours. Mr. Mike must take our orders and martial law or we arrest for treason and shoot. Then we come for you."

"You can't just take my store. That's my property. That store and everything in it belongs to FirstWal and the First Empire global retail chain. The money we earn belongs to China, so unless you're prepared to have a go with the government of China, I suggest you contact your superiors and turn control of the store back to Mr. Sanchez and me," Chet barks.

"These are orders, Mr. Chet. You listen."

After seeing the lieutenant click Mike's Lifelink shut, Chet turns to his security director. "What the hell just happened? We need to check out every other store in those states."

***

New Rite Compound, Utah

Sarah Osborne, the former Navy Seal who took over leadership of the Utah training and competition site last year, gets an emergency alert call from JT Alton. When not running the Utah compound, Sarah is part of New Rite's special operations unit, as JT calls the dedicated team that takes on isolated special missions against the Castillo cartel. During the past decade, JT expanded this team beyond intelligence gathering aimed at taking down Mexico's most powerful drug lord, a man JT blames for the death of his younger brother. In recent years, with Sarah, Ally and a dozen other military experts, New Rite has captured several targets in the Castillo organization.

Most of the Castillo employees had the lower part of their ear cut off after capture to remove tracking devices before being taken for interrogation. Once New Rite had what it needed, they let the employees choose whether or not to go back to Castillo. As far as they could tell, Cesar Castillo had any who returned ruthlessly tortured and impaled for being careless enough to be captured. Only on a few occasions did the New Rite team directly kill Castillo cartel employees.

Sarah locks her cabin back up and uses a secure connection device to call in to the special operations team. Ally is on the other end.

"We may have a mission. How quickly can you get to Colorado Springs?" Ally asks.

"Our camp is flooded with refugees. People coming north to escape the invasion and people coming south to help protect the new border," Sarah replies. "I don't know that the second in command here and the rest of the team can handle this on their own. Well, that's your call. I can probably get there in three to four hours if I can get a plane to get me close."

"Hold up, wait there. We'll call you back if we need you to get here. You might be in a good enough spot where you are."

***

Chicago

Tamika leaves her home, checking to make sure all the doors and gates are locked behind her. Walking down streets piled with snow on both sides, her boots quickly soak in the icy, salty slush that pedestrians share with cars. Sidewalks are never shoveled in Tamika's neighborhood. Plows come through here after a substantial snowfall, but always late, and never fully clearing the streets. She's shivering as she reaches the Metra Electric line train platform. Despite the bitter wind, she stands in the most open spot of the outdoor platform, with her back to the tracks and her head constantly searching for threat. Far too many of Tamika's friends have been robbed or raped. She's been lucky so far, but stays alert. While bitter cold usually deters criminals, there's really no safe time to be a young woman alone in her neighborhood.

When the train arrives, just a few minutes after its scheduled time, she gets on board, walks up another small set of stairs to the top of the bi-level car, and takes an open spot near a heat vent. After putting her feet against the heater, she instinctively opens her Lifelink to see if anything substantial has happened in the 20 minutes since she left home. Seeing nothing, she closes it and peers out the window of the train.

Getting off the train near campus, Tamika's bright orange hat, crimson earmuffs and scarf, blue gloves, black boots and Eskimo-like forest green parka won't win her any fashion awards. She only wears them when she can't take the cold in her normal winter coat. Even this outfit isn't warm enough to keep Tamika's teeth from chattering as she trudges through the 14 inches of snow that fell overnight. The Hyde Park neighborhood attracts street plows and sidewalk shovels far faster than near Tamika's home, but crews struggle to keep up even here.

Lake-effect snow is dissipating, but the brutal slicing winds racing over the ice-crusted lake cut deeply into her eyes, making them feel almost frozen in place. Tamika leaves the ice to form on her eyelashes, afraid wiping it away will snap them and drive her appearance down to her comfort level. Nearly 15 minutes later, she finishes the half-mile walk. Tamika fumbles for Rachel's apartment buzzer, not daring to pull her hand out of her glove to make a call from her Lifelink. The door buzzes. Tamika steps inside. After the door closes, she stands there, shivering, now hearing her teeth chattering as loud as the backbeat of a favorite song. Slowly, she strips the layers — the hat, scarf, earmuffs and gloves. Minutes later, she takes her coat off and her whole body shakes as violently as a longhaired dog after a bath. Tamika, though, is trying to fling away a deep interior chill rather than water.

Rachel worries Tamika isn't coming up and descends the stairs to meet her.

"I'm surprised anyone is out walking in this," Rachel states.

"Me too. I hope you're okay with me staying with you until it warms up," Tamika responds, only half joking. "I'm not walking home until it warms up."

"I'm fine if you want, but doubt you can handle living here," Rachel responds. "Three or four weeks of sleeping on the floor and I bet you'll be ready to battle the cold again. Are you sure you're okay?"

"Yeah, I'll warm up. But really I came to see how you're holding up and here you are worrying about me," Tamika says, entering Rachel's efficiency apartment. The one-room unit is sparsely furnished. A few folding chairs are open with the bags used to carry them strapped over each back. A futon that folds up to a sofa is in bed mode with a half-dozen blankets strewn about. The small kitchen area is perfumed with the scent of chocolate walnut coffee in a six-cup carafe.

"I don't know what to think. My dad is in jail. My boyfriend, or at least my convenient stand-in for a boyfriend, has defected to another country. Our country has been invaded. My mom and brother are supposed to try to make it through the worst of winter to come here until everything passes over. And I can't even think about an internship or anything I was planning to do when I don't even know if there is a future."

"I feel terrible for you Rachel," Tamika tells her, putting her hand on her forearm and gently massaging it for several seconds. "I thought I might come over and try and keep your mind focused on something else, like the paper we have due for Professor Stark."

"Oh, he can't possibly expect us to have papers done by then," Rachel says. "Can he?"

"Are you serious?" Tamika responds. "When have you ever known or even heard a story of Professor Stark giving students a pass from a deadline. I'm surprised he hasn't asked us to do another paper on how religion, culture, government and business can be used to solve this impasse?"

"Oh God," Rachel says. "Please don't say that out loud again and please don't write it anywhere he could find it. I couldn't stand it if he loaded up even more on us."

"I'd feel bad for you," Tamika responds, "if I didn't know we both knew what he was like and still were dumb enough to sign up for more punishment."

"I guess you're right."

"Okay, so on a more serious note," Tamika says. "Have you thought about telling Professor Stark or Jill about your relationship with Juan?"

"Seriously, what are they going to think of me, especially when I don't even know what to think? Juan's four years younger, barely out of high school. That's like Jeremy's dating age range. I'm not old enough to be a cougar already," Rachel says.

"That really should be the least of our concerns," Tamika responds. "Don't you think if there's something that could be done to help protect

Juan or convince him to change his mind, they would figure out how to
help you do that?"

"Like what?"

"I don't know. You're the one who grabbed his hand under the table at
my house."

"Yeah, but I haven't seen him in person since then," Rachel says.

"If you don't count the hour every day on video chat. Hours, I might
point out, that neither of you has really had time to spend."

Going back to refill both coffee cups, Rachel and Tamika continue to
talk.

Several minutes later, Tamika looks at Rachel and smirks: "And who
knows how close you get with him on video?"

***

Flagstaff, Arizona

Grandpa Coleman needs a break, and needs to warm up. After a couple
of hours sitting on the front porch, he steps inside holding his rifle in his
left hand and closing the door behind him with his right. He looks out
the window for several seconds to make sure there is no movement before
deciding it's safe. Grandpa walks toward the kitchen, puts his sealable
container under the dispenser and verbally orders hot tea. Seconds later, he
hears the drip of the coffee begin. The aroma quickly fills the kitchen area.

Minutes later, he is sitting on the toilet, rifle in hand, when he hears the
locked front door slammed open and a flash-bang grenade explode.

Eight fully armed SWAT team members come through the front door,
leapfrogging past each other for cover. They check off the front family room
to the right of the entrance.

"Clear."

Hearing the tea drip, the kitchen is checked next.

"Clear."

Then Grandpa's bedroom, converted from former garage space.

"Clear."

Startled by the loud noise, Grandpa is oriented enough to know he's under attack, but disoriented enough to react like he's back in a Hindu Kush mountain range.

"I'll kill every one of you towel heads if you don't turn and get out of my house now," Grandpa yells, firing a warning shot around the corner of the bathroom door.

The officer in charge orders the back-up SWAT members to pull back to the front of the house. He sends forward two officers fully encased in clear, bulletproof body cylinders to ram the suspect and knock his weapon loose. As these two reach the hallway, one crosses to the other side. Grandpa shoots. His bullet glances off a body cone. They'll have to make a 20-foot run at him, but they know what type of rifle he is carrying. The body cones deflect or absorb any bullets from Grandpa's Marimaster, even at close range.

"Three, two, one, go."

They make a charge for the bathroom door, one behind the other. As they do, Grandpa steps out from behind the door and is now standing in the middle of the hallway. He shoots rapidly, getting five shots off before he is battered to the floor by the first of the two officers, knocked flat on his back with his head whipping hard into the door jam of another bedroom. His hands release the rifle and his body goes limp.

"Crazy old man," one officer yells at Grandpa as both officers back up and lie flat to back out of their protective cylinders. Another officer pulls the rifle away and ties Grandpa's hands in front of him as they stand back up. The officer in charge comes up, picks the rifle up, removes the ammunition clip and calls for an ambulance.

"Is there a pulse?" he asks.

One officer reaches forward and places his hand on his wrist. He can't tell, so moves his hand up to start feeling around Grandpa's neck.

"There's a pulse," the officer says. "Well . . . , maybe."

***

Around the World

U.S. military reinforcements begin arriving at the southernmost military bases still within U.S. control. United Nations troops continue to flood north inside the Alta Texas states, adding reinforcements around the numerous bases that haven't defected or been abandoned. U.S. troops inside these bases are ordered to fire on any U.N. or Alta Texas troops entering weapons, ammunition storage or other areas where U.S. troops have gathered. President Phillipi orders these troops to call in air support if attacked, but not to move out from their existing positions to initiate battles with the U.N. troops.

Almost all naval fleets operating outside U.S. territorial waters are ordered to return to U.S. territory. With Egypt contributing a sizable contingent to the U.N. force, U.S. fleets in the Persian Gulf and Red Sea are denied access to the Suez Canal. The United Nations also convinces Panama to close its canal to U.S. ships trying to cross between oceans.

***

Traver, California

Mrs. Cruz is waiting at the door of the Traver, California police station when the doors open at 7 a.m.

"I came to get my husband, Victor Cruz," she tells the sergeant at the desk.

"You'll have to wait in line with the rest, but I wouldn't hold out a lot of hope because he hasn't been charged with anything yet," the sergeant tells her.

"So you're letting him go."

"I don't think so, ma'am. We're holding all our Mexicans over in the warehouse until we get orders on what to do."

"My husband's American. I brought his passport in case you needed proof," Mrs. Cruz responds, trying her best to control her anger at the "our Mexicans" insult.

"I'm sure he lives in America ma'am, but everyone in there has admitted they're Mexican," the sergeant states.

"You mean Mexican American," she responds with her voice starting to tremble with anger.

"Whatever. We can't let him go until we get orders on what to do. Nothing against you or him, ma'am, but we might be in a war so we need to make sure we're doing everything by the book."

"So, by the book now means it's a crime to have Mexican heritage, no matter how loyal of a citizen you are of the United States."

"I didn't say that ma'am."

"Then why are you holding my husband?" she screams, extending and shaking her hands at the officer.

"Ma'am, if you shut up and take a seat, you can wait in line for the chance to speak to your husband as a free person. If you continue to challenge me, I'm going to arrest you for disorderly conduct and then good luck getting approval to talk to your husband," the sergeant responds, pulling his handcuffs off his belt and holding them in front of him for added effect.

"This is ridiculous. I thought this was America," she says, as she turns and stamps her feet into the ground for the first few steps toward the waiting benches.

"Nasty bitch," the sergeant mutters, fully intending to be heard.

***

Cheyenne Mountain, Colorado

Set up inside the Cheyenne Mountain secure military compound in Colorado, Pete, Ally and the rest of the New Rite special training team map out alternative scenarios and responsibilities for a potential attack on Alta Texas leadership.

Ally is expert at flying New Rite's APB, a high-speed combo jet/helicopter that is so far invisible to all means of electronic tracking, though still visible at times and from the right angle to the naked eye.

Pete has proven himself an expert long-distance marksman and camouflage expert, with the ability to get in and out of tight environments without being seen and while hitting his target. He is the only member of the group without extensive U.S. military special operations training.

Four members of the New Rite team specialize in personnel extraction, with comprehensive weapons and hand-to-hand combat training. Clint specializes in untraceable improvised explosive device (I.E.D.) creation and deployment, but has a wide range of bomb-related skills. Lou, better known to her family as Luisa, is an expert in deploying and navigating small drones for surveillance and guided bomb deployment.

All have experience in taking out small targets – usually one target at a time. As the team discusses its capabilities, Pete suggests he knows what JT is going to ask them to do.

"With our skill set, we're best set to go after Senator Jones," Pete speculates. "We all know how to take out single targets. With a team, we have backup in case someone misses. I know I can get him."

"You can get him if he gets out in the open. What do you think the chances are that the Alta Texas leadership is sitting in an open field for you to go after them?" Clint asks in a way that makes clear to others he is annoyed to have Pete on the team.

"Well, that's what I do. So why else would I be here if that isn't what we're doing?" Pete replies, leaning further forward in his chair as he speaks. "They have to move sometime, and moving sometime means being in the open, even if just for a second. That second is all I need, and I don't even have to be close. I just need a sight line to lock in."

"It's not like they're really sophisticated. It's a bunch of wetbacks we're fighting," Pete says, drawing sharp and angry glances from everyone in the room.

"Hey, son-of-a-bitch, I'm one of those people so if you're here to get your kick out of killing Mexicans, you better not make any mistakes," Clint says.

"Clint isn't a Mexican name," Pete states with no apparent purpose.

Ally looks at Pete. She's known him longer than everyone else on the team and knows he can't possibly be as stupid as he sounds right now.

"Pete, you need to just shut up until your brain starts working again. This isn't a race issue and has nothing to do with you not getting a job because you don't speak Spanish. This is all about protecting freedom of speech, freedom to worship and our right to achieve success. If you are here for any other reason, I'm going to ask JT to drop you from the team," Ally says. "We can't work together if your hate divides us."

"All right, all right, all right, I was just testing you all to see how you would react," Pete says, trying his best to explain his statement away. "This is an America thing for me too."

Clint is clearly disgusted; forehead and eyebrows crumpled and eyes still glaring sharply at Pete. He looks at Ally, shaking his head and rolling his eyes toward Pete. "Really?" Clint asks her.

The group continues discussing scenarios they may be asked to undertake – individual kill, individual or small group extraction, small group kill, behind-the-line surveillance. Fifteen minutes later, Pete is hooded and cuffed for escort to the restroom by Branch, one of the official military officers assigned to the team. As Branch and Pete walk out of the room, Ally pulls Clint aside.

"I don't know what JT has in mind, but this kid could be a leave-behind to provide cover while we escape," Ally suggests, trying to get Clint to calm down. "He's more of a lone operator anyway."

"JT wouldn't want one of us abandoned in that situation," Clint responds.

"One of us, no. Him?" Ally says about Pete. "I don't know. Besides, it's not necessarily abandonment with Pete. If there's anyone who can physically hide in enemy territory, it's him. I'll give him that."

***

Washington, D.C.

The FBI thinks they've traced Congresswoman Jill Carlson's connection with Juan Gonzalez. They weren't able to fully track the electronic connections, but did find the last trace came in from a signal tower along the old U.S.-Mexico border. The original signal must have arrived at the tower by wire since nothing is visible around the tower.

Analysts reviewing the videotape determine that the flush handle displayed briefly on the screen behind Juan is the same type of flush handle used inside many Mexican military buildings. In addition, the wall behind

Juan appears to be constructed with a native Mexican stone from Northeast Mexico.

"We've got what we need," they tell Jill as they hand back her Lifelink and prepare to leave her office. "Hopefully, this will help someone."

***

New Rite Compound, Utah

Streaks of red and burnt orange are fading as thin, misty clouds begin to bake away in the slowly rising sun. It's a cool, crisp morning. A quick 30-minute nap and pre-packaged breakfast behind him, John Coleman joins the rest of the able-bodied volunteers at the center of the New Rite Utah camp. By the time compound leader Sarah Osborne joins them, more than 300 men, women and teenagers are assembled around the camp's outdoor training arena. With seating for just 50, the rest circle around the main podium area and strain to hear the discussion.

John wears a partial mask of black and grey stubble. His usually groomed hair is matted in some spots and sticking up in others. Darkness under his eyes is the clearest evidence of the strain on his body from sleep deprivation, both from driving half the night to escape an invasion and from facing the very real terror of searching for a daughter missing in the wilderness.

With the New Rite camp not far north of the Utah/Arizona border, those settled here are mainly Arizonans who already know they don't want to be part of Alta Texas. A few, however, came down from further north in Utah to see what they could do to protect the border. The Colorado River, including Lake Powell's Padre and Wahweap bays, provides a natural water-based invasion barrier on the eastern edge of the New Rite compound. To the west of Wahweap Bay lay stark, desolate lands that can be traversed in many spots at high speeds, but with real hazards along the way.

With the help of Clarissa's loud, shrill whistle, Sarah gets the group's attention.

"We have to assume the U.S. military will block off Route 89 and other main roads into the area. I've had some contact with former colleagues who tell me troops are being assigned to set up new border perimeters. So our primary purpose as we spread out around the camp will be to provide an added measure of security for you and your families. Right now, we have just over 300 volunteers signed up for scouting duties. That means we need to be selective in deciding where to put resources. We also need to think about whether the main compound here is in the right place to provide maximum security to you and your families along with access to native food and water," Sarah states, projecting a map of the compound and New Rite's full property.

"My initial assessment is that this camp site is not well-suited to a purpose for which it was never intended," Sarah continues.

Sarah outlines a plan, after taking input from several participants, to reshape the current main compound as a first day entry point, while relocating the rest of campers to an area south of Smoky Mountain Road that is within a one-hour walk of Warm Creek Bay and Wahweap Bay. From there, able-bodied volunteers will spread out in four-person camps at one-mile intervals, with each camp assigned to find high ground sites with long range visibility and protection from the elements. With two-person minimum patrols inside their intervals, these scouts will watch for water crossings. Each camp must maintain daily physical contact with the two camps to their east and west, in addition to exchanging Lifelink contact information for emergency-only use. A tech-savvy camper shows the group how to disengage and reengage Lifelink transmitter location devices.

"The other side can't know we have scouts out here," John Coleman tells the group. "It's going to be tough going if we can't burn fires for warmth at night and sterilize the water we take from the lake. Even going to get water can give our locations away if we aren't extremely cautious in how we approach."

Sarah listens intently to the discussion, trying to determine the best alternative to safeguard everyone she now considers herself responsible for protecting. After listening to 20 minutes of discussion, she speaks up again.

"So say we see someone who's probably not an American cross into Utah or try to take a boat to this side. If our response is to get military and police forces to stop them, and meet them with force if necessary, we'll reduce the likelihood of any action being in our area," Sarah says.

"We're ready for action, so I don't care if they come at us. I'm ready to fight," one young man yells out.

"That's because you think you're invincible. How old are you?"

"Sixteen."

"So, have you watched one of your friends being torn apart by bullets or bombs," Sarah asks.

"No, ma'am, I haven't."

"It's my hope that you won't have to. I appreciate that you're willing to fight for your family and fight for your country. But we don't want to send engraved invitations to come fight around our families, do we?"

"No. I guess not."

"The best way to win a fight is to have the other side decide they would lose if they took you on. So we need to either be invisible or look as menacing as we can."

Clarissa Coleman contacts her friends in Flagstaff to let them know why she can't meet up with them for lunch today. On King Day, the girls had planned to meet for lunch and shop at highway thrift shops.

"My family decided to go north to stay with our other family until this all blows over," she writes. "I'll miss you, but will see you soon. I hope."

Minutes after sending the message, Clarissa takes her Lifelink and heads to one of the elevated spots that Sarah told her would be best for rapid satellite connections. She starts searching for water sources, native foods and other survival tips, trying to make sure she and her family are prepared in case their Utah stay is extended.

***

Chicago

Rachel decides she needs to let Professor Stark know about her history with Juan. The two finally connect.

"Any news on your father?" Professor Stark asks Rachel after she says hello.

"Yeah, my mom says they're holding him, but he's not charged with anything. It just doesn't make sense," Rachel says.

"No, it doesn't. You'd think we would have learned, but maybe our collective knowledge is so limited that we can't figure out the important lessons history tries to teach us," Professor Stark says. "I know Jill is raising this issue with everyone she can." He pauses briefly before continuing: "How are you doing with all of this?"

"Okay, all things considered, but I need to tell you something, I think," Rachel says.

"What's that?"

"Well, first, any news on Juan?"

"Not since his press announcement. We don't know where he is or how he is," Professor Stark responds.

"Okay, well, anyway, I don't know if this means anything or helps at all, but Juan and I talked pretty much every day since we met," Rachel says. "You could kind of say he might be my boyfriend, except that we haven't really seen each other in person. I can't believe I'm talking to you, of all people, about boys."

"Rachel, it's fine, and I certainly appreciate your trust. It would be really important to know if you talked to Juan or had any contact with him in the last 24 hours."

"I don't want to say anything because I don't want anything bad to happen to Juan," Rachel says. "If I tell you, how do I know it won't be used against him?"

"You've just told me you've had contact," Professor Stark states. "I swear to you on my life that I won't let anything you tell me be used to hurt him. I can't take credit for saving too many lives, so I don't want the ones I do help save to disappear."

"Yeah, I know," Rachel responds in a quiet tone.

"So what did he say to you?"

"He left a whispered message that he was in a plane with Gabriel and he was blindfolded and headed east, if he didn't lose track of direction after he was blindfolded," Rachel says. "I think he was in an airplane bathroom."

"When was this?"

"Early yesterday. He told me not to tell anybody because he wasn't sure if he was being tested for loyalty or really in trouble, but he wanted me to know in case I didn't hear from him for a while so I could call the police in 24 hours."

"That's interesting. When he talked to Jill, it sounded like he wasn't happy with the invasion, but felt he might have no choice but to support it," Professor Stark says.

"Jill talked to him?"

"Oh, damn. I wasn't supposed to say that, but since you're telling me something vital, maybe it's only fair that you know. But you need to not say anything to anybody," Professor Stark says. "His life may depend on your silence."

"I won't. Of course, I won't," Rachel responds. "When did she talk to him?"

"In the middle of the night, before the announcement of his ambassador position."

"Do you think he might have been forced into taking that job?" Rachel asks.

"That's a good question. And, probably a critical one based on what you're telling me," Professor Stark responds.

"What do you mean?

"I mean we need to figure out how to keep Juan safe, and how to change his mind. He's probably the person in the country right now best positioned to tell the Southwest states that there's a better way to get control of their lives than to allow themselves to be invaded by the United Nations."

"Promise me you won't let him get hurt."

"I promise Rachel," Professor Stark responds, "to the extent I can control it. If I can do anything to protect him, I will. Anything else, from recent days or weeks or months that might be helpful?"

"I don't know. We've spent a lot of time talking about social justice lately," Rachel says.

"Is that it?" he asks one more time.

CHAPTER 10

60 Hours

Near Dallas, Texas

Morning rush hour commutes are extremely light in most cities and not just because of Martin Luther King Jr. holiday traffic. Inside Alta Texas, those who didn't hear about the secession invasion last night quickly focus on protecting family and friends. The Shady Shores area north of Dallas is one of hundreds of wealthier Southwest communities where police are torn between cooperating with and combating invasion forces. Both choices draw resources away from battling looting and assault surges, but cooperation is the avenue chosen in most departments.

Several criminal rings organize quickly once the invasion becomes public. The Pumas, a gang established at the behest of deceased cartel boss Cesar Castillo, reacts swiftly and harshly. Over several hours, the gang breaks into the homes of 196 anti-secession leaders, one home for each year since Texas became part of the United States. Six Pumas take part in each anti-secession home attack.

Charlotte Lee became a prominent anti-secession leader last fall. A native Texan, Charlotte grew up the daughter of an oilfield worker and a grade school teacher in West Texas. Strong, tough and independent, she made the transition from popular high school cheerleader to proud Aggie petroleum engineering graduate to even prouder stay-at-home mother of two boys and one girl. Bob and Charlotte Lee are raising their family in the largely Asian, Arab and white Forest Hills neighborhood on the other side of Lewisville Lake from Shady Shores. With her youngest daughter going into first grade last fall, Charlotte had been planning to return to at least part-time petroleum engineering work when the secession movement started. Instead, she dedicated herself to defeating an initiative she saw as threatening the way of life on which her family was raised.

For four months leading up to election day, Charlotte traveled within range of her home to speak to any group willing to hear her talk about or debate the value of remaining aligned with the United States. A few of Charlotte's friends, irrespective of race, chose the other side. To many, the secession move was an opportunity for Texas to separate from failed Washington policies and a chance to assert control over others in the Southwest.

After confirming that his business trip is cancelled, and the family's vehicles inoperable in any case, Bob Lee decides to spend time at home. Charlotte knows she and her family will be outcasts in the new Alta Texas nation, so she asks Bob whether it makes sense to move out of Texas. Leaving would be tough for two lifelong Texans.

The breakfast nook in the Lee house has a beautiful lake overlook. While feeling traumatized by the overnight event and the family's thwarted effort to head north, Charlotte decides to treat the family to a rare home-cooked Monday breakfast. She makes banana-chocolate chip pancakes, maple-flavored sausage links and a Portuguese potato hash made with heavy doses of paprika and onion. She starts squeezing orange juice by hand before Bob asks her to sit down.

"I know you're upset, but we can't cook our way out of this, so sit down and eat with us," Bob tells Charlotte as she continues to walk from room to room, trying to do everything she thinks might need to be done. When she goes to attach the vacuum hose to the great room vacuum wall socket, Bob takes her hand and walks her to the table.

Bob asks everyone to join hands. The kids look at each other and then their parents, trying to figure out what's going on. "I think we ought to take a moment to pray, okay," Bob says looking at everyone. They grab each other's hands and Bob starts to pray.

As Bob finishes, eldest son Kurt looks at him. "Are you and Mom getting divorced?" Kurt asks.

"What? Where did that come from?" Bob says, looking at Charlotte.

"Well, Mom's been gone a lot and we know you don't like it," Kurt responds.

"No, nothing like that. Actually, Texas may be divorcing the United States. That's what we're worried about," Bob says. Charlotte nods her head, maintaining a forced smile. Charlotte will do anything to maintain control.

Charlotte tries to hide her expressions, but Bob can see she's upset by Kurt's question. He looks at her for what seems like a day, but is only seconds, before she looks back at him.

"You weren't happy with me being gone? Why didn't you say this to me?" she says quietly to Bob as the children strain their ears to listen.

"I was proud of you. We all just missed having you here. It's nothing you should worry about," Bob says. "Believe me I never even considered divorce, let alone mentioned it."

"Kurt, why did you think we were getting divorced?" Charlotte turns and asks.

"A lot of parents get divorced when they get mad, and Dad was grumbling all the time, especially when you were out speaking at night. And I thought maybe you didn't want to be around us anymore."

Charlotte looks at her children, trying all she can to hold back tears. Given how much she had sacrificed to raise the children, the last thing she could handle was thinking they didn't believe she wanted to be with them.

"I'm sorry it wasn't clear to you, but I wasn't out speaking to people because I wanted to be away from you. I was out speaking because I want to protect you and make sure you have the same opportunities that your father and I have had," Charlotte says. "That's what parents do. They make sacrifices for their children. There is no way I could enjoy speaking to other groups as much as I enjoy my time with you."

Despite her best efforts to control her reaction, a tear starts to form on Charlotte's right eye. She tries to wipe it away while dabbing at her mouth with a napkin in an apparent attempt to hide her emotion, forgetting that no one has started eating yet. Kurt sees the tear, along with a noticeable lip quiver. He rushes over to hug his mother, realizing he must have hurt her. Kevin, Kerry and Bob join in to make it a family hug.

After a few minutes, they all return to their seats and start eating breakfast. A few minutes into eating, Bob reaches over and grabs Charlotte's hand. Finally he leans in and whispers in her ear, "The only thing I've ever said or even thought is that I miss you when you're gone." He kisses her gently on her cheek.

With breakfast over, the five are taking dishes to the sink when they hear a loud noise at the front door. Hearing what sounds like a gunshot, Bob yells at the family to run and throws opens the back door. Kurt is first out the door with Kevin and Kerry following close behind, racing down the deck stairs and into the water circling around the fence that separates their yard from the next-door neighbor's house.

Bob runs to the office to get his gun out of the safe when he hears Charlotte being tackled on the deck and dragged back into the kitchen. One of the intruders turns the corner of the office door and unloads a dozen muffled shots into Bob's chest and head. Hearing the shots, Charlotte screams and calls out Bob's name before she is dazed by a punch to the left side of her jaw. "Traitor bitch," an assailant yells at her.

One intruder starts to head back out the back door when the gang leader tells him to stop. "Let the kids go. We've got what we want."

Tying Charlotte up quickly, three of the men carry her out to their old, off-grid cargo van parked backed up to the garage.

Four houses away, Kurt, Kevin and Kerry knock loudly and repeatedly on the back door of a friend's house. The mother opens the door and sees them panting and frantic. "Quick, let us in," Kurt begs.

After running in the house, Kurt closes the patio door shades and the kids run into the interior of the house away from any windows.

"Burglars are in our house. I need to call 9-1-1," he says to his friend's mother, who quickly pulls out her Lifelink and connects to the emergency system. After a brief phone discussion, she tells the kids that police are on their way.

Twenty-five minutes pass before police show up to the house where the Lee children are hidden. After confirming the children are okay, the police walk over, guns drawn, to see what happened at the Lee home. Ten minutes later, the police remain inside the Lee home. The Lee children and the neighbor mother become worried. She walks over with Kurt, Kevin and Kerry to see that the house is blocked off for an investigation.

"These children want to see their parents. They're scared and need their parents," she tells the officer trying to keep her from entering.

"Do you know the people, here?" the officer asks the neighbor mother.

"Of course I do, Kurt and my son are best friends," she tells them as she looks over toward Kurt.

"Well, then, perhaps you can help us with identification," the officer says, giving the neighbor mother her first clue that this isn't a simple burglary.

"Identification?" she says quietly, hoping the kids won't hear.

"I'm afraid so. It's a male."

Entering the house, the neighbor waits for police to clear enough blood from Bob's face for her to see enough to identify him. Asking about the mother, they tell her that there are signs of a substantial struggle, with blood, long strands of blonde hair and fallen hangings along a 20-foot stretch of hallway and out into the garage. But the mother is not inside.

"Can you think of anyone who wants to kill these people?" the officer asks her.

"No, everyone loved her. She was the organizer for our community battle against the secession vote and we all loved her," the neighbor says.

"Oh no."

"Oh no what?" the neighbor asks.

"Oh no, now that we've seceded, this could be retribution," the officer says.

"Seceded. We haven't seceded."

"We did, apparently, in the middle of the night last night."

"We did what?"

"Will you tell the children about their dad?" the officer asks.

"I don't want to do that. And we don't know anything about their mother?"

"I think I better take the children into police custody for their protection, so I'll tell them."

"No, no, I'll tell them. And I'll keep the children with me until you find Charlotte," the neighbor mother tells the officer.

"I don't think that will be safe for you. There has been a rash of kidnappings of anti-secession leaders in the last hours. You might want to worry about your own safety."

Seconds later, the officer walks over to where Kurt, Kevin and Kerry Lee are being watched by another officer.

"I don't know how to tell you this, so I'll just tell you," the officer says to the kids. "Your father has been shot and killed. We don't know where your mother is, but we have police out looking for her."

All the neighbors gathered around the police perimeter turn to look at the children as Kerry's piercing scream is followed by her collapse to the ground. Kevin starts pounding on the ground and Kurt runs away. Grabbed by one of the police as he starts to run, Kurt is carried back to his brother and sister. The neighbor mother grabs them all in a hug and the four openly sob together. Many of the neighbors, figuring out what has happened, break down as well.

Between the time police were called and arrived at the Lee home, the escape van holding Charlotte was driven up inside a semi-trailer labeled as an official United Nations supply vehicle. Now, with the truck more than 20 miles away from the Lee's Forest Hills home, the Puma squad leader yanks the tape off Charlotte's mouth, leaving her chin and cheeks red, and her lips missing more skin than the punch tore from her face.

"Damn, looks like we picked up the hottie," the squad leader says to the others in the van. Walking over, he rubs his hands through her hair, then grabs two chunks of hair and yanks her up from the floor to a seated position. Now kneeling behind her back, he rubs his groin against the back of her head, causing the others to laugh, particularly after Charlotte does a reverse head butt that causes him to gasp and howl in pain. "I'm going to kill you," Charlotte yells at him.

Angered by being struck in the groin, he gets tighter behind her, moves his hands down to cup her breasts and lifts her onto the bench using his knee in her back for leverage. Now seated on the bench backing the cab of the van, he tapes her mouth shut again.

"I was going to let you die easy bitch, but now you made me have to do it the hard way. Too bad for you that you don't know how to keep your mouth shut."

Charlotte tries to mumble through the tape, but no one understands what she's saying through the tape and over the road noise.

"Pull the racist bitch out and strap her to the top of the van," the leader tells the others.

"Can't we all take turns with her first, to make sure she learns her lesson?" one attacker asks.

"I don't think lessons will do her any good," the leader says. "Besides, we're almost to the lot. If we're not ready, we'll be left behind."

At a large parking lot adjacent to an empty superstore front attached to a large mall, sixteen semis pull into the lot within 15 minutes of each other. The trucks maneuver, with the first four set at connected angles, a fifth straight on its own, and three more together. Beyond them is a row of eight more oddly positioned trucks. The first four are positioned the same as the first four in the back row. The other four are arranged as three trucks jutting out perpendicular to the first.

Dozen of loud noises can be heard between the trucks over the next 15 minutes. Then, on the hour, the drivers of the semis and all the Pumas from inside the trucks walk into the empty superstore and through the attached mall. Reaching the other end of the mall, they are picked up by waiting transport vehicles and driven into the adjacent Air Force base before driving away.

CHAPTER 11

55 Hours

New Rite Compound, Utah

The Coleman family decides to take an outpost together, with all but the mother staying together and manning a scouting location. Mrs. Coleman stays behind to help organize the main camp.

Carrying food, water containers, a tent and extra clothes in addition to the layers they wear, the Colemans hike to their Friendship Cove scouting location. Searching around, they look for an area where their tent can blend in with the surrounding scenery or be hidden from intruder view by rock formations.

With darkness approaching, John Coleman wants the protection of being invisible to anyone who might do harm to his family, and is equally worried about wildlife in the vicinity. Mountain lions, cougars and bears top his list of concerns, but getting crosswise with an elk could be disastrous as well.

It's down to 33 degrees and temperatures are falling fast as night settles in. Having not found an ideal location to set up their tent, the Colemans agree to hold until dark and then pitch the tent in an area protected from southern visibility. They know it means pulling the tent down before sunrise and setting up somewhere else tomorrow. Though they've gathered a small amount of wood, they see nowhere to build a fire that can't be seen from the south and decide they'll struggle through a night of cold. Clarissa, the youngest, is happy she'll at least have a tent around her when she sleeps tonight.

John and Clarissa agree to take the first shift of scouting the area and filling the nearly empty water jug for tomorrow's drinking and cooking. Their elevated campsite is several hundred feet above water level and a tough hike down rocky terrain in daytime. Partial moonlight gives them limited visibility, just enough to get by without a flashlight. Clearly, they'll need to scout their patrol paths in daylight tomorrow to make sure they know where to step and what spots to avoid. They need water for tomorrow – not enough is left in the family jug or their individual water bottles – so they decide to carefully descend the rocks to water level.

Though John orders Clarissa to follow him, after 10 minutes she tires of his slow, methodical pace and cuts in front.

"I can see just fine, Dad. Your eyes must be getting old," she says when he tries to get her to slow down and wait behind him.

"Nobody can see just fine in this light. All I need is for you to step into a hole and drop 100 feet to your death."

"At least the water and food will last longer if I die," Clarissa responds.

"Yes, Clarissa, my goal is to kill off my children slowly so I can eat and drink more," John says. "If I wanted to kill you off, I would have done it before any of you turned 13."

"God, you are so not funny," Clarissa yells back. "And you wonder why we're embarrassed to have you around our friends."

"Just slow down and take your time. It's not just our footing we need to watch. There are wild animals out here. Any human will be armed. We need to spot them before they spot us," John argues. "We agreed we don't have enough people to be menacing. So what did Sarah say was the other alternative? Invisibility."

"Do you really think the United Nations is going to send an invasion force to take control of barren rocks?" Clarissa asks.

"We're not watching for them to come take this land. We're watching for them to come through here to head north without being spotted."

"Fine, but I think this is all a waste of time. But, hey, at least it's not scho . . . . . oool," Clarissa says, as her feet lose traction, and she starts sliding down a rock formation. Fifteen feet later, the ground flattens out. "At least it's not school," she says more loudly from below, standing back up and dusting herself off.

***

Washington, D.C.

At FBI headquarters, a satellite surveillance review team now working closely with the Pentagon has spent the day searching for U.N. troop movements. During computer-based searches, a software system identifies an anomaly to be reviewed by an FBI analyst. Capturing an image of the unusual setting, the photo shows a large group of trucks in a parking lot aligned in a way that appears to spell out two words.

"This is a pretty bizarre way of bragging," the analyst tells his team leader, who takes the image to her managers, realizing that she can't just call local police anymore to investigate.

"Does anyone know anyone working near that store and have full faith in your relationship to get an honest response back on what this is?"

After searching around for 30 minutes, they find a contact.

CHAPTER 12

48 Hours

Washington, D.C.

With a short break in emergency response actions, President Marc Phillipi calls several top aides to an in-person meeting in the Deep Underground Command Center connected below the White House.

White House Chief of Staff Vijay Chinh sits to the President's left. Though physically in the room, he is engaged in more than a dozen simultaneous conversations – some oral and some written. Flipping nervously through the various discussions, he takes an audible breath as he moves between each discussion. In part, the breath is to keep oxygen flowing. In part, it reminds him that he has changed conversations.

Defense Secretary Xavier Mendoza rushes back using his tunnel running between the Pentagon and the DUCC elevator entrance. Homeland Security Secretary Ray Peyton joins from another passage to the DUCC entrance. Several top members of the president's National Security staff have been ensconced in the DUCC for the past 24 hours, sleeping on bunks, showering and eating without visiting the surface. Vice President Marcia Wilt connects from Fort Benning in Georgia. Less than 24 hours earlier, Vice President Wilt was moved to safety in case of attack on Washington D.C. At Maryland's Andrews Air Force Base, 20 transport jets were assigned 20 different destinations. Vice President Wilt selected which one to fly in without knowing its destination until seated for takeoff. The chairwoman of the Joint Chiefs of Staff also joins this discussion from her command center inside the Pentagon.

"Before we get lost in tactical response, let's step back and talk about strategy here," President Phillipi says as he sits down at the head of the elongated oval. "These are the days that nations either survive or fall. Any lessons from history here?"

"Senator Jones has invited you to join him at one of the military bases the U.N. controls in Texas," Chief of Staff Vijay Chinh says. "We turned him down immediately. There's no reason to believe we can trust anything about his assurance of protecting your safety."

"How'd we get the invitation?" Peyton asks.

"It came through the ambassador of Russia," Chinh replies.

"If we're not tracing every piece of physical and electronic traffic in and out of that embassy already, I'll get us on it. We need to find Jones," Peyton states.

"Absolutely, though this marks the fourth embassy to source communication from Jones. The CIA's on it electronically, but we have nothing from human assets. I'd love to bring in the dolts who gutted our human asset program thinking our eavesdropping technology advantage 15 years ago was going to last. I don't like flying blind," the President states.

"Mr. President, we have teams prepared to tackle any mission as soon as you give the go. We've secured the rest of our bases and equipment," Secretary Mendoza says.

"Fine, but what's their strategy play here?" the President asks.

"The play's pretty simple now. They have our territory. They've taken over many of our bases with some inside help. They have Americans surrounding their military operations, and have pulled in the townspeople as human shields around several sites. They have 75 percent of the world's serious national militaries in their coalition. We have no one else committed to our side yet. Through sheer strength, they think they can back us down. We not only need the sideliners to get with us, we need to pull apart their coalition."

"How?" the President asks.

"Marc," Vice President Wilt says to get the President's attention.

"Yes Marcia."

"Some of the countries joined with the U.N. are in this to protect loans. Some are in it to pay us back for sticking our nose in their business. But many of our natural allies have been fed a story that we would engage in genocide in the Southwest to prevent secession," Vice President Wilt says. Her foreign policy expertise, dating back to interest driven during her Mormon mission, is one of the main reasons President Phillipi selected her as Vice President. "If we want to peel them back, we need to consider how to convince them that we would never kill our own people and show them they were duped into joining the coalition."

"Okay, how."

"First, we publish results of the two-month investigation by the Justice Department showing that the secession votes in the states were rigged and fraudulent, making clear this was a set-up by Jones all along," Wilt says.

"Get Betty on screen. Do we have proof of this?" the President tells his small sub-team.

"I didn't say we had total proof," Vice President Wilt says. "This is about saving lives. We can issue indictments in the thousands of voter fraud cases she's been looking at and point to this as evidence of a mass conspiracy led by Jones. Who gives a damn whether it's a stretch or ultimately proves true? We've all made campaign ads attacking opponents with 10 percent of the data we have here. If we're willing to lie to get our jobs, but not to save the country, what does that say about our leadership?"

"I don't know that I'd advocate any outright lies, particularly ones that can come back to bite us before this is resolved," Chief of Staff Chinh says, "but Marcia's point is really that perception is reality and we need to win the perception war. We need to win it with every American, on both sides of this border if possible, and we need to win it with the countries we can pull apart."

"The big prize here is China," Mendoza contends. "If we can pull them out of the coalition, Jones will get nervous and so will the rest of the countries, especially if we can get them to come all the way over to our side."

"That's not going to come cheap. What could make it happen?" the President asks.

"They're continuously seeking food, water and energy security. We have resources they want right here. We could give up part of Texas or a state like North Dakota," Chinh says. "Then we go take Canada to give our people places to move to."

"Look Vijay, I'm still not interested in going to war with Canada."

"Do you see them taking our side? Have they thrown in with us? Then they're not an ally," Chinh says.

"I'm not going to sit here and decide what other country is going to rule our people. Americans elected us. We're the legitimate government here in all 52 states. Does everyone get that?" the President says.

"Understood, sir. Just trying to think practically for where we're at," Chinh responds, taking a drink from his hot tea before tapping back into his dozen ongoing conversations.

"China doesn't need to rule our territory," Vice President Wilt says. "They need a place to send people to reduce overcrowding and the stress on their resources. We can make that happen for them without giving up any land. Just agree to allow in five million Chinese each year to start the path to dual citizenship."

"That's an interesting thought. We need smart, hard-working people anyway to offset stagnating population growth, so this might actually be a good thing for this country and resolve an incredible crisis. Any objections? . . . No. Okay, Vijay, have our ambassador run this up the flagpole in Beijing and see what kind of response we get."

"Wait a minute," Chinh interjects. "Do you all know how few years it will be before China has effective control of our government anyway if we let dual citizens in at that pace? It's one thing to let the Chinese in, but we can't let them still be under communist government control as dual citizens . . . , and with relatives at home who can be threatened."

"Okay," the President says. "So amend the offer. We'll prioritize immigrants from China, and step up the pace of letting them in."

After a short restroom break, the group reassembles.

"I want to come back to the strategic perspective. How do we ensure our nation survives not just these next few days, but for the long haul?" the President asks again.

"Let me throw out some concepts," Vice President Wilt says. "I'm a big fan of work done by a Harvard professor on what makes civilizations successful. He broke it down to six issues – competition, science, modern medicine, work ethic and . . . , and . . . , and I don't remember what the other two were. Anyway, I started watching because my professors didn't look that good, but he really evaluated the history of civilization to find what determined winners and losers."

"So what's your point Marcia," the President says.

"My point is we're in this pinch because we've lost our military advantage. A key premise of this invasion is that we don't have major technology advantages that we can rely on to stop them. Hell, they've even figured out how to evade our electronic surveillance to get inside our borders without being spotted until it's too late. It won't help us now, but we need to always remember that the best deterrent to attack is a combination of superior strength and clarity of non-threatening intent."

"Great, what about something that helps us now?" the President asks.

Vijay Chinh turns off his Lifelink momentarily to weigh in on the discussion. "Since we're wading into the academic world, another former professor did a great historical review that raised concepts worth reviewing. I was intrigued by what a UCLA professor said about germs doing the greatest damage when the Europeans invaded the Americas, Australia and other previously isolated geographies. While superior guns helped win many of those wars, having 90 percent of the population die from an epidemic disease helped assure victory. If this becomes a protracted standoff, we ought to think about what diseases Americans in the Southwest have good immunity to that could be spread to kill off the U.N. invasion force."

"Are you suggesting biological warfare?" Secretary Mendoza says.

"If our goal is to ensure survival of the United States, all options have to be on the table," Chinh responds.

"That's pretty clearly a violation of our international agreements," Vice President Wilt interjects.

"I think this U.N. invasion negates all of our agreements," Chinh argues. "Don't you?"

"I would rather let the Southwest go than introduce something insidious that we won't be able to control into the environment," the President interjects.

"I'm not suggesting we carpet-bomb the area with a new smallpox or AIDS. I'm suggesting we look at developing diseases that only trigger with certain genetic codes. There's enough purebred Chinese, Russians, Mexicans and others here that we should be able to create and test laser-targeted diseases aimed at disabling big chunks of the U.N. troops," Chinh states.

"Exactly my point, Vijay. Anything we create to kill invasion troops is likely to kill Americans as well. Aren't you the least bit worried that you might carry a gene common in China that accepts whatever disease we might create and be killed accidentally in the process?" Vice President Wilt asks.

"I'm not saying this is Plan A, B, C, D or even R. I just think that compared to mass bombings, we might kill fewer people using a more invisible attack. I think we all agree that securing the borders we want with the least human catastrophe should be the objective. I can't see any reason to take germs off the table if they are the best way to achieve this objective since every international agreement we have has just been violated by our opposition," Chinh states, emphatically moving his arms to emphasize his points.

"Invade Canada. Unleash mass extermination diseases. I'm beginning to question your mental stability," Secretary Mendoza states while glaring intensely at Chinh.

President Phillipi reaches over and puts his hand on Chinh's shoulder. "We have to consider all reasonable options, and then evaluate them on effectiveness, efficiency and moral grounds. I don't have a problem with people raising even ridiculous ideas in this room, with this group, and for our ears only. But I don't want to hear a single sentence that leads me to believe any of this leaves this room or is acted on without my authorization," the President categorically states.

Leaning back in his chair, he rubs underneath his temples.

"Having said that," President Phillipi continues, "I do think we need to consider what diseases invading forces could bring to our people and get a mass vaccination program underway. Even raising the possibility of a Black Death or some new polio-like epidemic being spread and killing millions could deter Americans living in the four states from cooperating with the invasion force. Perhaps even defecting military units and new conscripts will recognize the risks and realize that they haven't been inoculated against potential diseases they now face."

"I'll get HHS on it right away and make sure the Secretary understands the military objective," Chinh says. "Before I leave the topic, one more thought. Is there anything we can do to the water system to cramp their plans?"

"Good God, Vijay. Is there anything you won't do to win?" Vice President Wilt says.

"I'm not saying pollute it. I'm saying a lot of water in these four states comes from up north. Can't we cut off the water supply and force as many people as possible out of the likeliest combat zones?" Chinh says. "This will minimize civilian deaths if we need to start bombing U.N. troops."

"As crazy as you are, Vijay, there might be something there," Secretary Mendoza acknowledges.

Homeland Secretary Peyton, a former U.S. Air Force General before being asked to run the Department of Homeland Security, had been watching much of the discussion, contemplating that he could have been on his way to soaking in the Caribbean if not for the invasion. He had planned to retire at the start of the president's second term but was asked to hold off until this crisis is resolved.

"We've done an extensive water security assessment and have a few experts on the topic. I doubt we ever looked at cutting off any of our states, but we can outline our initial concepts to you in 12 hours, Mr. President. Off the top of my head, I bet we could hurt South California and Arizona quickly," Secretary Peyton says.

"So we've covered disease, water, food, weapons, energy. Anything else we haven't covered?" the President asks.

"Communication systems jamming," raises the chairwoman of the Joint Chiefs of Staff, still participating in the discussion remotely. "These U.N. troops were thrown together in a hurry. But we didn't hear any coordination from what we could tap of U.N. communication channels. Each country had assigned targets so maybe they didn't need to collaborate until we already knew they were here."

"Okay, and what?" the President asks.

"Going forward, they'll need to coordinate using the U.N. communications grid if they need to do anything quickly. We know this grid. They've obviously adapted it and installed new code protection, but we'll be able to break it. I doubt they've had a mass technology upgrade since our last U.N. joint mission. Our techies pulled their units apart for us to see if there was any capability we don't have and we didn't see any," the Joint Chiefs chairwoman states.

"Good thought," says Secretary Mendoza. "We're already working on intercepting and breaking their protocols. I don't think it will be too long before we have this done. Is anyone here familiar enough with electronics to know if we can jam their systems and force them back to open communications? If we can jam them sporadically and destroy their advance warning, a counterattack might work."

Not hearing a response, President Phillipi takes back control of the discussion.

"So, in 12 hours, I'll expect reports back on options with communications jamming, water cut-off, and biological warfare defense. We should also contemplate nuclear risk. I want to understand what they could be thinking of doing to us," the President says, standing and walking to a smaller area to hear the latest intelligence update.

***

White Settlement, Texas

As midnight approaches, a lone detective pulls up in an unmarked vehicle to find 16 semitrucks and trailers positioned outside a vacant superstore and attached mall in White Settlement, a suburb of Fort Worth, Texas. The trucks are parked just as the detective had heard from a college roommate who now works in the FBI satellite surveillance department. Pulling up behind the trucks, Detective Jesus Arroyo is nervous about inspecting the scene alone. He's even more uncomfortable calling in colleagues to look at what may just be a bunch of parked semis.

Detective Arroyo isn't sure who is in on the secession movement in his department and who wants out, so he plans to stay quiet until he decides whether to stay in Texas or move north. He hopes his former roommate at the FBI is right that everyone who had been in the trucks had left and been driven away. He could easily be caught in an ambush in this dark, vacant lot.

Crumbled, pockmarked pavement means he needs to watch his footing. Chunks of rubble are built up around the sides of the lot; curbs serving as collection points for wind-blown pavement pebbles and assorted litter. None of the 16 parking lot lights operate, the store having been shuttered nearly 10 years ago during the middle of the second great depression. Parts of the area are rebuilding, but this superstore lot was bought by the Air Force for possible expansion. It remains empty and desolate.

Jesus points the high beams of his police cruiser at the back of the first two trucks. The tails of both trucks face toward him. Next to these two rests another pair.

While walking toward the cab of the truck on his far left, Jesus shines his flashlight in every direction and pulls a night vision lens over his left eye to help see if something comes at him from a dark spot. Dropping to his knees, he rotates the flashlight underneath all of the trucks, looking for anyone stepping toward him. He turns off the flashlight and goes back to turn off his headlights. Pulling on his other night vision lens as he walks back, he loads his semi-automatic weapon and releases the safety. From a 30-foot distance, he looks inside the cabs down the row closest to him and then goes up to the first row to check out the cabs for any sign of life.

After circling all 16 trucks, he returns to the rear door of the first truck. There's no lock on the truck, so he pulls up the lever and opens up the back door. Stepping back as he opens the door, he stands still for a minute waiting to be sure he hears nothing move inside. Eyeing what looks like a van inside, a view he confirms as he steps up in the trailer, his curiosity is aroused. Inside the trailer, he walks toward the van, stepping over metal ramps in the process. After a few steps, he turns back toward the door to be sure no one is coming at him. He goes all the way to the back door and out to look around. Then Jesus goes back up to the van.

Looking in the van, he sees nothing moving. Quickly dropping to the floor of the trailer, he looks under the van and sees nothing there either. He struggles to get around either side of the van, since the van only barely fits inside the width of the semitrailer. Instead, he opens the back door and pulls on his night vision lenses.

Dirt, dents and dried dark liquid on the inside of the cargo van trigger Jesus's intuition to elevate his tension level. Then, as he pulls the cloth apart between the back of the van and the driver's area, he moves his flashlight around until he spots dark stripes looking like dried liquid down the front of the windshield. Turning quickly, Jesus flashes the light out the back of the truck and still sees nothing. As he moves back out the rear of the van, he stands up, points his flashlight over the top of the van and reaches out to try poking the object in front of him with his automatic weapon.

It's too far way, but Jesus is horrified if what he sees is what he thinks he sees. Climbing back out of the trailer he starts walking toward his car.

"*Police! Freeze!*" comes the order.

Dropping both flashlight and automatic weapon, Jesus lifts his arms to the air.

"*It's me, Jesus,*" Jesus yells out to whoever ordered him to freeze.

Fellow officer Randy busts out laughing.

"*Got you man,*" Randy says. "*We need you on a call. You've been ignoring your calls for 20 minutes. Captain sent me to fetch you.*"

"*I may need you to fetch captain if I just saw what I think I saw on top of that van.*"

"*Doesn't matter. We have a couple of kidnapping and missing person cases to investigate. Captain is ready to tear everyone a new one right now,*" Randy says.

"*Just go up there and look,*" Jesus says. "*If I'm wrong, we can go.*"

Randy climbs into the trailer and up on the back of the van. Eight inches taller, he has a clearer view than Jesus.

"*Hey, you, on the van. Hey, can you hear me,*" Randy yells out loudly, trying to startle the person into responding if he or she is alive. "*Looks like we solved a missing person case,*" Randy says as he turns back to Jesus after letting go of the cold foot nearest him.

Randy and Jesus realize the ramps in the back of the trailer will allow them to back the van out. After setting the ramps, Jesus backs his car away and then walks back to the van. Going up to try shifting the van to neutral, he sees an old-fashioned key still inserted and starts the engine. Randy helps him slowly back the cargo van out and down the ramp, then climbs back up on the van.

"*That's what I thought. We've got a dead body here,*" Randy calls out to Jesus. "*I'll call it in.*"

"*Let's open a couple of other trucks and see how many we need out here.*"

Walking to other trucks, they open the back doors and see cargo vans in each. Quickly looking on top of the other vans, they find a dead body on each.

Randy goes back to his cruiser to call for backup. Jesus walks toward the edge of the lot, connects to his One World site through his police connection, the only connection that is back working, and sends a message to his former roommate at his personal contact address.

"You'll want to get pictures as we pull vans out of the trucks. Gruesome. Victims tied or bolted to top of vans," he writes.

An hour later, the last of the vans is backed out of the trucks. Eleven dead men and four more dead women are spread-eagled and loosely taped to the roofs of the vans. Two of these women have their clothes largely torn off and left inside the van. Bruising and cuts make clear they died painfully. A sixteenth victim, a partially clad woman, is also missing a large, circular section of her abdomen; an ancient skull mask bolted to her through the van roof in its place. As Jesus sees this woman, he quickly jumps off the back of the van and throws up, coating the scar-pocked pavement in half-digested food mass.

***

New Rite Compound, Utah

A sense of calm creeps in across Lake Powell, all the way to where the Colorado River is stalled by the Glen Canyon Dam. With almost no moonlight, only the stars provide any visibility. A light, dusting wind breaks the stillness, but seems meager compared to the deep piercing chill of last night. Clarissa learned yesterday that maintaining a socially acceptable appearance means nothing when her body shivers and her teeth chatter so loud that she can barely hear what's going on around her. Yesterday, she had to pace throughout her watch shift to keep from going numb. Temperatures today are a few degrees warmer than yesterday's low in the upper 30s. More importantly, the wind isn't trying as hard to shove the cold through her clothing to infiltrate every pore of her skin. In any case, Clarissa is better prepared tonight. A full body thermal bodysuit covers from her toes to the top of her head with only her fingers, eyes, nose and mouth exposed to the elements.

Yesterday, Clarissa decided the desert camouflage of her bodysuit would make her look ridiculously militaristic if someone interesting wandered her direction. Perhaps here, where other kids didn't know her history, she would meet people who didn't immediately dismiss her as bizarre. Tonight, she no longer cares, realizing that the inability to speak while her teeth chatter would be even more unappealing than an intimidating appearance. The Colemans keep nighttime watch shifts to three hours, much shorter than the daytime shifts. Clarissa's dad, John Coleman, doubles up on night shifts, finding it easier to nap during the day than the girls do.

John's hiking sticks stay with whoever is on watch. Though the sticks look like walking sticks, they really are John's multifunctional weapons. At one end, a large switchblade that turns the stick into a spear can be unleashed with a three-digit code entered on the mid-handle panel. Turned the other direction, the handle pulls down and shifts the hiking stick into a shoulder-mounted rifle, with a laser sightline pop-up. Folded in half, connected and triggered, the stick turns into a spike-ended club. John and his father created his multiple-defense hiking stick to improve their chances of survival if caught hiking by a pack of wolves or between a mother moose and her calf. When no threat exists, the stick looks and works like a normal hiking stick, alleviating potential worries of fellow hikers.

John hates leaving his daughters on watch shifts on their own, but trained them during the day on how to use the sticks for defense.

A bit bored, Clarissa does her weightlifting workout with the stick, doing curls with each arm, bench presses while laying her back against a rock and moves that look more like overhead baton twirls than any weight lift. She knows she doesn't want to attract too much attention, so drops below the sightline as she does each set. After 15 minutes of lifting and twirling, she decides that's enough and goes back to watching the skyline.

This would be a spectacularly beautiful night if the moon joined a full complement of stars in lighting the sky. Still, the stars are bright enough to create a modest shimmer off the stillness of the water. Clarissa believes she can see for several miles tonight from her elevated perch. She thinks about how amazing it would be to have this as the view from her room. If she could see this from her bedroom, her friends could stare out into the night with her as they talked about which boys they each want. Clarissa has already learned to throw a few distractions into the mix when she talks to her friends. She realized that Catalina seems to take a new interest in any boy she says she likes. It's weird, she knows, that a friend can be like that, but she finds it entertaining to see how she can manipulate Catalina into saying she likes boys none of them really like.

With an hour left to go in her shift, Clarissa walks back and forth along the watch line. Looking out over the water, she sees a ripple on the other side of the bay. A minute later, another ripple appears, then another, and another. Clarissa steps down from her watch station to walk slowly toward the water. She grabs the radio and hiking stick before hiking down to see if she can identify the ripple's source. Zooming in through her Lifelink with the screen glow dampened, she tries to identify the motion in the distance.

It doesn't look right. Although not sure she sees it right, it looks like there are six inflatable rafts floating in an almost straight line across the water and toward her shoreline.

"Coleman to lantern ASAP," she says breaking silence and immediately waking her dad and middle sister from sound sleep. Lantern is the station name for Clarissa's watch site.

John jumps out of his sleeping bag, stands up and starts to tear the top of the tent before realizing where he is and dropping back to his knees.

"What did she say?" John asks the middle daughter.

She looks at him as she clicks on a flashlight: "To lantern."

"Okay, go to the other watch site. I'll run to Clarissa."

Pulling on clothes as he moves, John takes off over the path to meet Clarissa at her watch station. His adrenaline is pumping full bore, realizing that Clarissa knows not to break contact silence unless it is urgent. With loose rocks, John stumbles several times on his way, but maintains his balance and keeps moving. After a 250-foot steep uphill ascent, he slows down, feeling his heart pounding so hard he feels pressure on his rib cage.

At a slower pace, John keeps moving and reaches the watch spot, but Clarissa isn't there. Nearly doubled over catching his breath, he looks around and gently calls her name. No response. Inhaling deeply, but with adrenaline pumping even faster, he risks standing up on the boulder that provides wind protection to the watch site. From atop the boulder, he has a clearer view of the area. Still not seeing her, he calls her Lifelink in panic.

"Where are you?"

"Heading to water, Dad. I'll wave and wait here," Clarissa whispers back.

John sees Clarisse emerge from a blind spot on a path down to water level. She spots him looking and waves. He immediately takes off after her, wiping sweat from his eyebrows, and feeling the first sense of cold not masked by an adrenaline rush. Surveying the area as he descends, John doesn't see what Clarissa is looking at. He doesn't have binoculars and his eyesight isn't turning up anything unusual. Several minutes later, he catches up to Clarissa.

"What do you see?" he asks.

She points her dimmed Lifelink to where she perceives rafts floating across. John looks at the screen to see what has Clarissa concerned.

"Those buoys?" he asks, as the two search while laying flat on the ground about 100 feet above the water line.

"Look again," she tells him. "They're in a line and they're moving toward us."

John watches for a minute and sees what she means, then spies heads bobbing up and down around the rafts. "They're manned."

"I thought those were heads too."

"One, two, three, four," John says. "One, two, three, four, five . . . and six. Looks like 24 people. We need to call in help. If they're armed, we can't handle them."

"What do we do, Dad?"

"We're calling for help and we're getting away until they get here."

"Don't you think we could hold them if we get to them as they come out of the water? You brought your other guns, right?" Clarissa asks.

"If they're military, they might be willing to sacrifice a few people if they have a critical mission. I'm not military anymore, but I know enough that we need to maintain a tactical advantage when we're 1-1/2 against 24."

"Half, my ass. I'm a grown woman."

"You're a 14-year-old girl with a dozen weekends of survival training. If these are foreign invaders, they are likely Special Forces teams with six years of training at a minimum. That puts us at worse odds than playing the lottery," John Coleman states before making a direct call to Sarah Osborne for help.

Sarah is awakened by John's call after just an hour's sleep and takes a few seconds to get her head clear.

"Sarah, John Coleman, 24 intruders coming over water at Friendship Cove. Intentions unclear, looking for area to get close, but need at least 100 armed support. Where do we gather?"

She walks out to the New Rite compound map and then outlines her strategy. She sees two likely egress locations and immediately puts out radio orders to get every available armed camp resident to those locations.

"John, we can put 100 at each site, but we need to know which direction they head so we can stream reinforcements to the right spot. Is there a scouting location you can safely call the intruders' direction from?" Sarah asks.

John looks around and looks back up at the lantern watch site. "Will do," he responds.

"Let's head back up, we can watch and call from there," he tells Clarissa.

"But if we call from there, we'll have to stay silent until they are well past us, won't we? Is that enough time for everyone up top to get prepared?"

"Crap, good point."

"Like I said, Dad. Half my ass."

"I'm not putting you at risk. You need to head back, get your sisters and get to safety."

"I'm the one in camouflage, Dad. I can hide and no one will ever see me. Besides, even if they catch me, what are they going to do to a girl?"

"It's one thing to be fearless. It's another to be stupid. What will a bunch of invading soldiers do to a girl? Yeah. Not to my daughter. Get going."

"Dad, we don't have time. The rafts are too close to shore. They'll see us going back up the slope."

John takes another look with his binoculars and sees the landing spot the rafts are heading toward.

"We're going to roll slowly down until we can get behind that boulder," John Coleman says, pointing to a large rock at water's edge. "Then we can be out of sight getting down to shoreline."

John points to a spot where the water's edge is hidden by a 12-foot rounded cliff face jutting over the water in a tiny cove-like formation. He whispers quietly to Clarissa: "If we can get in there, they won't see us and we can see what direction they head once they move. Let's go."

John and Clarissa scoot in an army crawl, pulling themselves forward by their forearms in prone position, then rolling over the rock surface until they reach the shore. At the shoreline, Clarissa strips down to her thick, desert camouflage bodysuit and pulls the hood back over her hair. John takes off shoes and socks and pulls his pants up as close to his knees as possible. Both take first steps into the shiver-inducing shore water to walk around into the cliff-face-covered hiding spot.

Waiting patiently, another 15 minutes pass before they hear the rafts reach the gently sloped portion of the shoreline just 400 feet away.

John and Clarissa are tucked under the ridgeline, impossible to spot from above or either side. They might have been visible from the water if the boats had come straight in, but John accurately reasoned that the rafts would not want to land in the area with the steepest climb up to dry land.

John continues to feel his heart pound, but now out of fear rather than his earlier exertion. He holds his hand over his heart, pressing down. As Clarissa hears sounds from the landing party, she bites the knuckle of her index finger to try remaining calm. She turns her head upward to make sure no one sees her.

With the quiet winds and calm waters, John and Clarissa can hear an increasing amount of movement. First, they hear the rafts being pulled up to shore. Then, they listen as the rafts are deflated, causing John to wonder if they really have no return plans.

Another 15 seconds pass, they start to hear celebratory cheering and high-fives being exchanged, before hearing a loud order barked out.

"We need to get out of range. Everyone to cover and dry clothes."

Clarissa turns and whispers to her dad. "It's English."

He mouths back an "I know," then holds his right index finger in front of his mouth to signal to her to stay quiet.

Footsteps approach, closing in on their position. John realizes they had probably left enough light imprints to be found, but hopes the absence of moonlight means it isn't bright enough to make their tracks visible. Hearing the sounds of wetsuits unzipping, Clarissa eases herself into the water and looks around the ridge toward where she heard the boats land. As she slowly, cautiously turns the corner of the rocks while pinching her bodysuit hood over as much of her face as possible, she sees 20 men in various states of dress off in the distance. She starts to move back toward cover, but peeks back around for a second look before backing out of the water and under the overhead ridge.

"They're naked," she whispers into her dad's ear. "This would be a good time to stop them."

As Clarissa whispers, the first of four women step around the corner into a narrow flat area near the cove they are standing in. John gives Clarissa his best evil look to demand her silence and quietly pulls his assault rifle into his hands. He eases toward the corner of the ridge. John swings around quickly to see three of the four women reach to cover themselves while the fourth reaches for a weapon.

"Stop," John says quietly. Now Clarissa is standing behind him with the hiking stick up to her shoulder in rifle mode. "Hands up," John orders.

"Daaadd," Clarissa says, recognizing that hands up would leave some of the women exposed.

"Okay, well, hands where I can see them anyway. Who are you and what are you doing here?"

"We're U.S. soldiers who escaped from Camp Navajo to get back to U.S. land," the still fully clothed soldier who had reached for her weapon says.

"Really?"

"Really. Do you mind if we put our dry clothes on now. We're freezing sir," one of the women says.

"Oh, sure, just don't reach for weapons."

"We mean without you watching."

"Oh, yeah. Well. I'm just trying to make sure nothing bad happens to my daughter. So tell me where you're from and how I can know you're American."

Very quickly, group members introduce themselves. John is comforted enough that he puts down his weapon and leaves Clarissa to watch them.

"Who are you?" one of the soldiers asks Clarissa.

"My name is Clarissa Coleman. I'm a high school student from Flagstaff. That's my dad," she says nodding her head in his direction. "We're watching this shoreline to provide warning in case an invasion force tries to come through here. Obviously, the border protection here isn't set up yet."

"Wow, well that's really reassuring," the soldier replies. "I'd feel a whole lot better, though, if you put that rifle or whatever it is down."

"Go ahead Clarissa," John says, with his back still turned. Clarissa shuts down the rifle and turns the unit back into its hiking stick form.

After the women finish putting on dry clothes, all six walk out from behind the rocks to join the rest of the soldiers. As they come out, a few recognize that two people they don't know are with the women in their unit and reach for their weapons.

"Stand down," one of the female soldiers orders. "They're Americans, watching the border for invaders."

"How about for Americans escaping back to America," one of the soldiers yells back, directing his remarks to John and Clarissa.

John asks if there is anything they can do to help, and then alerts the sergeant that 100 armed citizens would be waiting for them if John doesn't call them off. "What's your branch and unit? I'll alert our camp commander. Do you need food, water, shelter, anything?"

"All of the above would be good. More than anything, we need to get moving and get to warmth before hypothermia fully sets in."

***

Alta Texas Headquarters

Ramon Mantle relocates himself to the sub-ground security control room deep under the base serving as the Alta Texas command center. He patches in remotely to Perfect Logistics Company operating systems that manage Ramon's Easy Ride vehicle operating software. Ramon created his first version of what eventually became Easy Ride to evade police during his drag racing days.

With financial backing provided through obscured sources linked to Cesar Castillo, Ramon bought or designed the rest of the software components needed to provide total vehicle movement control. Once it proved that Easy Ride software worked, Perfect Logistics secured a federal requirement to embed the software in all vehicles using public roads, under the argument that the software reduced fuel consumption and enabled more vehicles to safely use existing highway space. The exclusive cartel version of Ramon's software includes 24/7/365 integrated satellite and communication scan programs that allow cartel drivers to identify and evade police, Border Patrol and other law enforcement vehicles. In places where evasion is difficult, cartel skip tunnels carry illegal drugs and weapons on belowground conveyors. When all of these measures fail, the Easy Ride system adjusts routing patterns for normal cars to interfere with police efforts to track or stop cartel vehicles.

From the deep underground room at Alta Texas headquarters, Ramon tests his configuration and development skills as he further adapts the cartel version of the software used in the U.N. invasion to a more robust system that also captures aboveground and waterborne U.S. military movements. The adaptation is simpler than he initially thought, benefitting from work his team had done to track all federal vehicle movements and from the U.S. encryption and communication technology stolen during the invasion by defecting soldiers and U.N. alliance troops.

Returning to the central command room, Ramon tells President Jones and assembled U.N. military officials that he's made quick progress: "I have an updated system. Looks like it should work, though we won't have 100 percent coverage for some time. It'll take a bit for the system to identify unmarked military craft and weapons with no onboard communication systems."

"If they're unmarked and don't communicate, how can you possibly identify they exist," President Jones asks.

"It's simple. I correlate movement of anything I think might have military use with known military weaponry and vehicles using algorithms I just adapted from my personal tracking software – the software I used to get you to New York," Ramon responds. "Anywhere we find movement correlations, we track future action continuously until we confirm an object's purpose."

"What does that mean?"

"I'm taking control of your wall screens on the east wall so I can show you," Ramon says.

"Who gave you access to our displays?" President Jones asks, seeing that Ramon is already replacing the satellite and other views that had been displayed around the room.

Ramon looks at President Jones and winks: "I don't need to be given access. How do you think I got this done so quickly?"

"What?"

"Look at the wall. You now see a map of Alta Texas and all the U.S. states surrounding us. The blue dots on the map are U.S. military assets — jets, tanks, boats, et cetera. The red dots are Alta Texas and U.N. assets. In real time, you now see the movement of any weapon-capable asset in this war, down to the troop level," Ramon says.

"This will let you see where they are moving, and helps you identify weaknesses that can be exploited," Ramon adds. "No one on our side should be surprised by any U.S. movements."

"Generals, what do you think?"

"We've always had the ability to watch what is happening on satellite. How is this any better?" one U.N. coalition general asks.

"Satellite tracks what you can see. Digital tracking finds what we can hear. This combines those capabilities, but also projects where vehicles are headed when we lose sight and they shut down all electronics. This tells you instantaneously where everything is and, more importantly, where it is all going. Once I give you controls, you can zoom in on hot spots for more detail on weapon type, et cetera. No one on our side should ever be caught unprepared," Ramon states.

***

Utah New Rite Compound

Walking inland, Clarissa learns more about the soldiers who floated up to the shores in her watch area. All had been on multi-day training exercises at Camp Navajo when the United Nations invasion troops took control of the base.

Given the futility of trying to engage a vastly outmanned and outgunned invasion force, they followed command to head for U.S.-controlled territory. As the troops ran through Kaibab National Forest, they ordered a semi-truck driver to take them to the Utah border. The truck driver had shut down to sleep for the night after hearing about blockades set up to cut off northbound traffic. Following discussions with other drivers, the driver took the troops up Route 64 into Grand Canyon National Park. The truck driver, sympathetic to their efforts to escape and equipped with a manual override so he could speed and reduce his driving time, was able to get the troops all the way to the Desert View overlook inside the park before he found out that U.N. troops were entering the park from Route 89 on the east.

Once they could no longer risk road transportation, the Camp Navajo escapees hiked at double-speed whenever possible to reach the border. The steep climb down to river level had been treacherous. Only a few of the troops were equipped with night vision. Slips on rocks and near slips off the edge of the narrow paths had been frequent at their accelerated pace. At river level, the Camp Navajo unit picked up eight soldiers running from a U.S. company that had been ordered to defect to Alta Texas by their commanding officer. Combined, the 24 circled south of the Glen Canyon National Recreation Area before stealing single person rafts large enough to just hold their gear. From there, they floated across to where they were spotted by Clarissa at the Coleman's watch location east of Friendship Cove.

The soldiers believed they had been in Utah for some time, but hadn't found any border security so kept heading north until they could find someone to retrieve them and reassign them for service. Only after realizing it would take at least a day to hike north around the backed-up bays from Glen Canyon Dam did they decide to swim across the 45-degree Lake Powell waters. The 16 soldiers training at Camp Navajo all had watertight thermals from their overnight training that made the water passage bearable. The eight escapees from defecting companies had been spread out two each on the four middle rafts so they could be watched for thermal shock during the crossing.

"Why didn't you just call for someone to pick you up?" Clarissa asks a female soldier who had minutes earlier been at the other end of her rifle stick.

"It didn't take us long after we decided we couldn't take back the base that we also figured out that our communication equipment could be traced by equipment inside the base. We had to drop and run, figuring the invaders would be after us if we stayed nearby," the soldier tells her. "Where are we headed?"

"There's a road on the other side of the cove," Clarissa tells her. "It's one of the sites where our troops would have lined up to battle if you had been invaders. But, since you're not, there's also probably enough vehicles that you can all get rides back to base camp."

"Is that where you stay?"

"No. Well we did. But my family has the watch location out here. After we drop you off with Sarah, we'll head back there."

"Who's Sarah?"

"Sarah's our camp director. Sarah Osborne. She's really nice."

"Did you say Sarah Osborne? As in Navy Seal Sarah Osborne?"

"Could be. I think she said she was ex-military," Clarissa responds. "Why? Do you know her?"

"If it's who I think it is, it's more that it would be an honor to meet her."

"Really. Well, she is really, really nice."

CHAPTER 13

42 Hours

Washington, D.C.

Homeland Secretary Peyton enters the DUCC. Without saying anything, he connects to the display system and displays a series of nine satellite photos on the wall. In the center is what appears to be an open parking lot, with semis arranged to appear, from satellite view, to spell two words.

"What's this?" the President asks.

"War crimes," Secretary Peyton responds.

President Phillipi drops the maps, papers and other data he had been reviewing with the national security team and steps to a closer view of the photos.

"Mr. President, these satellite photos show an empty parking lot outside Fort Worth, Texas. I apologize for the darkness, but our police contact was only able to get one overhead light brought in to the scene."

"What am I looking at?"

"Sixteen semis, arranged, we believe purposefully, to spell the words 'WE WIN' to an overhead view."

"And what about all the vans around the trucks in these other photos?"

"I'll zoom in Marc. Look at the tops of the vans."

"Oh my God, those are people."

"Dead people sir. All sixteen have since been identified unofficially as leaders in the anti-secession battle in Texas. They were kidnapped yesterday from their homes by armed gangs and thrown inside cargo vans. Each cargo van clearly drove up inside a semitrailer marked as U.N. property within minutes of the kidnapping and escaped local police. All of the semis arrived at this parking lot within a 30-minute time frame. Going back through satellite surveillance, we determined that all of the men driving the semis and the vans – seven in each vehicle – left their vehicles simultaneously."

"Where'd they go?"

"They all entered this empty store," Peyton says, pulling up a map of the area, "and it appears they left through this supposedly closed area to be taken to the adjacent Air Force base parking lot, from which they dispersed.

"So we have, what, 16 trailers, seven to a trailer, that's 112 killers. How many have we tracked down?" the President asks.

"We can't really track any yet, except by satellite, and every vehicle we could track from here went to an underground parking lot. Our contact on the ground can't go search for those vehicles without giving away that he's in contact with Washington."

"So what are we doing?"

"I haven't shown you the worst, yet," Secretary Peyton says. "This is gruesome, sir."

Peyton clicks up a picture of a dead woman on top of a van. He zooms in. Her shirt has been opened and her pants pulled halfway down her hips. Blood and organs are spread everywhere, with streaks in all directions over the side of the van as well. Her abdomen is sliced open in a circle. Zooming in further, Secretary Peyton points to what appears to be an Aztec skull mask inserted into her body where her digestive track once resided.

"Oh my God. What did they do to her?"

"Mr. President, that's a symbol often used by the Castillo cartel. They clearly were sending a message. They had to know we would find this."

"You think this is retaliation for killing Castillo. They clearly think the U.S. government got him and they respond by killing 16 civilians. What a bunch of sick . . .," President Phillipi says, catching himself before the curse leaves his mouth.

"You can say it, Marc, and it's not just 16."

"There are no words to describe what kind of person would do something like this to another human being."

"Keep in mind that these are people who think nothing of impaling one of their own in his back yard when he makes a mistake and tying his family up to make them watch as the pole slowly pierces every organ in his body. Can you imagine making a family watch that torment for three, four, five hours before they die, let alone doing it to someone? The Nazis used to do that to work camp gays. These people have the same morality as the Nazis and need to be destroyed with the same ferocity," Secretary Peyton says.

"We need to find the people who did this and take them all out. They've clearly opened war on us, so throw due process through the damn window."

"We'll work on that Marc, but there's something else you need to know."

"What?"

"You know some of these people."

"Oh no," the President whispers, standing up and walking around in a circle. He struggles to control his emotions, a struggle made all the more difficult by his complete exhaustion.

"These were all vocal leaders opposing secession in Texas. They were all taken here from several cities in Texas. In many cases, their spouses or families were slain as well."

"Good God."

"The one who's sliced open," Secretary Peyton starts. "That's Charlotte Lee. Her husband was found dead earlier in their home." The President shakes his head and cups his face down in both hands. Turning to Chief of Staff Vijay Chinh, the President tells him to call Secretary Mendoza and find a way for the President to be part of an assault team against a cartel target.

"Marc, I'm not making that call. We can't let you do that," Chinh responds.

"I need to kill someone. I'm ready to explode," the President yells, slamming his fist down on the table so hard that he feels a ringing up his arm and into his neck. After collecting his breath for a few seconds, the President turns back to Secretary Peyton. "What about Charlotte's and Bob's children?"

"From what we've been told, they're alive and were taken into protective custody by local police."

"Get me versions of these photos that can be shown to the public. We need to let the people of Alta Texas know what kind of sickness they voted for," President Phillipi directs. "Get me a place we can hold a secure press conference."

"A press conference will help get to our people, Marc," Chinh interjects. "But they've shut down communication in Alta Texas except for the bits in government control. Some of their attacking allies are expert in this and it sounds like they've done it well. We'll need to use tools that don't run through cables or satellites."

For the second time since the incident began, the first when he made sure they were safe hours after the invasion, President Phillipi asks to connect to his wife and family. The family is tucked away in a large underground bunker well beneath the Greenbrier Resort in West Virginia.

He shares the news about the Lee family with his wife.

"These are the moments I wonder if doing this is worth it, when I see what could happen to you just because some people hate," he tells her. He can't talk long, he adds, since there are still so many decisions to be made. "I'd give anything to be back home sitting on the front porch holding your hand," he says, preparing to end the call.

"Me too," the first lady responds. "With tea for me, a beer for you and maybe some warm pumpkin pie. You take care of what you must, and I'll be sure that's exactly what we're doing four years from today, with our kids and the rest of the family all around us."

***

Hours later, President Phillipi travels underground to the Pentagon for a press conference. As the President walks toward the podium, video screens behind him display three photos, one of the truck alignment, one showing the sixteen vans with bodies on top with the nude portions covered, and one-showing a close-up of the carving in Charlotte Lee's torso with other parts of her body blacked out and part of her face distorted.

After describing the events of what transpired during the past day, President Phillipi makes a plea to the people of Alta Texas that few there will see.

"I want you to see what your sham government thinks of freedom of speech and due process," President Phillipi states. "You think they are working for your best interests. Everything done in the past two days makes clear to me that Senator Jones, the governors and others in on this invasion are working entirely on their own personal agenda."

"I can't imagine that anyone who voted in November voted for men and women to be kidnapped from their homes, executed and gruesomely splayed, then displayed for the public in such a horrific manner. You need to turn now against these invaders and get back to sovereign territory. I urge all of you interested in being protected from these horrors, and others in the name of martial law, to get back into U.S. protected territory. These horrible war crimes will be prosecuted, through military action or the legal system, whichever comes first," the President adds.

After concluding his remarks, a reporter asks the President if he knows the identity of the dead people. To protect cooperating sources in the local White Settlement and Fort Worth area police departments, the President says he has no positive identification.

"Though we do not have positive identification, I can tell you from photos I have seen that I believe I know who some of these people are and I can guarantee you that I will seek vengeance for their deaths," the President responds.

"Can you tell us their names?"

"I would rather not do that since we do not have positive identification and I have no way of knowing whether next of kin have been identified."

"What do you mean by vengeance, Mr. President?" another reporter asks.

"I mean that we will hunt them down relentlessly, as we will with every war criminal using this conflict to settle personal scores."

Once the press briefing room is out of earshot, President Phillipi pulls aside Secretary Mendoza. "I'm serious Xavier. I want to be part of an assault wave against the Castillo cartel."

"Mr. President, I understand the emotion. Believe me. But I can't let you do that sir. We would have to assign too many people to your safety and would put any mission at risk or unnecessarily add complications. I can't do that to our troops," Secretary Mendoza responds.

"Whatever happened to leading from the front?" the President asks. "I can't ask soldiers to sacrifice their lives if I'm not willing to die for the same cause. Great leaders of history didn't sit on the sidelines, cheerleading and calling plays. They led their men into battle – and some women too."

Secretary Mendoza looks at the President, and knows his eyes are saying he's not going to back off on this demand. "The difference, Mr. President, is that kings and emperors trained to be soldiers in those days. You visit training facilities. You can't pass the physical requirements we require. I can't let you do that."

"I am the Commander in Chief and I'm ordering you to get me into an assault. I know how to handle a gun."

"Mr. President, with all due respect, sir, I have never heard of deer or pigeons shooting back. War isn't a turkey shoot."

***

Utah New Rite Compound

Clarissa Coleman spots someone approaching their camp from the west, pulls her Lifelink out of her pocket and zooms in through the camera lens to pull up a full screen view. Certain she recognizes the young teenager as being from the New Rite camp, she puts her arm up to let him know her location and yells out to him to hold his hands up as he approaches.

In his hand, he holds a folded sheet of paper with a handwritten message. It's addressed to her father. She opens it anyway.

"John, I've heard from friends at home that the police raided our house and your dad was taken out in an ambulance. I'm trying to track it down, but you need to get back here," says the note from Mrs. Coleman.

Clarissa heads out from their camp location to try figuring out where her dad went. An hour later, he spots her from his path and calls out to her.

"You can't run a stakeout by running around in plain sight," he says as she approaches. "Besides, you're supposed to be resting."

She pulls the note out of her pocket and hands it to him. John Coleman is torn. He can't leave his daughters here alone. He can't abandon the scout location. He can't stay here and do nothing.

"Dad, we're fine," Clarissa says.

"I can't leave you here."

"You have to go check on Grandpa. He's the one who needs you now."

"I can't leave my teenage daughters alone in the wilderness without protection."

"We know what to do out here, Dad. Don't you think all those New Rite weekends taught us something about taking care of ourselves? You saw how I handled myself when the troops landed here."

"The boy who brought the note can stay with us and be the fourth," Clarissa says.

"Sure, even better, leave my daughters to share a tent with a boy. Not going to happen."

"You don't have to worry. He can sleep at one of the scout spots next to us, but come over when we need relief."

"We need to all go in," John Coleman states.

"Then this whole idea of watching the borders is a waste of time if we open up a big gaping hole anytime someone thinks they need to leave," Clarissa says. "You can get back here in eight hours max. We'll be fine."

"But what if something is really wrong with Grandpa and I need to go see him, or we all need to go see him," John Coleman says, speaking more to himself than asking the question of Clarissa. "Worse comes to worse, we'll have to have your mother come out here."

"Whatever. We're fine."

***

Cheyenne Mountain, Colorado

Deep inside the Cheyenne Mountain base in Colorado, Pete, Ally and other members of the New Rite special operations team are well into contingency planning for the military options they may undertake. Assessing skill sets, they determine who will likely take each role in any assault.

Realizing that any operation will be officially unsanctioned, the team speculates on what they possibly could do that the U.S. military would not be asked to do.

"Best we know," Pete says, "the only thing the U.S. knows about our capabilities is our Castillo success. So it makes sense to me that they're planning another long-range assassination mission."

"Sure, possible," Ally responds. She's dressed in her New Rite operations gear, carefully designed to look like civilian clothing, but with more functional capability than traditional military uniforms. Tops fit tightly, showing off well-defined arm and shoulder muscles along with a tightly tuned abdomen. Ally keeps her red hair long to soften her look and make it easier to blend into civilian settings where most of her work takes place. "But if that's the case, my job is to fly you in and then what?"

"Out," Pete says. "What else?"

"Shocking that you would think it's all about you," Ally replies. "Is it any wonder that you're alone all these years?"

"Whatever it is with you two, stop it now," barks the military officer known to the group as Koz.

"I'm not going on a mission with two spatting lovers," fellow military officer Branch adds. "It's tough enough to come back alive when we're all on the same team."

"Trust me," Ally states. "There's no love here. Let's just run through our areas of expertise and see if we can piece it together. My specialty is evasive flight behind enemy lines. Pete is a marksman and expert at physical camouflage. Clint blows people up on the ground. Lou blows people up by remote. Koz, you're supposedly a munitions guy. Branch, you say you're a close-quarter combat and extraction expert. The other guys are all experts at surreptitious entry and close-quarter combat. And we've got one more person we can pick up on the way in if her skills are needed. Her expertise is water-based entry and either extraction or demolition."

"So, you put it all together," Pete says, "and it sounds like we're going to get ourselves into a close-quarter battle."

"I'm not sure that's what I heard," Koz responds. "What I heard was that most of us have great skills at getting into places where no one expects us. So, if I had to guess, they're going to send us after someone in the Alta

Texas leadership, civilian or military, with the hopes we can do our business without being seen."

"Sure, could be, but why all the close-quarter combat skill then?" Pete asks.

"Because we're probably going to be noticed when we get our kill shot and they want us to believe it's possible we'll get out alive after we do our business," Clint tells Pete.

"Don't be so pessimistic," Ally interjects. "We've all pulled off some pretty unbelievable stuff in our days. We can do it again."

"So tell me what kind of other stuff you're talking about?" Branch asks. "I'd be curious to really understand the capabilities of the team."

"I'm sure you would," Ally says, "but as far as we know, the extent of your knowledge of New Rite is the Castillo killing. I think it's best we leave it that way. As the saying goes, 'anything we say can and will be held against us,' and we don't know if you're really here to be on our team or to figure out what we've been up to."

JT's handpicked special operations team has grown substantially over the years, backed by a substantial intelligence team. Castillo's Protection Corps has grown much faster. The Protection Corps is the world's largest private military.

Working in close coordination with Islamic radical groups in the Middle East, North Africa and Western Europe, the Protection Corps continuously worked to draw attention away from drug enforcement. Islamic fundamentalists helped fund Castillo's operations, believing that drug addiction was one of the best methods of taking down the "Great Satan." Castillo was also the largest buyer of drugs sold by many of these fundamentalist groups, so was considered a critical customer who increasingly demanded adherence to his mandates from his suppliers. Often, these mandates were consistent with the objectives of the fundamentalists, manifesting in terrorist attacks against U.S. targets in the United States and abroad. For more than a decade, the string of terrorist attacks against U.S. targets financed by drug money served Castillo by distracting resources away from drug enforcement efforts.

"So we know each other's primary skill sets. That's enough for now," Ally says. "What type of mission could they possibly send us on with no time to practice when we haven't all worked together before?"

"I think it's pretty clear," Clint tells the group. "If we're the ones going on a mission, it isn't going to be one with a high chance of success. If there's a high chance of success, the President will send the military so he can take credit when it works. We'll be sent to do something no one really thinks will work."

"What happened to being optimistic?" Ally responds.

"I am optimistic. I'm optimistic that if we get sent out, I'll have the opportunity to die to help save my country. Anyone here not willing to die may as well take a walk right now, because I don't want someone on my back soiling his pants," Clint says, staring straight at Pete as he finishes his comments.

"Are you calling me out?" Pete asks, glaring back at Clint. "I may not have served in the military but I know how to fight."

"It's different when the bullets being shot back at you are real," Clint barks back.

"If I was afraid, I wouldn't have taken the assignments I've taken," Pete says.

"Was that plural assignments?" Koz asks.

"Don't think you're getting details from me," Pete responds.

"You've never had anyone shooting back at you in anything other than a game," Clint repeats, standing up and walking right in front of Pete.

"That's only because I've been successful. If I'd have sucked, I would have ended up in firefights. But I know what I'm doing and I get the job done," Pete says, standing up chest-to-chest with Clint and practically spitting in his face as he yells back at him. "Maybe if you were a little better at your job, people wouldn't shoot at you all the time."

"If you want to go, let's go now," Clint says in a calm monotone, before Ally jumps between the two and starts pushing them apart. Others in the group also step in to help keep them separated.

"Let me guess," Koz says to everyone. "Pete's the hothead of the group."

***

Alta Texas Headquarters

Photos of the White Settlement massacre reach Alta Texas President Manny Jones at nearly the same time as commanders from the various militaries in the U.N. peacekeeping delegation receive copies through their national military and political channels. While citizens inside remaining U.S. territory are instantly outraged by the photos, control of most media inside the four states substantially slows spread of the photos inside Alta Texas.

"Who the hell authorized this?" President Jones screams inside the Alta Texas command center.

No one responds.

"I'm asking again," President Jones barks.

After taking a close look, General Ramírez, leader of Mexico's official troop involvement, responds.

"I told you we could not afford to involve Castillo's Protection Corps. This is how they work. They think crazy violence will scare everyone away," General Ramírez says. "Why do you think President Suárez was insistent they not play any part in our peacekeeping? Because of them, this turned into an invasion. Before long you'll be known for leading one of the century's greatest massacres."

"You think they did this?"

"Of course they did this. Who else has turned cruelty into a science?" General Ramírez responds.

"*I need to get General Hernández back in line and right way,*" President Jones says, "*before he scares off my constituents.*"

"*Back in line? He'll never be in anyone's line, not even yours,*" General Ramírez states, speaking quietly and wiping a bit of sweat from his brow. "*He'll just bide his time until he can take you out unless you do what you're told at every step.*"

"*I am President. He'll follow my orders,*" Jones responds, slamming his fist down on the table, then standing, puffing out his chest and lifting his chin.

"*I'd like to think you're smarter than that,*" General Ramírez says, even more quietly so that only President Jones can hear. "*Because if you're not, he'll be running Alta Texas very soon, just like he does much of the north of our country.*"

"*Get me General Hernández,*" President Jones yells at an aide.

Once General Hernández is connected, President Jones yells loudly and angrily.

"*Did you do this killing, with the trucks? If you did, you're rallying our opposition and putting our allies in a very bad spot with perceptions at home,*" President Jones says.

"*Mr. President,*" General Hernández responds firmly and calmly. "*You said you wanted retribution at those who opposed secession. I followed your orders. No one else will get in your way now, not as long as they understand our connection. They'll know what happens to anyone who tries to stop you.*"

"*That's not what I meant, at least not like this. This is cruelty.*"

"*This might not be what you said, but I know it's exactly what you meant. I understand how to listen to powerful men, Mr. President,*" General Hernández says. "*My job is to understand what you mean without making you say it so you can worry about more important things and feel good about yourself.*"

Five minutes later, after concluding the call, President Jones turns to General Ramírez. "*Well, we really needed his communication systems and tunnels. We couldn't have pulled off the invasion without him, so I guess I need to just let this go.*"

"*Don't be so sure he'll do the same, sir,*" General Ramírez responds. "*Watch your back.*"

"*I'm not worried. He needs me now, for their new tunnels.*"

General Ramírez walks away. Out of sight of others in the room, he rolls his eyes and shakes his head.

***

Camp Navajo, Arizona

Only in the last few hours has word started to reach some U.S. troops in the Alta Texas states that they will be allowed to re-declare allegiance to the United States without being court-martialed in Alta Texas. At Camp Pendleton, a massive Marine base in California, word spreads rapidly. Troops barricaded inside to prevent entry by the U.N. weigh their desire to get back onto U.S. territory against protecting on-base weapons from theft.

Most recognize the importance of protecting the weapons inside and realize that having them captured could weaken the U.S. military for a decade. Encryption information is particularly valuable. When North Korea captured the U.S.S. Pueblo in the 1960s, they did so to steal code technology that helped the Soviet Union to decode U.S. naval communications for 20 years. That ship data was combined with code information provided by infamous spy John Walker and essentially turned U.S. military communication into an open book for the Soviet Union.

As U.N. troops overran many U.S. military bases in the Alta Texas states, U.S. soldiers scrambled to blow up communication devices on weapons they couldn't protect. At the time, none knew that enough defectors were involved in the secession that this code technology had already been captured. Various weapons units are already being shipped to China, Russia, Iran, Saudi Arabia, Pakistan and Egypt for analysis. U.S. allies in the North Atlantic Treaty Organization (NATO) who were also part of the U.N. alliance tried to prevent this technology from being removed and shipped to these countries, fearing its capture would affect NATO's already weakened security when a conflict occurs in Europe.

Now, with some communication restored to U.S. command centers, Camp Pendleton Marines are being told what weapons have already been compromised. A few uncompromised weapons remain on base, so the soldiers collectively decide to remain barricaded in base, protecting the weapons. The U.S. command is informed that all soldiers wishing to defect to Alta Texas have already left. Losses total less than five percent of Marines on base.

At Camp Navajo in Flagstaff, Arizona, few weapons of security concern are stored on base, one of the reasons Iran's poorly trained new recruits were given the chance to capture this base.

After Iran's military suffered massive losses in the Supreme Leader-ordered invasion of Armenia to wipe out Christian infidels living there, the Iranian military retook control of the country from Islamic clerics. Control of the country remains an ongoing battle, with religious fundamentalists having engaged in a series of suicide attacks against the new Iranian military and civilian coalition government. Iran's newly appointed Prime

Minister hopes that Iran's active involvement in the U.N. mission against the United States will stabilize his government.

When announced that Iran would send 100,000 soldiers to the U.S. border as part of the U.N. peacekeeping missions if enough new recruits signed up, the Iranian military gained an enormous surge of recruits. Iran's Prime Minister particularly focused on enlisting young men who had been fighting for Al Qaeda and its sister militias in the months following the military takeover and secular government's installation.

The peacekeeping mission was well timed from the perspective of Iran's hope of not returning to direct religious rule. By recruiting from militia ranks, the military was able to distract its primary internal rivals from massing an attack on the new government. New recruits are excited at the opportunity to go to the U.S. border and some pray for the opportunity to fight the Great Satan, as the United States is known in fundamentalist parts of the Islamic world. Most of the soldiers sent to take part in the U.N. mission came from these new recruits. The Prime Minister sees this mission as his chance to get opponents out of the country and focused on a greater enemy. If he can buy months, or even years, of stability at home, he can consolidate his power base and reduce calls for a return to fundamentalist religious government.

Surrounding Camp Navajo, more than 12,000 Iranian soldiers are joined by several hundred soldiers from other Arab countries. Camp Navajo was not among the strategic base targets for the U.N. mission, so the inexperienced Iranians, many with only 30 days of basic training at home and another 45 days of training in Mexico, were given the assignment to surround and control its occupants. Having sat around Camp Navajo now for nearly 40 hours, the young recruits from Iran are anxious to get into battle. They've been ordered to not fire their weapons unless directly attacked.

U.S. soldiers barricaded inside Camp Navajo are informed by the U.S. command that they have no strategic weapons on site and they can leave their posts without being declared Absent Without Leave. Under terms of a deal that affects only military bases with limited weapons on site, the U.S. troops will be allowed to walk to the new U.S. border with only their packs containing food, water and outdoor gear. No weapons or ammunition can be removed from the site.

Along a street inside the base property, soldiers are gathering with packs for the long march to the Utah border. A lieutenant colonel, commanding officer at the base, walks out alone waving a white flag and asking to talk to the U.N. commander. The Iranian commander assures him that U.S. troops will have safe passage. He sends a team of 50 of his best-trained soldiers inside the base to inspect the packs of the U.S. soldiers before they exit.

The first several hundred soldiers exit the base, starting a slow march until all of the soldiers planning to exit clear the camp gate. Several Cooper's hawks fly overhead, hovering above U.S. troops, circling in a way that draws the attention of a few soldiers. U.S. troops look to the right to see a platoon comprised of 40 of their ex-colleagues who defected to Alta Texas soon after the secession started. Some can't help but exchange words and gestures with the defectors. A few Alta Texas soldiers try to explain their defection, yelling to former colleagues that they have to be on whatever side controls their home and the lives of their families.

Past the Alta Texas soldiers, Iranian troops keep careful eye on the U.S. soldiers, watching to ensure no weapons are removed. As the last U.S. troops reach the gate, Camp Navajo's commanding officer orders the men to start marching just as a small missile pops open overhead, dropping small paper sheets around the area.

Several flyers land near the U.S. troops while others scatter across the area and reach the Iranian troops. Several U.S. soldiers pick up the flyers to see photos from the White Settlement massacre and a message, "This is what U.N. peacekeepers do to captured Americans." Thousands of these missile-like message distributors have been sent to explode above bases and urban areas throughout Alta Texas.

Before the U.S. soldiers can run far, the first gunshots ring out. Then more shots come from the new Iranian recruits. The Iranian commanding officer yells at his men to cease firing only to be shot down by his own troops. U.S. troops turn to run for cover back inside the base. Shouts of "Allahu Akbar" can be heard intermittently over blasts of gunfire. The few Iranian military veterans assigned to the Camp Navajo mission start shooting at recruits who refuse to cease fire, only to have the recruits shoot back at them before turning aim back to U.S. soldiers caught in an open field with no weapons.

Alta Texas defectors, seeing their former colleagues being slaughtered, begin firing on the Iranians, not knowing who is fighting on what side. As they do, other Iranian and Pakistani troops surrounding Camp Navajo begin running toward the fight. Gunfire echoes throughout the camp.

Within 20 minutes, several thousand remaining U.N. troops have full control of Camp Navajo. Hundreds of surviving U.S. soldiers sprint through nearby forests and open lands to escape.

With no Iranian officers surviving, dozens of ex-terrorists who now make up Iran's peacekeepers walk among the wounded outside the gate. Every few seconds, wounded U.S. soldiers hear the sound of a final bullet being shot through the head of another colleague, until each can hear no more.

CHAPTER 14

36 Hours

Washington, D.C.

In the Deep Underground Command Center, President Phillipi reconvenes his conflict strategy team to understand the potential uses of water, disease and communications jamming in defeating the U.N. if the dispute becomes protracted.

The Homeland Security team outlines a plan to shut off the California and Los Angeles aqueducts supplying the bulk of South California's water. They can also cut off the Colorado River once it reaches Nevada to prevent that water from reaching the Colorado River aqueduct that supplies Los Angeles, San Diego and surrounding cities. "We can turn South California dry in a heartbeat if we want. It won't take long for them to feel the pain," Secretary Peyton tells the group. "They'll have to shut down what's left of agriculture in the state, shut off all but the most essential industry use and strictly limit home use to keep people alive."

Arizona is a tougher challenge. Trying to shut off or redirect the Colorado River before it reaches Arizona will require big ecological gambles, with the side impact of cutting off a primary water source into southern Nevada. "If we do something here, we won't be able to undo it quickly." Peyton and team add that water flows into New Mexico and Texas can also be reduced, but without as devastating a short-term impact as can be had on South California.

"Is there a play here to cut off South California water and make it clear to the government and people that we'll turn it back on once U.N. troops leave and the people agree to abandon secession efforts?" President Phillipi asks. After some discussion, the group agrees to target South California with a water cut-off set to trigger as the President's 72-hour window expires. "Should we leak this to the press to pressure Jones, or just hit him with it with no notice?" Chief of Staff Chinh asks.

"It's bound to leak with the number of people we'll need involved, but if we can confine the leaks to the last couple of hours, we could gin up some panic that distracts Jones and his team," Peyton responds.

"Okay, let's go on this," the President orders.

"Don't we need to worry about people getting sick or dying of dehydration?" a national security analyst asks.

"That's Jones' problem if he doesn't figure out fast that he's in way over his head," Secretary Peyton says. "There will still be enough water for human consumption if he recognizes this as his priority."

"Okay, next issue. Biological weapons," the President says, turning to Defense Secretary Mendoza to lead the discussion.

Secretary Mendoza's presentation team includes an epidemic disease expert from the National Institutes of Health (NIH), as well as the Pentagon's leading experts on biological, chemical and nuclear weapons control.

"Mr. President, we need to clear the room of everyone except the presenting team, you, the Vice President and Secretary Peyton. This is special access program data," Secretary Mendoza begins. As President Phillipi waves, the national security and White House staff, including Chinh, leave the discussion for the main operations room in the DUCC. Chinh could have stayed if he had wanted.

NIH and Pentagon experts outline known biological and chemical weapons threats. They gain quick approval for water and air monitoring programs around secession state borders. Industrial sabotage risks are discussed briefly, but the President asks the team to focus on surreptitious attacks that might not normally invite immediate military response.

"I want to know what they can do to us without us being able to identify their involvement and respond," the President says firmly.

"Mr. President, we have two concerns. First, the exposure of large population centers in the secession states to foreign troops, some of whom are bound to be disease-contaminated, could spur disease epidemics that spread to our other states. Unintentional epidemics have played major roles in military victories for millennia. We need to consider that possibility here," the NIH expert states. "When we send our military overseas, we provide them full inoculation sets that anticipate local diseases, as well as those they might encounter from other militaries in the combat zone. We can't possibly create enough vaccine for people in the four states, let alone our other 48."

"What worries you most?" President Phillipi asks, leaning his backside against the edge of the table as he stares intently at charts projected around the room.

"My biggest concerns are diseases we haven't inoculated for in decades. Take smallpox, for example. We thought it was eradicated generations ago, but evidence suggests it continues to afflict people in an Indonesian island tribe and several countries around the Indus valley where religious objections and fears of western plots have limited vaccinations for deadly diseases. If this is true, and a soldier here contracts smallpox, we could be looking at death tolls in the tens of millions in just a few years. We've been trying to get samples of these cases, but the same fears that prevent vaccination have stopped us from getting samples. We don't have hard evidence that this is smallpox and not a more survivable version like chickenpox," the NIH expert continues. "If smallpox does exist, it has likely mutated in the 60 years since we thought it was eradicated. We may not be able to stop this mutated form from decimating our population."

"What about something intentional?" the President asks.

"Two comments, Mr. President. First, existing diseases could be intentionally introduced if governments knowingly send infected people here. Second, I'm particularly concerned about designer pandemics. We've long suspected that several countries are trying to create genetically encoded infectious diseases."

"Meaning what?"

"Meaning diseases that people carrying the primary genetic codes in their countries are immune from, but that could spread rapidly and wipe out other countries when introduced in areas where people aren't protected by genetic code."

"Give me an example," the President says while downing his third chunky peanut butter and chocolate chip panini in the past 12 hours. He'll watch his weight again when this is over, but comfort food is the only pleasure he has now.

"We haven't seen this used in our lifetimes, but think of it this way. The U.S. is genetically diverse. Our ancestors come from all over the planet. But that's not the case everywhere. So, if you run Kazakhstan or Mongolia and you see Russia on your northern border and China to your south or east, realizing that both crave the resources you have underground, you may think creatively about defending against invasion. If China attacks, you won't defeat them militarily. But if you can design an epidemic that takes hold in the Chinese troops, but has little effect on your own people, you might decide to unleash that epidemic to regain control of your country."

"Is there any evidence this type of research is occurring?" President Phillipi asks.

Secretary Mendoza pulls his chair closer to the President. "Yes, sir, and it's been going on for decades in a couple of countries run by dictators anxious to maintain power. A few defectors over the years have been involved in this research. We have tracked down, imprisoned and killed some of the human traffickers who kidnap U.S. victims to be used in trials. We believe that at least three potential epidemic diseases have been created and genetically modified to target parts of the U.S. population. Imagine if Hitler had been able to develop a pandemic targeting Ashkenazi Jews, recognizing that these people are genetically predisposed to certain diseases. That's the type of impact we're talking about."

"After four years in office, this is the first time the extent of this concern has been made clear to me," the President states. "How real is this threat?"

"We have no definitive data. Our concerns are based on what we believe we could achieve if we were in the business of creating this type of weapon from what we know today," the NIH scientist says. "Frankly, Mr. President, I don't sleep well at night knowing that at any moment an epidemic that could kill hundreds of millions could be unleashed, whether accidentally or on purpose."

President Phillipi cups his hands behind his head, pulls his chin down to his sternum and exhales audibly. As the room goes silent, he walks around looking at screens around the room.

"What do you need," the President asks, looking at the Pentagon and NIH experts, "to be sure something like this doesn't happen here?"

Both Defense Department experts look to Secretary Mendoza before responding, apparently seeking permission to say what they think. Before Mendoza reacts, the NIH expert responds: "We don't have the resources we need to identify, develop vaccines and inoculate as fast as we might need to do if any of these attempts succeed."

"When the 72 hours are up, we need a follow-up on this. Are we prepared for what the U.N. coalition countries might bring here?" the President asks, looking directly at the NIH expert.

"Not to my comfort, Mr. President," the expert says, doing his best to ignore the peanut butter resting on the side of the President's lip. "And we can't get there in a few days either."

Chinh codes in and shoves open the door to the closed meeting space. The thick, bulletproof glass on the door reverberates as it slides inside the wall and slams against its rubber stoppers. His face is ashen as he enters, but reddens quickly as he begins to speak.

"Sorry to interrupt, but more bad news. We just received word that the Iranians surrounding Camp Navajo lined our troops up there and slaughtered them," Chinh tells the President and others in the room.

"Say that again," Secretary Mendoza demands.

"U.S. troops stationed at Camp Navajo, lined up to depart based on the agreement to allow troops to leave low-weapons-priority bases in the Southwest, were slaughtered by the Iranians surrounding the base," Chinh repeats.

President Phillipi tenses his face, pulls his fingers in to make tight fists with both hands and closes his eyes. He rolls his lips inside his mouth and bites down sharply on his lips.

"How many?" the President asks, fists still clenched.

"Hard to say, but I thought you'd both want to know right away," Chinh adds, voice choking and right hand trembling as he looks at the President and Secretary Mendoza. "Initial estimates, from troops that escaped the slaughter, run into the thousands. The alert here says wounded who couldn't escape were executed."

"I should have made it 24 hours," President Phillipi states. "We'll come back to the nuclear assessment later."

***

Protection Corps Command Center

General Hernández, leader of the Castillo cartel's Protection Corps, receives calls from several North African and Middle Eastern generals following another outburst from Alta Texas President Manny Jones. For 15 years, General Hernández has been the cartel's primary liaison with nations and terrorist organizations intent on destroying the United States.

General Hernández's goal has always been to build the strongest military in the western hemisphere. His allies have diverse goals, all of which the general knows how to exploit. Some are primarily concerned with enriching their leaders through drug trafficking. Some nations partner with him primarily to weaken or destroy the United States. Many work with the Protection Corps to destroy U.S. degenerates they see as living in defiance of Allah.

General Hernández built relationships by providing the infrastructure to support terrorist attacks inside U.S. borders. For Hernández, these terrorist attacks are win-win collaborations. Terrorists groups bolster their financial strength by gaining tens of millions of followers as they proclaim each success. Militant Islamic nations who funnel financial support to terrorist groups are happy to keep U.S. military responses focused against terrorist targets rather than national militaries. The cartel gains as U.S. counterterrorism efforts subtract resources from drug enforcement.

By playing to the individual desires of each partner, Hernández built strong, deep relationships with top military leaders and heads of terrorist organizations.

"Are you sure this Senator is the right man to lead our victory?" one North African general asks General Hernández.

"Certain, no. But he will do what we need as long as we need him," General Hernández responds as he alternates between downing 30-year-old scotch, bacon-crusted filet mignon and moist jalapeno corn bread.

"He is losing control," the North African responds.

"Ah, the price of working with politicians. He does not understand discipline. It will not matter," General Hernández says. "We can finish the job whether he stays on path or not. Do not worry. Our plans are proceeding. The Americans will cave. They are weak and afraid. And for good reason."

***

Chicago

None of the students arriving in Professor Stark's graduate class are focused on the future. Instead, they come to class hoping for a bit of group therapy. A civil war – now perhaps 35 hours away – would at least delay their careers, and perhaps even destroy the value of all their hard work for some. Work and study with a long-term payoff can always be rendered useless by a careless accident, a bolt of lightning or a criminal. The odds that their studies won't create opportunities for a good life went from miniscule to meaningful in a matter of days. Renewed anxiety has many of the students mentally paralyzed.

Professor Stark is still tired and disheveled from Sunday's short night of sleep in which he shared a couch that barely fits one. Even sleeping back in his bed late Monday night didn't regenerate his energy. He tossed and turned contemplating the impact of the secession. Three cups of coffee at Heart and Soul Café haven't helped either.

Wearing black jeans, a black button-down shirt, a thick white, black and grey sweater and black high-top basketball sneakers, Professor Stark looks better dressed for a museum stroll than a professor's podium. He's scragglier than usual, having showered and left the house without realizing he forgot to shave. Normally, when Heart and Soul owner Margie reminds him that he forgot to shave, he races home before going to class. Not today. The weather remains brutally cold, enough that Professor Stark took a cab from the cafe to his campus office rather than endure a walk he typically enjoys.

Professor Stark's courses all run two quarters each. He starts his single graduate course in the fall quarter and two undergraduate courses in the fall and winter quarters. That leaves him teaching two courses in the fall, all three in the winter quarter, one in the spring and none in the summer. He purposely designed his workload to be higher in winter months with too little sun and too much snow and cold. That leaves him focused on research and writing in the spring and summer, work he likes to do outside.

"We're going to veer a bit off topic today since our minds are all focused elsewhere anyway," Professor Stark says, much to the relief of many in the class who are ill-prepared for the planned discussion. "We'll try to find the answer to the most important question we face over the next day and a half. That question is: 'What would justice decide if she were to determine what happens when President Phillipi's 72 hours is up?'"

With no one immediately raising their hand to offer an opinion on the topic, Professor Stark pulls his childhood tattered football rocket out, faces away from the class and throws it over his shoulder. He turns in time to see Jun Chen try to deflect it toward another student. Jun came to the United States to learn America's culture before planning to return home to enter China's government ranks. Jun's father is a successful business executive, so Jun worries that anything he says could be used against his father in addition to damaging his own career before it starts.

Though China has taken a lead role in the United Nations peacekeeping ranks, the nation has not asked its citizens to leave the United States. Jun is certainly apprehensive about anti-China sentiment that has begun to be shared through every media format, along with the rest of anti-Russia, anti-Arab and anti-every-U.N.-country sentiment.

Knowing he has put Jun in a tough spot, Professor Stark decides to give him a few moments to choose his words by asking a prolonged question.

"Jun, you are one of five students from a country that is part of the United Nations 'peacekeeping' mission," Professor Stark says, making quote marks with his fingers as he says the word peacekeeping. "If the nations entering under the U.N. banner truly believe they're here for peacekeeping, they would not have fired shots that killed American troops and many civilians already. I'm sure your government will say these killings were accidental or the result of troops operating outside their mandate.

And, to be fair, we know that this happens. U.S. troops have accidentally killed even our allies in war zones. Once a conflict starts, much can go wrong. So, with that context, what do you think is the just outcome from here?"

"I think you know, Professor, that I do not speak for the government of China on this topic and am very nervous to even discuss it," Jun responds.

"I understand, but would like to hear your perspective of what justice would dictate."

"I think justice is having the will of the Alta Texas people for freedom achieved with the very least loss of life possible. Sometimes freedom to be governed by our own people, people of our race, comes at a cost. I believe the United Nations action was accomplished in a way that saves the lives of Americans and Alta Texas residents compared to any of the other alternative methods of achieving that freedom for Alta Texas," Jun says. "And I think justice means the U.S. government should recognize the sacrifice China is making putting its own soldiers at risk to save lives of former U.S. citizens."

As Jun finishes speaking, Professor Stark sees Jeremy's tall, lanky body racing across the classroom toward Jun.

"Jeremy," Professor Stark yells so loudly that the entire class is startled and even Jeremy stops to look at him. "Get back in your seat right now or I will have you expelled by the end of the day," Professor Stark continues as he walks to intercept Jeremy if he decides to continue. "What the hell are you thinking?"

"I'm sorry, Professor, I wasn't. I just can't believe the crap I just heard," Jeremy says, face blushed with a mix of anger and embarrassment.

"And attacking Jun for expressing his opinion, an opinion likely expressed with interest in his own self-preservation, would do what?"

"I don't know, what?" Jeremy asks.

"If you don't know that answer, you aren't prepared to act, so sit down and shut up until I ask you to speak. This classroom has to be a sanctuary for honest and impassioned debate that focuses on finding solutions to problems. If we can't pursue logical, thoughtful debate here, we'll never learn to solve problems," Professor Stark states. "Back to the topic."

"So, is Jun right, that justice is determined by achieving the goals of a group of people, whatever those goals may be, in the least violent way possible?" Professor Stark asks as he looks across the entire class.

Tamika, the hard-nosed former City of Chicago debate champion and high school basketball star, suggests another alternative: "Let's think through this logically. The secession referenda gained majority votes in four states in favor of asking their political leaders to seek an amicable separation from the United States. This is anything but an amicable separation, and I would suggest to you that I doubt the majority of the people of these states would have voted for the resolution if it had been written to say, 'with several thousand people killed, foreign troops taking over our land, and martial law declared that strips the fundamental constitutional rights of the people.' Is there anyone who thinks the referenda would have passed if these conditions were openly asserted?"

Tamika pauses and looks around the room. No one disagrees with her point. She puts two fingers in front of her lips to hide a slight smile before continuing: "So if Jun is right that justice is served by achieving the will of the people in the least costly way possible – in terms of human and economic suffering – then we first need to determine what really is the will of the people. Is the United Nations here to protect the people from being harmed by their government? Or, have the people been purposely manipulated into expressing a will from which the consequences were hidden?"

"Interesting and thoughtful point, Tamika," Professor Stark says. "Any response, Jun, or anyone else who thinks the U.N. invasion is justified as the most sensible peacekeeping action?"

"I think I need to stay out of the rest of this debate, Professor," Jun replies.

"Understood Jun, but I want to be clear that this is why freedom of speech matters. We can't discuss and agree on solutions if we aren't free to discuss ideas and seek facts that might change our opinions," Professor Stark suggests. "Rachel, I know your mind is elsewhere, but wondered if you have anything to say in case particular family members or friends are able to see this livestream."

Rachel typically wears very little makeup, but has on more than usual today to cover the dark spots under her eyes from the combination of too many tears and too little sleep. She is enough out of the discussion mentally that she is still wearing her earmuffs from the walk to class, only realizing it when she sees Professor Stark staring at her, waiting for a response. She wasn't mentally in the classroom even when Jeremy was admonished for running at Jun.

"What's that Professor?" she says. "I'm sorry, I'm not very focused today."

"Do you have anything to say to the people you care about who are caught up on both sides of this? I'm hoping your father has access to the livestream and that others you care about will be able to hear from you by finding this feed."

Rachel purses her lips and then bites the outside of her upper lip as she looks to the ceiling. She turns her head down to the floor, turning to make sure no one catches her wiping the corners of her eyes.

"I was only coming here just to try not getting behind, but I guess I do have something to say," Rachel says, as the voice-activated cameras zoom to a tighter shot of her for the livestream broadcast.

"Papa, if you can see this, I want you to know that I understand now. I didn't realize how hard it must have been for you to go to a new country, learn another language and create a better life. But others want to break up this country and even have people killed to avoid doing the work you've already done. I realize now that if some people are willing to kill others to avoid what you went through, it must be tough," Rachel says. "But you did it. I've been mad at you for always working, but I understand now. You taught me to work hard and earn my success and that is exactly what I'm trying to do."

Tamika pushes her chair over and puts her hand on Rachel's shoulder, then holds her hand to provide comfort as Rachel continues to talk.

"Now I'm torn though," Rachel continues. "I have people I care about deeply on the other side as well. People I respect and admire and maybe even love. And when I think about what they're doing, trying to create a place where Mexican Americans and other Latinos can feel at home, I wonder why they came here. They don't need to integrate if they stay home. It's not that I don't want more Mexicans in America. This is a place that welcomes diversity, perhaps more than almost any other country. It's that America offers rights not found everywhere. We can't assume these rights will exist in Alta Texas. Rights like free speech, religious freedom, the opportunity to succeed even if you don't come from the right family. While the United States has flaws, it's still a far better country than most. So, to a person I care deeply about in Alta Texas, I ask you this question: How many people must suffer so you can take a shortcut to achieving the dreams your mother had for you? Think about it. Think about it."

***

Washington, D.C.

After instructions to track down more detail on the Camp Navajo assault are given, the President's full conflict strategy team gathers. Communications jamming replaces epidemic disease and water restriction as the primary discussion topic.

CIA Director Roland Rand joins personally, replacing the deputy director who had stood in during parts of earlier discussions. Director Rand is a rarity among agency directors, a life-long CIA employee who spent his first 15 years in the CIA running human assets in North Africa and the Middle East through the Arab Spring years and subsequent turmoil. Many of these human intelligence experts left the agency, voluntarily or otherwise, more than a decade earlier when electronic surveillance and sophisticated analytical software temporarily gave the United States strong intelligence-gathering advantages. Those edges, combined with a rapidly faltering economy, caused Congress and the White House to dramatically cut intelligence funding. The then-director responded to these cuts by eliminating 90 percent of the CIA's human intelligence program, hoping digital surveillance would be enough to prevent attacks.

When President Phillipi took office, digital intelligence leadership had already been proven lost by a series of successful terrorist attacks. Terrorist and enemy nation leaders recognized that the U.S. captured all above-ground and electronic conversations. They had gone back to basic discussions – talking out loud only in deep underground shelters or surrounded by intense, overlapping noises that would make their conversations impossible to discern. When those venues weren't available, they exchanged and burned handwritten notes only under roof. Eventually this practice evolved to a tradition of burning paper at the end of all meetings in large parts of the Middle East, North Africa and parts of the Far East in case smoke from paper burning was detectable by U.S. satellites and attracted attention.

Several devastating terrorist attacks on U.S. soil convinced Congress that human intelligence gathering needed to be reinvigorated. President Phillipi promised in his initial campaign to restore America's intelligence strength. He purposely put a non-politician in the role, having found Roland Rand only after he and his transition team interviewed more than 200 CIA staff.

After an introduction by Defense Secretary Mendoza, Director Rand takes over the communications briefing. "Mr. President, we conducted an emergency assessment of our failure to turn up advance notice of the U.N. invasion plan. As you know, the C.I.A. was over-reliant on electronic surveillance before I took this role. We have no evidence that any electronic communication occurred to launch the invasion. It appears the countries involved operate in a hub-and-spoke system, meaning that each country is assigned targets that require little or no cross-country collaboration. Because of this, we believe the instructions were all handwritten and distributed by couriers, or directly through the chain of command of each nation," Director Rand states.

"I didn't call for an assessment of what we missed. We'll do that, but I want to know what we can do now," the President states.

"Understood, sir, but I think this is important. We had believed the U.N. military operation was being run out of Mexico City. All the top generals for each nation's military had arrived to an underground bunker in Mexico City and Mexico's top military officials had been in and out of there multiple times since the U.N. was invited in for joint military exercises. However, it appears we've been watching the wrong planning site. Since we have no evidence of electronic communications launching the attack, we surmised it was launched by personally delivered messages, much as jihadist organizations have been operating almost exclusively the past several decades."

"And?" the President says, flipping his index finger in a circle to tell Director Rand to speed toward his conclusion.

"And, we tracked all 106 sites at which U.N.-connected troops are based. In the 24 hours prior to the invasion, we went back and looked at inbound traffic to all 106 sites and traced back the origin of that traffic. There's one site we found that was the origin of traffic to 102 of the 106 sites," Director Rand notes. "That origin site is in Monterrey, Mexico."

"So that's where the real military leadership is based?"

"Yes, but better than that, it appears that is where the Alta Texas leadership is operating from."

"How certain are we?" the President asks.

"We've gone back and traced other traffic in and out of Monterrey since the inauguration. We have a convincing case that every single Alta Texas leader could have made it to Monterrey through flights and other travel means, including a man a source tells us may be the new head of the Castillo drug cartel. The best proof came from pulling old satellite data to track the loading of this Gonzalez kid at what appears to be gunpoint into a plane that flew directly to Monterrey. We then traced calls exchanged between the kid and Congresswoman Carlson to that direction before we completely lost the connection flow. I suspect they initially forgot to seize and shut down his devices when they took him."

"How sure are you that this isn't a conscious effort to sidetrack us?" the President asks.

"We're putting our estimate of certainty that they're in Monterrey at 90 percent, as close to certain as we'll ever get," Director Rand responds.

"Mr. President," Secretary Mendoza calls out to get attention. "This information opens up military options for us. If we know where the invasion force leadership is located, we can take them all out with a bomb attack if we can circumvent their air defenses."

Mendoza outlines a series of military bombing options, from launching land- and sea-based missiles to bomber attacks. A nuclear strike is also raised, but with a quick recommendation that nuclear weapons not be used, given the proximity of Monterrey to Texas.

"If we kill the top generals from all these nations, don't we elevate the risk of full-scale war?" Vice President Marcia Wilt asks as the plans start to take shape.

"Interesting question, Marcia, but as you're asking this, I wonder if we aren't making a major mistake having this discussion using any electronic communications. How certain are we of the sanctity of our systems?" the President asks, turning to Secretary Mendoza and Director Rand.

"We can't be certain of anything, but we change main encryption codes every four hours and Marcia's link to us changes code every 90 seconds. "Just for safety, we sent the connection codes physically in cases that only Marcia can open."

"So, we're comfortable?"

"As much as we can be," Secretary Mendoza responds.

"Okay, back to the question of how to use what we know about TQ, which I ask that we use as the code for the target site in all future communications?" Director Rand says. "If we bomb TQ, we would have to announce that we have targeted a foreign site hosting secession leadership, and expressing our condolences and sorrow that Mexican military personnel may have been killed in the process. Of course, we'll want to condemn President Suárez for having used his soldiers as human shields for Jones and his team. This gets out the implication that we had no idea other nations had their generals in Mont. . ., in TQ, and perhaps mitigates the U.N. response."

"Risky as all hell," Secretary Mendoza says. "Any evidence that they've stepped up site security at TQ?"

"Only a few visible changes. Looks like some added anti-aircraft weapons," the CIA director responds.

"Can we implement a tactical assault with high likelihood of killing the Alta Texas leadership, and minimizing deaths among U.N. troops?" the President asks.

"There will be a high casualty load on both sides, especially if we need to fight deep into their structures," Secretary Mendoza responds. "I don't know that we can be in and out quickly enough before jet scrambles turn this into full-fledged warfare."

"What if we jam communications?" Director Rand asks. "If we interrupt U.N. coordination, they'll struggle to coordinate military engagement and shoot at each other as much as at us. Passing notes during a firefight would be like playing basketball on one foot while the opponent gets to use two. They won't stand a chance of stopping us if we just keep moving the ball."

"Let's step back," U.S. President Phillipi says. "Our strategic objective is clear. Stop the Alta Texas secession with as few American lives lost as possible, and no more civilian lives lost. If we can jam communications, can we get in and out with a strategic strike that captures or kills Jones, the governors and the rest without inciting full-scale war? I know you're all brilliant here, but I don't think we have all the expertise we need in this room. Get back to your teams, test alternatives, and let's gather in 12 hours to decide course of action."

***

Traver, California

Victor Cruz is held in a loosely fenced, makeshift prison that is rapidly overflowing with Latinos.

The meals cooked cooperatively by the prisoners themselves have been bland. Bread. Water. Rice. Beans. Some canned goods pulled out of nearby county jail storage. As one of the oldest prisoners, Victor organizes the primarily 16- to 40-year-olds into crews to cook food, arrange sleeping quarters and keep the area livable. His initial success is deteriorating as local police in the area have used newly taken authority to arrest any Hispanics with even suspicion of criminal activity in their past, whether they tried to head south or not.

As Salvadoran, Honduran and other national-origin-segregated gang members increase in number, Victor tries to avoid becoming a target.

The makeshift prison has none of the controls needed to keep prisoners secure from each other. A 16-year-old who flashed what was taken as gang signs was taken to the hospital several hours ago after being beaten with the metal legs of a cot. Three gang members who did the beating are still roaming the prison, with other inmates fearful of identifying them.

Victor tries organizing older prisoners, along with several gang leaders, to maintain control and safety for those inside. He asks for a meeting with anyone interested at the foldout tables set up near the makeshift kitchen.

"What is happening to us has to end soon. It would be a shame for us to hurt each other in the process. My daughter knows a Congresswoman who is working to get these arrests stopped. We should be out of here soon, and the only thing that can keep us here is if we commit crimes while inside," Victor tells the group.

"Old man. You're a fool. You think these white people care about a bunch of Mexicans and Salvadorans and Venezuelans?" one of the younger prisoners yells out.

"I think they're frightened right now, and will soon realize this is a mistake and let us all go. There are 100 million Latinos in the United States. They can't round us all up," Victor responds.

"Yeah, but we aren't all Mexicans," the kid yells.

"We're all Mexicans to non-Latinos. It's not like they can easily tell us apart," another says. *"Besides, some of us are New Texans now. I'm from San Diego. That's part of New Texas now amigo."*

"It doesn't matter where we're from. We have rights as Americans," Victor says, trying to get the group focused back on topic.

"Had rights, old man," the young prisoner responds.

"Regardless, we aren't fighting with each other. Our fight has to be to get released and to make sure we're safe and well fed in the meantime," Victor Cruz states, with those listening around him nodding their heads in agreement.

"They barely have enough food and water for all of us. I'm not going hungry just because some gringo is scared of my skin color," a well-tattooed prisoner says, standing up to make sure he is heard. *"The minute I feel even a bit hungry, I'm out of here."*

"I'll talk to the warden about letting our families bring us food and drinks," Victor tells the group, again drawing nods from those nearest to him.

"How about a case of beer while you're at it?" another man suggests.

"Well, we can raise that, I guess. But I wouldn't hold out much hope."

After talking to the warden, Victor Cruz gets approval to allow families to bring in food to loved ones, as long as it passes through security screening.

***

Alta Texas Headquarters

Juan Gonzalez, now Alta Texas ambassador to the United States, is severely limited in his ability to reach out to people he cares about. His last communication out that was not through official and secured Alta Texas channels had been more than a day ago. He wonders what his mother and others he cares about think of what he is doing. Juan questions whether he made the right decision, but can't really see any alternative.

At least now, Juan can listen to public reaction reported on Mexican news networks. He convinces his guard to let him switch channels, finding two Chinese satellite stations reporting in Mandarin. The pace of speech makes it difficult for Juan to keep up with what the reporters are saying, but he gets the gist of their comments.

"If I try to back out now, I'll just prove Gabriel was right about me," he mumbles under his breath in Mandarin, talking to himself in a new world where there is no one around he truly trusts and still conscious of backing up his earlier comment that he talks to himself when he's alone. *"But this, what's happening, just isn't right."*

***

Chicago

The debate on just outcomes to the secession effort in Professor Stark's class continues into the last 30 minutes of his 90-minute class session. After being angered by fellow student Jun Chen's support for the U.N. invasion, Jeremy settles back into his seat and prepares his thoughts, knowing that Professor Stark will give him a chance to speak. Finally, he gets that chance. "If you look at any sizable country in the world, there are groups of people who would rather be self-governed. There are a number of sections of China that have been in conflict with the central government for generations, places like Tibet. The people of Tibet don't want to have their lives run from Beijing. The same is true for some of the heavily Muslim areas of China. So if the justification for invading a country is to allow a people who want self-government to have it, we would be invading and dividing our nations into smaller and smaller subdivisions almost continuously," Jeremy says to the class before being interrupted by Jun.

"It's interesting to hear from an American about staying out of other countries' business," Jun interjects. "You constantly invade other countries and kill people in those countries under the pretense of protecting the rights of people inside the borders. Or perhaps you forget Korea, Vietnam, Iraq, Afghanistan, Grenada, Yemen, Libya, Bosnia, Armenia? Should I go on?"

"You are missing an important point, Jun," Jeremy says.

"I don't think so," Jun responds. "You've attacked more countries than any other nation in the past 100 years. What else can this be except imperial outreach?"

"Does that mean China invaded us as part of your imperial outreach? Are you planning to colonize our Southwest?" Jeremy says, face again turning bright red, hands firmly gripping the long table in front of his row of seats.

"I suggest no such thing, and am offended that you would even think such a thing of my nation," Jun says, waving his hand dismissively toward Jeremy and leaning back in his chair.

"Even so, what you're missing in listing the countries that the U.S. entered is that U.S. actions were to protect people from being killed by their own government or foreign invaders, sometimes, I might add, including your own country. There is no one suggesting that the U.S. government was bombing its own citizens or sending death squads out to kill political rivals. So the call for secession was entirely the ego trip of some politicians. The United Nations started a war on our land, and started killing people for political gain, not to protect people," Jeremy responds while folding the sleeves of his shirt up his forearm.

"I would remind you, Mr. Jeremy, that the United Nations only entered at the request of the legitimate government of the Republic of Alta Texas and its President," Jun adds, "as our government so clearly stated."

Jeremy stands over the desk in front of him, propped by both arms as he leans his lanky body toward Jun. "Legitimate. How can you even pretend Alta Texas is a legitimate government? The government is self-declared. If I find 10 people to make me their president, will the United Nations send its military to protect me and allow me to take land and life from other people?"

"Our government would only come to protect your people from racial hatred inside your own country," Jun responds. "You had the killings at your colleges in Texas, the assassination of the leader of Mexicans, riots in your own capital city. People have been dying because of their ethnic heritage, and the United Nations came to protect them from genocide."

For 10 minutes, the other students and Professor Stark watch this debate go back and forth, but with just 10 minutes left to go in class, Professor Stark interrupts to conclude the discussion.

It has been an unusual class, one in which Professor Stark thought the emotions of the day would keep students from contributing at the same high level he might normally expect. But having watched the intensity of the exchange between Jeremy, Jun and several other members of the class, he decides the best distraction he can offer is to keep his students focused on more work.

"I was going to give you until Thursday, but really, this is the kind of assignment where you either come up with a good idea, or you have no idea what to think. So 100-word papers are due in 21 hours. The subject: describe one critical concept necessary to win the peace. Assume the nation stays united. We'll discuss in class then," Professor Stark concludes.

As they walk out of the room, Tamika turns to Rachel: "Did you get all of that?"

"Yeah, right," Rachel responds. "Thank God this thing takes good notes," she adds as she holds up her Lifelink before inserting it back into its code-protected pocket.

***

Alta Texas Headquarters

Word of the U.S. troop massacre at Camp Navajo reaches Alta Texas President Manny Jones. He calls together all of the base invasion generals. Though five feet, eight inches tall, he stands towering above even the six foot, four inch tall Russian general. All of Manny's shoes have two-inch soles. His control platform is 12 inches above the rest of the floors. His deep, commanding voice captures the group's attention, aided by quickly flapping arms and pointed fingers.

Grabbing the shirt of Iran's general at his breast, he pulls the general forward, spewing saliva and phlegm with each word. "Who ordered you to kill all the U.S. troops at Navajo? Who?" President Jones yells between cigar puffs. "I know it sure as hell wasn't me."

Looking around at the other generals in the room, including General Ramírez from Mexico who is trying to take the coordinating role away from a defecting U.S. General, he continues to scream: "Did you order it? Did you order it? Did you order it?"

No one responds.

"Nobody ordered it, so how does this happen?" he continues, turning back to look down into the eyes of Iran's general, who is now reaching up to remove Manny's hand from his shirt.

"You give us a worthless base as our reward for giving you a country, and you think that gives you the right to yell at me," Iran's general barks back. Pushing away from President Jones, Iran's general sits down, sticking his feet up on a desk with the bottoms of his feet facing toward Jones.

"I know what you're doing," President Jones tells him. "I wasn't born yesterday."

"Then what makes you think war happens and people don't die?" Iran's general snaps back, his voice now slightly less elevated. "It happened. Get over it. If you want to win, you forget it and move forward."

"You don't get it," President Jones says. "I need the cooperation of my people to rule them. They must admire me for implementing their wishes."

"Stupid," Iran's general responds while waving his arms in the direction of Jones. "Just stupid."

President Jones throws everything on the table within reach at a nearby screen: "Are you calling me stupid?"

Iran's general stands back up and steps up on the command center platform to be eye-to-eye with President Jones: "Fear and power, Mr. President. That's what you need to rule. General Hernández understands this. Perhaps he needs to be here if we want to have any chance of winning."

***

Washington, D.C.

Inside the DUCC, President Phillipi turns to Chief of Staff Chinh. The President is barely able to keep his eyes open, with sleep having only come in 20 and 30 minutes stretches between important decisions. His chin rests inside his left hand with his elbow planted on the table to keep both hand and chin elevated. Whiskers prick the flesh between his thumb and index finger. Wrinkles around the sides of his eyes have deepened in recent days, spreading out like spokes. Forehead furrows appear permanently imprinted.

"You don't think I'll be known for presiding over the end of the United States as we know it, do you?" President Phillipi asks his long-time aide. His eyes are watery as he simultaneously contemplates the thought and fights exhaustion.

"It's not going to happen, Mr. President. You'll put this back together," Chinh responds. "We'll both do whatever it takes to make sure history honors you."

President Phillipi stands up and looks toward a wall, his face out of sight of everyone in the command center. Chinh watches him pull out a handkerchief from his pants pocket and dab at his eyes. After a few moments, Vijay Chinh decides to leave the President to his thoughts and perhaps some rest. He turns the lights off as he walks out.

***

Traver, California

Victor Cruz and other prisoners being held in Traver, California are brought together and asked to listen to an announcement from the makeshift jail's warden.

"I'd like to introduce you all to Sergeant Henry Ruiz of the North California National Guard," the warden says. "Those of you who are U.S. citizens living in North California who wish to be enlisted in the National Guard can be released immediately into the care of Sergeant Ruiz for transportation to your first official duties as temporary members of the National Guard."

A sizable group of prisoners try to shout down Sergeant Ruiz, led by the number of prisoners neither interested in joining the National Guard nor in becoming U.S. citizens. Because of the noise made by jeering prisoners, Sergeant Ruiz loudly and repetitively yells for those interested in joining the National Guard to approach. Almost one-quarter of the prisoners step forward, including Victor Cruz who sees this as his chance to defend his family.

The smaller group is pulled near a door and escorted out. Guards fire warning shots into the ceiling to get prisoners running to escape through the door pushed back. The National Guard group is taken outside under guard as Sergeant Ruiz explains the terms of the enlistment.

"Are we going to get to fight to defend our families if we're invaded?" Victor asks.

"While anything is possible, what we need are people who can support the supply chain behind the troops so our best-trained soldiers can go to the front line. We need drivers, cooks, mechanics, and just about every other skill. Since none of you have been through boot camp, and half of you wouldn't be able to pass a physical for entrance, we'll keep you where you can do the most good and put yourself and your unit at the least risk," Sergeant Ruiz tells the group.

"I can shoot a whole lot better than 90 percent of your men, I bet," Victor states. "I know how to use my weapons."

"Understood mister, but we have to put you where we need you. If that isn't acceptable, you can head back inside. If that works for you, sign these papers and you can load onto the bus," the sergeant says.

A few minutes later, Victor Cruz boards the bus.

Having received the message that she could bring food, Mrs. Cruz arrives at the Traver temporary prison a short time later with a thin plastic container of chile rellenos, deep-fried taquitos stuffed with shredded goat, Cotija cheese and diced jalapeños, and homemade salsa verde. She isn't much for cooking, and particularly is still taken aback at cooking goat. But Mrs. Cruz decided to make the special birthday dinner Victor used to request when they first married to remind Victor why he needs to come home.

Arriving at the gate, she waits in the long line for her turn to meet with her husband and deliver food to him. More than 90 minutes later, a guard takes her name and the name of the person she is here to visit.

"He's not here anymore ma'am," the guard informs her.

"What do you mean? Where did you take him?" she asks angrily.

"We didn't take him nowhere ma'am, if you would just calm down," the guard says. "He enlisted."

"Enlisted in what?"

"The Army or something like that," the guard responds, and Mrs. Cruz starts to walk away. "Hey, ma'am, if you could leave that food, there's a lot of hungry, angry people inside. It would be nice of you."

"Yes, it would," she says, still walking away a few steps. Turning around back to the guard, she hands the container to him. "Yes it would," she says more quietly to herself.

Walking back outside the gate to the family's car, she mutters: "The next meal that bastard gets from me is going to be poisoned anyway."

CHAPTER 15

30 Hours

Washington, D.C.

Homeland Security Secretary Ray Peyton had planned to leave tomorrow for St. Lucia. Soon after landing, Ray and his wife expected to head for waters connecting the Caribbean Sea and Atlantic Ocean. Instead, with the secession attempt underway and a sensitive investigation into Manny Jones under Peyton's direct command, President Phillipi withdrew approval of Peyton's resignation.

A retired Air Force General, Peyton had hoped to be named Secretary of Defense in a second Phillipi administration. He and Defense Secretary Xavier Mendoza, a former FBI director, battled over turf continuously through Phillipi's first four years. The President would have kept both on in their current roles despite child-like disputes he had to settle between the two. Peyton wasn't interested. He told the President he would retire post-inauguration unless he was named Secretary of Defense. With his resignation now rejected, Peyton is reengaged knowing his Homeland Security role is one of the nation's most visible and critical. Trying to discredit former Senator Jones is only one of his tasks. FBI investigators working in direct contact with Peyton have now developed a breakthrough in the months-long investigation of Jones and his role in the U.N. "peace-keeping invasion," as Peyton sometimes refers to inaugural night actions.

With President Phillipi ensconced in the DUCC Situation Room, Peyton, Chief of Staff Chinh and Attorney General Cooke gather in a side room to wait for the President to join them.

"Okay Ray, what have you found?" the President asks after taking a seat.

"We spent the last 36 hours using supercomputers to match Easy Ride location data to satellite visual references. We've done this to track suspects in the past and have sometimes been lucky to provide evidence for convictions and identify locations where bodies might be dumped," Peyton begins.

"I don't need the history, Ray. Just tell me anything actionable," the President orders, his patience now completely eroded with events of the past two days.

"Yes, sir. One path we explored was vehicle movement around the mall on the days we saw Jones heading there with his electronics off," Peyton says.

"Get to the point Ray."

"I'm getting to the damn point, Mr. President, but the context I'm giving is critical to your understanding whether it's usable. If you don't like my work, just say the word and I'll be happy to retire," Peyton snaps.

President Phillipi clasps his hands behind the back of his head and squeezes, trying to control his reaction. Everyone in the room grows uncomfortable.

"I understand the urgency, Mr. President. There really is a point to this," Peyton continues, realizing his initial reaction was overblown and measuring his voice more carefully.

"Get on with it then."

"We tracked all the cars in and out of the mall on days Senator Jones was sick. The travels of all except two of those cars matched with Easy Ride data, and none of the Easy Ride cars went anywhere near New York. Thirty minutes before Senator Jones arrived and parked underground at the mall, an off-grid car pulled into the same below-deck parking lot. After Manny left to go home, we tracked that car through historic satellite data all the way to the East Side of Manhattan, where it parked in an underground garage with multiple street-level exits."

"You think Manny could have driven that car?"

"That was the suspicion, so we checked security recordings. Interestingly, security cameras in that deck had mysteriously been disconnected the day prior and video feeds looped of old car and people movements. This wasn't discovered until the next Sunday, when a guard noticed an incredible number of cars still in the garage after Sunday close and went to see what was going on."

"So do we have video of Manny in either place? Can we connect him to the U.N. before the Security Council vote?" the President asks while gnawing at a vegetable tray brought in to help get his upset stomach under control.

"We found ground-level cameras along the path between Manny's home and the mall. Despite the heavy covering with the hoodie, sunglasses and thick, high-neck sweater, we were able to do facial analysis proving definitively that different people drove the car to and from the mall that morning and to and from the mall in the middle of the night. The person driving to the mall in the morning is likely the same person as drove the car home that night. Our facial recognition program has determined that the features are consistent with that of Senator Jones."

"So, who's the other face?"

"I'll get there in a minute. We know that he drove to Manny's home, likely sat in the home out of view all day, and then drove the car back to the mall that night dressed identically, but without the sunglasses."

"Even without the sunglasses, we haven't identified this guy?"

"Not yet, but we're working on it."

"So you came here to tell me you're working on it."

"No, Mr. President. I came here to tell you that we have tracked the off-grid car from the mall to New York City and have placed Manny in New York City. From two of the 48 cameras between where he and the man who drove him to New York parked, we have positive facial recognition of a man in a suit with an umbrella even though it was not raining at the time. We then checked satellite data again, and found an umbrella of the same shape and size tracking on streets between where he parked and entering the United Nations building."

"That son of a bitch. He played chess on a 3D board while we were playing 1D checkers," the President states.

"Our next step, Mr. President, would be to arrest the United Nations security guards, since we're not in the U.N. anymore, and interrogate them to confirm that they saw Senator Jones," Secretary Peyton says.

"What do you think Betty? I'm not worried about making a treason charge stick. I just need enough to show the people in Texas, Arizona, New Mexico and South California that Manny conspired with the United Nations all along to control them. Peacekeeping is the pretense, but the U.N. is effectively holding the Southwest in military occupation."

"There's enough here to convince me, but I'd sure like to know who drove Jones to New York and why we haven't found them," Attorney General Cooke says.

"Well, there, I think we have the other breakthrough," Peyton interjects. "We were able to gather a lot of facial recognition data on the guy who drove Manny to New York from highway, tunnel and other neighborhood cameras along the way. And here's the best news. A person with identical features turned up in the area of the Harvard Massacre just an hour before it started."

"I thought we determined that Castillo's military wing staged Harvard," the President says.

"We did, and they did. And Manny's driver, whoever he is, was part of it," Peyton says.

"What an arrogant little snake. God, I wish we knew this a week ago," the President says. "Now, with the secession, it could look like we made this all up."

As he stands up and paces around the room, he blurts out, "Better late than never. I need this cleaned up enough that we can get the friendliest of the peacekeeping countries to pull out. Vijay, I want the ambassadors from these 23 countries here in 90 minutes. We'll have to go up to the briefing room for that meeting. Any reason to believe we can't keep security extra tight while we're up there?"

"No reason," Secretary Mendoza responds. "We're down here as a precaution."

"Yes, sir," Chinh adds. "We'll get the ambassadors."

"Betty and Ray, get the presentation nailed tight. We'll take this to our allies and just a couple of key base invaders first. If they can see that they've been set up and their leadership will be humiliated at home for putting their armed forces lives at stake for a terrorist psychopath and a drug lord, we can get them to pull their troops out and destroy the coalition. We'll start tightening the noose around Jones until he turns blue or his neck snaps."

"What about telling the public?" Chinh asks.

"We'll keep that for later," the President says. "I think we can get China, Germany, Brazil, and many of the others to start turning their tanks and aircraft around and heading home. If we can get the big boys out, they might even leave us a few enemy countries we can weaken militarily on their way out."

"Since we've tied this now to Castillo, can we connect it to President Suárez?" Attorney General Cooke asks of Secretary Peyton.

"We don't have a connection made there yet, but we'll look into that next. Unfortunately, we can't ask Castillo anymore, though I doubt we could have gotten him to talk anyway."

"That reminds me," the President says, looking to Chinh. "Where are we on retribution for the White Settlement massacre?"

"The what?" Chinh asks.

"The parking lot trucks."

"What do you mean where are we?"

"Get Xavier on the line."

A few minutes later, Secretary Mendoza is back displayed on the screen in the DUCC command center. "Mr. President," he says when the President looks at him on the screen.

"Do we have an assault planned yet on the Castillo cartel, and what is my role in the assault?" President Phillipi asks.

"Mr. President, we will plan assault options, but your role sir is to manage the U.S. war against the entirety of the United Nations, not go off on a small retribution mission," Secretary Mendoza says. "Besides, we don't even have a plan in place yet that we can execute. Keep in mind that all their best sites are behind enemy lines."

Secretary Mendoza asks if the President is done with him for now. After getting the okay, he signs off saying, "If you keep asking me about going into battle, Marc, I'm going to have to leak your plans to the First Lady."

"I'd consider that a national security breach, Xavier."

***

Utah New Rite Compound

Fourteen-year-old Clarissa Coleman sits on a rock inset behind a boulder shielding her from continuing, cold air bursts. It's her turn again to watch for troops crossing the water from Arizona. She's particularly watchful knowing U.N. troops could have tracked the U.S. troops who escaped through here less than 24 hours earlier. Though cool, the early night sky is clear. It's remarkable how much brighter the stars are here, when not hidden behind an excess of street and building lights. Clarissa searches for the Big Dipper, Orion and the other stars she had learned can orient her when lost at night, though she doesn't remember how they are supposed to tell her what direction to go.

Clarissa is paying now for her thin frame, feeling the cold more sharply than she might with a little extra weight. Though layered up with her bodysuit and much of the clothing she brought to the remote watch site, her hands, feet, nose and eyes feel the brunt of the chilly night. When the cold becomes too much, Clarissa moves behind the boulder and paces in a circle, keeping her eyes trained along the edge of the water.

The quiet is remarkable, with little to hear over the sound of the wind pushing between tight rock spaces. Checking the clock on her Lifelink, she realizes she has two more hours to go before being relieved. Lying on the ground now, she does a few sit-ups, then 20 push-ups, all being sure not to lose sight of the horizon. Mentally, she walks through what to do if she sees a high-speed attack, something different than the soldiers who slowly floated across.

Once she signals an alert, a real military force with evil intent will know she's here and come after her. There's no way she's giving herself up, not after her father told her what would likely happen to her. So she thinks through the steps to take. Turn Lifelink off. Get around the corner to escape line of sight from the water. She estimates she can move 500 yards farther from the water line before someone could see her again. Racing to the water line and hiding in the covered small cove she and her dad hid in earlier won't work if an attack comes across the water at high speed. There's not enough time to get there unseen. During daylight, Clarissa identified four reachable rock crevices she can fit into without easily being spotted. She has enough water, and some food, to hide for a couple of days if needed.

"Clarissa," comes a whispered voice.

She jumps to alert, quickly scans toward the water, and then realizes the voice is coming at her from behind. Turning sharply, she jumps toward the boulder to grab the hiking stick. She triggers open the switchblade.

"It's me," the voice adds.

"Dad?"

"Oh my God. How did you sneak up on me without me hearing you?" she asks in quiet voice.

"I did learn a little from the training here," her father responds. "Clarissa, I have terrible news." John's voice shakes as he speaks.

"What?"

"Grandpa's dead," John says in halting, broken tones. "Killed by the police."

Despite all her normal strength, Clarissa was nowhere near prepared for this news. She starts to scream as she cries, before catching herself. Her wail sounds like a jackrabbit as a coyote takes its first bite, piercing the sky with the tormented sound of death. Hearing her scream, the few small animals searching for food in the night scramble for cover.

John holds his daughter's face to his shoulder, feeling the cold as he tries to comfort her. Quickly, his jacket accumulates moisture. Her body convulses as she tries to hold in both anger and sorrow. Her convulsions slowly relax, until many minutes later she composes herself enough to ask.

"Killed?"

"Sounds like it. The police started confiscating everyone's weapons. You know Grandpa and his guns. He wasn't about to give away his weapons while the country is under attack," John says, also tearing up again at both the loss of his father and, perhaps more so, the pain in his daughter's eyes.

"The only thing that makes it easier for me is knowing he went the way he would have wanted to go."

"So, are we going home now?" Clarissa asks.

"What do you think we should do?" John asks his daughter.

"Grandpa was a fighter. Don't you think he'd rather we stayed?"

"Yeah, I do. I think that's what he would want," John responds, voice still cracking.

"I'll take out whoever did this when we get back," Clarissa says.

"No you won't. It's my score to settle, if any settling needs to be done. If this was intentional, I'll figure out how to deal with it," John says.

"If you kill a cop, you'll end up spending the rest of your life in jail," Clarissa mentions.

"Says the hothead," John responds pointedly to his daughter. "Besides, it may not be the people who killed him who are really responsible for why Grandpa is dead. Okay? You're freezing cold. You need to head back to camp and get warmed up and get some sleep. I'll take the rest of your shift."

After they stand up and hug, Clarissa takes one more look over the water before turning and starting the walk back to camp. The stars are bright enough tonight to light her path, but watery eyes distort her vision. One hundred yards away from where she left her father, Clarissa turns and looks back at him, standing and staring toward the water. Turning back, she looks up to the stars.

Picking out the North Star, she stops and stares. "I love you Grandpa," Clarissa chokingly whispers.

Walking quietly the rest of the way, watching her step carefully, Clarissa listens intently to the sounds of the night. "He can live in this peace every night now," she says to comfort herself.

***

Alta Texas

The 24-hour news channels have globally shared more than two billion viewers at any moment since the Alta Texas crisis started. RNN, the Republican Party-owned news network, headlines its broadcasts as "Global

Invasion." Al Jazeera, CCTV and many global outlets use variations of "Preventing Genocide" as the moniker for their crisis coverage.

The secession effort twists.

Germany is the first United Nations troop contributor to announce it is pulling out from the peacekeeping mission. Germany's Chancellor cites evidence provided by the U.S. government that the widespread public support in Alta Texas for secession resulted from a carefully orchestrated campaign of violence and misinformation led by Alta Texas President Manny Jones and aided by the Castillo drug cartel. The Chancellor also cites Germany's belief – based on evidence provided by the U.S. government – that pro-secession referenda voting had been illegally inflated. When asked, the Chancellor refuses to add more detail behind this charge.

With only 2,000 troops in Texas, all sent to cities for what they believed was keeping peace, withdrawal of Germany's troops can be quickly accomplished. Germany's drop from the U.N. mission is more symbolic than tangible in impact. Seeing the news announcement, though, sends Alta Texas President Manny Jones into a tirade.

"How dare they abandon us, based on White House lies and without even the decency to secure agreement in advance," he says to everyone and no one inside the Alta Texas command center. He turns to General Ramírez, the highly skilled leader of Mexico's official military. General Ramírez has been successful at running Mexico's main military branch while avoiding involvement with the Protection Corps. "We can't let troops defect without punishment. Capture the Germans and try them for treason," President Jones orders.

"Mr. President. We can't possibly try the Germans for treason. They're here with the U.N. peacekeeping mission and have no sworn loyalty to Alta Texas," General Ramírez responds.

"We're only two days in and already you're challenging my orders," President Jones responds.

"Sir, it's my duty, from my President, to give you my best advice. My best advice is that if we don't let the Germans leave, we'll have Germany put troops on the other side of the border," General Ramírez says. "If, after hearing and understanding this, you decide that your order stands, we

will carry it out, but I tell you that such action carries with it grave consequences for the survival of your new country and perhaps that of my own."

President Jones puts his head down in his hands. Physically and mentally, he is already thoroughly exhausted and he has only been in this job
two days. "What was I thinking?" he asks quietly, but audibly, pulling out
another cigarette, lighting it up and drawing deeply on his first puffs.

"So you withdraw the order, sir?"

***

Washington, D.C.

Congresswoman Jill Carlson is stunned to hear that Germany, Poland,
Brazil and Costa Rica are pulling their modest peacekeeping troops out of
the Alta Texas states, and that many other nations are considering doing the
same. Working her contacts, Jill finally gets through to Attorney General
Cooke, with whom she has built a good relationship through Judiciary
Committee work.

"Betty, I need to know what is getting our allies to back out. Whatever
it is, if there's something I can use to try getting Juan Gonzalez to publicly
disavow this regime, he can further turn the tide against Manny and his
allies. But we'll need to get him the message, and then get him out to have
it do any good," Jill says during a quick, secure phone call.

"We aren't releasing anything publicly yet, so I need clearance because
it's been designated top secret. But I will tell you that these aren't the only
countries who know what we've found, so if you have good relationships
with any ambassadors from friendly countries, you might learn something
quicker that way," Cooke says.

"I appreciate this. But if I can get the message in, do we have any way
to extract Juan?"

"I don't, but I'll talk to the men who know if it's possible and get back
to you," Cooke tells Jill.

CHAPTER 16

24 Hours

Washington, D.C.

After several calls, Indiana Congresswoman Jill Carlson thinks she understands what initiated a steady stream of departures from the U.N. coalition. She needs to get a message to Juan, and soon. She's sure he doesn't know what really spurred the secession referenda victories and doesn't want a promising life destroyed by naiveté and youthful enthusiasm.

Though it's midnight in D.C., she calls Professor Stark to brainstorm.

"Paul, it's Jill."

"Jill, you're the only woman who calls me late at night, though I guess there is the rare exception of a panicked undergrad the night before a test. How are you holding up?"

"Fine, but I need your help."

"Anything."

"I need to get a message to Juan. Any ideas how we might get it to him?" Jill asks.

"What about posting a message on your One World site?"

"Thought of that. Too high risk. For the message to be effective, it would have to disclose Top Secret information."

"Well, that's certainly a challenge."

"I know. That's why I called."

"I don't know if it will work, but do you remember Rachel?" Professor Stark asks.

"Sure, the Fresno girl. Very smart, beautiful smile. And we talked with her just two days ago if you remember. She's definitely having a rough time, with her father and all."

"That's her."

"What about her?"

"She has had a relationship with Juan since our dinner at Tamika's house last fall, a fairly intense one at least in terms of time since they haven't actually seen each other in person since. But they were talking for an hour every day."

"Has she talked to him since this started?" Jill asks.

"She did before the secession was launched, but not since he talked to, uhm, you know," Professor Stark responds, realizing as he was speaking that he and Jill are not on a secure line.

"Well, then how can she get a message to him?"

"I'm not sure she can, but just because he can't get messages out to people doesn't mean he isn't able to see them. I would think it crazy to have someone you expect to be an ambassador held back from access to information he'll need to do the job."

"Okay, so what do you suggest?" Jill asks.

"Let's ask Rachel to post a message."

"That would be tough. Someone's bound to see it and then the secret is out. As far as I know, we could put lives at risk breaking confidentiality on this," Jill says.

"Then the message needs to be cryptic enough to get him to search for something more, not enough that anyone else can figure it out," Professor Stark responds. "So what should it say?"

"What do you think?" Jill asks. She starts to lean back, but catches herself when she realizes she has replaced her chair with a large exercise ball as the current seat of choice.

"Hard for me to do this. I don't know the secret you're trying to convey."

"Good point. Let me work on it and get back to you. Call Rachel and ask her if she's willing to do it. I'll call back when I have the message figured out."

"Will do. One last thought. Think about writing it to play to his insecurities."

"What do you mean?" Jill asks.

"I mean. We all have insecurities – things we're worried others will find out about us or we'll have to admit about ourselves," Professor Stark states. "Can you write the message in a way that addresses these insecurities; that helps him understand that what you want him to do is what he should want to do?"

"I'm still not sure I get what you're saying," Jill says.

"I know. I'm not being very clear. Put it this way: Each of us has attributes or skills that matter to us, as well as deficiencies we live with but aren't happy about. God shorts each of us on some attributes, but everyone has strengths. Some people are so obsessed with what they don't have that they fail to recognize, appreciate and take advantage of their strengths. Juan is young enough that, even with his outward confidence, he's bound to have insecurities – perhaps about failing his mother or maybe even that, as smart as he is, maybe he's being outsmarted for the first time," Professor Stark says. "And he might be worried now about disappointing Rachel."

"I get your point. I need to move fast."

Jill locks the closed doors to her office from the hall and the adjoining staff office. She turns off all of her electronic communicators and pulls out paper and pencil. She won't type this anywhere that Rachel's message could be traced back to her. Jill reminds herself to tell Paul to do the same.

She starts writing, putting parentheses around parts of the note she isn't sure are appropriate: "To the one I (love/care about). In the months we have spoken, you have made my world a better, happier place. I've been honest with you and shared everything about me, including my feelings (maybe that this connection is something more than a friendship). Not everyone in your life has been honest with you, particularly since your last flight. Please find a way to talk with the box-ing lady before it's too late for us to be together. She knows more than you can imagine and everything you need to be with me and pursue your dream peacefully."

After stewing about the words for 20 minutes, Jill calls back to Professor Stark with her proposed language. She asks him to write it down on paper that he can burn after reading it to Rachel. As she dictates, he writes until he completes it and reads its back to her.

"So you're the boxing lady now?" Professor Stark asks.

"Do you have any better ideas? I was trying to come up with something unique that only Juan would understand."

"I'm not sure I understand."

"You know, when you put us both in moving boxes to bring us into your house from your garage, just in case the house was being watched after we helped Juan escape."

"Oh. I didn't get that from boxing. I was thinking someone who's a fighter."

"How about if it just says box lady? It would be a stretch for anyone to figure that out other than Juan."

"Yeah, but remember my class sessions were livecast. Someone doing a search for box and Juan might get to that class session and figure it out," Professor Stark says.

"Can you pull that class session and transcript down?"

"I can, but I'll search to see if it showed up somewhere else."

"You know what, we have to take the risk. Time is running too short," Jill says.

"Consider it done. Rachel is happy to help. Is it okay if she modifies it to make it more personal?" Professor Stark asks.

"Sure. She can't give away a secret she doesn't know."

Rachel rewrites part of the message and posts it on her One World site, now the world's largest global social media platform.

"Knowing you has made my world a better, happier place, a world where I can see a future with you that is filled with joy. You will always have my total honesty, no matter the circumstances. I wish everyone in your life would be as honest with you as I am, because the dishonesty of others may cost us our future. Please call your favorite "box" lady before it's too late. People are using you. I love you and long to be with you. Please do what is right and come be with me."

***

Back in the DUCC, President Phillipi reconvenes his national emergency leadership team to draw out plans for attacking TQ. TQ is the code name given to the Monterrey, Mexico base believed to be Alta Texas and U.N. military headquarters.

Defense Secretary Mendoza is beginning to show the physical strains of the U.N. response action. He had already been up nearly 18 hours when the invasion was first launched during the President's inaugural ball. In the more than two days since then, he has slept just three hours. The skin under his eyes has sagged and darkened more than usual. His caffeine levels are now so high that his body visibly shakes from combined caffeine and exhaustion distress. With some countries dropping out of the U.N. coalition, his brief sense of relief is enough to remind him that his body can't take much more. Good news of progress toward a solution brings with it a drop in the adrenaline that helped keep him charged. But Secretary Mendoza knows the stakes and realizes any misstep or failure to act can results in thousands, millions and even tens of millions losing their lives.

"After this, you need to get three or four hours sleep, or your body and mind aren't going to cooperate," Homeland Secretary Ray Peyton says to Mendoza, putting his arm on his shoulder in an act of friendship the two hadn't shared in recent years. "I know the temptation is to put this all on yourself, Xavier, but you need to explain what you want to your team and trust them to deliver. You've got good people there. It's not like we know this ends tomorrow. It could just as easily intensify and you need to be alert if it does."

Mendoza nods his head to acknowledge he agrees. Perhaps Peyton was comfortable with no longer competing, since he now wanted to retire.

While pleased with progress in getting U.N. coalition countries to withdraw support for Alta Texas, President Phillipi still considers military action to take out its leadership. Mendoza, Peyton, CIA Director Rand, Vice President Wilt and Chief of Staff Chinh are the decision-making principals joining the President in the room.

"The U.N. coalition behind Jones is collapsing, so anything we do on TQ needs to be done now from the context of not reversing that progress," the President starts. "So that's the new ground rules. What do we have, Xavier?"

The screens around the room project a three-dimensional image of the TQ compound, with rooms, guards and protective weapons clearly displayed. Satellite images from earlier that day confirm a substantial ground force. A comparison of the location from days earlier shows new missile and air defense weapons installed at TQ.

"To get into the buildings, we need a full-scale assault and the element of surprise. We need to jam radar and other detection technology and shut down Mexican and U.N. communication channels for a 20-minute window. In minute one, communication jam starts. In minutes two and three, ship-based missiles take out the site's airborne defense systems, here, here, here and here," Mendoza says, pointing to the four primary missile defense sites. Mendoza points out that they would triple up on missiles at each site in case the U.N.'s new missile defense weapons catch several inbound shots. "There is a two-minute gap then with people on the ground believing nothing is happening, giving time for any follow-on explosions to settle before our attack chopper teams enter. The first two are New Rite APBs, with mixed New Rite and special ops teams on board. As far as we know, TQ won't know these are coming until they physically see them. New Rite drops in the extraction team and then the full-scale assault takes place."

Several express concerns that missile launches will be spotted early, attracting an immediate retaliatory strike inside the 48 states, or perhaps at bases in Alta Texas.

Mendoza walks through the schematics showing which choppers will land where, and which entrances will be attacked. He also goes through the base interior schematic, outlining expected battle points and the likely location of the Alta Texas leadership for extraction or execution.

"Casualties?" the President asks.

"If all goes well, best estimates are 500 to 2,500 on their side and one hundred or more of our men and women," Mendoza says. "That is if we can take out their missile and air defenses before the attack force goes in."

"Why the disparity?"

"Even with our missiles, we still gain an element of surprise and I believe a substantial first mover's advantage, just as they had when they attacked our bases. New Rite has some weaponry the other side hasn't seen, even when they chased it," Mendoza says. "Every bit of advantage helps. But, I need to be clear, we could lose everybody."

"Likelihood of success?"

"Seventy percent chance up to the extraction point. Less than 50/50 on getting the leadership out or eliminated before we have to get out."

"Explain."

"We estimate, even with communication jamming, that we have a total window of 20 minutes before we must be airborne to get our teams home. New Rite's APBs might be able to escape a fighter jet scramble, but once jets are on our tails, the rest of our forces don't stand much chance. We need to be near the U.S. border where we can provide air support before they reach us."

"How confident are you in your ability to jam communications?"

"I wouldn't bet the lives of the teams unless we were confident."

"Okay, get the teams ready to go. We'll want to go before the end of 72 hours. They'll be even more alert after that window," the President states.

***

Spring Valley, Illinois

Chet Leach, back in place with full operating authority as president of FirstWal in the United States, finishes typing an angry message to his leadership team and store managers. He sends it as soon as he finishes, without anyone else reviewing. When he selects the privacy key on his messages, they disappear from FirstWal's system four hours after he hits send.

"By now, it must be clear how disappointed I am in leadership's response to my directives. This conflict gave us an unprecedented opportunity to hit our numbers. With 48 hours behind us, no Alta Texas store has implemented the mandated price changes on essential items, and only 20 percent of our other stores are complying with my direct order. I know I gave everyone authority to find alternate ways to reach my targets. Perhaps this is too much freedom, because I see nothing in the daily numbers suggesting freedom is being used wisely," Chet writes in his message. "If I don't see progress in 24 hours, it's clear that I will need to start making leadership changes."

Mike Sanchez, long-time manager of the West Nogales, Arizona store, is awakened by the alert that accompanies every message from Chet. He had been delighted when Chet's replacement had cancelled the automatic alert response requirement. Now that Chet has been given full control again, the stress on everyone in the organization is ratcheting up.

Mike turns on his personal Lifelink camera and takes a picture of Chet's message displayed on his work device. Mike is certain he is one of the first targets in Chet's crosshairs, having already angered Chet when the West Nogales store was the site of a well-publicized protest against Chet's English-only policy. Calling one of his assistant managers at home – using a secure radio communication system that only works between store-assigned phones – Mike predicts what will happen.

"Lorena, this is Mike. I just received a message from HQ angry that we haven't jacked up prices in line with their orders and saying that heads will roll tomorrow if he doesn't see progress," Mike says.

"What can we do? If we raise prices, we violate terms of martial law and get arrested, or really have our heads roll. How stupid are they?" Lorena responds.

"I pointed that out when he sent his first edict, so he gave us the flexibility to meet his doubled financial target whatever other way we could make it happen," Mike says. "Can you think of anything else we can do, short of busing people in to drive up our volume?"

"We can't organize anything like that with all the troops running around here. Can you imagine them letting buses run around the neighborhoods?" Lorena says.

"I know. It wouldn't be safe," Mike responds.

"Hey, maybe we can get the government to force people to shop here," Lorena suggests, intending to be sarcastic.

"That might be our only hope. Is there any way to make that happen?"

"I was just joking," Lorena responds. "Does it really make sense to have the government tell people where to shop and what to buy?"

"I'm not worried about what makes sense right now," Mike says to Lorena. "I'm just trying to figure out how to keep my job and feed my family."

"Seriously, Mike, do you know how angry people would be if they found out we actually got the government to do this?"

"Maybe, but companies, unions, Wall Street, lawyers, political parties all get the government to do their bidding all the time. People rarely find out, and even more rarely get even. But you're right that it's wrong," Mike says, a dejected tone softening his last few words. "Well, then let me be the first to congratulate you on being the new manager of the West Nogales store."

"What do you mean?"

"I mean, I'll be fired tomorrow and you'll be the new manager with specific instructions on what Chet Leach wants you to do to increase profits. God help you if you listen to him," Mike says, before saying goodnight to Lorena.

"Don't worry, Mike," Lorena says before he hangs up. "We won't let you take the fall."

***

Alta Texas Headquarters

As midnight approaches, Juan Gonzalez faces another sleepless night. His detachment from everything he knows and exclusion from the key decisions of the Republic of Alta Texas government is clarifying for him how little this new government represents the ideals he dedicated himself to over the past year.

Juan, and several others in adjacent rooms, are being confined and kept from communicating with friends and family to protect the security of their location. Recognizing that he has no way left to communicate with anyone outside this compound, Juan schemes to get himself into the command center with President Jones to gain access to an outbound communication device. After spending 15 minutes convincing his guard that President Jones will want to hear from him, he is escorted to the war room, patted down, screened, and then allowed to enter.

"Mr. President," Juan says, after getting the attention of President Jones. "We're 24 hours away from the deadline President Phillipi set to resolve this. I think we need to issue a statement expressing our confidence that President Phillipi will show wisdom in not causing the deaths of millions of people by invading a U.N.-protected country."

"Fine idea Juan. Write something and let me look at it before we issue it."

"Can I use a regular computer? We want to get this out and I don't know how to hand write quickly," Juan says.

"He's our ambassador to the United States," President Jones tells the guard. "Get him access to a trace-protected computer."

Convincing the guard to provide him access to a fully enabled computer takes some doing, but the guard understands now that Juan will be a high-level government official in the new country. With the access, Juan does a series of additional searches for official government statements from various countries, all with the guard pacing around him, watching to make sure he doesn't do anything that endangers site security.

He mumbles to himself, loud enough for the guard to hear, that he needs to hear what average citizens think to know how to position the statement. As the guard watches, he types, "Alta Texas student stark reality" into the search and clicks through to discussions from Professor Stark's class. From there, he scrolls to One World writings of Jun Chen, and realizes quickly that the wording Jun has posted in English is simply a translation of official Chinese government statements. "I guess all that Mandarin study had some use," he mumbles to himself, as the guard turns his attention away.

Finally, with the guard distracted, Juan decides he has checked enough other sites to see what Rachel has posted. Her last message is clear to him.

Seeing "respect and admire and maybe even love" brings a smile to his face. But that adrenaline rush dissipates as he hears Rachel's question, a question he is sure is directed right at him. *"How many people must suffer so I can take a shortcut to Mama's dreams?"* he mumbles audibly in Mandarin, though even the guard is ignoring him now. *"Lies? What lies? How am I supposed to get in touch with her?"*

With the guard turning back toward him, Juan types his proposed statement. Once the guard turns away again, he clicks back to Rachel's site and responds: "Understood. Being watched. Will check back here for comment from 'box' lady. May be only chance. I want to hold your hand again."

Rachel had set her Lifelink for loud alarm if there were any responses to her posting and she is awakened from a dull sleep. Checking quickly, she realizes it must be Juan from the handholding comment. She calls Professor Stark right away, who relays the message to Jill.

"Damn, we don't have time to get clearance. What can I say? I'll post a response on Rachel's One World site," Jill says as she shuts down her call with Professor Stark and opens her Lifelink. Clicking through to Rachel's site, she sees the note to Juan and types a response.

"Glad to hear of the love between you two. Need to know that fleeing nations know MJ's role in shootings, massacre and bombings. Public will all know at 8 your time and effort will collapse. Get out any way you can."

Ten minutes later, another anonymous posting on Rachel's site reads: "Can't. Confined and guarded in deep basement utility room!"

***

Washington, D.C.

The U.S. Capitol complex is completely locked down. For 36 hours, a one-mile perimeter has been barricaded at street level and Metro subway trains have been prevented from going underground near the Capitol, the White House and other federal buildings. Capitol police have swept all the buildings for bombs and reduced the personnel allowed inside Capitol buildings to essential staff. Most of Jill's staff works from home to respond to panicked constituent outreach. Jill holds videoconferences with her team every few hours to guide her team on constituent response. For the most part, understanding their fears and relaying publicly available information are all the staff can do.

It's good Jill only has one staffer in the office with her, because the FBI and military have teams embedded now in her office. Confidentiality remains a critical concern. Despite worries she may have breached security, Jill shares her latest exchange with Juan with the FBI agents. She can't worry about risks she took contacting him. Quick database searches show that only one device that connected to Rachel's One World site also connected to several of her classmate's sites and to the classroom discussion on secession. That same computer also searched for official Chinese government pronouncements, and did so using Mandarin.

"That's either Juan or the kid in the class from China," Jill tells the FBI after they tell her about the connection. "Juan is pretty fluent in Mandarin for a non-native."

"We'll check it out," they tell her.

As the discussion with Jill ends, a message is relayed directly to Secretary Mendoza. He confers briefly with President Phillipi, gets his orders, and calls JT Alton into the small war room they are using to stay in contact with the New Rite team.

"Here's the plan, JT," he says as JT walks toward him. "We have a bead on the Gonzalez kid. The President and I are convinced that if he can be extracted, he could help shut down this movement with limited further bloodshed and then help rebuild damaged relationships. Given what we saw with your Castillo operation, we think your team has the best chance of getting in and out and bringing him in alive. Your APB escaped 100 scrambled jets so they clearly can't track you unless they see you. Can you get your birds in the air and work with my extraction team."

"How badly pulled apart is the one you took from us?" JT asks.

"All back together, in working order and on-site with your team in Colorado. We just need your pilot and our teams to do the extraction."

"With all due respect, I can't do that sir," JT responds. "We don't have time to train them together, so we need the team to be in place to give them a chance of getting out. Let's talk to my team and see what they need."

Secretary Mendoza and JT open a video call with the New Rite team and walk through the draft plan. Secretary Mendoza informs the New Rite team that Juan is being held at a military base in Monterrey, Mexico. A CIA team sent last fall as civilians to Monterrey will serve as on-ground eyes. The New Rite APBs will lead the insertion, be supported by a full-scale attack, and return to extract Juan and any survivors of the Alta Texas leadership.

"Castillo had a tunnel that started outside McAllen, Texas. We know the manufacturing plant 15 miles in on the other side that served as Castillo's warehouse that appears completely unguarded at the moment," JT says, referencing data confirmed by New Rite's border drones disguised as Cooper's hawks. "He's used that tunnel only minimally in recent years, so can it be taken and used as a staging point?"

"That still leaves us 125 miles from target," Ally calculates. "We're looking at six to seven minutes just to get there. Then what? We fly over the base, pull him up and take off without any eyes on us? We're invisible to electronics, not to the human eye from close range. Our gecko-skin needs to be fully enabled to hide, and even then we need to be some distance away for it to work. We need a different approach."

"I have a half-dozen teams in the TQ neighborhood. They can provide distracting fire and explosions. We've been putting people on the ground ever since U.N. troops started setting up shop in Mexico. Fortunately, we have a few cells around TQ," Secretary Mendoza tells the New Rite team at Cheyenne Mountain.

"What can they do if people are shooting at us?"

"Don't know. That's why surprise is so important and we're asking if you can do this. If you can't, tell me and I'll go back to my teams," Secretary Mendoza says. "But the President wants to give you a shot at it."

"By shot at it, what do you mean?" Pete asks.

"If it goes bad, we're bombing the place. We think the conspirators are all there. If we wipe 'em out, the whole secession falls," Secretary Mendoza says. "At least it falls apart unless Russia, Iran and the others have decided how to split the land until we take it back."

"So, let me get this, we go in, grab a kid off a roof of a military base and get out of there and then you start bombing," Pete says.

"If you get the kid out alive, my orders are to not bomb. The President thinks the kid can stop this whole thing and we can take a more peaceful approach less likely to kill generals from too many countries," Mendoza responds.

"Mr. Secretary," Ally Steele interjects. "Give us 20 minutes to define a plan, but we need to do this on the move. I need your teams to tell us where the cleanest air lanes are into Mexico." Over the next 20 minutes, the team discusses an option they think has a better chance of working, using an altered routing Ally suggests.

"Since we need to drop people in when we get close, we'll have to turn off our skin camo at the site. That means we need to make the APB physically look like it belongs at TQ. Our bird looks different than any they've ever seen," Pete suggests. "We have to assume people on the ground know Mexican military aircraft. And they have a pretty good idea of what American aircraft looks like. So we need to paint this up to look like a secret aircraft of one of the U.N. countries that the Mexicans would be afraid to piss off."

"So we settle on China," Ally suggests. "I wouldn't want China pissed off at me if I were them."

"Probably as good as any country," one of the ex-Rangers in the group says. "But we can't just land, pick a guy up, and take off, can we?"

"Maybe," Pete says. "But guards are going to come running as we get close to ground. If we run this at night, how far down can you drop me, Ally?"

"The hook cable runs 500 feet, but a pick-up at that height is dangerous. We can get caught in something. How about we lower you down as we're coming in, but have you inside a bullet-deflection cone, like we're delivering something. We lower you and the cone over the kid, you hook him up and we blast," Ally says.

"Only problems with that," JT says, "are that as long as the cone is outside the APB, radar can see it and it only fits one person. How long will it take to pull them in?"

"Ten seconds," Ally responds.

"That's 10 seconds for them to get a bead on where you're headed. They'll have birds in the air. You'll need to figure out how to lose 'em," JT states.

"Good point. We'll need to drop the cone," Ally says, gaining a stern glare from Pete. "We might be able to pull this off. We'll come in at 45,000 feet and then drop the bird with the package straight down. I'll start dropping Pete when we're 10 seconds clear of the roof. If the kid is there, we need 20 seconds for Pete to tell him who he is, strap him in, and then 10 more seconds before we're invisible to radar."

"Pete can't be yelling out in English," the ex-Ranger says. "That's a dead giveaway. We'll have every weapon in the place firing on us in a second. That's 30 seconds of enemy fire we will not likely survive."

"Can you speak Spanish?" Ally asks, though she realizes she knows the answer as she asks the question.

"Wouldn't matter if I did," Pete responds. "Every Mexican guard there would know what I was saying. It's just as dead of a giveaway."

Secretary Mendoza rejoined the conversation a few minutes ago, but stayed silent to hear their planning. Now, he's starting to see how the plan can come together.

"Do any of you speak Mandarin?" Secretary Mendoza asks.

"What good is that going to do?" Pete asks.

"Juan Gonzalez speaks Mandarin," Mendoza says. "The guy who picks Juan up has to speak Mandarin to him. It fits with the cover. It'll buy you valuable seconds."

"I don't suppose you speak any Mandarin, do you Pete?" JT asks.

"Not yet, but I can learn it."

Koz, one of Mendoza's assigned officers, speaks up. "I speak elementary Mandarin," he says.

"Then teach Pete on the way," Secretary Mendoza orders.

"Hey, Pete. You can camo us into looking Chinese on the way too," Ally says.

***

Shanghai, China

The United Nations coalition that invaded under the guise of providing protection as the Republic of Alta Texas formed is collapsing around President Jones. At least every 10 minutes for the past two hours, another national military leadership delegation has walked out of the TQ command center stationed deep below the Mexican Air Force base in Monterrey, Mexico.

In the last few hours, China and Russia began pulling troops back to the Mexican borders, setting off celebrations inside of Camp Pendleton, Dyess, Lackland and Holloman Air Force Bases, Fort Hood, Fort Huachuca and Naval Station San Diego, all of which had been largely surrounded by troops from these countries.

As soon as he hears of China's withdrawal, First Empire Chairman and CEO Chang Chen worries about the implications of China's U.N. endeavors on his company's FirstWal acquisition. Immediately, he calls a strategy session with his executive leadership team, including International Operations Executive Vice President Jia Lin.

The leaders gather hastily in the 95th floor conference room overlooking Changfeng Park in Shanghai's Putuo District. The view from the boardroom is spectacular, spanning thousands of high-rise residential, commercial and industrial operations. No one is looking outside now.

"We must be greatly worried about our investment in FirstWal and the potential great disaster that will befall us if Americans take on anti-foreigner behavior in the wake of the U.N. invasion, particularly now that we find out the invasion was based on a series of lies and perhaps even territorial promises," Chairmen Chen says. *"There is great risk that FirstWal, as one of the largest foreign-owned companies in the United States, will be the target of attacks or that Americans will stop shopping at our stores. This would put at risk the financial future of this company I have spent decades building, so I want to know our strategic alternatives."*

Jia Lin, or Lin Jia as said in China where the family name is emphasized as first and more important than the individual name, walks up to the front of the room and clicks on a piece of software that tracks a discussion and automatically creates lists, visuals and notations to capture its essence. The software has long since replaced taking notes in meetings. Projecting against the large screen that drops down to cover the floor-to-ceiling window in the conference room, she starts talking and notes start appearing on the screen. The notes change continuously through the discussion.

"The options seem pretty clear. We can continue to operate but make sure we're identified as a purely American company, removing any sign that FirstWal is Chinese-owned. Then, we hire American icons to be our spokespeople to make sure Americans think of us this way. We'll need to spend some advertising dollars to do this, but it'll be money well spent if it helps us protect market share. If we do it right, we can out-American even American-owned companies," Jia starts. Always a strong physical presence, Jia knows this is a make-or-break moment for her career. If she's going to go down, it won't be without a fight.

"This marketing campaign could include donations to U.S. veterans organizations and other charities Americans see as aligned with protecting America. I estimate that this will cost roughly two to five billion U.S. dollars in the next three years, with the returns coming purely in the form of protecting our existing position," Jia says. She looks more uncomfortable than usual as she speaks, having not dressed today for participation in a top-level executive meeting with Chairman Chen. Typically a conservative dresser on normal days, Jia always wears blouses a bit more open and skirts just a bit shorter when meeting with the executive team. She has long been expert at using her appearance and shoulder, arm and knee touches to exert her influence over First Empire's male-dominated executive leadership team.

"Lin Jia, you ask for a lot of money in order to deliver no returns. You should be ashamed of your weakness," states one of Jia's primary competitors to become number two to Chairman Chen.

"May I remind you that we invested more than $100 billion U.S. and borrowed another $250 billion to buy WalCo and turn it into FirstWal. The spending I propose is one method of protecting that investment. If you would be patient for a minute, I can suggest the other possibilities."

"Proceed," Chairman Chen directs.

"We must consider selling FirstWal's U.S. operations, or perhaps its U.S. and Canada operations together, in a public offering or to a strategic buyer," Jia says. *"The easiest and best way to avoid any repercussions or anti-China sentiment from the actions of our government is to not have investment in the United States. Of course, we will wait for the markets to recover once this is all settled, something I am certain will take a matter of months. It will take us that much time to prepare for the sale in any case."*

"I see no reason we cannot move faster," her competitor suggests, anxious to have the scope of Jia's responsibilities substantively reduced as quickly as possible while creating the impression that he would act quicker.

"It's easy to say such a thing when you have never had responsibility for a major acquisition or divestiture. Such rash behavior can destroy First Empire," Jia responds, always careful to never be positioned as weak. *"May I continue?"* she adds, staring down the competitor. After time passes and her question remains unanswered, Jia continues.

"My preferred approach is that we convince the government to create a close and immediate alliance with the United States. This will undo the risk of any damage from the rash action taken by our central government in supporting the secession without accurate facts," Jia says in a comment aimed as much at exposing the consequences of rash behavior suggested by her competitor as it was in condemning government policy.

"You disagree with the actions of the government," Chairman Chen asks, worried that Jia has spoken too openly of her disagreement with Beijing.

"No, no, no Mr. Chairman. I fully support current China policy. But, I believe we can suggest ways the government can repair its relationship with Washington and the American people while also helping First Empire," Jia says, noticeably taking a physical step backward as she speaks and crossing her arms in front of her.

"Such as what actions?" the Chairman asks.

"Well, I don't have specifics at this point, but believe we can quickly identify actions our government can take that will help First Empire, and, perhaps as importantly, have the funding come from the government," Jia says. *"For example, the marketing and donation campaign I spoke of earlier. Could such activity be just as valuable to First Empire if launched by the People's Republic, without direct financial costs to First Empire?"*

"What about the protestor who shut your stores down?" Jia's competitor interrupts again.

"The protestor is part of the secession movement, so he will not be a factor," Jia responds.

"But didn't you just give him a one million U.S. dollar scholarship – a scholarship for a traitor? What a terrible decision – in hindsight of course," Jia's competitor states.

The strategic debate inside of First Empire continues for 45 additional minutes before closing with Chairman Chen asking everyone to sleep on the ideas for the night and return in the morning to make a decision.

***

Protection Corps Command Center

General Raúl Hernández, leader of the Castillo cartel Protection Corps, works his contact list arduously. He starts with his closest allies – top generals in 15 countries.

"Don't run when the weaklings pull back," he tells them all. "The rest have done what we needed. We'll finish the job with just our core if we must."

As he urges the generals to remain strong and hold their nation's troops in place, he steps up the timetable for activity he has not coordinated with President Jones. He orders Protection Corps soldiers to place nuclear bombs in Los Angeles, Dallas, Houston, Phoenix, San Diego and a city in Mexico.

Al Qaeda and two other terrorist groups secured the material for these bombs through Iran, Pakistan and remnants of North Korea. Hernández insists on maintaining final trigger control as his condition for hiding the bombs, but, as usual, commits to allowing the terrorist groups to take full credit when attacks are executed.

"*One way or another, Alta Texas will end up back with Mexico and Mexico will be stronger. We'll hold them hostage if we must,*" General Hernández tells a top aide. "*The Americans are too weak. Their politicians will not let millions die.*"

His aide looks at him. "*You look so happy General,*" the aide says.

"Sí . . . . Sí . . . ," General Hernández responds. "*There is nothing quite so exquisite as inflicting deep, tortured pain on those we hate.*"

CHAPTER 17

18 Hours

Washington, D.C.

As a show of openness, President Phillipi asks the Alta Texas government to pull U.N. border troops back at least 20 miles from the state borders. The President hopes to create a no-man's-land to reduce the risk of unintended conflicts.

The message is cabled to Mexico and quickly rerouted to the Alta Texas leadership. After reading the message, Alta Texas President Manny Jones sends an immediate reply.

"The great Republic of Alta Texas, in recognition of the importance of treating its neighbor to the north with respect that is returned in equal parts by the United States, will agree to ask the United Nations to move its border troops to spots 10 miles from borders with the United States if the United States will also move its troops 10 miles away from its borders with the Republic of Alta Texas," the message reads.

Upon delivering the message to the White House, the Mexican ambassador is asked to wait for a response while the Alta Texas message is relayed to the DUCC Situation Room.

Within seconds, President Phillipi personally writes a response for delivery to the ambassador. As he hands it to an aide to take up, he turns to Chinh: "Manny may be wrong as hell on this, but I have to give him credit. He's totally committed to his delusion."

The Mexican ambassador reads the three-word message addressed to Jones.

"I don't think that's humanly possible," the ambassador tells the aide after reading the message. "Should I just tell them that President Jones' proposed solution is not acceptable?"

"No," the aide responds. "Send the message exactly as the President wrote it. He was very explicit that this is the message he wants sent."

"I think I'll save the original," the ambassador says. "This could be valuable some day."

***

As this note exchange takes place, Protection Corps soldiers, part of General Hernández's elite assault unit, finish placing nuclear bombs at select targets in the five Southwest cities. The targets are all locations owned circuitously by the Castillo cartel, or more accurately now, by General Hernández. Another Protection Corps soldier takes a sixth nuclear bomb to a city inside of Mexico where President Suárez's family is now held in protective custody by the Protection Corps.

General Hernández calls all six back to the Protection Corps command center to celebrate their achievement.

Upon their arrival, the six are taken into custody by other Protection Corps soldiers and imprisoned in a cell deep within one of the cartel's production and command center compounds. General Hernández resets the entrance codes to the cell so only he can enter.

Before leaving the six behind, he tells them: "*I need to be sure no one knows where you have placed these until they are used. Once they are used, I will release you and pay you well. In the meantime, you should pray for my safety.*"

***

Beijing, China and Washington, D.C.

Worldwide media break into coverage of the conflict to hear China's Premier personally issue a formal apology to the United States for its role in invading U.S. territory, while also committing to building close ties with the United States.

"The People's Republic of China expresses its sincere regret for its decision to join the United Nations in what we had believed was a humanitarian effort to prevent genocide against your Latins," the Premier is translated as saying. "We later discovered, through research we are sharing with the U.S. government, that the secession is an effort by a corrupt politician and the Castillo drug cartel to steal a nation. We must establish a deeper and closer relationship with the United States going forward to ensure such misunderstandings of intent never take place. I have demanded the resignation of the Secretary-General and military leadership of the United Nations, and will work with the United States to ensure the United Nations plays a positive role in the world's future."

After reading the statement, President Phillipi asks the CIA and other intelligence organizations to determine whether China's statement represents a true statement of contrition. "It has always seemed to me that China's first principle is that it needs to win, and that other principles fall secondary to the first principle. Perhaps this is our opportunity to help convince the government of, and the people of, China that free and fair elections may help avoid such terrible decisions in the future," the President says in relaying his request to Chinh.

"Perhaps, Mr. President," Chinh says in response. "But I wouldn't hold a vigil waiting for it to happen." Knowing that Chinh only calls him Mr. President in private when he disagrees with him, the President prepares himself for a rebuttal.

"Democracy doesn't keep leaders from making bad decisions," Chinh continues. "But it does limit the length of time over which those bad decisions are endured. Whatever the mechanism, our hope must be that China's government is shaken up, election or otherwise, to remove those from office who have made such a bad decision that will be seen by China as a stain on its reputation."

Chinh, of mixed Punjabi Indian and Han Chinese descent, was the most surprised member of the President's inner circle when it was announced that China was taking part in the U.N. peacekeeping delegation.

"China is the world's longest sustaining self-controlled nation, and they have gotten that way largely by avoiding expensive intrusions into foreign territory. I realize they have moved away from this at times in the past century," Chinh finishes telling the President, "but I think this has been more based on desire for food, water, energy and military security, rather than a direct desire to control other people."

"Doesn't matter whether a country intervenes for gold, oil or slaves. The trauma to those being invaded is the same!" President Phillipi responds with an angry tone. "In any case, I realize they've largely tried to protect what they believed was theirs to protect. The problem is that, in some cases, the beliefs are based on cherry-picking facts."

"So what do we do now?" Chinh asks.

"We take them at their word while building the capabilities to protect ourselves as if they don't mean it," the President responds. "It's in the interest of both nations to be allies, not enemies. There's no better time to work toward building that type of relationship than today."

***

Chicago

Seated in the back corner at Heart and Soul Café, Professor Stark finishes up his breakfast as the deadline arrives for his graduate students to submit 100-word papers. Pushed to the side now are the remnants of a sweet potato hash mixed with onions, pork sausage and fried green tomato chunks. Though he had asked to keep the sausage gravy in a side bowl to try controlling his fat intake, the gravy bowl is largely empty as well. Owner Margie checks with him to make sure the food is up to his expectations. Her new chef started just a few weeks ago.

"Delicious as always," Professor Stark responds. "If it wasn't, I might not have so much trouble keeping weight off every semester."

"You're looking good Professor," the owner and his long-time friend tells him. "Though you could use a little more meat on those bones."

"Breakfast alone will add five pounds, but it won't show up as meat," Professor Stark replies. "Now I'm going to have to stick to cottage cheese, celery and lettuce the rest of the day just so I can come here again tomorrow."

"Some more coffee?"

"Sure, I'm going to hang out and read here the next couple of hours. If you don't mind, of course?"

"Not at all, read away," she tells him.

Opening his Lifelink, Professor Stark connects to his secure class site and downloads the papers submitted by his class. The benefits of smaller graduate school classes are that he has only 30 students in each class. The downside is he has no teaching assistants to help with graduate course grading.

He starts by reading the papers of foreign students first, anxious to see if their perspectives differ meaningfully from his views, or the views of the American students.

The first statement he reads is from Sophia, a native Italian.

"Freedom of speech is the cornerstone upon which other critical elements of long-term peace are built. Competition can only develop in societies that value freedom of speech. Science develops only when contrasting views are encouraged and debated. Freedom of speech helps unseat despots using political power for evil or personal gain, particularly if an honest and committed media understand their role in challenging every source of societal control that can best be challenged by them. Abuses of religion can only be stopped when challengers are protected from being branded and executed as heretics," Sophia wrote.

Jun, the son of a wealthy Chinese business executive who hopes for a career in China's government, wrote the next piece Professor Stark reads: "Knowledge is the crucial differentiator between successful societies and societies that fail. In addition to knowledge of science, business, and other elements of a successful economy, it's important for everyone in society to understand his or her role and contribution to the broader nation. Farmers must not only know how to farm, but they must know the important place they hold in feeding others. Power plant operators must know how to run plants, but also know that it's not their place to gain fame. Everyone in society must learn the world enough to know how they fit."

After a few sips of coffee, Professor Stark opens the next paper, a perspective from one of two Canadian students in the class.

"A culture that values a strong work ethic has more to do with a nation's success than any other single attribute. When people have incentives to work hard, over time that work creates national strength," the first Canadian wrote. "Most attributes of a strong nation – competitive environment, advanced technology, military strength – require individuals with strong belief in hard work to develop. In nations where work is punished, or even just not fully rewarded, too many people focus on enjoying life and treat innovation and effort as a responsibility for others. When this happens, progress stalls."

The other Canadian student starts her paper with a very different perspective. "Sacrifice is the critical element of national success. When the people of a nation are willing to sacrifice to help others in the country, it helps to build strength as a community. Selflessness helps lead the nation by example. When people see others giving their time and money to help others, they also want to help. The people who receive this help appreciate it and are more willing to accept their circumstances, providing for greater social stability. By ensuring that everyone understands that they must sacrifice of themselves for the whole of society to grow, you build a true community."

Professor Stark types in notes on questions he plans to ask each student, either during the in-class debate or during the 15-minute review discussions he has with each student whenever he asks them to provide him with such short answers. These individual discussion sessions allow him to quickly determine the depth of a student's knowledge and insight on the assigned topic. Equally important, anyone with either a superficial or plagiarized understanding of the topic and their paper is quickly exposed.

Given the circumstances of recent days, Professor Stark is particularly curious to find out Rachel's thoughts, so reads her summary first among the American students.

"Advanced cultural knowledge is critical to the long-term success of any nation, particularly multi-cultural countries. Pro-active efforts are required to tear down walls of segregation, with barrier-removal responsibility shared between governments and individuals. When life is confined to like-minded individuals, our views aren't challenged. For example, viewers of either MSDNC or the Republican news channel miss the complexities of many stories, or may be totally unaware of crucial stories that don't conform to a single political viewpoint. I learned this last fall. When we don't study others, we gain no understanding of what drives people to approach problems differently," Rachel wrote.

With the Heart and Soul Café now fairly empty, Professor Stark is no longer concerned with annoying other patrons by doing his note-taking verbally. Inserting a small, wrap-around receiver around his bottom lip, he dictates his questions for Rachel.

"Could one construe your perspective as restating the concept that all individuals have a responsibility to seek disconfirming evidence? You argue that segregation is inherently a problem, but throughout world history, people have generally segregated physically for security reasons along economic and even racial lines. Would required integration discourage wealth creation by removing enhanced physical security as one of the benefits to be obtained through hard work?" Professor Stark dictates.

The next paper that catches his eye comes from Jeremy.

"While military power is important to national survival, it's not the only security that's crucial. Along with protecting citizens against foreign invaders, nations must protect citizens from each other. Evil does not always cross borders. 'Ensuring security' is a critical national survival capability. If citizens do not feel protected from each other, it's the natural instinct of men to seek security. When the government fails at this, other methods of ensuring security are created. Some even think gang membership provides better protection and security than can be provided by local police. That's intolerable," Jeremy wrote in his summary.

***

Republic of Alta Texas Headquarters

Having finished his work, Ramon Mantle drops in on Juan Gonzalez. Juan's guard lets Ramon into Juan's room, a place with all the visual appeal of an oversized crawl space.

"I don't know if you remember me, Juan," Ramon says as he shakes hands with the exhausted-looking Juan.

"Yes, of course. You're Ramon Mantle. Everybody knows you," Juan says, having long since figured out that Ramon must be in on the secession.

"Actually, Juan, everybody knows you. And now you get to be ambassador of our new country, a pretty impressive achievement for a young man who hasn't even started college," Ramon says.

"Quite a compliment from a billionaire inventor, business executive and philan . . , philanthropist," Juan replies, struggling to recall a little-used word in his third language without the benefit of his Lifelink translator.

The two talk for some time about how Juan is feeling. It's clear to Ramon that Juan is not trusted by the leadership as much as he is, but Juan has an important position in the new government.

"Juan, you seem like a smart kid," Ramon says after some time. "Do you have any people you trust completely, you know, with your life."

"Well, yes," Juan responds. "Mama, my girlfriend Rachel . . ., Professor Stark and a congresswoman."

"Jill Carlson right?"

"Yeah. That's her."

"But no one here?"

"Well, sure, I can add people here I guess," Juan says.

"You'd be wiser not to," Ramon tells him.

Ramon pulls up close to Juan and whispers lightly in his ear.

"Juan, this might not all go as planned," Ramon says very quietly. "Take the paper I'm giving you and remember that the number is a One World account number. If it goes bad from here, get this to someone you trust with your life who can check it without being traced. The people who trust me with their life may need to depend on the people you trust with yours."

***

Washington, D.C.

President Phillipi is growing increasingly confident that the U.S. borders will be secured under U.S. control. His two-hour nap is interrupted by a dream that he failed to fix the nation and a new secession attempt is underway.

He calls several of his cabinet members with instructions and then asks to speak to Professor Stark.

"Paul, this is President Phillipi," he says when Professor Stark opens his Lifelink.

"Yes, Mr. President. I was told it would be you, but must say I'm surprised to hear from you now."

"I understand you are talking with your class about an agenda for winning the peace," the President says. "Would you mind sharing what you come up with? I want to be sure we don't go through this again at least as long as memory of me exists."

"We'd be honored," Professor Stark responds. Hearing the call end, he shuts his Lifelink, sticks it back in his secure, code-protected pocket and continues his walk.

Only as he starts walking again does he realize that his fingers, nose and mouth are numb. He shakes his head when he realizes he just received a call from the President in the middle of America's most threatening conflict since the Civil War.

***

Utah New Rite Compound

Clarissa Coleman hears a female voice heading toward her watch location that is clearly not the voice of either of her sisters. She converts the hiking stick back to rifle mode, lies down behind a sizable rock formation, and intently watches with just the top of her head and the rifle exposed to whomever is coming toward her. At still a distance, Clarissa sees the person walking with arms in the air and intentionally making noise. It's not the way to sneak up on a person. Clarissa relaxes a bit. Suddenly, she spins to make sure no one is coming at her from any other direction. No one else is around.

With full daylight Clarissa realizes it is Sarah Osborne while Sarah is still a distance away. She converts her weapon back to hiking stick mode and walks to greet her.

"What are you doing here?" Clarissa asks while hugging Sarah. "Not that I don't want you here, but I hope you don't have more bad news."

"No. No. Nothing like that," Sarah responds. "I think you've had more than enough bad news and tough challenges for a year, let alone a couple of days. I just came out to check on you and your family. Your dad and sister said I'd find you here."

"Well, that's good. Why don't you come on up to my watch spot and see what you think."

The two walk back up to an elevated stretch of rock set several hundred feet above water line and with a clear view to the south and east, as well as parts of the west and north. Behind the watch spot is a sunken area with even greater wind protection.

"This really is a beautiful spot," Sarah says. "Just look at how peaceful it is, with such a big open span of water protected by the rocks."

"Yeah, I was thinking this would be a great spot to have my bedroom window. Can you imagine looking at this every morning and every night?"

Clarissa had triple-folded blankets on the ground for comfort while she lay in the prone position for parts of her watch. She unfolds the blankets to create more blanket space so Sarah can join her in at least some comfort.

"It's really nice of you to check on us," Clarissa tells Sarah, happy to have company to break up the boredom of the watch.

"Hey, after all that you've done and what you've been through, I think it's only right. Besides, you remind me a lot of me when I was your age."

"Really? How's that?"

"You know. You're gonna do what you're gonna do," Sarah responds. "And like I was at your age, I don't know whether you're fearless or just oblivious to the risks you take. Either way, I thought it would be good to check in on you."

"Well, I'm glad you did. It gets kind of boring sometimes," Clarissa says, lying prone on the blanket with her chin propped up on her fists, eyes focused on the water line. Sarah is doing the same with their elbows nearly touching. "Hey, I wanted to ask you, one of the female soldiers who came through said it would be an honor to meet you. Did you know her?" Clarissa asks.

"No. My guess is she may have heard of some of the work I did as a Navy Seal, if it's the person I talked to."

"Why, what did you do?"

"Really, I just did what I'm trained to do. But a lot of people made a big fuss about it. Anyone who had the chance would have done the same thing," Sarah says.

"Still, it sounded like you were a superstar to her," Clarissa says. "That has to be cool, knowing you've done something that someone else thinks is that awesome."

"It's no different than how I feel about how you and your dad handled those soldiers coming here," Sarah tells Clarissa. "That was pretty smart, pretty intense and level-headed work. You would have made a trained soldier proud."

"Oh, well, they weren't trying to attack, so it wasn't really that hard," Clarissa says.

"But, if they had," Sarah replies, "you put yourself in the perfect position to protect everybody around you. That's all I've ever done. You just did it at a lot younger age when I'm not sure I would have reacted as well."

Clarissa and Sarah talk for another 15 minutes about life, the military and fitting into the world before Sarah tells Clarissa she needs to go.

"It was really cool of you to come out here. I imagined maybe my mom would join me on this watch sometime, but she really doesn't like to be outdoors and she's not very athletic. So to have you here . . . . You know . . . . It's just really nice of you."

"One thing I've learned Clarissa," Sarah says, "is that people in our lives have different purposes. Some are part of our lives for only a short time, but still mean something or contribute something to our lives. No single person can be everything to you. Your mom and dad are important, but even they will never be able to provide everything you need to grow and be happy. If you're open, other people will help fill gaps – providing friendship, competition, challenge, mentors and whatever else you might need to be the best possible person. There are people in my life – like my first drill sergeant, a few friends from high school, teachers, mission commanders, even old loves – that I haven't seen in years and may never see again, but they still helped make me the person I've become. I still think about them."

Standing up, Sarah gives Clarissa another hug and then tells her to stay alert.

"I have a feeling something really cool is going to happen right in front of your eyes as long as you keep them open," Sarah says, turning and walking away.

CHAPTER 18

10 Hours

Chicago

Students from Professor Stark's graduate-level course roam in, shaking off the dusting of snow and the shivers of cold that penetrate deeply this time of year. Several step out to grab coffee, tea, hot water and hot chocolate before class begins.

Professor Stark fills one wall screen with a list of critical concepts to maintaining national unity and peace. Another screen displays the main points of 30 summaries, which he asks each student to read and validate that their opinion is properly condensed. Photos and charts supporting various points are displayed around the rest of the room, through an automated visual display program Professor Stark uses to spice up his lectures.

"I appreciate that each of you completed the assignment on time and with what appears to be a reasoned level of thought. We'll talk through the issues over the next 90 minutes and then you each need to get on my calendar by next Monday for a 15-minute personal review session to discuss your concepts in greater detail," Professor Stark says to audible groans. Even those who do well in these individual sessions often walk out feeling exhausted. What's worse is that he holds open 30 minutes for each 15-minute session and even 30 minutes isn't always enough. To get 30 people in by Monday likely means many of these discussions will happen over the weekend.

"I know we're all completely disoriented by what's going on with the secession move. Even if it looks now like we may not career into world war, the impact of this dispute is unsettled and troubling," Professor Stark tells the class. "So I understand if you are a little distracted. I'm going to try to give you good reason to focus. Often, in war, governments are fully engaged in winning wars, but fail to exercise the same diligence to win peace. So, the question I want us to focus on is how do we twist the clear trauma of the last several days into as positive an outcome as possible by creating an agenda for peace?"

Near silence of the next several moments is interrupted by rattling of Rachel's chair. Professor Stark looks at her and sees her left leg rattling up and down at a pace that would make a hummingbird proud. Seeing the professor looking at her, Rachel refocuses on the classroom.

"A positive outcome?" Rachel asks. "The only positive I can see is figuring out how we avoid this ever happening again."

"Exactly," Professor Stark says. "As much as it's important to fight to win, it's equally important to sustain victory. We should always look for ways to turn negatives into positives. So, what went wrong to get us to this point that we need to avoid in the future?"

Tamika responds: "We allowed ourselves to be torn apart by politicians who put their own personal interests ahead of the interests of the nation."

"That may be the single-most important mistake, but what created the conditions some self-centered individuals were able to exploit?" Professor Stark asks.

Jeremy sits on the back edge of his chair, waving his arm to get Professor Stark's attention. Professor Stark spots him.

"We let ourselves be divided," Jeremy says. "We allowed the nation to get to a point where we were so segregated, and our political leaders segregated with us, that we stopped working to resolve disputes and instead let hostilities build until we reached our melting point. All Senator Jones and H2M had to do to get us to split was to stick a fuse in the right place. We were already prepared to blow apart."

"There's a good deal of truth to what you just said Jeremy," Professor Stark states. "So, if that is the problem that created this issue, how do we make sure we never get to such a point again?"

Rachel twists her hair into a hand-wrung ponytail with her right hand as she partially raises her left hand to get Professor Stark's attention.

"We figure out what we need to do to be united," Rachel says. "It's the United States of America, yet we've stopped trying to create national unity. We've let people go their own way under the notion that multiculturalism and segregation are identical twins. Identical twins, though, don't try to harm each other. They stay connected. Different, sure. But with a bond that is much more difficult to break than the bonds we've had broken here."

"I agree with Rachel," Tamika interjects. "The debates we hear in Washington or during campaigns present us with either-or solutions like there are only two ways a problem can be solved. That's almost never true, but too many people make their living off of ensuring that issues are unresolved so these issue advocates remain relevant. Somehow, we need to force our political leaders to be brave enough to work together to solve problems."

"So what I would like to ask you, as a class, is whether you are willing to help create the debate on what we need to do differently?" Professor Stark asks, holding his arms up and spread wide. "We have a very important client interested in having us do this work. Are you willing to help write a manifesto for change to make this a better and more united nation?"

***

West Nogales, Arizona

Mike Sanchez steps outside his FirstWal store. He walks to a nearby street vendor for his favorite lunch. Eating at his desk won't do on a day he expects to be fired. Mike figures he has a couple of hours to enjoy the afternoon before the firing happens. Chet Leach is well known for firing people at the end of a workday, never wanting to leave any work undone that he can extract from even employees he plans to fire. Since there is no way he can meet Chet's elevated financial targets and still comply with martial law, Mike is prepared to be the example Chet uses to prove he is serious about his expectations.

Mike opens the pressed paper and foil container with the comfort food he turns to whenever he is stressed. While biting his first slice of pepperoni, sausage and banana pepper pizza, he scans the horizon from his hilltop location. Quickly, he forgets his employment concerns. A long line of tanks, armored vehicles, jeeps and other military vehicles are lined up at the Nogales border. They're all heading south.

Mike scans back to the FirstWal parking lot and realizes that the Chinese military officers who have been at his store the past two days, and who were there when he arrived this morning, are gone. Mike pulls out his Lifelink and zooms in to look at the line at the border. Vehicles from China, Russia and dozens of other countries are moving back into Mexico, though at a much slower pace than he recalled seeing when they arrived.

Pouring on crushed red pepper and shoving the pizza in his mouth as quickly as he can, Mike rushes through his food and downs his cola as he walks at an elevated pace back to the store.

Running up to his office, he searches quickly for an update. There is nothing in official Alta Texas news about U.N. troops withdrawing.

***

Cheyenne Mountain, Colorado

Ally, Pete and the rest of the New Rite team finalize extraction plans. The New Rite APBs will run at TQ from its southwest. This attack route is chosen to increase chances that the APB's Chinese disguise works, as well as to distract ground-level attention from the full assault by U.S. troops attacking minutes later from the northeast.

Flying from the southwest means Ally and a second New Rite team pilot will need to fly the APBs unseen deep into Mexico before starting their move to Monterrey. Ally is confident she can stay off radar and out of visible site for much of their initial run. The only real visibility risk, she tells the team, occurs when they pick up their final team member on the way. Once the pick up is done and the APBs are elevated again out of visible sight, they won't be seen again until the APB approaches Monterrey.

Several of the New Rite team members begin final preparations. Two of the New Rite team members kneel to say a few short prayers. One lays down his prayer mat, faces toward what he believes is the direction of the Ka'ba Shrine in Mecca, and begins his series of prayers. Pete takes a nap.

***

Washington, D.C.

A military vehicle parks at the Cannon House Office Building. Several soldiers enter, show their identification and are escorted by the Capitol Police to 419.

Knocking on the closed but unlocked main office door, the soldiers don't wait for a response before entering. Hearing the commotion, Jill walks out of her attached office to ask what is going on.

"Congresswoman Jill Carlson?" one soldier asks.

"That's me," Jill responds.

"You need to come with us," she's told.

"What for?" Jill asks.

"You need to come with us," the soldier repeats. "Now ma'am."

Jill goes to her desk, grabs her Lifelink and pulls her coat out of the closet.

"Okay, where are we going?"

"You'll know when we get there," the soldier says, pointing her arms toward the door and the nearby elevators, then instructing Jill to walk with the soldiers surrounding her.

As she is driven away, Jill sends a message to Professor Stark. "Paul, please get to D.C. right away. I think I need you here," she writes, showing the message to the soldier next to her for approval before hitting send.

The military transport vehicle carrying Jill stops at the Pentagon. The female soldier leading her asks Jill to follow quickly and quietly as she clears several layers of security. From there, Jill is brought to an office where Defense Secretary Mendoza eventually greets her.

"Can you tell me what I'm doing here?" Jill asks Secretary Mendoza.

"I thought you might want to watch," he says. "Follow me."

Jill follows Mendoza through a series of halls and secured doors, before entering an elevator unlike anything she's ever seen. Eye, bone and dental scans are conducted, and verified against the security system in the Deep Underground Command Center.

Secretary Mendoza goes down to the DUCC with her.

"What am I watching?" Jill asks on the way.

"We're going to try to get Juan Gonzalez out of where he's being held, and you're going to verify from visual feeds whether we have the right person," Secretary Mendoza tells Jill once they reach a secured area. "The mission is launching now, but nothing exciting should take place for a while. In the meantime, relax for a bit. I know the President said he'll stop over to say hello as soon as he has a moment."

Growing up on a dairy farm, Jill Carlson never imagined watching history unfold in the way it has happened to her over the past year. "Don't screw this up," she mutters to herself.

Secretary Mendoza hears her comment. "You'll be fine. Just remember to breathe when we get started. Nobody does well without oxygen."

***

Utah New Rite Compound

In late afternoon, Clarissa Coleman is back at her watch position. From the highest elevation point overlooking Friendship Cove, Clarissa paces back and forth to stay warm. Though daytime temperatures are relatively mild even in the middle of winter, as the sun drops, intensified chills sweep over the landscape.

Staring across bays formed by water backed up from Glen Canyon dam, Clarissa's job tonight is to make sure that no U.N. boats use the bay to enter Utah and attack U.S. military personnel from behind at the more populated towns where National Guard troops are stationed.

The last few days have been eventful. First, Clarissa spotted a group of U.S. soldiers escaping back into U.S. controlled territory. Then she learned that police killed her grandfather. She's still devastated, and slept poorly during her extended eight hours off duty. Her father, John Coleman, has just headed back to base camp to catch a few hours sleep after checking to make sure Clarissa is okay.

While Clarissa is pacing, John is one-quarter mile away, walking on a slippery path still slightly visible despite deep shadows. Both are tired but alert, searching their surroundings for any sign of danger – military or wildlife. A high-speed air blast passes over John's head and behind Clarissa's back, forcing both to move. Clarissa looks up in time to see two white fires coming from the back of something she has never seen before. Seconds later, long blades extend from the aircraft and start spinning. By the time John turns around and looks up, he sees little, but immediately starts running back to Clarissa, slipping several times on the way and rolling his ankle badly over a rock. With the adrenaline rush of fear, he ignores the ankle pain and hobbles forward, putting as little pressure on his rolled ankle as possible.

Nearing Clarissa, he yells out ahead, "Clarissa, Clarissa."

"Yeah, I'm here. Quiet, Dad."

By the time she finishes speaking, he's in front of her and now noticing the searing pain from his ankle.

"Are you alright?" she asks as he responds by shaking his head vertically.

"Did you see what that was?" he asks, now much more quietly.

"I saw something, some kind of jet, white hot. Or maybe a helicopter," she responds. "Either way. It came in really fast."

"You didn't see anything else?"

"Hard to be sure, but the wings sure looked funky, almost like you know how the inside of a cardboard box looks, with nothing solid and everything crossing everything else. It looked like it came to a dead stop for a second over the water, dropping right to water level for like a minute, and then just took off again."

"We need to call this in," John Coleman says, "but it might be one of ours so we can't risk alerting the other side to one of our guys."

"But it looked like another country to me."

"Really?"

"It looked like another flag on the side, but it was too far away to tell for sure," Clarissa says.

"I didn't get a good view. Anyway, we have to assume since it came from the north that it's got to be one of ours," John says. "We don't want to broadcast it."

"So I'll run it in," Clarissa says. "You're clearly not going anywhere on that ankle."

John has hobbled over to sit on the boulder, unable to put any pressure on the leg.

"It's one thing to have you here alone, but I can't have you running through the night alone in this environment. Go back to camp and get your sister to go with. She's on a rest turn."

"There's no time, Dad. We agreed to do a job and we need to do it. You see the camp over there," Clarissa says, pointing. "I'll pick up someone there to go with me the rest of the way if it makes you feel better. You should be able to see me from here most of the way until I get there."

"That'll have to do."

John hands her his water bottle and his hiking stick.

"Why didn't you let me use this on our trips before? This stick is cool," Clarissa says.

"It's not cool. It's a weapon," he tells her. "Be safe and keep your eyes and ears open."

"Cool. . . . Cool . . . . Eyes open . . . . Something cool is gonna happen if I stay alert," Clarissa says quietly to herself. "I bet that was Sarah."

CHAPTER 19

4 Hours

Friendship Cove, Utah

After Sarah Osborne is pulled on board the APB with Ally, Pete and three other members of the New Rite team, the craft elevates and reaccelerates to ultra-jet speed. The New Rite APB is designed with adjustable-direction jets that allow it to hover at altitude as efficiently as it accelerates forward. However, heat from the jets mean top-end rotary blades need to be deployed near ground level to avoid starting fires or, more importantly this day, incinerating passengers entering from below. Ally's team has three assignments: Drop in Sarah to get to Juan, divert the TQ defense attention away from the main attack force, then return to pick up passengers while the main assault is engaged on the ground.

Ally runs her APB hard south, deep over the Mexican desert before turning east and running from the southwest to TQ. TQ is the presumed headquarters site of Alta Texas and likely also the main coordination center for the U.N. invasion force.

After picking up Sarah, Ally rapidly gains altitude, wanting to be sure to avoid being spotted before they get to Monterrey. Her run out of Mexico with Pete after Pete's successful kill of Mexican drug kingpin Cesar Castillo proved to her that Mexican and U.N. defense systems can't track her digitally. But, as she knows all too well after being spotted returning to the Colorado New Rite camp, visual identification at low levels is possible.

As she ascends, the assault team is masked to optimize oxygen intake. Travelling five miles an hour below the speed of sound, the APB quickly traverses Arizona and heads deep into Mexico.

***

Alta Texas Headquarters

Extraction plans for Juan Gonzalez have changed considerably in recent hours as Secretary Mendoza decides that extracting Juan is just one aspect of the mission. Ally, Pete, Sarah and the other three members of Ally's diversion and extraction team are already deep in Mexico and turning northeast.

Everyone in the APB puts on the thin covers that look to be Chinese uniforms. Pete works to put make-up on team members as they fly, with the exception of Sarah, who can't have make-up interfere with her air mask function. The camouflage should make them all appear Chinese, supporting the Chinese flag Ally can project when they are in range of being spotted visually. When picking up Sarah, Ally flashed the projection to test that Sarah could see it as they approached. Ally tries to minimize Pete's work around her face, both because she's flying and because she'd still rather knock him out than work with him. Still, she lets him do enough to avoid drawing unnecessary suspicion if she is seen.

For the diversion to work, Ally needs to avoid being recognized until she is near TQ, then drop down, release Sarah for her mission, attract every available fighter jet to chase her by advertising her U.S. connection, and find a way to lose them. Her 20-minute window to do this starts five minutes ahead of the main assault.

As they near Monterrey, Ally makes clear to the team that they all better strap in. The APB carries few attack weapons to ensure high-speed escape. She projects a Chinese flag on the sides of the APB. Everyone inside has their camouflage on, assuming they will be watched visually as they near TQ.

Once the APB is just outside the Monterrey compound, Sarah drops encased in plastic material from 300 feet into a pond near TQ, making her fall look like she had been shot to anyone viewing from ground level.

Meanwhile, Lou releases 10 Cooper's-hawk drones, electronically arming the highly explosive material in bombs disguised as northern grasshopper mice.

While Ally flies the APB away at 220 miles per hour faster than the nearest jet, Lou concentrates on flying the Cooper's hawks clutching mouse-shaped bombs into anti-aircraft missile launchers. She takes six of the targets, while Pete flies four drones into their targets using techniques he perfected playing New Rite games.

If Alta Texas scrambles its stolen jets, along with Mexico and the other U.N. nations with fighter jets, the fastest they can get airborne is estimated at two minutes. It takes them another two minutes to reach full speed, meaning Ally can put nearly 100 miles between herself and her trackers in the 10 minutes before she turns. During the first 10 minutes, Ally flies high while transmitting digital signals that make her appear like a full-size U.S. bomber. At the 10-minute mark, she cuts the APB off the digital grid, drops at high speed to just 100 feet above ground, reverses direction, enables the gecko-like camouflage coating and blows past the chasing jets under their visual sight range.

A ground-sensing bullet-resistant enclosure inflates around Sarah during her descent. As the enclosure hits water, Sarah quickly opens the bottom hatch, drops below the surface and pulls up her breathing tube. Sarah swims 150 yards underwater to where she expects an inbound water pipe, based on the schematics the team reviewed. She cuts through the metal bar exterior with an internally ignited acetylene torch and follows the tunnel until she finds a big open tank holding area that then splits into pipes too narrow to fit through. At that point, Sarah pulls out her first explosive pack, sets it for one minute and pushes off to get separation from the blast. If timing is right, the main military assault on the compound should be underway by now, providing noise cover for her explosion.

The pack blasts a hole in the floor. A startled guard who has come over to check out the hole stares in amazement and terror as the black-coated, soaked Sarah pulls him into the water and cuffs him before he has any idea what's happening. Sarah emerges from the floor and pulls the guard up out of the water by his hair to let him catch his breath.

"Where's Juan Gonzalez?" she asks.

He shakes his head that he either doesn't know or won't answer. Sarah dunks his head back below the water, still holding him by the hair on top of his head. Counting to 20, she pulls him out again.

"Where's Juan Gonzalez?" she asks again, this time a little louder and with much more menace in her tone.

He shakes his head and feels her starting to push him back down into the main tank, when he blurts out. "Juan Gonzalez. Sí."

She stops pushing his head into the water, pulling him back out by his hair.

"No hablo inglés."

"Dónde está Juan González?"

"¡Quiero vivir!" the guard spits out, begging for his life.

"Dónde está Juan González?"

"¿Señor Gonzalez?"

Sarah lets the guard go, jumps over to the wall and pulls over a long metal bar. Kicking his legs furiously, he struggles to keep his nose above water. She places the bar over the middle of the hole, reaches in and pulls the guard's head back out of the water to rest his chin on top of the metal bar. After making sure he is secure while holding himself up on the bar by his chin, Sarah pulls a mission communicator out of her bag and projects a schematic of the facility against the wall.

"Dónde está Juan González?"

"Está allá," the man says, looking with his eyes and pointing with his nose toward a series of rooms four stories below ground level, and two stories above where Sarah now kneels. She confirms where he is pointing through a back and forth exchange, then pulls the remainder of her weapons out for ready use as she starts her assault upward, hoping the rest of the American assault team is making its way down simultaneously. Before leaving the room, the guard asks for help, not sure he can continue to hold his chin on the bar. Sarah understands, but doesn't have time to worry about him now. She's already 30 seconds behind plan. She pulls a breathing tube out of her pack and shoves it in the guy's mouth before departing.

Working her way up, Sarah encounters no resistance until she reaches sub-floor four. Most of the military on site have moved toward ground level to fight the assault. One guard remains outside the room where she expects to find the Americans. Sarah puts a bullet squarely through the back of his head, runs over to kick his guns away from him and checks the door.

Looking inside, she sees only one person. The young man is trying to build a stack of chairs in a corner to pull himself into a ceiling vent as Sarah blasts the door open. Startled, the young man turns and falls off the chairs, hitting his head against the side of the wall as he falls and cutting himself open.

"Juan? Juan Gonzalez?" Sarah asks.

"Sí."

"I'm Sarah, I'm here to help you escape. Come with me and stay on my back. We need to get you to a rooftop in 210 seconds for extraction."

Juan does as he's told. A little stunned by the fall, and bleeding from his head, he simply follows his instinct, and Sarah.

Sarah breaks radio silence. "Drummer boy secure. Moving to target now up stairwell six."

"Hold for stairwell clearance," comes back the response. In the time following Sarah's water jump, more than 100 U.S. attack helicopters had fought their way into the Monterrey base. With 700 U.S. soldiers on the ground, facing a defense force depleted by defections from three-quarters of the U.N. peacekeeping countries, the U.S. team is able to break through initial defenses. Ground-level forces had purposely been kept close to standard base levels to avoid attracting satellite and local spy attention. On-ground U.S. forces are facing continuous fire, however, from U.N., Mexico and Alta Texas forces emerging from the underground command center and staging areas. For nearly 10 minutes, Sarah and Juan hold inside the room where he had been held hostage.

The "stairwell six clear" message finally comes.

Sarah and Juan race up six flights of stairs, then find the pull-down ladder enabling them to reach the rooftop opening. Juan's blood is covering the side of his head and soaking the white button-down shirt he's wearing. His tie and suit coat have long since been removed from his well-attired start to this tumultuous experience.

As she enters the rooftop, Sarah kneels to check for threats and sees ground combat continuing below with U.S. forces in solid control. Lying back flat, she helps pull Juan through the roof access and then tells him to stay low and on his belly until she orders him to move.

"Ready for extraction," Sarah calls out.

When Ally returns with the APB to TQ, she finds that the assault has worked. Ally brings the APB in hot to 1,000 feet, comes to a dead stop, then extends the overhead rotary blades. Two seconds later, the blades are engaged and running. She turns off the jet engines now facing the ground to avoid incinerating Sarah and Juan as she drops. As Ally quickly descends, Pete drops 50 feet below the APB on a cable latched to a torso harness. Pete latches Juan in, calling out to him in hastily learned Mandarin. Pete and Sarah return fire to Alta Texas troops continuing to fight their way up stairwells to repel the U.S. attack.

Inside the DUCC Situation Room, Jill confirms that Juan is the person being extracted. President Phillipi is standing next to her as she gives this confirmation. He pumps his fist, then jams a chocolate and peanut butter candy into his mouth.

With Juan's location confirmed, U.S. forces increasingly drop grenades and bombs into identified sub-ground entry points, and concentrate fire on building exit points.

Pete straps Juan in front of him, much as a skydiving instructor would strap in a trainee, though with Juan facing him. The only other difference is that Pete secures Juan in just three seconds and now has his hands clasped around Juan to make sure the straps hold for the upward pull.

As Pete and Juan are yanked toward the APB, several Alta Texas and U.N. soldiers recognize what is happening and start firing aggressively at the APB. Pete grabs the metal rope above and swings himself around to shoot back and be sure his body is between Juan and those firing at him. Pete yells at Juan to grab Pete's helmet, take it off and put it on his own head. Pete and Juan rise quickly toward the APB, but not quickly enough. Pete is hit several times. His bulletproof gear deflects most of the bullets, but several bullets find gaps as Pete extends himself to protect Juan.

With Pete and Juan inside the APB, Ally takes off. Sarah shoots her way back to the roof access, engaging an Alta Texas force that is still fighting up the stairwell. This roof is not one of the main extraction sites, so Sarah wants to get through the building and out onto the main grounds to be picked up by one of the U.S. attack choppers. There are too many Alta Texas soldiers still in her way.

Ally triggers the jets firing in hover mode below, shuts down the rotary blades and accelerates 20,000 feet straight up before rotating the jets to fly parallel to the ground. With the departure order given, Sarah climbs backwards up the roof access ladder, shooting at each head, arm or weapon that turns the corner of the stairwell below as she ascends. Back on the roof, she kicks the roof access closed behind her and runs to an edge of the roof. Gravel on the rooftop kicks up behind her as she runs. With 20 feet to go before she reaches the edge of the roof, Sarah hears the roof access door slam open and turns while running to see shooters taking aim.

Almost to the edge, she feels multiple hits as she prepares to jump three stories to the ground below. The hits knock her balance off enough that Sarah lands nearly flat when hitting the ground. She lies still on the ground, bleeding as Alta Texas and Mexican soldiers get to the edge and start firing rocket-propelled grenades at the final U.S. attack choppers leaving the base. Three choppers remain on the ground trying to extract bodies, but dozens of dead soldiers are left behind as the last chopper departs under heavy fire.

Sarah Osborne is on the ground, her body being torn apart by Alta Texas soldiers taking out their anger at the few targets they have remaining.

Inside Ally's APB, Juan tries holding his fingers over Pete's bullet wounds. He ignores the wound from a bullet that went through the bottom of Pete's feet as they were pulled up. Juan also has several new flesh wounds, but doesn't notice.

The worst of Pete's wounds is on his neck. Pete had forgotten to take a helmet and neck guard for Juan down with him, so ordered Juan to wear his instead. Juan presses two fingers on each side of Pete's neck to try stopping the bleeding. Then he presses both sides with his palms. New Rite team member Luisa, or Lou as she is called, opens the medical kit and starts a fast field patch on the wound. Pete is still breathing, but the amount of blood covering the floor of the APB makes clear to those with battle experience that it will be tough to keep Pete alive.

Lou asks others on board for their blood type. No matches. She takes a quick sample of Juan's blood to check his type. A match. She starts a draw for Pete from Juan, and checks vitals for both every two minutes all the way to Louisiana.

***

Alta Texas, Mexican and what remains of U.N. military jets have since been told they've been duped by Ally's southwest run from TQ. Jets are screaming back toward Monterrey. Arriving just after the last American assault team departs, the jets pursue the raid force. Secretary Mendoza scrambles 100 U.S. fighter jets over Mexican territory to provide protection and a deadly battle is engaged over Mexico and the Gulf of Mexico, before U.N. and Mexican military commanders order their jets to retreat. With these retreat orders uncoordinated as U.S. efforts to jam U.N. communication channels continue to succeed, defecting Alta Texas pilots who came with confiscated U.S. military jets are left alone to engage the U.S. force. The only survivors among the group are picked up out of the Gulf of Mexico.

During the battle, Ramon Mantle and his Protection Corps bodyguards run away from the shooting, eventually hiding surrounded and covered by bags of corn meal and cases of canned foods. Ten minutes after the last sounds of shooting and explosions, Ramon emerges from the kitchen. He and his men search for and eventually find a working vehicle, then start the long drive west to cartel headquarters.

As soon as the success of the extraction is announced, President Phillipi heads up from the DUCC and then to the tunnel connection to the Pentagon for transport to Andrews Air Force Base.

Jill's shirt is soaked with sweat accumulated while watching the attack. At first leaving her coat off to cool down as she is escorted back to the Capitol, Jill quickly begins to shiver in the military escort vehicle. The female soldier who brought her to the Pentagon escorts Jill back alone.

"Have a good rest of your day Congresswoman," the soldier says to Jill as she drops her at the entrance across from the Capitol South Metro stop.

"I think I just might," Jill responds, before heading to the House gym for a quick shower and change.

CHAPTER 20

3 Hours

Sinaloa Province, Mexico

General Hernández, leader of the Protection Corps, demands that Mexican President Suárez pass on a message to U.S. President Phillipi that he will call him in 15 minutes. President Suárez initially objects before Hernández tells him he has nuclear bombs placed in the United States and in Suárez's own hometown that he will start exploding if President Phillipi does not talk to him and agree to his conditions.

Exactly 15 minutes after taking the call from President Suárez, President Phillipi is connected to Hernández.

"I would like to be the first to congratulate you, Mr. President, on your stunning success in repelling the United Nations invaders," the general states as his opening comment.

"Tell me what this is about," President Phillipi responds, angry that he is speaking to a man he considers vile and immoral.

"I want you to know, Mr. President, that you have every reason to believe you have won. But your victory will be a painful one if you do not meet my conditions."

"We owe you nothing."

"Perhaps, but the nuclear bombs you planted in Alta Texas could explode at any minute."

"We planted no such thing."

"It's a shame you cannot acknowledge your cruelty," Hernández states. "How could you decide to detonate nuclear bombs at the end of your 72 hours? You see, I have been told of your arrogant, self-indulgent plans. I know you will retaliate against freedom fighters just as you have won the right to keep them enslaved. Or perhaps your people will come to see your explosions as incompetence in forgetting to disarm your nuclear weapons at the crucial hour. Or maybe you will act stupidly to let these dangerous weapons fall into the hands of a vicious enemy for later use. I don't know which of these options you are following, but I want to avoid letting any of them happen to my people."

"Your people?"

"My people. Always, my people." Hernández assumes the call is being taped, so chooses his words carefully.

"How can I make you stop whatever you are doing?" President Phillipi asks.

General Hernández sighs: "Ahh . . . , I heard you were a man who would bow to powerful reason."

***

Chennault Air Force Base, Louisiana

As soon as Ally's APB lands, Pete is placed on a stretcher and rushed to emergency surgery.

Juan is washed down, has his flesh wounds treated and stitched and is loaded into the back of an X-72 Wave medical jet for high-speed delivery to Andrews Air Force Base, taking blood and oxygen on the way.

Ally, Lou and the other soldiers arriving here congratulate each other on their success. Ally searches for Sarah.

CHAPTER 21

2 Hours

Washington, D.C.

A short time later, a press briefing is hastily called at the Pentagon. With two more hours left until the deadline for the Alta Texas secession to be abandoned, tensions remain heightened, particularly for the very few aware of General Hernández's latest threat.

While the largest countries involved in the U.N. peacekeeping mission have since pulled out, nearly a dozen frequently anti-American countries maintain their alignment with Mexico and particularly General Hernández. Mexican President Suárez sends a message to the White House that he would like to withdraw Mexico's military from the encounter, but the combination of the U.S. attack on Monterrey and the control on the military exerted by the Castillo cartel makes that impossible unless all sides, including General Hernández, can reach a cease fire.

President Suárez does not mention that his family is now confined by the Protection Corps and under nuclear extermination threat.

Video of the intense air skirmish over the Gulf of Mexico raises concerns that, despite abandonment of U.N. peacekeeping by most nations, the secession attempt may still only be settled through full-scale war.

Every national network interrupts what has been nearly 24 hours news programming the last three days to cover the President's press conference. The few sporting events not already cancelled are stopped mid-game to broadcast the press conference live once the public is told that information critical to the end of the secession and withdrawal of U.N. and Mexican troops from U.S. soil will be announced.

At 10:05 p.m. Eastern time, five minutes after the announced start of the press conference, President Marc Phillipi walks to the podium with his arms on the shoulder of Juan Gonzalez. Juan's head is stitched and covered with a hat to avoid startling viewers with the large gashes on his head before those gashes can be explained. His small flesh wounds have been patched or stitched.

Around the nation and the broader world, audible gasps are heard at the sight of Juan and President Phillipi together.

"Ladies and gentlemen, I have a substantial amount of news to share with the citizens of all 52 states, as well as with the rest of the world. But before I do this, I would like to introduce Mr. Juan Gonzalez to make his remarks."

The President steps back, shakes Juan's hand and pulls him toward the podium.

"Thank you, Mr. President. For those who don't know me, my name is Juan Gonzalez. As you may know, I've spent the better part of the past year as an avid supporter of Southwest independence and Spanish language mandates. However, I am here to tell you, of my own free will, that I am fully opposed to the secession effort undertaken by Senator Jones with the misled cooperation of the United Nations."

"Early on the morning of President Phillipi's inauguration, I went to the Tucson airport intending to make it to Washington, D.C. to represent Honor to Mexico at the President's swearing-in ceremony and subsequent events. Instead, Gabriel Herrera and his men kidnapped me at gunpoint, cuffed me, put a bag over my head and kept me that way until I was locked in an empty room under armed guard. Only after I was rescued by U.S. Special Forces did I learn that I was being held at a military base in Monterrey, Mexico that served as the launch base for the United Nations invasion of the Southwest states."

"I said during the past year that secession needs to be non-violent, with the other states convinced it's in their best interest to let our four states govern ourselves. I thought non-violence was the H2M way all along. It turns out, I was wrong," Juan tells a packed press conference.

While a few reporters are already trying to shout questions, President Phillipi asks that they wait until Juan finishes and the President speaks, assuring the reporters that the two will stay until the last reasonable question has been answered.

"I accepted the position as ambassador to the United States for the Republic of Alta Texas because it was clear to me that if I was not part of the secession team, my body would likely never be found. Once I told Senator Jones, who was also in Monterrey along with the United Nations invasion leadership, that I would accept the position as ambassador, I was permitted some modest freedoms, though always with an armed soldier watching over me."

"Now, before I go further, I'll remove my hat and explain what you see before my mother or anyone else gets too concerned," Juan says, skipping to Spanish to let his mother know that she should not worry about what she sees next.

Juan pulls off his hat to display a shaved area of his head around which he now has 24 stitches and a glossy wound sealant applied. The hat had been given to Juan to put on just before he walked out to the press conference as Chief of Staff Chinh realized that the initial visual impression of Juan walking out wounded next to the President would be that the United States had done this to him.

"During the course of rescuing me from the Alta Texas headquarters in Monterrey, I had been piling chairs up to try to reach a high ceiling vent to escape when a U.S. soldier blew the lock on the door and came into the room. She scared the living, uh, well, scared the heck out of me and I fell against the wall and into the fallen chairs on the way down. This woman escorted me to the rooftop where I was pulled up into a jet or helicopter or . . . ."

"Juan, please don't describe the vehicle any further," the President directs.

"Oh, okay, I was pulled up and we blasted out of there. On the way here, I learned that the woman who saved me was likely killed as the battle at the Monterrey site continued for some time after my rescue," Juan says, his face turning pale. Grabbing both sides of the podium for balance, he asks if anyone minds if he sits down for a moment. Juan's facial muscles twitch as he tries to speak again, eyes clearly watering. A tall stool is quickly brought over and Juan pulls it up underneath himself, then reaches up with a tissue and wipes his eyes.

"Anyway, I guess I can't say the name of the soldier because her family has not all been notified yet, but when you hear her name, I want everyone to know what a remarkable hero she and everyone else involved in my rescue is to me. I also realize that rescuing me was not the main reason for the assault on Monterrey, but I'll leave it to the President to talk about that."

Juan steps back, takes a deep breath and gathers himself before returning to the podium.

"So, what was I talking about? Oh yeah, I want family, friends, H2M followers and all those who trust that I want what's best for them to know what I've learned that has convinced me we must abandon this secession."

"First, it turns out that the secession votes were rigged, and that only New Mexico passed the vote legitimately. I learned that Senator Jones' team manipulated computerized voting, as well as exit polling data to obtain what appeared to be clear majorities in all four states. In my meeting with President Phillipi before coming out here, he let me know that a full-scale investigation had been underway and was approaching indictments when the invasion was launched. So even our people did not support secession, except in New Mexico. That is the first reason I ask that all secession supporters stand down immediately."

"Second, an invasion by the United Nations was never something I considered part of secession. Already, thousands of innocent lives have been lost with an attack spurred on by the political ambitions of Senator Jones, the governors and several generals. In just the short time these countries were in our lands, it became clear to me that Russia, Iran and several others intended to establish permanent military bases on our lands as compensation Senator Jones agreed to pay in return for their support of his secession effort. The United States has imperfections, but agreeing to things like Sharia law around foreign-controlled bases in order to get control of a country shows the extent to which President Jones, I mean Senator Jones or whatever he is now, will hurt people to achieve his own ambitions."

"Third, I ask you all to abandon secession because it is clear to me now that the largest financier of H2M and the secession effort was recently killed drug kingpin Cesar Castillo. I'm told Castillo envisioned reuniting Alta Texas and Mexico, then ultimately becoming dictator of the two countries. There is much that needs to be changed about America, but not at the expense of dictatorship or martial law or whatever else we might have ended up with," Juan continues. "Finally, the fourth reason I'm abandoning attempts to secede and ask others to join me is that President Phillipi has made clear that he understands what we need, and will start addressing the very real concerns of our community immediately once the U.N. troops have left U.S. territory. With that, let me turn it back to the President."

President Phillipi reaches out to shake Juan's hand again, then pulls him in for a hug. The two had only spent significant time together once last fall, but the President felt an instant connection with Juan during that meeting. The President pulls the stool back to the side for Juan to sit on before moving back to the podium.

"Good evening, fellow citizens of the United States of America. It's my pleasure to tell you that our states will continue to indeed be united," the President states, pausing for nearly a minute to let his message sink in. "In the last hours, I have been informed by China, Russia, Germany, Brazil and most other major nations that they have pulled their troops out of both the United States and Mexico, or are in the process of doing so. A few nations, including Iran, Pakistan, Egypt, Saudi Arabia, Syria, Afghanistan, Indonesia, North Sudan and two or three others, say they will withdraw to Mexico but plan to leave troops there. This is progress, but we will demand at an appropriate time that all invaders leave our vicinity."

"Equally important, during our raid on Monterrey, in addition to rescuing Mr. Gonzalez, we were able to capture and return to the United States with Senator Jones and several of the U.S. generals who defected. These men and women will be tried for treason. I want to point out that once we breached the Alta Texas command center, Senator Jones made no effort to fight. He was willing to send other men to die, but was unwilling to fight himself. Our courts will decide his fate from here."

"As a result of our raid, we are taking government control of Perfect Logistics and have started an aggressive manhunt for Ramon Mantle. For those who don't know, Perfect Logistics makes the Easy Ride software that controls most of the nation's vehicles. Perhaps more importantly, we believe that Ramon Mantle has recently won an internal battle to succeed Cesar Castillo as head of the Castillo drug cartel. I don't have to tell you what type of money can be made in the drug business when an entrepreneur worth billions decides he wants in on the drug business instead."

"But the really important news is that the secession effort will be abandoned, without further loss of life. That does not mean that great sacrifices have not been made and I want to particularly honor the men and women who held control of several U.S. military bases in the four states throughout this crisis, as well as the men and women who risked and particularly lost their lives in the raid on Monterrey. Juan has described just one of the heroes who sacrificed her life to save him. Dozens of the best and brightest of the U.S. military lost their lives during the raid on Monterrey and we will fully honor all of these heroes once families have been notified," the President tells the room, the nation, and billions around the world.

During the next hour, the President and Juan Gonzalez answer several dozen questions.

***

"Mr. President, why wouldn't you let Juan describe the plane or helicopter he was picked up in?" the MSDNC anchor asks.

"When you have a military advantage, as we now do, you don't just readily give it away. So I think we want to keep some of our weapons capabilities to ourselves."

"Could this new weapon be the U.F.O. that was spotted in Mexico on New Years Day?" the anchor asks as a follow-up question.

"We can identify all the weapons we have in U.S. military control so we don't call anything we have a U.F.O."

"But would others call it a U.F.O.?"

"I'm not going to speculate on that," the President responds.

"How did the U.S. know you were a prisoner and not part of the secession leadership?" a reporter asks Juan.

"I guess through contacts with my girlfriend, Congresswoman Carlson and Professor Stark, from what I understand."

"Are you saying Congresswoman Carlson is your girlfriend?"

"No, no, no. Those are three different people."

"So, you have a girlfriend?"

"If she's still speaking to me, I do."

"Mr. President, will any retribution be taken against the leadership of Mexico or the United Nations for their roles in this fight?"

"Militarily, that is not my preference. I will ask the Attorney General to consider whether criminal or civil actions can be taken, either in U.S. Courts or an International War Crimes setting. I do expect that the Secretary-General of the United Nations will resign before the end of the day, and have been assured by the leaders of China, France, Germany, Brazil, India and many other countries that their continued involvement in the United Nations is dependent on his immediate removal. As for President Suárez in Mexico, I believe the only honorable action he can take now is to resign for the damage he has inflicted on his nation and to save his people from further harm."

"Do you both think the issue of secession is settled now for the next 100 years?" asks news network anchor Brody Maguire. Juan met Brody during an interview last year at which Juan first met Jill and Professor Stark.

"Issues like this never go away," the President responds. "Governments are, by their very nature, kleptocracies. We take from people. In return, though, good governments provide services worth more collectively than if each individual tried to acquire these services independently. When we do it right, we provide for defense, infrastructure and life-sustaining transition and support services in ways that the people we service are satisfied with the value we deliver for their tax dollars. But we all know governments with the power to serve also have the power to abuse. More importantly, governments can fail to find the right balance between enabling success and enabling dependence. As I told Juan, we have a long way to go to create a better deal for the American people."

Brody turns to Juan: "Great to see you safe Juan. Your thoughts?"

"As far as I'm concerned, the issue of secession is settled, certainly for now and certainly with these leaders and this approach," Juan adds, a small trickle of blood still dripping from the back of his wound. "I'm encouraged that the President understands the problems of this country are much more than heritage and language. It's interesting to me that he will turn control of many programs and operations for the people back to the states. State control brings government closer to the people, reduces bureaucracy and spurs competition. An interesting lesson of history to me, one I have to thank Professor Stark and his class for helping me to understand, is that societies where competition is encouraged do better and last longer than in places where too much is centralized and government becomes stagnant and self-absorbed. It may seem, I think the word is ironic, that the best way for the United States to stay united is to send responsibility for as much as possible back to the states."

Maguire appears perplexed by Juan's last statement and waves to get the President's attention for a follow-up. Seeing his exaggerated waves, the President points back to Brody and press conference audio controllers turn his microphone back on.

"I have to admit Juan, that you lost me with that last statement. You're agreeing with President Phillipi that we need to turn more programs back to the states as a way of building unity. That sounds to me like you are agreeing with attempts to re-segregate America," Brody states.

"I can see how you might think that. This is just my opinion, but I think a nation needs to share values and fundamental beliefs and agree on outcomes we want. How we implement programs to achieve those outcomes needs to be subject to competition so we always can find ways to get better at achieving our objectives," Juan responds.

"What do you think, Mr. President?" Brody asks.

"I think I should just shut up and let Juan talk," the President responds.

"But when you leave this stuff to the states, aren't you sentencing someone in Arizona to a lower quality of service than someone in New York when they face identical conditions? I'm surprised you would support any form of discrimination," Brody continues asking Juan.

"You may be right that, for some period of time, someone might receive slightly better treatment under a program in one state compared to if they lived in another. But, as Americans, we choose what state we live in so if the difference is substantial enough, it's easier to change states than to change citizenship – as we just saw," Juan says, as several reporters chuckle at the irony of Juan's talking about the difficulty of changing citizenship after supporting secession for the past eight months. "Most importantly, if there's only one way to achieve an objective, it gets tough to make that program better. There's nothing to compare it against."

President Phillipi steps back to the microphone panel.

"I have to say, I'm glad I can't seek reelection when Juan turns 35," the President says to loud, tension-relieving laughter.

"I still don't get how having the states act differently isn't a form of segregation and discrimination," Brody asks again.

"It's simple really," Juan says. "Discrimination and segregation are driven by the words 'can't' and 'must.' What I'm saying is that it's better to give people options on how they want to achieve what we collectively agree as a nation is what all people should be able to achieve."

"And the language issue," Brody continues. "How does this fit nationally? Do you agree that all people should speak English, or that each state should decide it's own language?" Brody asks, his microphone clicking off as he ends the question.

"Throw that into the mix of issues on which I'm still trying to figure out the right answer. All I know is that I want to prevent people from being discriminated against because of who we are at birth," Juan responds. "And I can understand now the importance of being integrated and having a shared language, as long as we also appreciate diversity and the benefits of a multilingual society."

"Mr. President, are there any people or groups you can name who were particularly important to the success of the Monterrey Raid?" another reporter asks.

"The reality is that there are so many to whom the nation is indebted that I do not want to diminish the contributions of these heroes. With that, I think we need to end this press conference. There are thousands of loose ends that must be attended to and, more importantly, hundreds of families I must now call with heart-wrenching news that takes away from the joy of keeping the nation united."

***

As they exit the press conference, Secretary Mendoza catches Juan and the President to let them know of another casualty, one he is told Juan will want to know about. Pete Roote didn't make it through surgery.

The President turns to see Juan's anger taking control of his emotions. He puts his arm around Juan's shoulder.

"I know this is tough news, Juan," President Phillipi says. "We heard what this guy Pete did to take the bullets to protect you. Since he's passed away now, I'll tell you that the man who helped save your life isn't even military. He was one of New Rite's elite survival gamers. More importantly, he completed the most remarkable individual assassination effort of which I have ever heard when he snuck into Mexico, killed Cesar Castillo in his compound, and managed to escape back to the United States, completely without the aid of the U.S. government. His life clearly had a purpose Juan, and I think that you are standing here now is clear evidence of that purpose."

***

Utah New Rite Compound

The Coleman family, along with all the other watch teams across Wawheap Bay, Padre Bay and the other waters backing up from Glen Canyon Dam, are alerted by radio that the war is over; the last of the U.N. alliance countries have agreed to withdraw their troops. Everyone at New Rite's compound can return to base camp.

For John and the rest of the Coleman family, it's a bittersweet moment. John's feeling of incredible relief that his wife and children are safe is off-set by recognition that his father was killed during the invasion. Grandpa Coleman was just one of thousands who will be counted as collateral damage in the three-day war. As the Coleman family all converges at their base camp, John asks that they all take a moment to pray for Grandpa – and for the men who killed him.

"Dear Lord, thank you for the blessing you bestowed upon Grandpa by taking him in full dignity and honor, battling to save everything that he had fought to protect as a soldier, a father and a grandfather. We do not understand why this fight had to occur, but we hope and believe that his death has served a purpose greater than any of us can understand. We honor the sacrifices Grandpa made for all of our freedoms and thank you, God, for granting him the ability and freedom to live a life of which we are all proud. Amen."

As the other members of the family say "amen," Clarissa stands up. She walks away crying, wiping tears with the outside of her sleeve. Her mother follows her and pulls Clarissa's head down to her shoulder. "Grandpa would have been tremendously proud of you and how you handled yourself these last few days, Clarissa. You know that, don't you?"

"Yeah, I know that Mom. I think he was already with me when I saw the rafts coming across, telling me what to do. I wasn't even scared."

"That may be, sweetie, though I wish you would be a little more scared more often. Life doesn't always work out the way we wish it would."

"You and Dad keep telling me that. I guess I needed to see it for myself."

After they finish packing the tent, sleeping bags and other supplies, they look around to be sure they haven't left any garbage. Then the family takes off on the hike around the rim of Friendship Cove to Grand Bench Road, where they wait for someone to pick them up.

"Let's go home, ladies," John Coleman says as a flatbed truck meets them at the road to drive back as many as can pile on.

***

Washington D.C.

With the press conference concluded, Juan Gonzalez asks to speak to President Phillipi privately. The President agrees and asks his staff and Secret Service guards to leave the two alone.

Within seconds, the room is cleared. The small conference room is barren, except for a table and eight chairs. President Phillipi loosens his tie, unbuttons the top button of his shirt and takes off his suit jacket. He sits in the closest chair and points toward another chair to invite Juan to sit.

Juan starts sweating. Through most of his public appearances and even the press conference they just concluded, Juan maintained a remarkable level of calm. Only talking to the media the morning after his mentor was assassinated had him publicly unnerved.

His nervousness makes the President uncomfortable.

"Take a seat Juan. What's on your mind?" he asks.

Juan continues to stand in front of the President, looking his direction, but with a blank stare. Then he starts looking around the room for cameras in the ceiling.

"Juan. Juan." President Phillipi tries to get his attention, then stands up and gives his shoulder a gentle shake.

Juan reaches his right hand down the front of his pants, causing the President to back up and look down to see what Juan is doing. He hears an interlocked strap pull apart and questions whether Secret Service could have missed something in screening Juan. Before he calls for Secret Service to come in, Juan's hand is out of his pants and holding a hand-written note.

President Phillipi relaxes. He sits back down.

Juan's face is still pale.

"Mr. President, someone you are interested in gave me this piece of paper and told me to only give it to someone I could trust with my life," Juan says, wiping sweat from his forehead with his sleeve.

The President looks at the paper.

"2,718,281,828," the paper reads.

"What does this mean?" the President asks.

"He told me the number has something to do with bacteria growth," Juan responds. "But that's not what matters. It's meaningless without my added piece of information."

"Which is?"

"Which is . . . " Juan starts to respond, finally taking a seat in the chair next to the President. "Which is. I need to ask you first. Can I really trust you with my life?"

"I think I've earned that trust," the President responds, staring intently at Juan, trying to figure out what this is all about. He rubs his eyes trying to get them to focus.

Nodding, Juan asks for a pen.

He takes back the piece of paper and adds to the note: "One World #"

As he shows the President what he wrote, he looks back at him: "He told me that whoever I gave this to had to only involve one more person in tracking it. He said too many spies are buried in our government."

"What, exactly, does it mean?" the President asks.

"This is the account for this place," Juan says, pointing at the number and the words One World. One World is the primary interconnected social media site in the world, used by nearly three billion people globally. "There will be a message there."

CHAPTER 22

0 Hours

Washington, D.C.

Two-thirds of the U.S. cabinet members gather in the DUCC, with the others under orders to remain at other locations until full security is restored. President Phillipi opens the cabinet session passing around champagne glasses and personally opening two champagne bottles. He passes the bottles around the room for everyone to fill their glass.

"A toast," he says, "to honor every man and woman who sacrificed to protect the freedoms of the United States of America."

"Here, here," all respond, voices reflecting a mix of solemnity and elation.

"And a thank you to each and every one of you and your teams for your extraordinary success and dedication through this crisis. America owes you tremendous gratitude and I, personally, thank you for your service," the President continues, though his mind still races knowing the conflict is far from over. Glasses again clatter around the room. Handshakes and hugs are exchanged around the room before President Phillipi asks for attention again.

"In front of everyone, I want to thank Ray for delaying his retirement to help ensure we have a country to enjoy. So thank you, Ray. I promise I will let you retire if that is still what you want to do, but I think everyone here would join me in begging you to stay."

"I certainly echo that, Mr. President," injects Secretary Mendoza. "Ray and I haven't always been on the same page, but I have gained great admiration for his leadership and talent."

"Thank you, Mr. President . . . , Xavier. I really appreciate your kind words, but if I don't retire soon, I will not be able to sleep at night without worry that my wife will slit my throat," Secretary Peyton states to nods of agreement.

After the meeting breaks up, President Phillipi pulls aside Secretary Mendoza. "Xavier, I'm asking you now for one more personal favor," he says.

"What's that Marc?"

"I want to be part of the assault team that goes after the Castillo cartel."

Secretary Mendoza shakes his head and sighs heavily.

"I thought you would have given that up by now. How many times do I need to tell you I can't, in good conscience, do that, sir?"

"Xavier, I'm not asking. I'm ordering. We'll work out the details."

"What happens if I leak this to the first lady?"

"Any leak of my involvement will jeopardize the mission, Xavier, and I know you understand the importance of mission security," the President says. "Consider this my penance for mistakes I've made that put this country at risk."

***

Jill has convinced Capitol Police to make an exception for her. The police let Jill and Professor Stark through an old door hidden away at the base of the Capitol dome to climb old, rickety stairs that run inside the dome of the U.S. Capitol. Cut off to general public use for generations, Members of Congress gain occasional approval to walk the steps to the top of the Capitol from inside the dome. As they walk, they see the ceiling murals painted in a way that is distorted up close, but appears proportionate from the floor below. Repairs to the steps have happened regularly over the years, but the narrow steps, short railing and occasional creaks leave all but the most fearless a bit nervous and awestruck on the climb up.

At the top, a door takes the pair out to a ridge just below the top of the Capitol's dome. It's midnight now. The 72 hours have expired. It looks like the United States will again be united – at least for another generation. Tens of thousands lay dead around the country from terrorist attacks, military assaults, race-based conflicts, war and the effects of mistaken communications.

Jill and Professor Stark decide that ending this string of violence deserves celebration. Against the rules, Professor Stark has brought up two small bottles of wine tucked inside his jacket.

He opens the first and hands it to Jill. Then he opens the second and proposes a toast. "To an America that breaks through past divisions to work together, play together and succeed together," he says, clanking his bottle against hers as the two look across toward the Washington Monument.

Jill takes a sip, thinks for a moment and then offers her own toast: "To all the heroes who sacrificed to save America for future generations, and to all the families who must now repair lives torn apart by the greed and ambition of politicians who think the best solutions always involve us."

With the city lights off for the third straight night, the stars stand out against the cold, dark backdrop. Where normally a few dozen stars are all they can see from the city, the view tonight takes Jill back to her nights and early mornings on her family's dairy farm.

"There's something about seeing the real night sky that gives me a sense of peace," Jill says, grasping Professor Stark's hand.

"There's something about holding your hand that does that for me," Professor Stark says, looking at her, cupping his hands around her cheeks and leaning in for a passionate kiss.

In the distance, three choppers make their way up the Potomac River, cross behind the Washington Monument, and descend toward the White House.

"Has to be the first family heading back home," Jill says after Professor Stark pulls back his lips. "Nice to know he feels safe enough to bring them back to the city tonight."

"I just hope they're smart enough to stay away from theaters," Professor Stark says. "The last civil war didn't end well for the president who led us through it."

"God, you're humor is so deadpan sometimes," Jill says.

"I'm not saying it to be funny. I mean it. He needs to be careful."

***

Utah New Rite Compound

Clarissa Coleman arrives back at the New Rite camp headquarters looking for Sarah Osborne. Not finding her, Clarissa asks where Sarah went. The man at the front desk doesn't want to answer. He stutters through several attempts at starting a sentence before responding.

"I took her down toward the bay yesterday. She went out in a boat on a scouting trip. She was searching for others who might be trying to escape back into America," the man tells Clarissa, hoping that is enough to end her questioning.

"Oh, okay. Where did she put in, and where was she headed?"

He pulls out the scouting map used to track assignments of who was watching what part of the border and points to a spot on the map. "She went in here and said she would circle up all the way to Bullfrog Bay. Why?"

"Oh, I thought I saw something small in the water. I bet it was Sarah. Was she in a tiny motorized boat?"

"Yes, she was."

"Had to be her then. Did she leave a way to get in touch with her?"

The man at the desk turns his head away and bends over to pretend he's moving documents around. After several minutes, without looking back up, he responds: "No, there's really no way to reach her now."

Clarissa leans over the desk to try looking at him: "Can you give a message to her that Clarissa saw her on the water and really admired her cool ride. I think she'll know what I mean."

It's clear now that he can't just dismiss this young girl.

"Did you really know Sarah?" he asks. "Are you related?"

"No, but she helped find me when I got lost and we became friends. I just like her," Clarissa says, smiling at the man. "And she told me that I would see something cool if I kept looking. Can you give her my message so she knows I saw it?"

The man delays for another minute or two. He looks at Clarissa, trying to find a way to tell her gently.

"I really wish I could, miss," he tells her, "but we just found out that Sarah didn't make it."

"What do you mean by 'didn't make it'?"

"She, um, was part of a group that fought for our country and, well, we just found out that she didn't make it." He can barely get the words out and is talking so softly by the end that Clarissa has to concentrate to understand what he said.

Clarissa sits down on a chair, puts her head down to her knees and clasps her hands behind her head. The man at the counter watches as her back heaves up and down.

Not knowing what to do, he stands there watching, shedding tears of his own.

"I'm really sorry Miss. I didn't want to tell you, but I didn't want to lie to you, either," he says.

"This whole thing is so unfair, . . . so stupid," Clarissa yells out, standing up and slowly, weakly moving toward the door. "So . . . not . . . cool."

***

Mexico City, Mexico

As the 72-hour deadline passes, Mexican President Daniel Suárez announces he is resigning effective immediately.

"*U.S. President Marc Phillipi has made clear that the United States could invade our country and take vengeance on our people if I do not immediately remove myself from office and leave Mexico,*" President Suárez tells a nationwide audience. "*I am appointing as my replacement the only man I believe who has the military expertise and proven leadership to protect Mexico from the United States, without threatening U.S. territory.*" Substantial amounts of sweat drip from his face. Each new wrinkle reflects a traumatic moment from months of hosting U.N. troops and weeks of planning peacekeeping responses. Grey around his temple appears to have expanded exponentially from the moment President Suárez discovered that military base attacks were part of the overall U.N. plans. Peacekeeping plans were made in Mexico City. Invasion planning took place in Monterrey, with a smaller group of nations included.

"I introduce to you your new leader, President Raúl Hernández."

"Thank you, Daniel," General Hernández says. *"In the interests of protecting our people from an invasion by the United States, I must immediately announce the declaration of martial law over Mexico. The constitution is suspended effective immediately and will remain suspended until we have again strengthened our nation. I have secured the commitment of many nations to keep troops in Mexico to protect us from attack until such time as this support is no longer necessary to protect all of Mexico."*

***

Washington, D.C.

President Phillipi convenes his top national security team to discuss strategy. JT Alton is the only outsider brought into the planning session.

"If we dedicate every resource imaginable, how quickly can we build 1,000 of your APBs, several thousand of your miniature drones and thousands of missile launch rifles and any other weaponry you haven't shown us yet," the President asks JT. JT responds that each APB took a dedicated team of 30 more than a full year to build even with substantial robot-assisted assembly. Plans to move to larger-scale production have already been developed, but it will take at least a year to make that many APBs, JT predicts. The other production could also be done in a year or two.

"I need 1,000. I need them in a week. And I need 1,000 people capable of flying your APBs without being spotted and thousands more capable of shooting your weapons without missing," the President demands.

"You're asking the impossible Mr. President. Even with all the money and all of the people in the world, I can't do this," JT responds.

"If you can't do this with 0.1 percent of the money and even fewer of the people," the President says, sternly looking JT in the eyes, "we will watch tens of millions of people die because of our failure."

JT stares at the President blankly to process what he just told him.

"Tens of millions?"

"Tens of millions."

"I assume then that all of this needs to be done without any leaks?" JT asks.

"Correct."

"Well, then, how many people can we trust to help us?"

"We trust no one. We'll have to confine every worker in lockdown until we've finished the job and executed the mission."

Retired Homeland Security Secretary Peyton is given one hour to have dinner with his wife before taking over mission command. Retirement again must wait.

CHAPTER 23

February 1, 2041
Utica, Illinois

FirstWal Executive Chet Leach stops half way through his frigid morning walk, with temperatures in the 20s, to follow an eagle as it soars above his head looking for prey. Snowpack on the ground has an icy sheen from recent daytime highs reaching well into the 30s. Animal life is still largely in mid-winter doldrums. Still, Chet is optimistic that the eagle will find a mole or squirrel or mouse and treat him to a wildlife kill scene he enjoys as a diversion from daily life.

Reaching an overlook after 25 minutes of hiking, he moves closer and closer to the edge. The further out he steps, the more complete his view of the eagle's attack. Standing near the edge, he watches as the eagle swoops high over the river, then drops closer to tree top height as it crosses over these elevated cliffs 70 feet above river level.

Chet's new winter mustache holds mini-icicles across his lip line, as sweat from his hike is captured and chilled by the early dawn air. He has unzipped the top third of his winter coat, now that his body has warmed up from hiking. Checking to be sure his footing is strong, Chet turns as the eagle swoops down just 200 feet to his right, digs its talons into what remains of snow pack and pulls back into the air with a small rabbit, weakened through the winter, writhing and squirming. Less than a second later, the eagle is soaring over the Illinois River with breakfast firmly in its clutch.

Chet watches intently, and smiles as he hears the shrill shriek of the rabbit as the eagle's talons pierce deeply into it. The rabbit bleeds out quickly. "Time for me to go kill someone in the office," Chet says to himself as he steps back from the ledge. He heads back to his Right Size adaptable car, complete with human-weighted dummies and fingerprint and eye replicas for his children to keep his car from shrinking to one-person size as it would if the car knew he was the only live human inside.

Stepping through the snow, Chet lifts his knees high in spots with snow drifts still more than 18 inches high. As he approaches the parking lot, four men stand outside their black gas-powered vehicles, with the cars blocking Chet's exit from the lot. Chet stops to consider what they might be doing, and starts to step backward to get out of their sight. The last thing he needs is to walk into the middle of a drug deal.

As he backs away, four other men come up from behind him, weapons drawn.

"Chet Leach?" one of the four asks.

"Yes, I'm Chet Leach. Can I help you?"

"Yes, sir. You can help by slowly lifting your hands up over your head, dropping down to your knees and staying still while we handcuff you. You are under arrest, Mr. Leach."

"Who are you?"

"I'm Agent Cortes from the FBI, and these are fellow agents. You are under arrest for conspiracy to engage in war profiteering, Mr. Leach. You have the right to remain silent . . .," Agent Cortes tells him, reading the rest of his Miranda rights and asking Chet if he has anything he wants to say.

Chet says he is happy to talk.

"FirstWal made money, sure, but it wasn't my direction. Everything came from Shanghai down or from the store managers out. I'll be happy to provide you the files that prove who is responsible," Chet tells the agent. "You don't need these cuffs to get my cooperation."

"So, no direction on raising prices came from you?"

"No sir," Chet says with confidence that digital evidence of his communications had been erased from the FirstWal system within four hours of each message being sent. His wrist alert system ensured that managers saw his notes before the digital destruction took place. Chet had this destructive capacity built into the system just for his own selected messages.

"That's quite interesting, Mr. Leach," Agent Cortes states. "Let me ask you, do you know a gentleman named Mike Sanchez? He runs your West Nogales store."

"Of course, Sanchez has been at FirstWal for a long time. He could have been one of the ring leaders raising prices at the stores to maximize his bonus," Chet responds, maintaining his confident presence. "Of course, we'll need to look at the system to know for sure."

"Really?" Agent Cortes asks, pulling out his Lifelink and unfolding it to produce a larger screen for Chet to view. "Because he thought these photos of messages you sent might tell us a different story."

Chet looks at the messages. His head and shoulders slump. He feels the FBI's claws piercing his skin, digging into his organs and pressing his life away.

Gathering himself a few minutes later, he looks at Agent Cortes.

"Can you call my wife and let her know? She'll be expecting me home soon. I don't want her to get worried," he responds.

"We'll be able to do that after you're processed, Mr. Leach."

***

Washington, D.C.

As he has done personally every two hours since meeting with the President in the DUCC to get instructions, JT Alton uses an untraceable account to check for messages on the One World site of Lecia Skater – account number 2,718,281,828.

Though Juan refuses to confirm the note writer's identify to the President, JT is fairly certain it came from Ramon Mantle. Ramon's little sister Celia is a talented ice skater, and JT has long known that protecting Celia is Ramon's top priority. The name isn't a particularly clever disguise, but perhaps Ramon didn't want his identity to be too difficult to discern. Through his sources, JT has known for years that Ramon is involved with the Castillo cartel. He surmised from tracing signals from Ramon's earring that this involvement might not be voluntary.

The account number is the number *e*, something few lacking Ramon's mathematical and programming wizardry would consider important. Anyone could figure out that Lecia uses the same letters as Celia.

Finally, a message pops up on Lecia's site.

"Skating new program in Chicago today. Have a real shot at winning. Must follow patterns in program order or trigger terrible fall. Plan to celebrate victory with my family if we can keep them safe. Give me a sign."

JT puts his forehead down into his hands.

"What the hell does this mean?" he says to himself. "This is what I'm losing sleep over."

JT calls the President.

***

Chicago, Illinois

A small jewelry-sized package arrives at Professor Stark's office. He looks at the package carefully, wondering whether he should open it.

Nearly a decade ago, Professor Stark suffered a series of muggings while speaking around the nation in favor of a constitutional amendment that implemented the most fundamental political reforms in the nation's history. The Political Freedom Amendment, as it ultimately became known, required open primaries and 60-day election cycles with no fundraising or spending outside of the cycle among its many reforms. All of the changes were designed to eradicate a political system more concerned with money and political party advantage than with the health of the nation and its people.

Only the depth of the second great depression created enough pain that Americans rose up and forced the constitutional amendment through the political process as their price for reelecting any incumbent legislators. Professor Stark was credited with intellectual leadership behind the amendment. He dedicated several years to promoting its passage.

Once he became known as the primary enemy of incumbency and entrenched political power, Professor Stark was targeted with vicious personal and professional attacks. Several of the accusations nearly derailed his career. In addition, four physical muggings in four different cities in the final year before the amendment passed left him with an assortment of scars. Though police treated the muggings as robberies, he remains convinced they were efforts to scare him away.

Nearly a decade later, Professor Stark still tries to blend into his physical surroundings to avoid drawing too much attention. He keeps his eyes constantly alert for danger. His table at the Heart and Soul Café, for example, allows him to see everyone coming into the restaurant while being steps from a side-door emergency exit and a door to the kitchen that leads to a rear exit. His office is built to convert into a safe room, with a secondary escape if the safe room is breached.

As he stares at the package, deciding whether to open it, he looks back at the address.

"To Professor Stark and Rachel," it reads. He decides to open it. He'll call Rachel and figure out who Lecia is later.

Inside, he finds a small shot glass with a platinum exterior and a crystal lining. Embedded into the platinum is a pyramid with two shrines sitting on top. Separate staircases lead up the pyramid to each shrine.

Inside the shot glass, he finds something else unusual. It looks like a diamond stud earring with multiple, melted connection points. The diamond is shattered.

Professor Stark calls Rachel, asking her to come to his office immediately.

When she arrives, Rachel is out of breath; worried that Professor Stark needs to give her bad news about Juan and wants to do it in person. As soon as she sits, Rachel reaches up, grabs her hair in the back and starts twirling it so rapidly it's quickly in a tight ponytail. She continues to twist her hair anyway. Rachel's legs move up and down at jackhammer pace as well.

Professor Stark walks around and grabs Rachel's hand while telling her to relax, then immediately pulls his hand away. Keeping a professional distance from students is one of his core commitments. Still, Rachel, Tamika, Jeremy and the other students in his class have been with him through a disproportionate amount of trauma.

When he moves back behind the desk, he can see Rachel is breathing more normally. He explains the situation and shows her the shot glass, earring, envelope and address.

"Is this from Juan for you?" he asks.

"I can't imagine. He knows my address if he wants to send something to me," Rachel responds. She pulls out her Lifelink to call Juan.

Professor Stark continues to look at the shot glass, spinning it around. He scans a picture of the shot glass and searches for a match. Less than a second later, images of the Templo Mayor appear on his screen.

Continuing to look, he turns the shot glass upside down and sees the crystal lining separate slightly from the platinum. Looking closely inside, he can see seams around the bottom. Platinum shouldn't have seams if it's molded properly, he decides. Then he pulls at the glass. The crystal pops out of the platinum exterior.

Meanwhile, Rachel confirms with Juan that he didn't send the glass.

With the glass removed, a piece of the platinum bottom falls out. Looking at the piece, Professor Stark realizes it will connect to his Lifelink.

The item might contain a virus or be something to steal his identity and financial control. It's a risk to connect it. He calls Jill to ask for advice.

Jill was just preparing to call him, having received a message from Professor Stark asking her to call.

"What is it Paul? You ask me to call and can't wait five minutes for me to get back to you," Jill says when she connects in.

"What do you mean?" Professor Stark asks. "I didn't send you any messages today."

"Sure you did. Five minutes ago on my Lifelink," Jill states.

"What? From my number?"

"Yes, from you."

"But my Lifelink has been sealed in my pocket for hours," Professor Stark says, feeling to make sure it's still there.

"Well, that's odd. So what's this about?"

Finally, the two realize they won't know what to do unless Professor Stark looks at the chip's contents. He folds out his Lifelink, inserts the chip and knows immediately what they need to do.

Jill calls President Phillipi.

Minutes later, JT Alton departs for Chicago, accompanied by FBI agents who had worked in Jill's office through the 72-hour standoff. Professor

Stark and Rachel are instructed to lock his office, remain there, talk to no one and allow no one to enter until JT arrives.

Professor Stark triggers the safe room mode for his office.

***

North California

Victor Cruz is brought on board a military exercise as part of a supply team supporting training in the cleared out Death Valley area. The National Park is closed to visitors. The public is told that intense explosives were accidentally dropped in the park during the secession battle and must be located and disarmed.

Three days into the training exercise, Victor offers to take the place of one of many diseased, bed-ridden soldiers in an exercise. After proving himself fully capable on the ground with a New Rite missile bullet launcher, a weapon he had never before seen, he is loaded onto a helicopter, taken to 20,000 feet, and asked to fire at human-sized targets on the ground. All five shots hit their target.

Back on the ground, Victor signs papers and makes one supervised phone call to his wife to inform her that he has been asked to take part in a National Guard rescue mission across the Pacific.

***

Washington, D.C.

With the chip in hand, JT arrives under heavy armed escort to join Defense Secretary Mendoza, Homeland Security Secretary Peyton and President Phillipi in the DUCC Situation Room.

"How confident are we that the information on the chip is accurate?" the President asks, looking toward JT.

"I only know one person who could confirm this, and you have him locked in federal prison," JT responds.

"Who's that?" President Phillipi asks.

"My top cartel source. Max Herta, the top tunnel builder for the Castillo cartel. The FBI arrested him at the Detroit Salt Mine right after New Year's," JT responds.

"Wasn't he the ringleader for the bombings and Harvard Square?" Secretary Peyton asks.

"That's what he's accused of, but I suspect his Protection Corps watchers did that while he was brought back to Mexico to build more tunnels. Give me a few minutes with him, and we'll know if it's real," JT says.

"If we show it to him, won't he figure out where it came from?"

"If he sees me come in to talk, he'll talk, particularly if you give me permission to offer him a publicly staged execution and a privately concealed pardon and new life," JT claims.

"You're sure of this?" the President asks.

"I trust him enough that he's the man who designed my tunnels," JT responds. "We've had our lives in each other's hands for almost 20 years. That's how we knew we could trust each other. He's been my most important cartel source."

"If he confirms the plans, we need to move as fast as we can," the President says to Mendoza and Peyton.

"We need a month," Peyton says.

"Three weeks – maximum," the President responds. "Every day we wait is a day millions could die."

CHAPTER 24

February 19, 2041
Washington, D.C.

In the President's box above the House floor for the State of the Union speech, Juan Gonzalez sits next to the first lady, thinking about how much his life has changed in the little more than a year since FirstWal refused to hire him because his English wasn't fluent enough. He turns around to look at his mother, who sits beaming despite being startled again to be in such intense media spotlight. While Juan is perfectly comfortable now with the media hordes that have followed him since his return to Washington, D.C., Mama Gonzalez is too uncomfortable speaking English to feel relaxed here. Besides, every tremendous honor Juan has received has been offset by deep and terrifying tragedy.

Seeing her nervousness, Juan grabs his mother's hand, pulls it toward him and kisses it. Releasing her hand, he watches as she sits back in her chair and smiles. Standing as the Speaker of the House introduces the President for the State of the Union, he reflexively reaches with his left hand to grab the hand of his date. Rachel Cruz reaches back, spreading her fingers between his and looking up. Exchanging smiles, they turn to look back to the President.

As the President walks up the aisles, he stops to shake hands with legislators from both parties, reaching in several rows and accepting congratulations from many who are seeing him at this delayed speech for the first time since the end of the war. Nearing the front, he turns and looks back to his right. Seeing Jill, he waves hello. He looks toward the presidential box, smiling, waving at his wife and giving a thumbs-up signal to Juan, Rachel and Mama Gonzalez.

The atmosphere is substantially more relaxed than it was just four weeks earlier, when even holding a State of the Union session with so many of America's elected leaders in the same building would not have been considered. Earlier in the day, President Phillipi publicly dropped the defense condition warning to DEFCON 3, stating that he hopes to drop it further when the last United Nations alliance troops leave Mexico. DEFCON 3 is an alert level still above normal readiness.

As the President reaches the podium and finishes greeting everyone up there, the House floor again erupts with cheers from most members of the U.S. House, the Senate, most of the President's cabinet and several Supreme Court justices. The galleries are packed with admirers who made this State of the Union the hottest ticket in the city. After several attempts by the President to quiet the crowd, the audience sits and the President begins his address.

"It's a common expression here to say that 'you never know how good something is until you lose it.' This is another way of saying we don't, as imperfect human beings, always appreciate the good in our life until that good no longer exists. I'm as guilty of this as anyone. I ran for President of the United States because I believed I could make a difference. We suffered too much through the latest depression and it has seemed at times that America has lost much of what once made this the greatest nation on earth.

"What I didn't fully realize until we risked being torn apart was that we have a tremendous advantage over many others. It's not just that we have extraordinary people here. I can tell you from my travels, and from meeting people from all over, that the world is filled with a large number of exceptional people. No, our advantage is in the values that founded this nation, created its Constitution and Bill of Rights, and enabled us to adapt as the world changed.

"As I thought about what losing full freedom of speech, freedom of religion, freedom of assembly, the right to bear arms and other core principles would mean to Americans in the four states dragged into the secession battle, it was clear to me that these and others are principles worth fighting and dying to protect. While all of us, in our own way, fought for these principles, we lost more than 10,000 American soldiers and citizens before and during the three-day war over secession. That the losses were so few compared to the last Civil War is perhaps a relief to the nation, but not to the loved ones of all those who perished."

For the next 10 minutes, the President talks about several of the people who lost their lives during the war, including several whose loved ones are seated in a Presidential box to the right of the first lady.

"Finally, I want to thank a woman who has now twice saved the United States from devastation. As a Navy Seal, Sarah Osborne was responsible for individually enduring a deep and extended dive to sneak up and sink a renegade Pakistani nuclear submarine located just 250 miles off our eastern coast nine years ago. Last month, Sarah lost her life while helping to extract Juan Gonzalez from captivity in the Alta Texas command center in Mexico. Sarah succeeded in her mission, then remained to fight off every attacker who threatened Juan until finally succumbing after Juan was safely away."

Broadcast cameras pan up to the presidential box, showing Juan biting his lip, while Mama Gonzalez and Rachel have already lost the battle to restrain tears. The first lady puts her arm around Juan's shoulder and gives him a gentle hug.

"It would be a shame if we did not honor the sacrifices of so many, not just with words, but with actions. After World War II, the United States was the true global leader. We used to be more educated, more innovative, more inclusive and less corrupt than almost any nation on earth. Our ideas were proven to be right. Democracy outshined communism. Where Communists once ruled over more than a third of the world's population, the failure of communist philosophy has been proven. Today, only a small portion of the world's people must endure the horrors of mutually assured failure that comes from a system where success is never rewarded. Capitalism took hold and created a nation with a growing economy that raised the living standards of almost everyone. Still, in a matter of just a few generations, the rest of the world caught up and many have now vastly surpassed our success by following principles we once proved to be superior, but then somehow decided to too-frequently abandon.

"So the question I ask us all to consider is why have we fallen behind? Have 'we the people' become less capable? I don't think this is the problem. Have we become lazy in our comfort? While we can find examples of this, this is not our fundamental flaw. So what is the fundamental flaw that stands in our way? What do we need to change to honor the sacrifices of the Americans who fought to preserve our union?"

The President pauses for dramatic effect and looks around the room from end to end.

"I hope everyone now sees that protecting our liberties is government's paramount obligation. But it's not enough. We also need to repair the foundation of our nation, the laws upon which we are governed. We have a legal code so riddled with loopholes, subsidies, evasions and uncertainties that we, the people, have lost faith in the decency and integrity of government. Too many run businesses and programs in legal terms, asking questions such as: Is it legal? If not, am I likely to get away with it? Instead, we need to ask these questions: Is it ethical? Am I acting with integrity? Is it fair? Would I be okay if someone did this to me?

"In simpler terms," the President continues, "we must be a nation where we do unto others as we would have done onto us. Some of you may see this as mixing religion and government. I see it as creating an environment in which this government succeeds for its people, not at the expense of its people. So, in the coming months, I will turn this concept into a sweeping reform of our laws I will refer to as God's Law."

A gasp from many lawmakers goes up as they hear the President suggest a law that could favor one religion over another or, perhaps as bad to some, the religious over atheists.

President Phillipi is undeterred by the number of dropped jaws: "Our faith informs our views of right and wrong. But the God's Law concept is not an attempt to create a national religion. Far from it. Religion must not run government. Faith is part of our humanity, but reason is a gift we must exercise in conjunction with faith. I believe we must consider our faith in the context of a deep, studied understanding of what it takes for societies to survive and prosper for millennia. Only then, building from faith and reason, can we take the steps to build a better, lasting society.

"By the time this presidency comes to an end, I hope to have returned the laws of our nation to a clarity, simplicity and justice that can be understood by and honored by every American. I know this is an extraordinary challenge so ask each of you to work with me to make it happen."

After going through a series of other issues and recognizing dozens who've made extraordinary contributions during the past year, the President returns to the language and related issues that elevated the nation's tensions.

"I've been working with congressional leaders, Congresswoman Jill Carlson and issue advocates such as Honor to Mexico Honorary Ambassador Juan Gonzalez and Professor Paul Stark to find a way to resolve language issues. We believe we have achieved agreement on a new national language mandate that makes clear English is our official language, but ensures that those not fluent in English are accommodated through training, development and transition translation assistance programs funded federally, but implemented through the states.

The President points at Juan: "I am also pleased to announce the creation of one of the few new federal programs I will introduce during my second term, a block grant program to support language instruction. This program, to be administered by the states, will be used to teach English in areas where English is not the predominant language so that every opportunity available to children in Seattle and Cleveland is also open to children in Puerto Rico, Miami, San Diego and, yes, West Nogales. This same program, however, can also be used to support foreign language instruction of each community's choosing in areas where English is the primary language. The program will include school-based programs for children as young as three years old, community-based programs for adults and on-line, self-paced instruction programs.

"In one generation, it is my hope that we will be able to look back and see this program as promoting cross-cultural respect and building language capabilities that allow America to regain our economic leadership."

As the President ends his speech, he is met with louder and broader applause than followed any State of the Union in recent decades, with congressional leaders well aware of his strengthened popularity for his success in saving the nation. As he makes his way out, he spots Jill several seats away from the aisle and motions for her to get through. Jill walks over to the aisle to shake the President's hand. Instead, he hugs her and moves his mouth close to her ear.

"Thank you for everything you've done Jill. I hope Professor Stark told you that I'll be calling you to help with the God's Law concept, since I'm sure you helped him develop it for me," he tells her before releasing the hug and patting her on her shoulder.

As the speech ends, Rachel asks the first lady if she can do her a favor and have someone find out what rescue mission her father was sent on and when his National Guard unit will be done and he can come home.

"Give me a few days," the first lady responds, "and I'm sure I can find out for you."

***

Isla San Juanito, Mexico

Three Protection Corps guards pace the perimeter of this tiny island to ensure its first permanent resident remains in captivity. San Juanito Island, the newest branch of a Corps-run penal colony island to its south, was established to ensure that former Mexican President Daniel Suárez is lost and forgotten by those who might follow him or seek retribution.

The isolation, ordered by replacement President Raúl Hernández, was poorly conceived and executed.

Ally Steele drops her APB to 15,000 feet and steadies it so the two shooters inside can focus on their targets. Two other APBs operate along-side, with three shooters in each of those APBs. Victor Cruz, having proven himself one of the top shooters in the final week of testing with New Rite's missile-bullet rifles, is on board one of those APBs. His target is the fourth guard now resting below the island's guard shelter.

A final APB from the attack group focuses on jamming communications from the island to prevent the Protection Corps from becoming aware of their mission.

Ally gives the go signal. Six missile bullets scream for the three roaming guards. All six hit their targets. Seeing one of the guards go down, Suárez moves suddenly, rattling the chain attached to the metal collar on his neck. The fourth guard awakens. As that guard steps out from his shelter, Victor and another soldier shoot. The four kills are quickly visually confirmed.

Ally leads the APB contingent in a steep drop to ocean level, then proceeds southeast until hovering just above the modest shelter that leaves Suárez largely exposed to the elements. One of the attacking soldiers rappels down and comes at Suárez from behind. He uses the neck collar to pull Suárez's head down, slices his ear lobe off just above where a Hernández-ordered monitoring earring was installed. The soldier then slices his own lobe off in the same place before grafting Suárez's lobe to his own ear with a medical adhesive.

Once his head is released, Suárez turns to look at the soldier in shock. As he does, another soldier turns Suárez around, powders his ear to stop the bleeding, picks the lock on his collar, re-hooks the collar to the soldier dressed to look like Suárez and leads the former Mexican President to where Ally is now hovering her APB two feet above ground. Twenty seconds later, Victor and others have loaded the four dead bodies on board, three American soldiers with appearances to match the Protection Corps soldiers are roaming the island's perimeter and a fourth is lying down in shelter. The replacement for ex-President Suárez, carefully groomed to look like him, starts following the routine Suárez had followed since being confined on this island.

Ally and the other two attack APBs leave the island. Ten seconds later, the communications-jamming APB departs, heading northwest. Two Cooper's hawks leave their treetop nest, heading straight north to their home at New Rite's Utah compound.

As the APBs fly back to Camp Pendleton, Ally fills Suárez in on what is happening to him and what U.S. forces are planning to do about his family.

***

Washington, D.C.

The President's motorcade heads back to the White House with the first lady, Vice President Marcia Wilt and Defense Secretary Xavier Mendoza inside.

The President is driven in Secretary Mendoza's vehicle to the Pentagon.

From the Pentagon, the President rides by helicopter to Andrews Air Force Base. As he does, Vice President Wilt and Secretary Mendoza drop to the Deep Underground Command Center, where preparations inside the Situation Room are ramping up.

Arriving at Andrews, the President enters one of six transport flights headed to Camp Pendleton.

CHAPTER 25

February 20, 2041
Camp Pendleton, California

Four hours after leaving Andrews Air Force base, President Phillipi puts on his new bullet-resistant fatigues, helmet and face shield. He greets and hugs special operations pilot Ally Steele before boarding her New Rite APB and taking instructions on using his body cone for protection and his weapon to shoot. When the last of the 10,000-strong initial attack team is set, the President gives Ally the honor of asking for authorization to launch.

The authorization comes directly from Defense Secretary Mendoza and Vice President Wilt in the Situation Room.

Mission "Charlotte Lee" is a go.

If the operation fails to shut down the six nuclear devices placed by Hernández, tens of millions of Americans could be dead in hours. President Phillipi can't stomach the idea of putting that many American lives at risk without risking his own.

The first twelve APB attack squads launch in sequence, targeted to arrive simultaneously at cartel-owned buildings in San Diego, Los Angeles, Phoenix, Dallas, Houston and the hometown of former President Suárez, where Suárez's family is being held by the Castillo cartel's Protection Corps.

Using the map of nuclear bomb locations provided as part of the file sent to Professor Stark, two APBs approach a high-rise building just west of the Gaslamp Quarter. From a three-mile distance, two soldiers take out the roof guard using New Rite's missile bullet rifles. The APBs trace behind the missile bullet paths, quickly landing on the high-rise roof. Eight Special Forces soldiers enter the building from the roof and quickly kill the surprised guard outside the top floor room where the soldiers expect to find a nuclear bomb. In just a few seconds, they locate the weapon.

As it is confirmed that the nuclear bombs are located, Ally leads 986 APBs from Camp Pendleton flying 100 miles northwest before turning over the Pacific Ocean and flying full speed at 60,000 feet above sea level toward Sinaloa Province in Mexico.

Once the bombs are located, the three nuclear disarmament specialists brought to each site work to disable the weapons. Within minutes, the lead specialist in San Diego confirms disarmament. The incapacitated nuclear bomb is lifted to the roof and loaded onto one APB. That APB heads straight west, where it will land on a near-empty ship anchored halfway between San Diego and Hawaii. This success is repeated at the five other sites, though the Dallas and Houston nuclear bombs are transported to a ship anchored in the Caribbean Sea.

The 986 airborne attack APBs are racing toward Sinaloa Province to target a series of deep tunnel command centers, drug production facilities and escape routes from which Mexican President and Chief General Raúl Hernández is believed to be running what he now calls Nuevo México. Schematics for the compounds were embedded in the computer chip hidden under the crystal in the shot glass sent to Professor Stark.

Three minutes before they reach the drop spot 60,000 feet above the cartel compound, Secretary Mendoza confirms to Ally that assault teams have all taken control of and disarmed all six nuclear weapons placed by Hernández.

Inside Ally Steele's APB at the head of the assault wave sits President Phillipi. Next to him is former Mexican President Suárez, with what remains of his ear now properly bandaged.

Ally calls back to the team: "We have bomb deactivation confirmation."

Suárez smiles, clenches his fists and shakes his arms back and forth in triumph. His family will not be obliterated today, at least not if this attack succeeds in executing the rest of the U.S. plan.

President Phillipi looks at former President Suárez, whose uniform contains a patch that reads: "Sarah Osborne." President Phillipi's patch reads: "Charlotte Lee."

Victor Cruz is one of 500 snipers on the first 100 APBs who fire missile-launch rifles from 20,000 feet to take out key aboveground targets before the rest of the attack is seen or heard.

"Time to take back control of our countries," President Phillipi says in matter-of-fact tone, just before feeling the pit of his stomach leap through his throat.

Ally takes her APB into a rapid downward dive.

Suárez and Phillipi take deep breaths from oxygen tubes. New wrinkles developed in recent months no longer show as their flesh presses tightly backward. They grasp their weapons tightly around the shoulder harnesses holding them into their seats.

Nearly ten thousand other U.S. Special Forces soldiers, all wearing patches with the names of Americans killed in the secession attempt, are in rapid descent.

Military vehicles are dispatched to pick up Juan, Jill and Professor Stark.

One of the last two APBs made in the most massive, secretive military construction ramp-up since World War II approaches the Suárez family home. A final APB races toward Punta Mita, Mexico followed by a 100-person special operations force to extract Celia Mantle and her parents. The troops are under order to protect and extract Ramon's family, while killing all Protection Corps guards at the estate.

Deep underground inside the cartel's Sinaloa Province command center, Ramon appears to be working on an updated logistics system when the first explosions are reported above ground.

With his Protection Corps guards running toward the explosions, Ramon signs into One World as Lecia Skater to post a second message.

"When you're skating to win, you can't leave any competitors standing, even me," the post from Lecia states. "Tell my father that I hope he's finally proud of my program."

JT is immediately alerted to the message and responds.

"Just picked your father up with the rest of the family. All are safe and flying away," he writes. Seconds after clicking to post that message, JT decides to post another message to Lecia. "From those few of us who saw your program, thank you for what you have done."

Vice President Wilt, acting president for the duration of Marc Phillipi's combat involvement, orders Defense Secretary Mendoza to send the nation's military to DEFCON 1, the code announcing to all U.S. troops that nuclear war is imminent. Mission Commander Ray Peyton puts his hand on Mendoza's shoulder as Mendoza issues the DEFCON 1 order to U.S. troops globally and simultaneously launches a series of global attacks on terrorist targets and rogue nuclear weapons sites.

No one knows for sure how many nuclear weapons the Castillo cartel and terrorist allies might still be able to deploy. The U.S. attack, aimed at the cartel's operations and at terrorists operating in seven nations with the strongest ties to Raúl Hernández, won't stop until this nuclear threat is eliminated.